ANGELINA;

OR,

THE MYSTERY OF ST. MARK'S ABBEY.

A TALE OF OTHER DAYS.

BY THE AUTHOR OF

"THE MANIAC FATHER; OR, THE VICTIM OF SEDUCTION," "EVELINA," &c. &c.

"Child of myst'ry, be warned and flee;
This is no place for peace and thee;
Danger surrounds thee, guilt is nigh,
And views thee with designing eye.
Then mark the warning, maiden fair :—
Child of myst'ry, beware !—beware !"

LONDON:

PUBLISHED BY E. LLOYD, SALISBURY-SQUARE, FLEET-STREET,
AND SOLD BY ALL BOOKSELLERS.

PREFACE.

PREFACES, from time immemorial, have been made the mere vehicles of puff; but when the work is completed ere the Preface is written, it becomes the pleasant medium of expressing the author's gratitude for the support his efforts to please have met with. The latter is again the task of the author of "ANGELINA," which, thanks to the liberality of the public, has been one of his most successful productions, and not, he trusts he may be allowed to say, without deserving it. This romance was originally published in that most popular of all the cheap periodicals, "THE PENNY SUNDAY TIMES, AND PEOPLE'S POLICE GAZETTE," and the extraordinary favour with which it was received, induced the proprietor of that excellent journal to republish it in a form similar to the present. The continued application for it after its second edition was out of print, induced the proprietor to again publish it; and the author feels that he should be very much wanting in gratitude, did he not take the present opportunity of returning his sincere thanks for the flattering encomiums bestowed upon it by the press, and the public in general.

The encouragement he has received, will stimulate him to fresh and increased exertions to please; and he takes the liberty of informing his friends and patrons, that, in a few days, he will have the honour of offering to their notice, A TALE OF ROMANCE AND PATHOS, with very superior engravings, under the title of "EVELINA; OR, THE PAUPER'S CHILD," which the author feels confident will please and instruct those readers who have hitherto so ably appreciated his humble labours. Once more, therefore, returning his heartfelt thanks to a liberal public, the author respectfully takes his leave.

December 10th, 1849.

ANGELINA;
OR,
THE MYSTERY OF ST. MARK'S ABBEY.

CHAPTER I.

"Come, Angelina, pray let us return home; see, the sun has sunk behind the western hills, and the bare contemplation of these gloomy ruins is enough to fill one's mind with frightful apprehensions. I am sure I cannot see anything about these black and moss covered walls, which frown so dismally upon the passengers, and offer only a retreat for the melancholy bat, or dreary screech-owl, to admire; and it is a matter of perfect astonishment to me, that you can be so fond of visiting them every day."

"Hush, Laura," interposed the fair companion of the first speaker, placing her finger upon a pair of the prettiest ruby lips that the imagination of a limner could depict. "I thought I heard a sound; it seemed to me like the tone of a guitar, touched by no unskilful hand. There, again! Did you not hear it? Surely this venerable fabric, dilapidated as it is, must be inhabited."

"Yes, with ghosts or robbers," retorted the other, shuddering and looking timidly around her; "as to the sound you fancied you heard, it was nothing more than the wind whistling along the solemn avenues of the old pile. Come, come, Angelina, let us hurry home, the sky looks black and lowering, and portends a coming storm. Besides, my father will have returned ere this and will be angry at our remaining out so late."

This dialogue took place beneath the crumbling walls of an ancient abbey, which stood on the summit of a gentle hill, and commanded a romantic and extensive view, between two young girls, who, although they were clad in the neat, but simple garb of peasants, were of such surpassing beauty, that they might have created a feeling of envy in the bosoms of the damsels who moved in the highest ranks of gaudy fashion.

Laura was apparently the youngest, and was evidently not more than seventeen. She was a laughing, black-eyed brunette, with a skin soft and transparent, and a figure, which, though delicate, was exquisitely shaped. But the beauty of Angelina was of a far different character. There was a grace and elegance in all her actions that was inexpressibly fascinating, and strongly impressed the beholder with the idea that she was born to a far more elevated situation of life than that she moved in. Her countenance was perfection itself, and there was a meekness of expression in her lovely blue eyes, which spoke more than language could have done of the intrinsic virtues she possessed.

Laura and Angelina stood in the relation of cousins to one another, and were seldom seen apart. The affection between them had never suffered the least interruption, for they had been brought up from childhood together, the parents of Angelina having expired in her infancy, which placed her under the protection of her uncle, humble, but honest Arthur Woodfield, who, having been very unfortunate in life, was now reduced to a small cottage in the neighbourhood of the abbey ruins, where we have introduced the lovely cousins to the notice of the reader.

Saint Mark's Abbey had evidently been a splendid edifice, but it had been left to decay for many years, and few persons in the place would venture to approach it after night-fall, for, like most old buildings, it was reported to be haunted, and many appalling legends were related by the old gossips, as they sat trembling before their blazing fire on a winter's evening, concerning the dreadful crimes which had been perpetrated within its mouldering walls. The more reasonable, and less superstitious portion of the community, however, accounted for the noises that had been heard to issue at various periods from the gothic pile, in a far more probable way; and it was strongly suspected that the abbey was, in fact, the retreat of a gang of robbers or smugglers—more particularly the latter, and although the proper authorities had hitherto failed in making any satisfactory discovery, it was still hoped that they would succeed ere long in doing so, and in setting all doubts on the subject at rest.

Notwithstanding these marvellous and alarming reports, and the cautious injunctions of her uncle, Angelina, who was strongly susceptible of the beauties of nature, felt a pleasure in visiting the abbey ruins upon every opportunity, but had never been able to prevail upon Laura to accompany her until the present occasion, and more emboldened by her presence, she was now anxious to gratify her curiosity to the fullest extent, by taking a minute survey of the interior of the building, and in spite of the timid solicitations of her less enthusiastic companion, had advanced to the hall, when a sound, as of music, suddenly vibrated on her ears, and gave rise to the conversation we have quoted at the commencement of the chapter.

"What a timid little simpleton you are, Laura," said Angelina, trying to urge her forward, "you are always running upon ghosts and hobgoblins, which foolish notions are instilled into your mind by poor old Dame Gertrude, whenever you visit

her, and who would almost endeavour to persuade those who will listen to her awful stories, that she is in the habit of seeing more phantoms than were ever conjured up by the invention of a romance writer."

"Well, you may say as you please, cousin," replied Laura, " but I am certain there are such things, and there cannot possibly be a more likely place for them to resort to, than this frightful old abbey. See how the darkness increases; we shall never be able to reach home before the storm commences, if we do not hasten from hence directly."

"It will only be a shower," exclaimed Angelina, "and therefore it will be more advisable for us to remain where we are, under shelter, until it has passed over. My uncle will not be alarmed, for he will think we are only paying a visit to Dame Gertrude, who is ill."

At that moment, a vivid flash of lightning darted in at one of the broken casements, and was quickly followed by a loud peal of thunder, which reverberated above their heads, and seemed to shake every stone in the venerable fabric. Laura trembled, and clung to the arm of her cousin, and the next moment the rain descended in torrents.

"There, Angelina, I told you how it would be," ejaculated Laura, " how obstinate it was of you to persist in remaining here; how shall we get home now? and I'm sure if we stay here it will be at the risk of our lives, for we shall have the old walls rattling about our ears directly."

Angelina endeavoured to appease the apprehensions of Laura, and consented to postpone the object of examining the ruins to a future day; and she had scarcely formed this resolution, when, between the pauses of the thunder, a strange noise, like the banging of a ponderous door, followed by a loud volley of rude laughter, from the farther end of the hall, sounded in their ears, and made them both start with amazement and alarm.

"Oh, Heavens!" ejaculated Laura, " what is that?—Let us fly, Agelina, do not delay another moment—hark!"

"Hush, Laura, I pray," said her cousin, who, having in vain looked around her to discover if there was any object present to justify their fears, had become more collected ; " it was only the wind, after all; compose yourself," we cannot venture forth in such a storm as this."

Another awful flash of lightning now darted in at the broken casement, and Laura uttered a faint scream, and clinging to Angelina, with terrified gestures directed her attention to the centre of the hall. Angelina gazed as the frightened girl pointed, and the object which her eyes encountered, standing in the ghastly light which the elemental fire ever and anon darted in at the large gothic window, transfixed her to the spot in mute astonishment and awe.

It was the tall and majestic figure of a female, clad completely in white, and bearing in one hand a white wand. Her countenance was ghastly pale, and her eyes, which were fixed upon Angelina, had an expression so unearthly, that it thrilled the soul with horror to behold them. A thin blue vapour seemed to envelope the lower part of her form, and a brilliant star blazed on her forehead. There was something so supernaturally awful in the appearance of the mysterious figure, that the two beauteous cousins were transfixed to the spot without the power to move a step, or to utter a single cry; while the strange being remained in the same attitude, and her piercing eyes were never for a moment removed from their countenances.

Unable to endure the deep feelings of horror that crowded upon her mind, Laura sank senseless to the earth, and Angelina was thus left to combat with her own terrors, and to unravel the awful mystery which attended the apparently supernatural being.

Angelina was not one of those weak and affected

beings who pretend to faint at the sight of their own shadow; but her situation had now become insupportably alarming, and her whole frame trembled with surprise and apprehension. But the ghastly form moved not, and as the blue lightning's flash ever and anon made it more distinct, a smile seemed to overspread its unearthly features, as though it was exulting in the fears it created.

By degrees, however, Angelina regained her presence of mind, and fancying that she might have been deceived, ventured to advance towards the strange and unearthly-looking object, in order that she might scrutinise it more narrowly, and finding that it did not then offer to move or to change its position in the slightest degree, she became convinced that her eyes had not deceived her, and with a firm determination to fathom at once the mystery, she exclaimed in a voice of courage—

"In the name of Heaven, who are you, and what seek you with me?"

"Approach me, girl," exclaimed the woman, in a voice of sweetness, but command, that ill accorded with her appearance; "approach me, I say, I must speak with you. Nay, do not fear me, I will not do thee harm; virtue and innocence need not dread me; come hither, maiden."

Encouraged by the woman's words, and the tone of her voice, Angelina became more assured, and did as the strange-looking being had desired her, who, grasping her by the arm with gentle violence, drew her closer to her. In the meantime, Laura had recovered, and, unable longer to endure the terrors of the place, called upon the name of her cousin, entreating her to follow, and hastily fled from the ruins.

"Maiden," said the mysterious woman, "thy visits to these lonely ruins are not unknown. I have secretly watched thee, and I have now hastened to warn thee that they must not be repeated. Beware, beware, thou knowest not the danger thou runnest into to gratify thy curiosity."

"What mean you, my good woman?" inquired Angelina, shrinking beneath the intensity of her gaze; "whom should I fear?"

"I may not tell thee, maiden," replied the woman, "but rest assured that what I speak is truth; Angelina, thou art not what thou seemest."

"Good God!" ejaculated the astonished girl, "what strange ambiguity is there in your words; tell me, who are you, and why are you interested in my welfare?"

"Seek to know no more at present," said the woman; "and above all, as you would save yourself from future misery, mention not a sentence to any one that you have heard from me. Your own life, and the lives of others depend upon your secrecy. The day may come when you may know more; in the meantime, know that I am your friend, and will watch over your safety."

"Mysterious being!" exclaimed Angelina, trembling violently, "your words alarm me. For heaven's sake, explain them. How, and what know you of me, and who are the persons against whom you would caution me?"

"Hist!" ejaculated the woman, in a tone nearly approaching to a whisper, and darting her eyes through the deepening darkness which now obscured the building, as though she feared the approach of somebody; "speak low, damsel—speak low. Do not tremble so, poor girl; again I tell thee thou hast nought to fear from me; no, no, no, the all-seeing and benignant Being who watches our actions from above, can bear witness that I would even die to serve thee! Oh, maiden, little canst thou imagine how well I know thee,—with what anxiety, what care, for months, nay, years, I have watched thee, unknown, followed thee as thine own shadow! What know I of thee! Oh! that this tongue dare reveal all I know! But at present it must not be—the web of thy fate is

not yet complete—the dark deeds of the guilty must yet a little longer be concealed beneath the cloud of mystery. But let them tremble, for the day of retribution will arrive—the voices of the murdered even now shriek for vengance from the tomb—they strike mine ears — they continually ring in them! Hark! girl, dost thou not hear them now? There again! what is't they say? 'Blood for blood! blood for blood!' Silence, silence, thou shalt not cry for ever in vain."

During the utterance of this wild and incoherent speech, the mysterious woman seemed to be worked up to the greatest pitch of frenzy; her frame was dreadfully convulsed, and her countenance was distorted with various emotions. Angelina, who now believed her to be a maniac, felt a renewal of her alarm, and tried to extricate herself from her grasp.

"Pray let me go," said Angelina, "my uncle will be greatly alarmed at my absence from home at this hour, and——"

"I see," interrupted the woman, retaining her hold of Angelina's arm, "I see thou thinkest me an impostor or a mad woman; but thou wrongest me, girl: no, no, I am not mad, I am not mad; 'twould be well for some if I were. But enough, I will not longer detain thee, girl; get thee home, and remember what I have said to thee, and scorn it not. Beware, I repeat.

"Beware of one of pomp and pride,
Or crime and sorrow will thee betide;
Beware, beware, of one whose crest
Is a blood stained shield and a raven's nest!"

As the wild woman of the ruins uttered these ambiguous words, she gradually receded from Angelina, and emphatically repeating the last line, she darted hastily from the spot, and was almost immediately lost in the obscurity of the abbey ruins.

Surprised, bewildered by what she had seen and heard, Angelina stood for a minute or two after the disappearance of the woman, transfixed to the spot; but at length, recollecting the caution which had been given her, and feeling a melancholy stealing over her senses, she hastened from the dreary fabric, and made the best of her speed towards home, with the hope of overtaking her fair cousin before her arrival, and to caution her to keep their visit to the ruins of St. Mark's Abbey, and the mysterious adventure they had met with there, a secret from Arthur and his wife.

Fortunately, Laura, on recovering her senses, had made her way to the cottage of Dame Gertrude, to shelter herself from the storm, and Angelina encountered her. therefore, just before she arrived at home. It was not without many entreaties on the part of Angelina, that Laura could be induced to remain silent upon what they had seen in the ruins, but at length Angelina prevailed upon her, although she had already detailed everything to Dame Gertrude, whose loquacity and extreme love of the marvellous, made her listen to the story with delight.

CHAPTER II.

OUR narrative commences about the year 1525, at which period the town of Redcar, in Yorkshire, was quite notorious for smugglers and dealers in all kinds of contraband goods.

Not far from this place, and in one of the most delightful parts of that romantic county, at the time we mention, stood the small but neat cottage of Mr. Woodfield, who, as well as his family, which consisted only of himself, his dame, one daughter, and Angelina, his niece, had excited considerable interest and curiosity since they had resided in the neighbourhood, (a period of about three years,) but to the vexation of the inquisitive and the scandal loving Mr. Woodfield, and the members of his family, were so reserved in their manners upon the subject of their former life, that very little could be elicited of their history. It was merely known that Woodfield had formerly been a seafaring man, but in what capacity no person could discover. That he had been unfortunate, might easily be guessed, for his means were now evidently limited, and yet his fortunes had rather seemed to improve than otherwise since he had resided at the cottage, he having cultivated a large expanse of ground with much care, and having, as it was thought, some annuity besides, for though he was poor, he never seemed absolutely to want anything, and always kept his family with much respectability.

The beauty of Angelina was a subject which had excited more curiosity than any other circumstance connected with the family of the Woodfields, and there were many of the busy gossips who ventured to hint their doubts of her being actually related at all to Arthur, inasmuch as it was the opinion of the sagest of these worthies, that she was by far too pretty, and too genteel, and too lady-like to be the niece of a poor cottager; and indeed the general conduct of Angelina was not at all calculated to do away with these surmises. She possessed natural accomplishments that are generally supposed to belong to the higher ranks of society only;—reading, music, and drawing, she was passionately fond of, and her general deportment and conversation was of a higher order than is usually acquired by a person in humble life.

Angelina's sweetness of disposition, and the extraordinary beauty of her face and person, had captivated the hearts of many young men in the neighbourhood, who had made proposals to her uncle for her hand, but were all civilly, but peremptorily declined; and it was also observed, that any overtures of the kind never failed to throw him into a state of great agitation, from which it was often a considerable time before he recovered.

All these remarkable traits in the character of Mr. Woodfield, had not failed to excite considerable wonder in the bosoms of those who knew him, and various were the conjectures that were formed upon them; but, notwithstanding the mystery attached to them, such was the appearance of him and his family, that they commanded universal respect.

We must now return to Angelina, whose mind had received a deep impression from the mysterious adventure she had met with at the ruins of Saint Mark. In vain she tried to solve the ambiguity of the woman's words, but the more she sought to do so, the more did she become lost and bewildered in the labyrinth of wonder and uncertainty. The strange being had declared that she knew her;—that *she was not what she seemed to be !* and yet she had never seen her before: nor could she imagine how she could possess the knowledge of which she had boasted, and of what service could it be to her to take such an interest in her fate? Then the inexplicable lines the woman had uttered—what could they mean? What could be the meaning of *the blood-stained shield and the raven's nest ?* In vain did Angelina thus rack her brain for several days after her visit to the ruins, but could not arrive at any satisfactory conclusion. Had she been superstitious, she would undoubtedly have set the woman down as a being of another world ; but as it was, she tried to persuade herself that she was a person who had assumed the appearance either from aberration of intellect, or for the purpose of a hoax. Laura, however, was not so easily to be convinced—she would have it that the being which had appeared to them, was a spirit, and that it had come to apprize them of approaching death, either to themselves or a near relation.

In this *reasonable* conclusion she was ably supported by Dame Gertrude, whose memory was amply stored with legendary lore, and who held all disbelievers in the marvellous in complete horror. Angelina found 'it was no easy task for her to prevent Laura from divulging the secret of what they had seen at Saint Mark's, and poor old Gertrude was actually upon thorns to go and tell the story to all her neighbours.

For several days did Angelina continue to think of this singular event, and the more she reflected, the stronger became the impression on her mind of the woman's mysterious warning. But yet, in spite of the caution she had given her, she felt a curiosity to inspect the old abbey, which she, with great difficulty, could resist.

It was on the third evening after the adventure, that Laura being on a visit to the cottage of Dame Gertrude, and her aunt being deeply engaged with a book, Angelina left the cottage, and walked through Redcar, towards the sea-beach.

It was a beautiful evening ; the sun was gradually sinking beneath the ocean, while his last rays still lingered on the hills, in dying splendour. The moon had also just shown her silvery countenance, and mingling her soft beams with the sun's refulgent rays, shed a pleasing melancholy over departing day. The gentle breeze scarcely moved the dewy foliage ; all nature seemed hushed in a tranquil slumber ; no sound was heard, save the plaintive voice of the nightingale, soothing the soul to pensive thoughtfulness.

The scene harmonised with Angelina's feelings, and she walked on indulging in poetic thought.

Absorbed in the pleasing delusions of fancy, she had proceeded a considerable distance in a wrong path before she perceived her error. The day having closed, and the moon more faintly glimmering through the trees, awakened her to recollection. She would instantly have gone back, but that would prolong her walk and retard her return. A break in the path that she was now in led directly to the sea-beach, and this having gained, she thought she could find her way by another route to the cottage, but she looked for anything like a road in vain.

A sudden cloud now obscured the moon, and spreading gloom darkened the atmosphere. A sultry heat filled the air, while the rising breeze over the distant ocean foretold the coming storm.

Unable to form any decisive plan, Angelina ran forward, and finding a path among the rocks, struck into it, hoping it would lead towards her home, but in vain did she look around for some familiar object to direct her wandering steps. Her eye could not penetrate through the increasing darkness of the night. Slowly and fearfully she moved on; the wind increased and the waves dashed tumultuously against the rocks.

The thunder now rolled; the rain poured in torrents, and the lightning flashing along the horizon, discovered a small cavity in a huge rock, into which Angelina crept for shelter.

The place widened the farther she advanced into it, and presented to her eyes, as well as the lightning occasionally permitted her to see, a spacious cavern, evidently the work of nature. To the right and left, several subterraneous passages or narrow caverns opened, which filled the mind of Angelina at first with apprehension, for she began to think it was some smugglers' retreat, and she doubted not but that if they discovered her there, she would either fall a sacrifice to their suspicions, or be subjected to their brutality and lewd ribaldry.

Impressed with this idea, she was about to quit the cavern, notwithstanding the storm was raging with redoubled violence, but listening, and hearing no other sounds but the wind howling through the hollow cavities, and the waves dashing furiously against the rocks, she took courage, and resolved to remain where she was until the storm had abated.

Angelina was very much concerned at the alarm her absence from home at such a late hour, and in such a storm, would excite in the bosom of her friends, and often did she cast her eyes wistfully across the troubled surface of the ocean, with the hope of seeing some symptoms of the tempest subsiding; but still did it rage with frightful fury, the billows rolling their infuriated crests to the clouds, and the thunder rattling, and the lightning blazing athwart the horizon, rendered the terrors of the scene complete.

About half an hour had elapsed in this manner, when Angelina thought she heard a rustling noise behind her, and turning round, her attention was attracted to a faint glimmering light which streamed from one of the smaller caverns before mentioned.

The maiden trembled with apprehension, and scarcely knew how to act; to fly the cavern would, probably, expose her to great danger from any of the gang, (to which she firmly believed the cavern formed a haunt,) lurking outside. She had scarcely been there two minutes, when the light grew stronger, and revealed to her astonished gaze a tall, and apparently, female figure, clad in long flowing garments of white, and bearing a lamp in her hand.

With difficulty repressing a scream, Angelina watched the actions of the supposed phantom, which having stood for a few seconds at the entrance of the cavern, and appearing to gaze vacantly around, uttered a deep sigh, and advanced to the centre of the outer cavern with noiseless footsteps, where, raising the lamp above her head, the lamp streamed full upon the countenance of our heroine, and uttering a shriek, the light was extinguished, and the apparent spectre vanished. Bound up to a pitch of desperate resolution to solve this mystery, the maiden sprang forward towards the narrow cavern, but struck her head violently against the rock, and fell prostrate to the earth, stunned and insensible.

How long she had remained in this state, she had no means of judging, but when she recovered her senses, the storm had subsided. The roaring of the thunder was hushed, the rain had ceased to pour, and the vivid lightning no longer darted its forked fury. She had scarcely reached the outside of the cavern, when a soft train of plaintive music vibrated on her ears, and arrested her footsteps. She looked around for the minstrel, but although the moon was riding proudly, and undimmed by the smallest speck, she could not discover a human being. At length the music ceased, and she was aroused by a gentle sigh, which seemed to proceed from some person near her. Alarmed she involuntarily raised her eyes towards a projection of the rock which overhung the spot on which she was, and to her surprise and confusion beheld standing on the summit the tall and graceful figure of a man, who, with his arms folded in a thoughtful mood, was gazing earnestly and fixedly upon her.

The stranger was young, and his features were remarkably striking and handsome. The rays of the moon fell full upon his high and open forehead, and his dark and piercing eyes seemed to sparkle with mute astonishment and admiration. A profusion of black and glossy ringlets descended luxuriantly to his shoulders, and his figure, which was noble and commanding, yet devoid of pride or haughtiness, was enveloped in a large blue mantle, which was thrown in graceful folds over his right shoulder.

Bewildered and surprised by the attitude and intense glances of the stranger, Angelina was unable to move for a minute or two, when fear taking the place of admiration, she started hastily under the rock on which he was standing, and bounded

as fast as she could along the only path which presented itself to her eyes, unconscious whither it led. Fortunately, it led her on to a heath, which she knew, and here, almost exhausted, she paused to take breath, and looked back to see if the young man was pursuing her. She was very much alarmed when she beheld him running rapidly along the path, and calling upon her to stop. Terror now put redoubled speed to her footsteps, and she again hurried along for about half a mile, when unable to proceed farther without resting, and leaning for support against the withered trunk of a tree, she had the satisfaction to find that the stranger had abandoned his pursuit.

Overcome by the singularity of the events she had that evening met with, Angelina bent her way towards home, but found it impossible to account for the form she had seen in the cavern of the rock. But above all, she could not get the person and features of the handsome stranger from her mind, and as she thought upon him she felt a sensation fluttering at her heart, which she had never before experienced.

It was ten o'clock when she reached home, and her uncle, who was terribly alarmed at her absence, had gone in search of her. Having accounted for her remaining out so late, by attributing it to the storm, and having lost her way, Arthur was satisfied, but enjoined her to confine her rambles in future to such places as she was thoroughly acquainted with.

Visions of the most remarkable description haunted the sleeping fancies of Angelina that night, in which the handsome stranger, and the supposed phantom of the rocky cavern, acted prominent parts, and she arose at an earlier hour than usual on the following morning, unrefreshed and spiritless.

CHAPTER III.

The mysterious occurrence we have related in the previous chapter, gave rise to many reflections in the mind of our heroine, but she could come to no satisfactory conclusion. Was the place she had wandered to inhabited, or was the form she had seen that of an earthly being? She was lost in a chaos of conjecture. But, above all, the form of the handsome stranger she had seen was impressed indelibly upon her recollection, and she was at a perfect loss to account for the interest he excited in her bosom.

The day after this adventure she did not go out, as she felt rather indisposed, and at an early hour in the evening she retired to her chamber, but did not feel inclined to sleep.

She seated herself at the casement, which commanded a view of a large expanse of country from the back of the cottage; hills and valleys, meadows and rivulets, were all seen dancing in the moonbeams, and in gazing upon the tranquil scene, our heroine endeavoured to divert her thoughts from the subjects that engrossed them.

While she was thus wrapt in contemplation, she suddenly beheld the dark shadow of some approaching object moving across the earth, and upon straining her eyes, she distinguished the tall form of a man apparently wrapped in a mantle, walking across the lawn towards the cottage.

Having advanced to within a few yards of the house, the man paused, raised his head, and appeared to be gazing intently up at the window. Surprised and abashed, Angelina involuntarily withdrew her head, and was about to close the shutters, when the melodious tones of a flute broke upon the stillness of the air, and listening with breathless astonishment she recognized the same plaintive air which had been played by the handsome stranger she had seen upon the rock. Completely lost and enchanted, Angelina once more approached the casement, aad looking out, beheld the figure she had before seen, still standing there, and was convinced from his position that he was the musician. The instrument was played with the same exquisite skill which had on a former occasion so delighted her, and the maiden listened to every note with the most unbounded wonder and admiration. At length he ceased, and then approaching almost immediately beneath the casement, raised his head, and the bright beams of the moon revealed to her gaze the handsome features of the youth she had seen upon the rock.

Fearful that he might observe her, although she could have looked upon his noble and expressive countenance for ever, Angelina hastily closed the shutters, and throwing herself into a chair, gave way to the thoughts which the circumstance occasioned.

It was evident that the stranger had watched her to her home; and yet what could be the motive of his curiosity, and who and what was he? Could his designs be bad?—Oh, no! there was not the smallest mark of guilt in the noble lineaments of that open and manly countenance! Angelina was surprised at her own thoughts, and the sensation that involuntarily fluttered around her heart, and at length tired of thinking, she resolved to retire to her couch, but before she did so, she was tempted once more gently to unclose the shutters and to peep from the window, but the stranger was gone.

Angelina tossed for some time restless on her pillow, before sleep fell upon her eyelids, when the following remarkable vision flitted before her imagination :—

She thought she was wandering among the rocks in which she had sought shelter on the night of the storm. It was midnight, and an almost impenetrable darkness was upon the earth and the ocean. No star shone in the firmament to illumine her way; and yet some invisible power seemed to urge her on into the intricacies of the place. The air was piercingly cold, but all around her was still—not even the slightest murmur arose from the waves—an awful silence like that of death appeared to reign over everything. Suddenly, however, the storm arose—the waves roared and rolled, and dashed with inconceivable fury—the lightning blazed in the heavens, and casting its ghastly light across the broad expanse of the ocean revealed to her gaze a vessel tossing and battling with the waves! She fancied she heard the awful shriek of the persons on board for help, and saw them clinging to the shrouds to retard that fate which seemed to be inevitable! one moment more, one terrific whistling through the waters was heard, and the vessel disappeared. Angelina imagined that, bound up to a pitch of distraction and desperation, she rushed to the utmost extent of the beach, till the waters washed over her feet, and the moment the form of a man was dashed ashore! She raised his head, and the lightning darting across his face, showed her the features of a man which bore a remarkable resemblance to the handsome stranger she had seen upon the rock, only he was apparently much older and seemed to be in the agonies of death. For a moment, Angelina imagined in her dream, the expiring man opened his eyes, and fixing them affectionately upon her, exclaimed " *Bless thee, my child!* " and immediately fell into her arms a corpse. In the terror and agony of that moment, she awoke.

Scarcely conscious where she was, and still trembling from the terror created by this mysterious dream, Angelina rubbed her eyes, but her candle was burnt out, and the room was involved in utter darkness. Once more her senses became steeped in sleep, and again she dreamed.

She now imagined herself at the entrance of the cavern, in which she had sought shelter a night or two before; but the storm had abated—the waves were calm, and the form of the drowned man had disappeared. Suddenly raising her eyes to the rock which overhung the entrance to the cavern, she imagined she beheld in characters of fire the following words :—

" *Enter here; search well, and you will be rewarded!* "

In a moment, she thought she entered the cavern, and a supernatural light seemed to dance before her, and guided her way. Through innumerable rocky caverns and subterraneous passages she imagined she walked, until at last she found herself in a lofty gothic chamber, hung with arras, in which were the portraits of a lady and gentleman, the latter of whom was exactly like the drowned man she had seen in her previous dream. At one end of the room hung a coat of arms, on which she imagined was " *a blood-stained shield and a raven's nest!* " and casting her eyes to the floor, she was horror-struck on beholding that it was marked with stains of blood! She started back a few paces when she saw this, and before she could recover, felt herself in a rude grasp! Turning round, she discovered the ferocious features of a strange man, whose eyes were fixed awfully upon her, and he held a dagger in the air, which he prepared to plunge into her bosom.

" Wretch! destroyer of my peace! curse of my hopes," she thought she heard him say, " die! "

She thought she struggled convulsively to escape from his hold, but all her efforts were futile, the dagger's point was within an inch of her bosom, when suddenly a dismal groan was heard, which arrested the stranger's arm, and a selpulchral voice cried—

" *Hold, murderer!* "

The next moment, Angelina fancied in her dream, that casting her eyes towards the portraits they seemed suddenly animated with life, and, stepping from their frames, confronted the stranger, from whose hands the dagger fell, as a peal of thunder reverberated above, and she once more awoke.

Again sleep fell upon the eyelids of Angelina, and again fancy wove around imagination its magic spell. She now thought she was in a dark and dreary passage, the walls of which were damp and loathsome, and were dimly lighted by a lamp depending from the front. She thought she was struggling in the grasp of the stranger she had before seen, whose cheek seemed flushed with wine, and whose eyes sparkled with the most alarming passions. In vain she tried to rescue herself from his hated embraces, and her strength was rapidly becoming exhausted. Another moment and she must have fallen a victim to his guilty desires, when suddenly a door behind them was thrown back on its hinges, and the same handsome stranger of the rock rushed in, sword in hand, to her rescue. Immediately on beholding him, she imagined that the man released her from his hold, and drawing his sword, rushed with great fury upon the stranger, who met him with a cool and determined courage, at the same time he desired Angelina not to fear, that her oppressor should speedily meet the punishment due to the outrage he had committed. The following moment he plunged his sword into the body of his antagonist, who fell and expired with a groan. By a sort of magic so natural to dreams, the scene now in an instant seemed to change, and she found herself before the altar in a chapel, while her deliverer was also kneeling by her side, and a priest had commenced the marriage ceremony. Before, however, he had uttered many words, a strain of heavenly music seemed to burst forth from the organ, a silvery vapour arose from the earth, which, gradually dispersing, revealed to the imagination of Angelina the form of the drowned man in her first dream, and by his side stood the spectral figure she had followed through the rocky avenues. Angelina thought they smiled benignantly upon her and her companion, and seemed to be calling down a blessing upon their head, which, having lasted for a few seconds, the phantom of the man thus spoke in a hollow sepulchral voice—

" It must not be ; nature forbids the union ! "

Again an unearthly strain of music swelled from the organ, the forms seemed gradually to melt away, and Angelina awoke !

The dismal bell of a neighbouring church now tolled forth the hour of two, but Angelina slept no more. The curious visions that had haunted her slumbers occupied her thoughts till daylight, and she in vain sought to elucidate them. With a mind not imbued with superstition, still Angelina could not help thinking that they were forebodings of what was going to happen to her; she connected them with what she had met the last two or three days, and her mind received a very strong impression that she was marked out by Fate to be the heroine of some strange and painful adventure. The mysterious words which she imagined she had seen at the entrance to the cavern, in her second dream, particularly struck her, namely, " *Enter here—search well—and you will be rewarded !* " and she was induced to believe that it was really a supernatural warning given to her, to bring about some mysterious event and discovery. The form she had seen in the cavern the more convinced her of the justness of this idea, and she resolved, in spite of the consequences which might occur to her, to attempt to penetrate the mystery of these subterraneous avenues the next day.

Having come to this determination, her thoughts reverted to the handsome stranger she had encountered in such a singular manner, and his remarkable behaviour.

In vain she tried to conjecture who or what he was ? The more she thought, the more did she become involved in perplexity, and the more anxious was she to have that perplexity removed. That he was of no mean rank, his noble bearing sufficiently convinced her, but whatever could be his motives for following her footsteps, she was perfectly at a loss to imagine.

CHAPTER IV.

FIRM in her determination to search the subterraneous caverns, Angelina seized the opportunity of her uncle being absent from home the following day, and having provided herself with a lamp, and the means of lighting it, made her way towards the rocks.

As she approached the sea-beach, the mysterious events of her dreams recurred to her recollection, and she looked timidly across the ocean, almost expecting to see them realized, and to behold the dying man cast at her feet. But the waves were calm, and the golden rays of the sun streamed full upon the surface of the deep, giving it the appearance of a vast expanse of liquid fire.

After looking cautiously around her for a few moments, to make sure that she was not observed, Angelina mentally committed herself to the care of Providence, and entered the outer cavern, where she paused to listen ere she ventured to proceed. Recollecting the ghastly form she had before seen there, a momentary sensation of fear crept over her, which, however, vanished, when she found that a profound stillness reigned around, save the dismal murmur of the waves as they dashed against the rocks ; she became firm, and smiled at her former apprehensions.

She stepped towards the small cavern, whence she had seen the form issue, and there again listened, but no sounds broke upon her ears. All was buried in obscurity beyond, and Angelina prepared to strike a light; and while she was thus occupied, she thought she heard a noise like the closing of a ponderous door, but all afterwards was as still as death. Having lighted her lamp, she was enabled to discover that the cavern, or rather passage, was very long and narrow. The rays of her lamp could not penetrate to the full extent of this dreary passage, along which she proceeded, frequently pausing to listen and look around her; and as she advanced, it became lower, until at length she was compelled to stoop to prevent her head from coming in contact with the roof.

Upon arriving at the end, it branched off to the right into an avenue, much wider and loftier than the one she had been traversing, and which received light from various natural apertures in the rocks above. As far as Angelina could see, there was not the least signs of any human being having been there before her, and she trembled, for the air around her was keen and damp, and the earth beneath her feet was moist and muddy.

Having arrived at the end of this place, Angelina was surprised to find a large door, with massive hinges, locks, and bolts, but which was standing partially open. Here she paused, and meditated how to act. It was now evident to her that the passage led to some place of habitation or retreat, and the words of her dream recurred to her with greater force than ever. But what might be the character of those who would choose such a strange place for an abode or refuge ?—Perhaps robbers or smugglers, who, doubtless, if they found her there, would, in self-protection, prevent her having the power, if she had the inclination, of betraying their secret. She was nearly resolved to return and abandon her project, but still her curiosity prevailed over her fears, and she was determined to run all hazards to gratify it.

Hearing no noise beyond the door, she took courage, and peeped in, and found that it opened into another subterraneous passage. that seemed to be beyond the chain of rocks, and dug out of the earth. It was very low, and was descended to by two or three broken steps. Angelina boldly threaded this gloomy passage, and found another door at the extremity closed, but it yielded with the slightest effort, and revealed to her a narrow flight of ruinous steps, that appeared to lead to a corridor above. More astonished as she advanced, to find such places, apparently buried in the bowels of the earth, Angelina became completely insensible to fear in her anxiety to penetrate the mystery, and began to ascend the steps. This was a task of considerable difficulty and danger, for they were very much broken, and she had nothing to lay hold of; however, at last she arrived at the top, and fearlessly opened an iron door opposite to her, the key of which was in the lock.

She now found herself in a kind of cell, in one corner of which was a straw mattress, and in another an old chair and a table.

She was positive that the place had been lately occupied by some person, and she began to imagine that the form she had seen had been no phantom, but some unfortunate human being who was either confined there by force, or had become disgusted with the world, and fled to that dismal place to waste its declining days in solitude and meditation.

As these thoughts passed rapidly in our heroine's mind, she felt her resolution increase, and some instinctive power seemed to urge her on, which she found it impossible to resist. She passed through a door on the other side of the cell, into a stone passage, arched over. and winding. Here she once more paused, for she thought she heard a footstep, and holding the lamp above her head, was almost certain that she saw a white object moving in the distance. Once more her fears predominated, and she turned round to hasten back into the cell, but to her surprise and consternation, found that the door had closed with a secret spring, and resisted all her efforts to open it.

Completely at a loss what to do, Angelina wrung

her hands in despair, and upbraided herself for her imprudence, in venturing upon such a wild and dangerous undertaking; then again she tried to discover the secret spring, but in vain, the door was effectually closed upon her, and she had no means of returning by the way she had come. To remain where she was, however, without any effort to escape, would be the height of folly; she therefore determined to pursue her way along this passage with the hope of finding some outlet. With a palpitating heart, she traversed its narrow and intricate windings, frequently pausing as the wind in hollow murmurs whistling through the place, to her disordered imagination sounded like the dismal moans of some troubled spirit : at last, arriving at the end of the passage, she once more thought she beheld the white robes of the form she had seen on a former occasion, flit through the doorway as she reached it.

Confident that she was not this time mistaken, Angelina mustered up resolution to call, and desired the supposed phantom in the name of heaven to stop : but the dismal echoes of her own voice along the gloomy avenues alone answered her, and she rushed with precipitation towards the low archway that seemed to be the only outlet.

A sudden flood of light now burst on Angelina, who extinguished her own, and to her utter astonishment found that she was in a long and lofty gothic gallery, supported by marble pillars, but in a state of decay. She was confident that she was no longer traversing underground, and she was eager to know with what building the secret passages she had tracked communicated. The gallery was lighted by a large window of stained glass at each end, and round the stone frame-work of which the moss and ivy thickly crept. Several oaken doors opened into this gallery, which Angelina tried, but found them fast, until at length she came to one that was open, and she entered without fear. The furniture in this room had evidently been extremely handsome, though antique, and was in tolerable preservation considering the number of years it had been left there in neglect. Angelina now felt convinced that she was in some ruined gothic pile, but could not form any idea what it could be. Many noble paintings and portraits of " knights and ladies fair," were yet hanging on the walls, but so decayed by damp, that it was impossible to make out the subjects.

Passing through this apartment, our heroine found herself in a room of rather large dimensions, but in worse condition. The tapestry was entirely destroyed, and both the casements and shutters broken nearly to pieces; the columns which supported it seemed also rotten and decayed. Issuing from the room by a large oaken door, she stepped into a small dark gallery, and proceeding to the further end, descended a winding staircase, and flinging back a pair of folding doors at the bottom, what was her astonishment to find herself in the Gothic Hall of Saint Mark's Abbey!

Completely thunderstruck at this circumstance, and more than ever convinced that the Abbey was inhabited, not by spectres, but some unfortunate being who sought seclusion from the world, Angelina forgot the injunctions of the unknown woman she had formerly encountered there in so mysterious a manner, and pondered with delight over the crumbling relics of the days of old. Magnificent in the extreme had once been that mouldering hall, and Angelina stood lost in admiration of the immense columns, by which what remained of the roof was supported. There could not possibly be a more striking picture of feudal greatness. In one place the eye rested upon a headless column, its base buried several feet in the earth, and as firm as the monarch of the forest; in another place lay three or four capitals, around which might be seen the mutilated faces of several hideous monsters, bringing to the mind the barbarous ideas of their creators. Here might the idea feast and revel over an heterogeneous mass of broken columns, pilasters, capitals, and dilapidated pinnacles, together with innumerable other striking mementoes of the labour and ingenuity of our ancestors. Our heroine, as she contemplated with sublime admiration and wonder everything around her, became absorbed in a dreamy reverie of the deeds and beings of other days, until she was aroused by the falling of some of the rubbish, which alarmed the birds, who, to the number of several hundreds, sought shelter in the ancient fabric. She now recollected where she was, and the wild woman's warning came fresh upon her mind, but still her insatiable curiosity to explore the Abbey made her disregard it, and she hurried on to the upper end of the hall, and passed through a gothic archway, was soon descending some broken steps, at the bottom of which was a pair of large iron gates, through which she beheld the remains of an extensive and noble chapel. The gates were very heavy and rusty, but after considerable exertion, they being unlocked, she forced them back on their hinges and entered.

A sacred awe was stealing over Angelina's senses, as she gazed upon this once holy building, but she was very suddenly alarmed by hearing a low murmuring sound, as of a human voice; and holding her lamp above her head to facilitate her view, its faint rays fell upon the long flowing white robes of some object that was kneeling before a small altar, as if in devotion.

Fixed immoveable to the spot with amazement, Angelina felt a deadly chill creeping through her veins, mingled with a mysterious curiosity to satisfy her doubts; and before she had time to recover herself, the object before the altar arose, looked around the chapel, and observing our heroine, fixed like a statue, uttered a shriek, bounded behind the altar, and immediately vanished.

" Stay, mysterious being, I conjure thee," cried Angelina, regaining courage when too late; " if thou art some unhappy being of this world, I commiserate and alleviate thy sufferings; and if thou art a spirit of that sphere, the eye of mortal must not penetrate, still have I courage to inquire why thou wanderest from the silent tomb ?" But the dismal echoes of Angelina's own voice were all that answered to her; and rushing towards the altar, she looked in vain for some aperture through which any human being could so suddenly have disappeared.

" Good Heavens ! what awful mystery is this ?" exclaimed Angelina, looking timidly around. Unable to resist the superstitious feelings which were gradually stealing over her, and apprehensive of some new horror, she upbraided herself for the imprudence of which she had been guilty, and determined to quit the ruins with the least possible delay. She was making her way towards the iron gates for that purpose, when she was terrified at hearing some door close heavily in that direction; and presently afterwards the noise of approaching footsteps burst upon the stillness of the gloomy place. What could she now do ?—They were evidently descending the broken steps which led to the gates, and therefore the maiden cou'd not pass that way, without encountering those who had excited her fears; and she could not find any place of outlet on the other side of the chapel. There was no time for deliberation—she heard the rusty gates creaking on their hinges, and almost sinking with consternation, hastily secreted herself behind a broken column, and awaited with a palpitating heart the termination of the singular and alarming adventure. She had not been in this situation a minute, when the gates were thrown open, and two men entered, wrapped up in large dark mantles, who, looking around the chapel with cautious glances, stepped towards a column opposite the one behind which Angelina was concealed;

and the light from a small window streaming full upon their persons and faces, Angelina's astonishment was not a little augmented, when she recognised in one of them the Baron de Morton, who lived near the spot, and in the other his repulsive domestic, Rufus!

Scarcely venturing to breathe, lest they should discover her, although she knew not why she should fear such a circumstance, she crouched down behind the column, and watched their actions.

"Well," exclaimed Rufus, "I suppose this spot will do for the communion; you have no fear of listeners here."

"Right, good Rufus," replied the baron, "we need not indeed fear that the prying eye curiosity will watch our actions in this old abbey, and for that purpose did I resolve that our future secret consultations should be held here. We might have listeners in the castle, and already have I fancied that the baroness begins to——hark!—was not that a voice?"

"Nonsense, 'twas only the wind," returned his servant, "come, to business."

"This is a gloomy place," said the baron, looking around him with something of fear in the expression of his countenance: "report has filled it with frightful forms, and——"

"Psha!" interrupted Rufus, "report is a common liar. Is it possible, my lord, that you can begin to feel qualmish and timid after all the daring deeds you have performed?"

"Be silent, Rufus," returned the baron, in a tremulous voice, "would that those daring deeds of which you speak could be recalled—would that they had never been performed."

"And," rejoined Rufus, in a contemptuous voice, "that you might be the living model of virtue and integrity, and see another luxuriate in that rank and wealth which you now enjoy! Bah!"

"Enjoy!" cried the baron, in a tone of bitterness; "alas! can there be any enjoyment in the fruits of crime—mur——hark!—again! I could have sworn I heard a sigh!"

"Are you going mad?" said Rufus; "however I came not here to listen to a sermon, so, my lord, I'll e'en leave you till you are in a more fitting mood to talk upon the business in which you require my aid. 'Tis only fools who talk of conscience! Psha! the cant of priest-craft—the coward's bugaboo. What is the use of repenting of what has been done years ago, and which nothing can alter now?"

"Well, well, be it so—perhaps I am weak—foolish, good Rufus," replied the baron, in a firmer tone; "but enough, to business at once. Rufus, dost thou remember that dreadful night when, near this spot, thou didst, by my orders——"

Here a hollow gust of wind that swept through the chapel completely drowned the voice of De Morton, and Angelina in vain tried to catch the concluding sentence.

"Methought your lordship's *conscience* was ready enough to remind you of the events of that night, and two or three other circumstances," sarcastically replied Rufus, "but to prove to you that my memory is not in any way impaired, if it please you, I will recapitulate——"

"Nay, nay—hold, Rufus," hastily interposed De Morton, "I meant not that; but I would ask you, are you certain that your arm was sure, and that——"

"Sure!" interrupted Rufus, in a savage voice, "what now? Did not the disappearance of——did not my reeking dagger offer sufficient proofs how truly I had kept my word—how certain had been my aim? Have you grown suspicious, my Lord de Morton?" If so, the sooner we part the better."

"You mistake me, Rufus," said the baron, in an agitated tone, "I——"

Here the whistling of the wind again rendered the words of the baron inaudible, and it was several minutes ere Angelina could make out a syllable they were uttering; she noticed the violence of the baron's gestures, who every now and then looked fearfully around the chapel, as though he was apprehensive that some one was watching them.

"Both, I tell you," at length Angelina heard Rufus say, "why should you doubt?"

"'Tis strange," returned the baron, "and yet the astonishing likeness that rustic beauty bears to——; I was thunderstruck the moment I beheld her, and I felt a deadly chill run through my veins. Her uncle, too, I like him not; there is a mystery about him that convinces me he is not what he wishes to appear to be!"

The conversation was now carried on in so low a tone, that not a word could be overheard. Angelina trembled with excessive terror, like an aspen leaf. The allusion to herself and her uncle filled her bosom with the most acute anguish; and the warning of the mysterious woman of the ruins struck more forcibly on her recollection. In the agitation of her feelings, she disturbed some of the crumbling rubbish which lay around her, and it fell down with a rustling noise, that made both Rufus and the baron start.

"Did you not hear that?" cried the latter.

"I did," returned Rufus, looking fiercely around.

"This time, I am certain I am not deceived," ejaculated the baron, "somebody is here besides ourselves."

"Then their lives shall answer for their curiosity," cried Rufus, drawing a dagger from underneath his mantle, and stalking hastily towards the spot from whence they imagined the noise had proceeded. Who shall attempt to describe the terror of Angelina, when she heard the villain's threat, and saw him advance towards the very place where she was concealed? She held her breath, and tried to crouch beneath the rubbish around her. Rufus walked past the column and almost touched her, but fortunately he saw her not; and after the lapse of two or three moments more, he returned to his trembling companion.

"We were deceived," said he; "it was only the wind that had blown some of the ruins down."

"Probably it was," replied the baron; "but I forgot—this abbey, as you are aware, was formerly in the possession of my family, and I have got the key of those gates with me. I will lock them, and that will secure us from being surprised that way, at any rate."

"Good God! what will become of me? I'm lost!" thought Angelina, as she heard the baron lock the gates.

They now resumed their conversation, but Angelina was in too great a state of agitation to listen to it. At length they prepared to depart by the way they had entered; and as the baron unlocked the ponderous gates, his companion said in a loud tone—

"Enough, my lord—you know you may depend upon me. I will keep a vigilant eye upon them; and should our suspicions be verified——"

"You know how to act," added the baron. "Get thee gone, it may not be prudent for us to depart together."

"Rufus bowed, and following the baron, the gates were locked on the outside, and our distracted heroine found herself a prisoner in the chapel of the abbey ruins.

CHAPTER V.

FOR a few moments Angelina stood and wrung her hands in despair, totally at a loss what to do. The wind whistled cold throughout the chapel, and she was so overcome by her fears and the chilliness of the place, that she could scarcely support herself. The words that she heard pass between the baron and his villanous colleague, and the allusions they had made to some deeds of darkness perpetrated by them in former days, were strongly impressed upon her memory, and the unintelligible threats they had held out to her and her uncle, brought to her recollection the warning she had before received from the mysterious woman in the ruins. These then were the parties she had to fear; and yet how could she or her uncle have incurred their enmity? She was unconscious of having wilfully deserved the hatred or persecution of anybody, much less the Baron de Morton, and therefore was she the more perplexed. But this was no time or place to reflect, for

the day was waning apace, and what would become of her if she was unable to escape from that dismal fabric, which her disordered imagination now filled with the most awful forms? Again lighting her lamp, she searched around the chapel, and more particularly inspected the altar; behind which she was positive she had seen the form that had alarmed her, vanish; but she looked in vain—no signs of an outlet met her eyes, and she clasped her forehead in despair.

Looking up above the place where she was standing, she perceived an aperture in the wall, large enough to admit of a human form, and which had been broken away by the ravages of time; but it was at such a height that she knew not how she could clamber up to it; and even if she succeeded in reaching it, she might be in the same dilemma, not knowing into what place it might open. Desperate situations suggest desperate measures, and accordingly Angelina determined to make an effort to reach it. She hastily collected some of the pieces of ruins, the largest she could lift, and piled them one on top of the other, until she thought she should be able to reach the opening, and then with cautious and trembling steps, prepared to ascend it. With much difficulty she reached the top of this pile, and then with a desperate effort the affrighted maiden clambered up to the aperture, and looking below, found that it opened into a gallery. To descend was a task of more danger than the ascent had been; but at last she accomplished it in safety, and pursued her way along the gallery to a gothic apartment at the end, the door of which was standing open. She entered it—it was lofty and spacious—and what was her surprise to find that it in every respect corresponded with the one she had seen in her dream! There were the portraits of the lady and gentleman; and what the more surprised her was, that the likenesses were complete. Thunderstruck at this remarkable coincidence, she stood and gazed around her, quite unconscious for the moment where she was. Casting her eyes above the arras on the western side of the apartment, she beheld the mouldering remains of a coat of arms, on which she was enabled to trace the devices of a *blood-stained shield and raven's nest.* Induced by these singular coincidences to search, she cast her eyes towards the oaken floor, and was horrorstruck to behold deep stains of what appeared to be human blood!—transfixed to the spot with terror, she continued for several moments to look upon these dreadful marks.

"Good Heavens!" she cried, "what deed of darkness has been perpetrated in this chamber? Alas! whither have my footsteps led me?"

She was startled by what seemed to be a dismal moan and to issue from the opposite side of the room. She trembled, the lamp almost fell from her hand, and her heart palpitated with emotion in her bosom. But nothing met her eyes, and after a second or two, endeavouring to persuade herself that the sound she had heard was nothing more than the wind, she tried to regain her courage, and make her way from the chamber. She looked around her, but perceived no other door by which she had entered, and she had almost given herself once more up to despair, when a thought struck her that she would try the wainscot. She passed her hand underneath the decayed arras; at length her fingers came in contact with a hard substance, which, upon a closer inspection, she was rejoiced to find was a spring. She pressed with all her strength against it, and at last a panel in the wainscot glided gently back, but she started from the opening in alarm, when the rays of the lamp streamed full upon her, and she beheld the form of a man seated on an oaken table with his back towards her, and his head resting on his hand in a disconsolate manner. Trembling with apprehension, she hastily closed the secret panel, and glided back without the slightest noise, and then stood uncertain how to proceed.

While she was in this situation, the man muttered some unintelligible words, and being induced to listen, she heard the following uttered in tones of the most poignant anguish—

"Oh for some oblivious draught to drown the awful recollections of the past!"

The tones of the voice immediately struck Angelina, and she was certain it was the Baron de Morton. Curiosity, which often supersedes the most imminent danger, now involuntarily prompted her to push back the panel, and to watch the baron's proceedings. He was still seated with his back towards her, and appeared to be completely absorbed in his own painful reflections. Frequently would his bosom discharge the most heart-rending sighs, and then he would strike his forehead with his clenched fist, seemingly in bitter agony.

"The ways of guilt," he at length said, "are indeed those of pain and sorrow! Oh, that I could recal the past—that I could blot out from the dark tablet of memory those deeds that have made me accursed and wretched! Lust, ambition, jealousy, pride, oh, what damned passions are ye; into what crime and misery will ye not lead your unhappy victims! But fool! why do I now repine? If I have boldly dared, have I not boldly won? Have I not wealth and rank?—Courted by the great and feared by the humble? Dissatisfied wretch, what more would'st thou have? Why should'st thou murmur at the past that has brought thee so much? And who is there that dare to accuse thee of——? Psha! I will banish this womanish weakness from my mind! Conscience, that hideous scarecrow, shall no more torment me!"

As the baron thus spoke, he suddenly arose, and before Angelina had time to retreat from the opening, he turned, and the rays of his lamp darted upon her. A dreadful tremor seemed in a moment to palsy all his limbs, the lamp dropped from his hands, his eyes rolled wildly in their sockets, cold drops of perspiration stood upon his temples, and in a hoarse voice, he cried—

"Away, dread shade of her my word consigned to death! Mine eyes cannot gaze upon thy ghastly features!—Hence, hence I say, to the grave with thee! Ah!—horror! horror!"

Overcome with the excess of his terrors, the wretched man uttered a frightful shriek and sunk senseless to the floor; while Angelina, with wonderful presence of mind, considering the singularity and awfulness of the event, stepped hastily into the apartment, and glided towards an open door on the other side. It opened upon a flight of stairs, down which she fled with the utmost precipitation, and had the satisfaction to find herself once more in the hall of the abbey.

Breathless with agitation, and almost sinking with exhaustion, she still continued to run towards the path that conducted to her home, and never ventured to look back until she arrived at the cottage door.

CHAPTER VI.

DE MORTON CASTLE was a fine old gothic structure, which had stood the test of many generations, and now seemed, with its lofty battlements, blackened towers, and sturdy moss-covered walls to frown defiance upon the devastating scythe of time. It covered an immense tract of land, and the scenery surrounding it was of the most picturesque description. Hills, dales, woods, lakes, and rivulets met the eye, which ever way it turned, in endless diversity.

But if the external beauties of the castle and its surrounding scenery were striking and enchanting, the interior of the fine old fabric was not less magnificent and imposing. There, all the pomp and pageantry of feudal splendour was displayed in endless variety. Its numerous apartments, its intricate passages, its spacious halls, its armoury, its rare old paintings, richly worked arras, and all the other paraphernalia, too numerous to mention, were all objects of interest to those who delight in such things, and showed the wealth and power its former possessors must have enjoyed.

The present Baron de Morton was said to be possessed of all that wealth that his ancestors were renowned for from time immemorial, but his character was viewed with detestation by all well-intentioned men, and with dread by his dependents. He was haughty, stern, passionate, and overbearing. He seemed to look upon those who were placed in an inferior situation to that he himself occupied, as being even beneath contempt, and upon every opportunity exercised an authority that was thoroughly disgusting.

The baron was now about fifty years of age; his form was noble and commanding, and his features were what might still be termed handsome, yet withal they were stamped with the forbidding aspect of pride, and there was an air of haughtiness in his whole demeanour, which was anything but prepossessing.

Orilia, Baroness de Morton, was by birth an Italian, and still bore the traces of that surpassing beauty which had made her so celebrated in her younger days; but there was an expression in her piercing black eyes, a certain bearing in her whole behaviour, which plainly told that inordinate vanity and passions of the most dangerous nature still predominated in her bosom. Her's was a beauty that rather seemed to command admiration as a right, than to win it; a power of fascination which held her votaries in her chains, without engaging their esteem.

The baron and his lady had abandoned the seat of his ancestors for several years, and had been residing on the continent, leaving the castle and his wealthy domains in Yorkshire, to the care of an old and faithful steward, who had been in the family for a number of years; and seldom wrote to know how his affairs went on.

There were strange stories circulated concerning the present baron; it was even whispered by many that he had come into the possession of the title and estates of de Morton in a suspicious manner. However, be that as it might, certain it is that his brother, the former possessor of the castle, had disappeared in a most mysterious way, and his death had never been satisfactorily accounted for. Soon afterwards, the present baron was united to the widowed baroness, notwithstanding she was then *enciente*, and had ever appeared to view him with a coldness approaching almost to repugnance. The baroness was delivered of a child, but what the sex of that child was, was never known, as it was said to be still-born, and a very short time subsequent to this event the baroness herself died suddenly, and it was at the time thought under very suspicious circumstances.

Soon after this occurrence, the baron quitted Yorkshire in the manner which we have before described, and nothing more was heard of him for several years, during which he did not even so much as correspond with his steward; when suddenly, without giving any notice, he returned to his castle, with his present wife, whom he married in Italy.

When the baron returned to the castle on the evening of this singular meeting with Angelina his extreme agitation was visible to every one —his countenance was deadly pale, and his eye looked wildly around, as though he expected to behold some frightful object. He declined the evening repast, and giving the baroness a stern reply to her question of whether he was unwell, he abruptly left the room and retired to his own apartment, locking himself in, to prevent the intrusion of any one. There, for hours, he was heard to pace the room with the most disordered footsteps, and to utter incoherent sentences, which the baroness, who was induced to listen, in vain sought to conjecture the meaning of. At length he hastily summoned the attendance of one of his domestics, and commanded him to send Rufus to him immediately.

"What means this agitation, my lord?" demanded Rufus, when he entered the chamber and beheld the ghastly hue which overspread the baron's features, and the violent emotion which agitated his whole frame; "what has happened that could have taken such a singular effect upon you?"

"Rufus," replied the baron in a hoarse tone, clasping the arm of his myrmidon, and looking solemnly in his countenance. "Rufus, I have seen her, but this night did her restless spirit cross my path, and fill my soul with horror!"

"Are you so weak, my lord," said Rufus scornfully, "as to believe in such old womanish nonsense as this? Psha!—but your mind is disordered; you are not well; you had better retire to rest!"

"Rest," reiterated the baron, with a laugh of derision, "rest for one who has——"

"Bah?" interrupted Rufus, "I am sick of this superstitious cant; forsooth, my lord, if you give way to these idle chimeras, nothing but disgrace and infamy can be the result of it. You must have been labouring under some wild and sickly delusion."

"Oh, no, Rufus," returned the baron, "it was no delusion; I saw her as plainly as I behold you now; just as she looked when first I knew her, so young, so lovely; her eyes were fixed upon me with an expression of reproach that smote me with horror. I tell you, Rufus that I am positive I was not mistaken. When you left me, I could not resist a strange temptation I felt to wander over these chambers, in which such deeds of iniquity have been perpetrated; and while pondering over the horrors of the past, I suddenly raised my head, and, gracious Heaven! there, gazing upon me, stood the form of——"

"Nonsense!" said Rufus, "your weakness deceived you, and conjured up the hideous phantom; come, my lord, arouse yourself; this conduct is unworthy of you. It is only old women and children who believe in such stories as these, and—ah, now I think of it—you remember the noise we heard while we were conferring in the abbey ruins?"

"I do! I do!" hastily replied the baron, "what of that?"

"As I came hither," answered the other,

" I beheld that peasant girl, Angelina, as they call her, and with whose singular likeness to——"   ,

" Ah ! I know," gasped forth the baron " b ut proceed, proceed !"

" She seemed to have come from the direction of the abbey ruins," observed Rufus, " and was running quickly, apparently in great agitation ; I should have spoken to her, but, on beholding me she increased her speed, and was soon out of sight."

" And what of that ?" demanded De Morton ; " what has all this to do with the subject we were conversing upon ?"

" What has it to do with it, my lord ?" repeated Rufus, " why, everything—mark my word, this same girl it was who had been wandering over the ruins, and probably she overheard what we were talking about."

" Ah !" exclaimed the baron, as the opinion of Rufus seemed to strike him forcibly ; " by my soul, this is not improbable, and if so, it was her that I beheld, and who so much alarmed me. But what an extraordinary likeness. And yet 'tis impossible ! By heaven, if I thought that ——I must see this Arthur Woodfield, and question him, and if my surmises prove correct——"

" The girl dies !" added Rufus, in an under tone.

CHAPTER VII.

THE alarm which Angelina felt after her strange rencontre with the Baron de Morton was noticed by her uncle, for, on her arrival at the cottage she was completely breathless and exhausted. He questioned her as to the cause, but she returned an evasive, an unsatisfactory answer, and complaining of headache, requested to be allowed to retire to rest.

" I suppose, coz," said the giddy an d thoughtless Laura, in her usual tones, " if the truth was known, you have been paying another visit to those haunted ruins, and have been frightened, in spite of all your pretended courage ; mark my words, Angelina, if you do persist in disturbing the hobgoblins in their retreat, some of them will run away with you one of these days, and we shall never see you again."

Angelina in vain, by significant glances at her loquacious cousin, endeavoured to stop her tongue, but Laura either would not, or did not observe her, and went on till she had divulged the whole secret of their visit to St. Mark's Abbey.

" Angelina," said her uncle seriously, " you did very wrong to wander to that gloomy fabric, wherein the most depraved wretches are reported to hold their haunts, and I trust you will not repeat your visits for fear that any harm should befall you."

" Indeed, my dear uncle," replied Angelina, who had now recovered herself, " I think your apprehensions are unfounded, for I have been all over the ruins, and saw no signs of the lawless men to whom you allude."

" Well, but you know, Angelina," said her cousin, " that we have had convincing proof that if the abbey is not inhabited by mortal devils, it is the haunt of supernatural ones. Dear me ! —I shall never forget what we saw there the other day, as long as I live."

" What do you mean, Laura ?" demanded her father, whose curiosity was excited by her words, " what is the awful adventure to which you allude ?"

" Oh, it is nothing worth mentioning, uncle," said Angelina hastily, " but my silly cousin, who is so very superstitious, is apt to attach importance to the most trifling events."

" Oh, indeed," said Laura, " but the event to which I allude was no trifle, though, and you was frightened enough at first as well as me ; though you did brave it out so heroically afterwards."

" Well, let me hear it," said Mr. Woodfield, " and then I shall be better able to judge which of you is in the right."

" Oh, no, my dear uncle," exclaimed Angelina, with much confusion, " it is not worth listening to ; it is a foolish story, and——"

" Well, then, as foolish as it is, I shall relate it, and then hear my father's opinion upon the matter," said the pertinacious Laura. " I maintain that it will go far to prove that the spirits of the departed are allowed to revisit this earth. Well, father, you must know, that about a month ago, me and Angelina paid a visit to the ruins of St. Mark's Abbey ; I confess that she had no little trouble to persuade me to accompany her, for the many strange accounts I had heard of it, did not prepossess me much in its favour ; however, she was so coaxing and wheeling, that at last she did prevail, and I went with her. Well, we remained there some time, and looked about us, without anything particular occurring, but I was in a terrible state of uneasiness, expecting every moment to see the grim spirit of some old monk dart forth from behind the ruins. Angelina was so wrapt up in the contemplation of everything around her (though, for my part, I cannot see anything to admire in broken pillars and statues without heads), that I begged in vain to return home, and presently a storm arose, and we were compelled to remain in the dismal place until it had abated. Presently we heard a strange noise, which Angelina at first attributed to the howling of the wind through the different apertures, but at length it was repeated, and th flashing of the lightning the next moment revealed to us——"

" Beware !" at that moment uttered a hollow voice. The female screamed, and Mr. Woodfield, astonished at the singular interruption, immediately turned his eyes towards the casement, upon which he perceived those of his daughter and niece were fixed, and was completely thunderstruck at the object which there met his view.

A supernatural light seemed blazing outside the cottage, and standing in the midst of it was the figure of the mysterious woman who had appeared to Angelina and her cousin in the ruins of St. Mark's Abbey. The blue reflection of the light imparted a most ghastly aspect to the countenance of the mysterious being, whose eyes were fixed upon the astonished and terrified group, and one hand was held out in a menacing attitude towards Laura, as though she would enjoin her to silence.

For a moment or two, so surprised was Mr. Woodfield at this singular appearance, that he had not the power to move or speak, while his wife, Angelina, and Laura, were all, as it were, petrified to the spot, but at length, determined to fathom the truth, and to know the reason of the woman's visit to them, he darted out of the cottage.

As he quitted the porch, the woman fixed upon him a singular indescribable look, and walked, or rather seemed to glide to some distance from the place where she had before stood, and there she fixed herself in an attitude, apparently determined to await the approach of Mr. Woodfield.

The woman continued unmoved until he had nearly reached her, when she uttered a wild laugh, and darted into the wood, which commenced not far from the cottage, and was soon hidden from his view, in spite of the precipitation with which Mr. Woodfield pursued her footsteps.

Mr. Woodfield hastened to the spot where she had disappeared, but the darkness of the wood, which was almost impervious to the light of the moon, prevented him seeing anything at more than two or three yards' distance, and he was consequently unable to discover any traces of her; he, therefore, returned to the cottage, bewildered and disappointed.

This incident had very much alarmed Angelina, who was at a loss to imagine the motive the woman could have for thus so closely following her footsteps. The interview she had had with her in the abbey ruins, and all that she had said to her, recurred to her memory with redoubled force, and she could not help thinking that her fate was in some way or other connected with her's. Her uncle, who knew her delicate nature, and saw the alarm into which the visit of the woman had thrown her, much as he was himself astonished and perplexed at the circumstance, endeavoured on his return to the cottage to persuade her that the woman was only one of their neighbours, who had assumed the wild dress and mysterious behaviour for the purpose of a hoax; but had he known what had previously taken place between the awful looking stranger and his niece, at St. Mark's Abbey, he would have seen that all his attempts would be futile.

"Hoax, you may call it, if you please, father,' said Laura, who had now partially recovered from the terror into which the circumstances had thrown her, "but I mean to say that it is no such thing; I have very good reason to know and so has Angelina, that——"

Here the simple girl was again about to reveal the secret of their adventure at the abbey, when Angelina hastily interrupted her, and by a significant look recalled her to recollection.

"Well," returned Laura, " I was only going to say that Angelina knows very well, if she likes to confess it, that, as sceptical as she pretends to be, she really does not disbelieve that there are such things as supernatural visitations, and——"

"Ah, Laura speaks very true," interrupted Mrs. Woodford, who had been anxious to give vent to her opinions upon the mysterious subject, "and I hope none of us are such sinners as to think that the spirits of the dead are not allowed to revisit this earth. Goodness me! they do say that this neighbourhood has been the scene of some shocking transactions, and who knows but this may be the ghost of some unhappy wretch who met with an untimely end here?"

"Nonsense, wife!" returned Mr. Woodfield, "you are ever fancying something of this sort. Any one would suppose that you had been born in a church-yard, and cradled in a tomb. If a mouse only stirs in the cupboard, you imagine it is some terrific spectre or other, coming from the other world to frighten us all out of our wits, and if a cricket but rattles against the wainscot, it is construed into the death-watch directly."

"I don't care what anybody says," observed Mrs. Woodfield, " but nothing shall alter my opinion. Why didn't I hear old Mrs. Ambrose call me three distinct times, the very minute she died, although we were at the time nearly two hundred miles away from the place; and didn't our old dog, Bluff, howl——"

"Psha! enough of this," interrupted Mr. Woodfield, affecting to laugh, and once more endeavouring to restore his niece to her wonted cheerfulness. Angelina, however, could not divest her mind of the impression made upon it by the adventures of the evening, and the more she reflected upon it, the greater was she at a loss to elucidate the mystery.

Mr. Woodfield's curiosity was also excited by the words of Laura, and also the singular appearance of the woman, and he was about to interrogate his daughter farther upon the subject, when he was aroused by a tapping at the casement, and, glancing in that direction, they beheld the honeysuckle pulled aside, and the tac-

of the mysterious being who at present occupied their thoughts, gazed full upon them.

For a minute or two that piercing glance—that wild, unnatural look, was fixed alternately upon Angelina and her uncle, but before they could recover from their confusion and astonishment, she forced up the casement, and in a voice of deep and impressive solemnity, she commanded Mr. Woodfield (calling him by his name) to follow her.

" Why do you visit my cottage at such a late hour as this, woman?" demanded Mr. Woodfield, " and what is your business with me?"

" I will not satisfy your questions here," replied the woman; " what I have to reveal must be to your ear alone. Follow me, I say."

" I know you not," said Mr. Woodfield, " and I cannot think of complying with such a singular request from a stranger."

" You had better obey me," returned the woman, or you may repent that you did not avail yourself of the information I can give you when it is too late."

" Why not impart what you have to say, here?" asked Mr. Woodfield.

" I have told you; there are listeners."

" But they will retire."

" That matters not, the walls have ears."

" Whither would you I should attend you?"

" To the wood."

" At such an hour, with a stranger, and alone?"

" Are you afraid that a woman will harm you, Mr. Woodfield? But I promise you that there shall be nothing wrong."

Mr. Woodfield paused and hesitated. The request was a singular one, and especially when it was made by a complete stranger, the ambiguity of whose appearance and behaviour were sufficient of themselves to create a doubt and suspicion, and a sentiment very nearly allied to fear. Mrs. Woodfield and Laura, who had been trembling with consternation all the time the woman had been speaking, looked at him with a significant expression, which was meant to persuade him not to comply; but after a few moments' deliberation, his curiosity overcame his doubts, and he told the woman he would attend her. The woman smiled and made a motion with her hand towards the wood, and Mr. Woodfield having put on his hat, and, taken with him his stout cudgel in case of danger, left the cottage, and they were both soon hidden from the view.

For several moments after Mr. Woodfield had departed, the three females were so confused and amazed that they could not speak, but Laura having at length got once more the free use of that garrulous member, her tongue, expressed her firm belief that her poor father would never return again, and that she was confident he would be spirited away by the

awful-looking being who had so much alarmed them, and who she was certain did not belong to this world. In this sensible opinion she was backed by her mother, who wrung her hands, and a thousand times denounced the folly and imprudence of her husband, whom she never expected to see again. Angelina endeavoured to quiet her apprehensions, though she scarcely knew what to think herself; she was in a state of inconceivable suspense and wonder till he returned.

More than half an hour had elapsed before Mr. Woodfield again appeared to the anxious eyes of the party in the cottage. His countenance was pale; his lips quivered, and his whole frame evinced the most violent emotion.

" Good gracious, Arthur!" cried Mrs. Woodfield, alarmed at his manner, " what is the matter with you, and what has occurred to agitate you thus?"

" Question me not," replied Mr. Woodfield, in a tone of asperity the good dame seldom had before heard him assume; " let us retire to rest immediately, it is late."

Seeing the agitation of her husband, Mrs. Woodfield did not for the present venture to question him further, and the three females in vain tried to conjecture what could have been the nature of the mysterious woman's communication to him, which had so unusually excited and alarmed him.

When Angelina retired to her chamber, she ruminated for some time over the singular events of the day; her adventure in the abbey ruins; her encounter with the Baron de Morton; the appearance of the mysterious woman at the cottage, and what could have been the purport of her secret communion with her uncle. The more she dwelt upon these perplexing subjects, the more did she become bewildered in the mazes of doubt and uncertainty. She felt a presentiment of some impending evil, but in vain tried to imagine what it could be or who could wish or have any interest in annoying their humble and inoffensive family.

The following morning's repast was scarcely over, when looking out at the cottage door, she was astonished to behold the Baron de Morton approaching. She shuddered involuntarily as she gazed upon him, and remembered the words she had heard him utter the night before, and the terror he had evinced on beholding her. What had passed between him and Rufus, in the ruins, fully convinced her that the weight of some dark deeds of former days weighed heavily upon his conscience, and strange as the idea appeared to be, she could not help imagining that she was in some way or other connected with him.

Anxious as she was to learn what could be his reason for visiting the cottage, she did not like to meet him again, she therefore excused herself to her uncle, and left the cottage by a back way just as the baron entered it.

The Baron de Morton greeted **Mr. Wood-field** with unusual condescension and politeness, but there was something so repulsive in the restless glare of his eyes, that Mr. Woodfield could not help feeling uncomfortable in his presence.

"To what may I attribute the honour of this visit, my lord?" asked Mr. Woodfield.

"Simply to a wish to put a few questions of the utmost importance to you, Mr. Wood-field," replied the baron, "can we be alone?"

Mr. Woodfield bowed, and led the way to the room upstairs, where the astonished dame and her daughter heard him lock the door. They remained here for above an hour, and frequently spoke in loud tones, and seemed as if they were quarrelling; but neither Laura nor her mother could distinguish any more than a disjointed sentence here and there, which served only to involve them in still greater mystery. At length the room door was opened, and the baron descended the stairs, followed by Mr. Woodfield. His face was flushed—he looked stern, and was evidently much excited, and Mr. Woodfield betrayed scarcely less emotion. As the baron was about to leave the cottage, he turned round to Mr. Woodfield, and said—

"You will do well to think better of this business, sir, or you may have cause to regret it."

"No further reflection, my lord," replied the other, firmly, "can alter my resolution; and knowing that my conduct is dictated by probity and justice, I do not fear the result."

The baron frowned; fixed his eyes for a moment upon the countenance of Mr. Woodfield, and then, without uttering a word, left the cottage.

CHAPTER VIII.

MR. WOODFIELD maintained the most profound silence upon the subject of the baron's visit to him, and what had been the purport of their conversation; but it was noticed he was very dull and thoughtful for many days afterwards, seldom left home, and particularly cautioned his niece not to go near de Morton Castle any oftener than possible. He also expressed considerable uneasiness whenever the baron's name happened to be mentioned, and did not appear to wish to converse upon such a subject, or to make any allusion to that nobleman.

Mrs. Woodfield was in a perfect fever of excitement at the mystery of the events which had taken place within the last few days, and she racked her brain in vain to endeavour to elucidate them; but that which created her astonishment and anxiety more than all, was the baron's visit to their cottage and the secret conference he had had with her husband. The words they had made use of at parting, and the expression of the baron's features, showed that the interview had been anything but an amicable one, and the threat which the speech of the latter seemed to convey, raised in the old woman's mind the most serious apprehension; for she recollected the character which he bore, and she dreaded the effects of his vengeance, should her husband act in any way contrary to his wishes. But what could be the nature of the business he wanted Mr. Woodfield to perform, and why should he so particularly select him from among all his many tenants and dependents, for the accomplishment of a task, which evidently, by the secret manner in which it was conducted, was of such vast importance? The old woman continued to ponder over these curious circumstances for some time, and by the period she had become tired of thinking about them, she was more entangled and bewildered in the mazes of conjecture than ever. She would have questioned her husband upon the subject, but she knew his disposition, and would not venture to inquire into that which he did not seem disposed to explain.

In the meantime, Angelina's mind was as busily engaged in ruminating and trying to unravel the mystery of the occurrence that had taken place, but with as little success as her aunt. One opinion, however, she could not help coming to, which was, that she was in some way or the other connected with the business on which the baron had sought an interview with her uncle; but in what way, she could not form even the most remote idea. She recollected the agitation de Morton had betrayed on encountering her in St. Mark's Abbey, and the strange words he had uttered, and the conversation which she had partly overheard in the vaults beneath the Abbey, between him and Rufus; and the warning the mysterious woman had given her, together with the crest of the baron, which so exactly corresponded with part of it—and the more she dwelt upon these things, the more was her opinion strengthened. She needed not a second warning from Mr. Woodfield for her to avoid the vicinity of the castle, for there was something so revolting to her in the countenance of its haughty owner, that she involuntarily shuddered whenever she beheld him, and always avoided him as much as possible, from an unaccountable apprehension of danger, whenever she saw him.

Thus passed a fortnight, and as nothing more occurred to strengthen the fears of Mrs. Woodfield, and Mr. Woodfield having relapsed into his general mode of behaviour, she began to drive it from her recollection and never even hinted anything upon the subject to the latter. During this interval Angelina had seldom left the cottage for any distance, only wandering occasionally in the meadows adjacent, or reclining with a book under the foliaged canopy of a shady tree in the neighbouring greenwood.

The stranger she had twice seen often arose to the damsel's thoughts, and when he did so, she would feel the blush mantling to her cheeks, and her heart throb with a sensation she was at a loss to understand the meaning of, and which she never remembered to have experienced before. Sometimes she could picture him in her mind's eye as she first beheld him, and then all the graces of his person, and the manly beauty of his countenance, would return to her memory in colours so vivid that she could not obliterate them. In spite of her endeavours to think to the contrary, she could not help feeling that she should like to behold him more than once.

If Angelina during this time obeyed the wishes of her uncle, by not re-visiting the ruins of St. Mark's Abbey, it was not because she feared to do so after the alarming adventure she had met with there the last time, but because she was fearful of offending him by acting in opposition to his will. Yet did she often feel an ardent desire to examine its numerous vaults and chambers, to ascertain whether they were really inhabited by a human being or not; a supposition she was inclined to encourage from the circumstance of the form she had once caught a hasty glimpse of. But what motives could induce any person to seclude themselves in that wretched and dismal place? Angelina knew not then that there were sorrows that would drive the sufferer to any act of desperation.

At length, however, unable longer to resist the impulse which urged her on, she resolved once more to examine the ruins. She could not help thinking that by some strange means or the other, her fate was mixed up with the mysteries of the abbey, and in spite of whatever danger might accrue to her for her hardihood, she determined that nothing should induce her to waver in her resolution until she had arrived at some satisfactory result.

She entered the abbey by a doorway in the northern wing of the building this time, and found herself in a gothic hall similar to the one she had before traversed, only it was much more gloomy. It was a heavy piece of architecture, in a state of rapid decay, and the stone pavement was completely overgrown with rank weeds. Around this hall were to be seen, fast mouldering to decay, the banners and escutcheons of the family of De Morton, and in various niches were the tall, black, coarsely executed statues of the famous former members of that ancient house. This place was dimly lighted by four small casements overgrown with ivy, and a very lofty one of stained glass at the extremity, which was finely executed, but covered with dirt, ivy, and cobwebs. Ever and anon the wind whistled in fitful gusts (for the day was lowering and chilly) through the several chasms in this dreary hall, and Angelina felt a secret awe stealing over her as she contemplated the grandeur of everything in decay, but still no fear possessed her mind.

She entered beneath a low porch at the left-hand side of the hall, and finding that the place was very dark, although it was in the middle of the day, she lighted a lamp which she had taken care to bring with her, and ascended a flight of stairs beyond. This led her to a small gallery, upon which three doors opened, leading apparently to different chambers. Angelina tried two of them, but they were quite fast; the third yielded to her hand, and entering the room, she found the key was in the lock on the other side. She looked around her, and found herself in a handsome apartment, very lofty, and hung round with full-length portraits. The furniture was very elegant, and not in such a state of decay as that she had before seen in some of the chambers of the ancient fabric. Three lofty casements descended to the floor, and opened upon the terrace, which overlooked the ocean.

In this apartment Angelina paused and looked around her: all was still as death, save the dashing of the waters against the rocky shore, and, occasionally, the rumbling noise of a portion of the falling ruins which was driven down by the wind. Suddenly, she fancied she heard a noise at the further end of the apartment, and looking in that direction, what was her astonishment to behold the full length portrait of a lady pushed back from its frame, and a female figure in white stepped from it, but perceiving our heroine, it uttered a faint scream, and glided back; the portrait closed again without a sound, and Angelina, in a frenzy of astonishment and eager curiosity, rushed to the spot, but the portrait seemed quite sound, and resisted all her efforts to force it back.

Surprised, bewildered, and confused, Angelina, vainly trying to discover the secret spring by which the portrait was forced back, stood for a moment or two uncertain how to act. That she had not been deceived she was certain; and now, confident that the abbey afforded shelter to some unfortunate being or the other, she resolved to prosecute her search until she had discovered her. As this determination rushed upon her mind, she lighted the lamp, and quitted the room, proceeding along the gallery to see if she could find any other outlet which might lead to some of the rooms or vaults beneath the abbey, in which she imagined it was most likely the recluse would conceal herself. The gallery terminated by a circuitous flight of steps, and after passing along a narrow passage, and descending some more broken steps, Angelina found that her conjectures were correct, for she was in the dismal vaults beneath the chapel of Saint Mark.

She shivered with the cold air of that loathsome place, and holding the lamp above her head, as its faint rays fell upon the damp and gloomy walls, she could almost imagine that she saw the grim phantoms of some of the monks of old, who formerly inhabited those lonely cells. She was not allowed much time for thought, for she was startled, and somewhat alarmed, when she remembered what she had overheard between the Baron de Morton and Rufus, by hearing a heavy door creaking upon

its hinges, and looking up, she beheld a door open at the very extremity of the vault, and standing there she again saw the form she had seen not long before in the apartment upstairs. —She seemed apparently in the act of emerging into the cell, when the light from the lamp which Angelina carried, streamed across her eyes, and uttering a shriek, which sounded dismally through these subterraneous apartments, she darted back, and ere Angelina could reach it, the door was closed with a loud bang, and resisted all her efforts to open it.

Angelina's curiosity and suspense were now almost insupportable; she paced the vault to and fro with hurried and impatient footsteps, and then knocking at the door, ejaculated in the most earnest tones—

"Mysterious being, whatever you are, do not fly from one who has not the power, had she even the will, to harm you; and who has a heart that can sympathise in your sorrows, and would pour the balm of consolation into your bosom."

No answer was returned to this appeal, and, after waiting a few moments to no purpose until the damp, unwholesome vapours of the place began to curl around her lamp, and to have a powerful effect upon her, Angelina, finding that she could not proceed any further in that direction, with cautious footsteps reascended the steps, and once more returned to the apartment in which she had first seen the female form. She was not a little surprised when she beheld the secret panel open, and stepping lightly towards it, she listened, but hearing no sound, she ventured to enter the room into which it opened.

It was a small dark closet, and contained no articles of furniture, save a couple of chairs. She could perceive no place of outlet beyond, and while she was wondering in what way the female had effected her escape, she felt the boards tremble under her weight, and she had only just time to step aside when a trap door fell in, upon the spring of which she imagined she had trod, and revealed to her a small depository underneath the flooring, which contained a large iron chest. Angelina tried to open it, but it was locked, and she was about to give up the examination in despair, when her foot kicked against something, and stooping, she found it was a rusty old key, which seemed to have been dropped there by accident and not design.

Angelina paused ere she applied it to the lock, and a strange sensation came over her, but soon recovering herself, and knowing the justice of her intentions, she felt firm and undaunted, and with a mental prayer, she put the key into the lock. Instantly the lid flew open, and to the horror of the intrepid girl, revealed to her gaze the mouldering bones of *a human skeleton*!

With a loud shriek, she let fall the lid of the chest, and starting into the chamber, closed the secret panel, the spring of which she had previously discovered, and hurried down the stairs into the hall. Here, for the first time, she paused to recover breath, to reflect upon the dreadful spectacle she had seen, and to decide what course it was best to pursue.

At length, as it was getting late, she resolved to return home, and at another time to prosecute her search still further, hoping that she might again encounter the mysterious female, and be enabled to discover some clue to the perpetrators of a crime, which had evidently been for so many years hidden, and which she could not help thinking she was ordained by an in-scrutable Power, to be the means of disclosing to the world.

CHAPTER IX.

WITH the utmost precipitation, and appalled at what she had seen, Angelina quitted the chamber, having, however, the presence of mind first to fasten the chest and close the trap over it, taking the key of the former with her. As she descended the broken stairs, her heart throbbed, and she frequently looked back, expecting to see the ghastly shade of the murdered person pursuing her; or fancying that she heard its dismal groans.

Evening had now spread its sombre mantle over the earth, and when Angelina had reached the hall, her lamp being exhausted, she was involved in complete darkness. She had very little difficulty, notwithstanding, in finding her way to the door, but no sooner was she about to quit the place, than the light from a lantern blazed across her face, and she started back with considerable alarm when she beheld the Baron de Morton. But if Angelina was alarmed, the terror of the baron appeared to be tenfold; he fixed his appalled gaze upon her countenance, his face became deathly pale, his eyes were distended, his whole frame trembled, and he exclaimed, in a voice hoarse with agitation—

"Avaunt, dread phantom! Why again do you cross my path? My eyes become scared in gazing on! It was not I that did the bloody deed—why then do you haunt me? Ah!—a light dawns upon my brain; fool I was to be so deceived. By hell, I will know whether you are a mortal or a being of the other world! Ah! I grasp your arm, you are not what my coward conscience conjured up; no, I know you now; you are the girl whose strange likeness to her has so haunted my fancy. Nay, attempt not to leave me; you have heard too much, and——"

"My lord," ejaculated Angelina, as the baron grasped her arm. "What means this violence? ... have I incurred your displeasure? for heaven's sake do not grasp my arm so vehemently, but suffer me to depart."

"Never!" cried the baron; "never shall you leave me, until I am satisfied who you are, and for what purpose you visit these ruins so frequently; tell me, girl, and without equivocation, Mr. Woodfield is in no way related to you;—is it not so?"

"Why do you ask me such a question, my lord?" said the astonished Angelina; "and why should you take such an interest in one who——"

"Answer my question, girl," cried the baron,

fiercely, while an indescribable expression darted from his eyes, and he held her arm with a tighter gripe than than before; "think not to deceive me. Who and what are you?"

"Your lordship knows who I am," answered Angelina, making a powerful effort to regain her firmness; "I am but the niece of a humble cottager, but who would not fail, were he present, to resent, even to you, or the king himself, any insult offered to me. Unhand me, my lord, and let me pass; this conduct to an unprotected female redounds not to your credit."

"Yes, it must be so!" exclaimed De Morton, as his agitation increased; "the very looks, the expression, the whole demeanour is the same! They would lay a snare to entrap me, and bring me to disgrace and ignominy, but it shall not be. Girl, either divulge to me the truth, or this dagger shall pierce your heart!"

Angelina screamed aloud with terror, as the baron drew a dagger from beneath his cloak, and with a look of ferocious determination, held it to her breast, and seemed ready in an instant to fulfil his diabolical threat. At that critical moment, however, when Angelina had given herself up for lost, she heard a rustling from behind, and as the baron repeated his threat, and raised the dagger in the air, a commanding voice exclaimed—"Hold, villain!" and his arm was immediately arrested by a powe... .   Angelina looked up and recognized in her preserve. ... all and noble figure of the young stranger, who she had ..... and who had excited such an una......ntable interest in her bosom

"Tr... ..y ruffian!" he exclaimed, as he forced the murderous blade from the baron's hand, and dashed him from him; "away with you, or you shall pay dear for this outrage on a defenceless girl."

"Ah! who art thou?" demanded the baron trembling with rage and disappointment; "presumptuous varlet, and darest thou to attempt to foil me in my purpose? But beware, rash fool, you know not the power I possess; dread my vengeance!"

"I despise both you and your empty threats, Baron de Morton," said the young man, scornfully; "even now, in spite of boasting, I could, at a signal, place you in a situation that would soon make you repent having aroused my anger. Away with you, proud noble, and bear in mind this caution—dare not, on your life, attempt to harm in future this damsel, for know that there are those who can trample your power under foot, who will be ready to fly to her protection."

The baron paused for a few moments, apparently petrified at the boldness of the young man's words, and gazed upon him with looks of doubt and apprehension; then turning a threatening glance upon Angelina, he muttered some incoherent sentences, and rushed from the spot.

"Fair damsel," said the handsome stranger, in tones whose sweetness penetrated to the heart of our heroine, while he gazed upon her with looks of the most ardent admiration, "how happy I am to think that I should have been the means of rescuing you from the violence of that ruffian. Be not alarmed, while I am with you no harm can happen to you: with your leave I will see you in safety to your home."

With what rapture did Angelina listen to every sentence which fell from the lips of the noble stranger, whose features, as he spoke, seemed to be lighted up with double energy, ... expression of the most exquisite feeling. Hastily, however, regaining her usual equanimity, she returned to him in suitable terms her acknowledgments for the service he had rendered her.

The stranger seemed to hang with delight upon every word she spoke, and proffered her his arm, which with a deep blush, and in an embarrassed tone, she declined to accept, as she said she was so near home, that she would not further intrude upon his kindness.

"Your pardon, fair lady," observed the stranger, "but when I recollect the danger from which I have so lately rescued you, and the probability there is that the baron, or some of his myrmidons, may still be lurking about the neighbourhood, I cannot suffer you to return home by yourself. But if I may make myself so bold, I would seriously advise you to discontinue your rambles among these ruins, in the evening especially, for you know not the danger that lurks around."

Angelina could no longer object to his importunities, and suffered him to accompany her towards the cottage. As they proceeded, her manner became less embarrassed towards the stranger, and she listened with the most earnest pleasure to his conversation, which was polished, and bespoke the gentleman

He was a young man, apparently not more than twenty-four years of age; his complexion dark, his features regular and expressive; his eyes beamed with intelligence, and his high pale forehead bespoke the expansiveness of his mind. His figure was tall, but admirably formed, possesse of all manly dignity and grace. His attire was neat, and a large mantle was thrown over all, which gave him an of nobility that immediately impressed self upon the attention of the beholder, and prepossessed them in favour of him.

"And why should the Baron de Morton feel this enmity towards you?" asked the young man.

"I have not the slightest idea, sir," answered Angelina; "indeed, although I have seen him often before, this is the first time that I have ever spoken to him."

"And yet would he have taken your life," observed the young man, "had I not fortunately come to your preservation. Is not this strange?"

"It is indeed," answered our heroine, "and I am at a loss to account for it. To me, however, the baron appears to be labouring under some painful delusion, and imagines me to be a person whom his conscience accuses him of having done some former injury to."

"He is a villain, I know well," said the stranger, "and no doubt has many heavy crimes upon his conscience. I would again warn you to avoid the vicinity of the castle as much as possible, and never to venture to these ruins again after dark; for when you least expect it, the greatest danger may befal you."

Angelina thanked the stranger for his advice, and being now in sight of the cottage, she observed that she would no farther encroach upon his kindness.

The stranger seemed loth to leave her; he gazed earnestly and tenderly in her countenance for a few moments, and then in a respectful manner, he said—

"Lady, twice before we have met, and ever since, never have you been absent from my thoughts. But I am too bold. Excuse me, fair damsel; we shall meet again; and rest assured that in me you will ever find a friend and a protector. Farewell, and all good angels guard you."

As the graceful stranger uttered these words, he pressed his lips respectfully upon Angelina's hand, and hurried away. Angelina reached the cottage door, and then a secret and irresistible impulse urged her to look back. The moon was shining brightly, and she was therefore enabled to see the form of the young man distinctly. He was standing in the path with his arms folded, and his mantle wrapped closely around him, and apparently watching her with the most intense earnestness. When he beheld her looking towards him, he waved his hand. Angelina, with a blush, hastily entered the cottage, where her uncle was anxiously awaiting her arrival, having been surprised at her long absence from the cottage, and the lateness of the hour. He immediately observed the unusual paleness of her countenance, and the extreme agitation of her manner, and he seriously questioned her as to what had happened to excite her alarm in such a powerful manner.

Angelina could not dissimulate, therefore, much as she dreaded the reprimand she would receive from her uncle, for not having attended to his injunctions, she related to him the whole truth.

Mr. Woodfield seemed greatly astonished by the account she gave him, and paced the room for a short time with considerable agitation, muttering to himself—

"This, this, the more confirms my suspicions; the villain! but I will see him, and demand an explanation; let him not imagine that——; but, Angelina, you have acted very wrong, very imprudently in visiting the ruins of St. Mark, after the strict injunctions I gave you to the contrary; I told you that danger lurked there, and you have now found that my words were correct. I tell you it is not the baron (whose conduct is perfectly inexplicable) you have to fear alone, but there are others who may be even more dangerous. I know that there are smugglers in the neighbourhood, and I have good cause to suspect that they make the abbey ruins their haunt, and the place where they conceal their contraband goods. I must, therefore, once more request, nay, insist that you do not visit it, for should any of these lawless men find you lurking about, they would probably think you were a spy upon their actions, and your life would be sure to be sacrificed for their security."

Angelina could not but see the reasonableness of these ideas, although she was not of the same opinion as Mr. Woodfield—namely, that, although there might be smugglers in the neighbourhood, they had made the ruins of St. Mark's their retreat. She, however, promised him faithfully that she would adhere to his wishes, and he expressed his satisfaction, and also his determination, to demand an explanation of the outrageous conduct of the Baron de Morton on the following morning.

With regard to the awful discovery which his niece had made in the chamber, Mr. Woodfield, after having deliberated for some time upon it, gave it as his opinion that the skeleton had, in all probability, been placed in the spot where she had discovered it, purposely by the smugglers, in order to keep up the report of

the abbey being haunted, and to frighten any person away, who might be bold enough to intrude upon their retreat. In this opinion, however, our heroine did not coincide, and it was moreover very strongly opposed by Mrs. Woodfield and Laura, who maintained that it was undoubted proof that there had been some horrible crime perpetrated in the abbey, and that it was, therefore, certain that it must be haunted by the dread phantoms of those who had been murdered.

CHAPTER X.

ANGELINA passed a troubled night, for she found it utterly impossible to erase the events of the day from her mind; and when she dwelt upon the attack made upon her by the Baron de Morton, her breast became the abode of apprehension. But why he should seek her life she was at a total loss to conceive; for in what manner was it possible she could have injured or given him cause for offence? His alarm, when he at first beheld her, and the words he had made use of, next recurred to her memory, and filled her with astonishment and perplexity. Oftentimes she could not help thinking that her uncle knew more of the baron than he pretended he did; and she did not forget the mysterious interview which the latter had sought and obtained, and the inviolable secrecy which Mr. Woodfield always maintained as to what had been the purport of it.

Completely worn out with harassing thoughts, she threw herself upon her couch, and dozed off to sleep, but quickly awoke again in a terrible fright, having seen in imagination the murderer's poniard presented to her breast, and beheld the Baron de Morton glaring revengefully upon her. She arose, resolved not again to venture to go to sleep, and, taking up a book, endeavoured to divert her mind from the gloomy thoughts that at present occupied it, by reading; but, no, she could not; they would crowd upon her imagination, in spite of all her efforts; and, putting down the volume, she walked to the window, and looked out upon the scenery beyond, lighted up with the beams of Luna, who was riding majestically through oceans of fleecy clouds. All was still and calm around: a gentle breeze wafted up the odour of many shrubs, and came refreshing to the senses of our heroine, who seated herself by the window, and gazed upon all the objects her eyes could scan, with feelings of the warmest admiration and delight.

Her thoughts became more tranquillized in the contemplation of the beauties of nature, and wandered almost unconsciously to the youthful stranger, who had that day rescued her from the violence of the baron, and whom she had once before seen from the same apartment from which she was at present gazing. As she recalled his noble and handsome features to her memory, she felt a burning blush mant_ling to her cheeks, and her heart throbbed violently against her side. But why she felt these emotions she could not account. She re-membered every sentence he had uttered, every expression of his countenance; and she could not deny that he had created a great interest in her mind. But was it not natural, she asked herself, that she should feel grateful to the preserver of her life?

From the casement she could just catch a glimpse of Saint Mark's Abbey, as the light of the moon fell strong upon its ancient walls, and the adventures of the day came vividly upon her memory again. The figure she had followed through the vaults, the old oak cham-ber, and the skeleton in the chest, all rushed again upon her thoughts, and she was once more involved in dread and perplexity, when she was suddenly aroused by hearing a voice im-mediately beneath the casement murmur in an under tone—

"Hist! maiden, hist!"

No sooner had the alarmed damsel recognised in the person who addressed her, the woman of the ruins, than she pushed the wand she always carried with her up to the casement, and Angelina beheld a piece of paper fastened to the end of it, which the more surprised her when she discovered by the light, that it was addressed to her.

"Take the paper, maiden," said the woman, "it is from a friend; be silent—farewell!"

And our heroine had only just time to comply with her request, when she bounded from the spot, leaped over the low palings that separated the garden from the fields beyond, and was soon out of sight.

Angelina was in such a state of surprise and confusion at the singularity of this event, that it was some minutes after the woman had made her hasty exit ere she could compose herself suf-ficiently to examine the letter. It was written in a male hand, and in beautiful characters, and was addressed to "Angelina Woodfield." With a trembling hand she broke the seal, and to her utter astonishment read the following lines—

"Will the beauteous Angelina grant the individual who was so happy as to rescue her from the violence of the Baron de Morton, an interview alone, in the sycamore grove, at four in the afternoon of to-morrow, when he will impart something that may be highly important to her happiness and his own? Do not be under any apprehensions, dear lady, at this strange request from me, whom you know not, and rest assured no harm is intended you."

Angelina was indeed surprised, and read the note a second time, thinking she had been mis-taken. What could he want with her? What could he have to impart, when they were total strangers to each other?—and how could he think that she could ever act with such impro-priety as to comply with his wishes, and accept of a secret assignation with a stranger? The bare thought was preposterous; and she was about to fold up the letter again, when another piece of paper fell from it on to the floor, and picking it up, she read, in a different hand-writing the following lines—

"Maiden of myst'ry, be warned and flee,
This is no place for peace and thee;
Danger surrounds thee, guilt is nigh,
And views thee with designing eye:
Then mark the warning, damsel fair,
Maiden of myst'ry, beware, beware!"

"What can be the danger of which I am warned?" said Angelina to herself, after she had perused this singular composition, "and who are they who take such an interest in my fate? I cannot solve this mystery; and the more I attempt to do so, the more inexplicable does it appear to me."

One thing, however, she was convinced of—namely, that the stranger, and the woman whom she had several times encountered in the ruins of Saint Mark's Abbey, were in some way connected together; and thus she afforded fresh food for rumination. But who were they, and what were the motives of their conduct? The appearance of the young man bespoke nobility, while the mystery of the woman's behaviour was sufficient to excite suspicion; and she was, therefore, the more at a loss to imagine what could have caused any association between two beings so decidedly opposite in appearance.

Angelina, however, was not long in coming to the decision that she would not, by any means, comply with the young man's request, and that she would make her uncle acquainted with *one* part of the circumstance only in the morning, namely—the warning she had received in so strange a manner. Although she could not account for it, she felt a strange repugnance in disclosing the wishes of the handsome young stranger, trusting that he would soon perceive by her not attending to his appointment, how high'y she disapproved of his boldness, and that he would not again make the request.

Buried in reflections such as these, the night passed away almost unconsciously; and daylight peeping suddenly in at the window, Angelina left the chamber, and walked forth into the tastefully arranged garden, to inhale the fragrance of the opening flowers, until such times as the family had arisen. So much did she benefit by this, that by the time she heard Laura and the others stirring in the cottage, notwithstanding she had had no rest all the night, and her mind had been so harassed, she felt quite refreshed.

When she appeared at the breakfast-table, her uncle, however, easily remarked the paleness of her countenance, and inquired if she was ill. Angelina replied in the negative, but admitted she had been rather alarmed; and then, much to the apparent wonder of Mr. Woodfield, and to the inconceivable terror of her aunt, she related the particulars of the woman's visit, and gave him the lines of warning only to peruse.

Mr. Woodfield read them over two or three times, and examined the hand-writing minutely, to see if he had any knowledge of the characters, and was afterwards buried in thought for several minutes. At length he suddenly arose from his chair, and stalking once or twice across the room, he muttered—

"This mystery I am determined to fathom, for should it be *he*——"

"*He!* who?" eagerly demanded his wife; "of whom in the name of wonder are you speaking?"

"Ask no questions," returned Mr. Woodfield, angrily, carefully folding up the paper, and placing it in his pocket; "you know I hate inquisitiveness, dame."

"But surely a subject of such deep interest to us all, husband," replied Mrs. Woodfield, "and one which seems to threaten us with danger, must be——"

"Psha! enough of this," interrupted her husband; "you are always conjuring up some apprehensions or the other before there is any occasion: get me my hat and stick, Laura, I will away to the Baron de Morton, and, proud and haughty as he is, insist upon an explanation of his conduct yesterday."

"Well, you may treat all these things as lightly as you please," remarked the dame, "but I think there is plenty of cause for fear, or else it's very strange indeed. At one time we are frightened at the appearance of a ghost, who insists upon your holding a private conversation with her; then the Baron de Morton' with his forbidding countenance, comes here and demands a private interview with you, and you are both locked in for more than an hour, talking about the deuce knows what. After this, the same nobleman makes an attempt upon the life of our niece; and then she is almost scared out of her senses by the appearance of another ghost or a witch, who warns her of God knows what approaching calamity; and yet you say that I am conjuring up apprehensions before there is any occasion. For my own part, I only wish we were far away from this spot, for I have never had a moment's peace since we have resided on it, what with ghosts and hobgoblins—haunted ruins—desperate smugglers—skeletons in old chests, and one thing and another."

Before the good old dame had half finished this harangue, her husband had left the cottage, and was on his way to De Morton Castle. The morning passed away without anything worth noticing taking place, Angelina's thoughts being occupied with thinking of the events of the previous day, and the probable result of her uncle's visit to the baron. Dinner time came, and yet Mr. Woodfield did not return; but this excited very little surprise, as they knew he had to transact some business a few miles off, and they thought it was not at all improbable that he had gone there before coming back to the cottage.

In the afternoon, Laura and her mother went to old Dame Gertrude, to make her acquainted with all that had happened, and our heroine was left by herself, Mr. Woodfield having given her strict injunctions not to quit the cottage during his absence upon any account whatever.

At length, tired with reading, she walked into the garden, and entered a small summer house at one end of it, which her father had erected, and which was her favourite retreat. She was examining some carnations with her back towards the door, when she was startled by feeling her hand pressed by somebody, and turning round, she beheld the handsome stranger with one knee bent gracefully to the earth, and looking up in her countenance with an expression of the most intense admiration.

CHAPTER XI.

ANGELINA, with the utmost confusion and astonishment, endeavoured to withdraw her hand from the stranger's ardent grasp, and her beauteous countenance was deeply suffused with blushes; while he retained his hold with gentle violence, and, after a brief pause, he ejaculated in tones of impassioned fondness, and so sweet that they imparted an irresistible sensation of delight to her bosom while she listened to them—

"Beauteous girl, pardon the boldness of one, who is a complete stranger to you, but who feels that he could worship you, even as a being of the other world. Yes, fairest Angelina, from the first moment my eyes beheld you, my heart became devoted to you; but fearing that my love would not meet with a return, I tried to stifle it in its infancy. Vain effort!—every day it grew stronger; I could not help cherishing the recollection of your lovely features in my mind; you were the object of my thoughts both day and night; in the daytime you followed me as my shadow, and at night fond visions presented you to my imagination in all the bright effulgence of your beauty. You became indeed a part of my thoughts, a very portion of myself; and, made presumptuous by the impetuosity of my love, I determined to seek an interview with you, to divulge my thoughts, and——"

"Sir," interrupted the blushing damsel, whom surprise had hitherto rendered silent, "unhand me, I beg; this language, and from a stranger, I must not listen to. Let me go, sir, and by your forbearance, prove to me that you are worthy of my forgiveness for the liberty you have taken."

"Fair damsel," exclaimed the young man rising and bowing gracefully to Angelina, "I feel indeed that I deserve your rebuke, but may I not hope—oh, tell me, may I not ?"

At that instant, Angelina was alarmed by hearing the sound of approaching footsteps. She looked imploringly at the stranger, he bowed his head in obedience to her wishes, and he had scarcely time to bound over the palings into the field, when Laura was seen coming along the path. Just then, the trembling maiden, casting her eyes towards the earth, beheld a small miniature in a golden frame, lying on the spot whereon the stranger had stood, and which he had doubtless dropped. With trembling haste she picked it up, and had only just succeeded in concealing it in her bosom, when her cousin approached her.

"My dearest cousin, here you are then, moping by yourself as usual," said Laura; "well, I declare, you are the dullest creature I ever knew, and if it were not that you are at the same time the kindest hearted soul in existence, I should absolutely be out of temper with you. But, bless my soul, how pale you look, my dear; why what in the name of wonder is the matter with you ?"

"Nothing, nothing," faltered our heroine, with evident confusion, "I—I—it is rather sultry, and I feel faint, that's all."

"Sultry," returned Laura, "why, dear me, I feel quite chilly, and I'm sure the air is very cold. You certainly are a mysterious girl, Angelina, and any one would suppose you were in love."

Angelina blushed deeply, but made no answer.

"Nay, my dear cousin," said Laura, "you need not blush, love is not such a very uncommon thing among girls of your age, and I do not know but that it is very natural after all, and that's exactly what Edwin Rushfield has told me at least a dozen times. Now let me know, Angelina, whether I have guessed right, and if I have, I think it is very unkind of you not to make me acquainted with the fortunate swain. I would not be so secret with you. But now I remember, when I left the cottage this morning, I did see a fine, tall, handsome young man, with black eyes and black silken hair, enveloped in a cloak, waiting in the meadows yonder, and, as I thought, looking very earnestly towards the cottage; but, as he could not have been——"

"Ah !" interrupted Angelina, thrown quite off her guard by what the loquacious Laura had said, "have you then seen him ?"

"Oh, oh !—so the cat is out of the bag then, and I think I have managed this very cleverly," said the provoking girl, laughing heartily, " if that is him, I have seen him, certainly, and I must say that I admire your choice, at least, so far as looks go, but there is no judging a person by their appearance."

"Laura," said Angelina, seriously, having regained her composure, "you mistake me, and I cannot suffer you to entertain any such erroneous suspicions; I certainly do not feel very highly flattered by the opinion you seem to entertain of me, to think that I should ever so far forget the modesty and propriety of our sex, as to make secret assignations with a man, and encourage his addresses, without the knowledge of your father."

Laura was abashed, and as she knew not what answer to make to this reproof, she endeavoured to conceal her confusion by singing a verse of a song, as she tripped into the cottage.

Angelina did not immediately follow her cousin, but paused to reflect upon what had occurred, and more particularly to examine the miniature. With a strange indefinite feeling, she took it from her bosom, and gazed intently upon it ; it was an excellent likeness of the stranger himself, and every lineament, every feature, every expression, was traced with such admirable skill by the artist, that it almost seemed animated with life. In vain did the damsel try to remove her eyes from this miniature, and as she continued to look, her admiration increased. So completely absorbed was she in the contemplation of the likeness, that she noticed not the lapse of time, and it is uncertain how much longer she might have remained so occupied, had she not been suddenly aroused by a jocund laugh, and turning hastily round, she once more consigned the miniature to her bosom; she was vexed and bewildered to behold Laura smiling at her elbow.

"Ah, my fair cousin," said the merry girl, "I thought I should find you out at last. Oh, you sly girl, to be desperately in love, and carry the likenesses of young men in your bosom, and never to say a word to me about it; well, I declare, if I have not a good mind to make you jealous, and set my cap at him myself, for I am certain it is the young man I saw this morning; I knew the likeness directly."

"Laura," said Angelina, angrily, her heart having throbbed with emotion all the time that she was thus speaking, "I must beg of you to choose some other subject to jest upon, I am not disposed to listen to such absurdities."

So saying, Angelina walked into the cottage, and Laura, who did not feel inclined "to get the mulligrubs," as she expressed herself, by sitting with her gloomy cousin, walked forth, thinking to meet her mother as she came from old Dame Gertrude's.

Shortly after this, Mr. Woodfield returned home, and he seemed more vexed and disturbed than when he had departed in the morning. To the anxious inquiries which his niece ventured to put to him, he replied, that the baron had quitted the castle, and that he had not been able to ascertain where he had gone, or when it was probable he would return; and that was the only information she could elicit from him.

Angelina was surprised, but pleased, to learn that the baron had left the neighbourhood, and she hoped it would be a long while ere he would again return to it; she then talked to her uncle upon different subjects, and endeavoured to restrain the agitation she was thrown into as much as possible, by the adventure of the afternoon. In this she succeeded much better than might have been expected, and her uncle either did not, or would not take any notice of her emotion. On retiring to her chamber, she found much to occupy her thoughts, and, taking out the miniature, she again became completely absorbed in the contemplation of the handsome and benevolent features. Yes, there was the same intellectual countenance, the same graceful contour of features, the high, pale forehead, the raven hair, and piercing bright eyes that had so forcibly struck our heroine the very first moment she had beheld the stranger. She could not remove her eyes from it, her frame trembled with agitation, and thoughts she had never before known, darted upon her imagination."

"Surely," she ejaculated to herself, "the being possessed of such a face as this, must be all that is good, noble, and generous. Oh, yes! I cannot think he is otherwise! But what am I saying? Why should I encourage a thought of one who, to me, is a perfect stranger? Of what consequence is it to me, that—But did he not save my life? Yes, and gratitude demands that, as my preserver, I should always think of him with kindness and esteem."

What was to be done with the miniature? Of course, she could not think of keeping it; but then, how was it to be returned? She could not help thinking that he had dropped it purposely, and if she did not take the earliest opportunity to give it him again, he might probably construe it into an encouragement of his passion; but then she was at a loss to conceive in what manner she could get it conveyed to him. Was she not acting wrong, she asked herself, in not making her uncle acquainted with all that had taken place, so that he might seek an explanation of the young man, and put a stop to his importunities, if they became too pressing? She felt she was, but yet she could not make up her mind to broach the subject to him. She at length came to the determination that she would herself, the next day, walk in the direction the stranger had before come, and, if she met him, return the miniature; but she did not come to this resolution without feeling a certain regret, for which she could not account.

The following afternoon, Angelina went from the cottage, and took the road before mentioned, but she walked on without meeting the person of whom she was in search. With a mixture of disappointment and pleasure she continued her walk, and was so wrapped in meditation that it was not until she found herself near the chain of rocks, upon the summit of one of which Saint Mark's Abbey stood, that she looked up and found that the shades of evening had gathered around.

It was a beautiful moonlight evening, and Angelina could not resist a wish she felt to get to the top of one of the rocks and view the ocean as it danced in the silvery light of heaven. While she was thus occupied, she suddenly beheld a dark object at a distance on the waves, and presently the moon shedding forth a broad flood of light, she clearly distinguished a small vessel coming swiftly in the direction of the very rocks she was standing upon. But a few seconds more, and her anchor was cast, boats thrown over her side, several men jumped into them, after depositing numerous heavy casks, and then they pulled towards the rocks with all their might. Although Angelina felt convinced they were smugglers, she had such a strange curiosity pervading her mind, that she was completely rivetted to the spot. She concealed herself as well as possible, but yet she was enabled to observe all that passed below.

The boats soon got beneath the rocks, and the next minute there was a low whistle, and several sturdy fellows, who seemed to spring out of the earth, made their appearance, and flew to assist the other men in the boat to land the casks and deposit them in a large hollow immediately under the rock upon which Angelina stood.

"Quick, my lads, or we shall have the land sharks down upon us."

The voice was familiar to her ears; she looked eagerly towards the speaker; he was enveloped in a large mantle, and turning his face towards the full light of the moon to give these orders to the men, she was enabled to see his features distinctly; but what was her astonishment, when in him she recognized the mysterious stranger who had for so many hours occupied her thoughts!

The fellows seemed anxious to obey him, and the boats were therefore soon emptied of their contents; the men, with the stranger, entered them again, and rowed off; they soon reached the vessel, which weighed anchor directly, and quickly became a speck in the distance.

Wonder-struck and pained at what she had seen, and the discovery she had made, Angelina hurried down the rock, and was proceeding into the path which led towards her home, when suddenly two men rushed upon her, and seizing her violently by the arms, held their daggers to her breast, and threatened to plunge them into her heart if she ventured to utter the least outcry.

———

CHAPTER XII.

"RELEASE me, villains!" exclaimed Angelina, in spite of the threats they had given utterance to, "what is your purpose with me? If it is robbery, you will be disappointed in your object, for I——"

"We have no time to waste words with you," said one of the ruffians, "and once more I caution you, as you value your life, to be silent; resistance will be useless. You must go with us."

"Liar!" shouted a loud voice. The next moment the report of a pistol was heard, and the man who had spoken uttered a yell of agony, and releasing his hold of our heroine, sunk bleeding to the earth.

The other ruffian started round in consternation, and Angelina glanced eagerly towards the spot whence the voice seemed to proceed, and beheld, standing in a threatening attitude, the mysterious woman of Saint Mark's Abbey, from whom she had received so many warnings. She approached the place where they stood, and confronting the villain, who still grasped the arm of our heroine, exclaimed—

"Away, wretch, or the same hand which laid low your companion, shall also deal you your death blow!"

"Foul hag! who art thou?" cried the man, who, perceiving that she had no other pistol than the one the contents of which she had just discharged, became emboldened, and looked fiercely upon her.

"One who will protect that trembling maiden with her life!" answered the woman; "release her, I say, or take the consequences."

"Take thou the consequences of thy daring!" said the man, as he let go the arm of Angelina and rushed upon the strange being, who had so often excited the wonder of our heroine. A fierce struggle ensued, the woman attempting to wrench the dagger from the ruffian's hand.

"Fly—fly for your life!" cried the woman, speaking to Angelina, who had been petrified to the spot with the astonishment created by this singular and unexpected circumstance. This aroused her to action, and bounding over the blood-stained corpse of the other man, she fled, with the rapidity of a startled hare, in the direction of the high-road which led to the village. She had not, however, proceeded far, when she was alarmed by a shrill whistle, which was immediately answered from the direction from whence she had fled, and directly after two more fellows leaped over a gate from a neighbouring field, and she found herself once more so firmly held, that to attempt to fly, she was confident, would be completely futile.

"Oh—oh, my dainty miss," said one of the fellows, who were well armed, "so you have attempted to fly, have you? Well, well, you will be safely caged anon, so there will be no necessity to clip your wings. Ah! Martin, how is this?"

This was asked of the man from whom Angelina had fled, and who at that moment came running up in a state of great trepidation.

"How is it?" cried the other, "why she had nearly slipped through my fingers, and I have a good mind that I would stop her run_ ning for ever. We were interrupted by some hell cat, and poor Dare-devil Will now lies a corpse at the foot of the Suicide's Rock."

"Confusion!" exclaimed the other two fellows, in a savage tone: "Dare-devil Will murdered?"

"Oh! for the love of Heaven release me!" implored Angelina, almost fainting with terror as the ruffians fixed their savage glances upon her, and seemed half inclined to plunge their murderous weapons into her bosom; "what can be your object in thus seizing a poor defenceless girl who——"

"Stop her d—d clack!" shouted the third wretch, who looked more ferocious even than the other two: "gag her!—gag her!"

His advice was immediately followed, and our heroine, completely overcome by her terrors, became insensible.

When she recovered herself, she was astonished to find that she was in the cabin of a vessel, and she could plainly hear the waves as they dashed with a hollow sound against its sides. A lamp was burning on the table, and standing by her side, and who had doubtless been applying proper remedies to restore her, was a middle-aged woman, whose countenance was far from being an unprepossessing one.

Angelina started from the place on which she had been reclining, and staring wildly around her, she exclaimed—

"Merciful God! where am I? and why am I brought hither? Oh! tell me, I beseech you, for what purpose am I thus clandestinely torn from my friends and my home?"

"Be silent, young lady!" said the woman, in an under tone, and with a look of compassion, which emboldened our heroine. "You are on board a ship, but any outcry on your part would be useless, and might be attended by the most dreadful consequences, for you are surrounded by wretches who would not hesitate a moment to steep their hands in your blood, should you arouse their anger."

"But what is their purpose with me?" demanded the distracted damsel. "Oh, why am I, who know no one that I have offended, or ever injured by word or deed, exposed to this painful trial?"

The woman shook her head, and answered in a whisper—

"Indeed I know not, or I—but I dare not

answer your questions ; should we be overheard, both our lives would be the forfeit."

"But who is my persecutor? Surely these men do not act upon their own responsibility?" observed our heroine, wringing her hands with the intensity of her anguish, and looking into the countenance of the woman with the most earnest supplication.

"I dare not—must not answer your enquiries," said the latter, "but pray endeavour to appease your anxiety, and rest assured that no harm will come to you. All that I can do for your comfort I will. Come, come, be composed; you need refreshment ; take a glass of wine."

"Oh, no, no," exclaimed Angelina, "I cannot—cannot. Merciful God! for what am I reserved? Alas! my dearest friends, what is now your misery—your anguish?"

Her feelings now choked her further utterance, and in a paroxysm of grief she covered her face with her hands, and sobbed convulsively.

The woman seemed much moved by her sufferings, and endeavoured several times to soothe her, with words that shewed she was not that depraved being which her apparent association with the wretches who held her (Angelina) in their power, might have led any person to suppose.

"I must leave you for the present," said the woman, as she kindly took the hand of our heroine, and pressed it in token of her commiseration; "but do not give way to despair—no harm can come to you here; and," she added, in a low tone, "there is no knowing what may occur to release you altogether, and restore you to those friends from whom you have been so cruelly and unjustly torn."

"As you hope for mercy," implored Angelina, grasping both the hands of the woman in her's, and fixing her tearful eyes with ardent entreaty upon her countenance; "your heart does not seem callous to humanity and pity, oh, tell me, then, who has caused this outrage, and whither are they taking me?"

"Would that I could comply with your request," said the female, "but——"

"What, ho! Bridget!" exclaimed a gruff voice from above, at the same time a loud knocking was heard on the deck.

"It is my husband calls me," said the woman. "I must leave you for a short time; but, depend upon it, all that I have the power to do towards ameliorating your grief, I will: —your question I dare not answer!" At this moment, the voice of the man was again heard calling upon the name of his wife, in tones of of greater impatience than before, and, after curtseying to Angelina, and trying to re-assure her with another look of pity, she hastily quitted the cabin, and the door was fastened securely after her.

To what a state of misery and despair was Angelina now reduced; language could not do adequate justice to her feelings. She wrung her hands, and wept bitterly ; then she paced the cabin, and called aloud for help; but the hollow sounds of the waves, as they dashed against the sides of the vessel, or the rude laughter of the men upon deck, alone answered her. What motives could have induced any one to the perpetration of such an offence? In whose power could she be, and what were their intentions towards her, and whither were they conveying her? These questions suggested themselves to her mind immediately; but her imagination could not supply even the remotest idea in answer to them. One thing, however, amidst all this cause of sorrow, gave her some relief, and that was, that the woman who had just left her seemed to possess something like feeling ; but, then, should she not be permitted to remain with her? Angelina clasped her hands to her aching temples, and rocked her body to and fro in a state of the most violent agitation. At length, she threw herself upon her knees and offered up a prayer to the Almighty, after which she arose more composed, and was enabled—with some degree of calmness—to reflect upon her situation, and the probable cause of her being taken away from her home ; but she could arrive at no satisfactory conclusion, and she therefore gave it up in despair.

Two hours elapsed, and Bridget did not return to the cabin. The motion of the vessel, which was evidently scudding rapidly before the wind, made Angelina feel very ill, and her head ached violently.

The men upon deck were apparently enjoying themselves, for their loud shouts of glee, and their coarse roars of boisterous mirth, frequently vibrated on our heroine's ears. How she shuddered to think she was in the power of such wretches.

At length, Bridget re-entered the cabin, bringing with her a repast, which she placed before Angelina, and endeavoured to persuade her to partake of it, which the latter complied with, more from a wish to conciliate the woman's favour, than from any appetite that she possessed.

In answer to some inquiries which Angelina made, Bridget said that she believed they were near the end of their voyage, when they were going ashore, but to what place, or in what part of the country, she declined to answer. In about another hour there was a loud shouting from the men on deck, and it was soon evident to our heroine that the ship had arrived at the place of her destination. A few minutes afterwards, two of the ruffians who had borne her away, knocked at the cabin door, which being opened by Bridget, they entered, one of them bearing a large mantle over his arm, and the other one carrying a dark lantern.

"Now, young lady," observed the first one, "you must prepare to go ashore. However, as you gave us such a specimen of your screaming abilities before, we do not mean to run the risk this time; we will therefore take the liberty of gagging you again."

Angelina knew it would be of no use appealing to such heartless scoundrels as these, she therefore submitted in silence, and after they had placed the gag in her mouth, they covered her head with the mantle, and each laying hold of her arms, they hurried away, followed by Bridget. She soon felt that she had left the ship, and was walking upon *terra firma*, and

shortly afterwards she was assisted into what appeared to be a carriage, and the two men each took a seat beside her, and Bridget placed her herself opposite.

The mantle was now removed from the head of Angelina, but the blinds being up, she was unable to see the country they were travelling through. At last, after proceeding for about an hour at a rapid rate, the vehicle stopped, and when our heroine was assisted out, she beheld herself in the court yard of a gloomy looking castle, whose black and flinty walls seemed to frown upon her.

CHAPTER XIII.

WE must now leave Angelina for the present and return to the cottage of Mr. Woodfield' where the utmost consternation prevailed at her absence; and when hour after hour had elapsed and evening closed in, and still she returned not, the alarm of her relatives became insupportable. Laura could not give any account of her, as she was herself away from home at the time Angelina left the cottage. In a state bordering upon distraction, Mr. Woodfield prosecuted his inquiries among the neighbours, but with no better success; they could none of them afford him the least information upon the subject but Angelina was so universally esteemed, that her disappearance created a great excitement in the village, and several persons volunteered their services in assisting Mr. Woodfield in his search after her, and immediately went in different directions.

It was now quite dark, and two or three hours beyond the latest time that our heroine had ever been known to be from home, and still she returned not.

Mrs. Woodfield wrung her hands and cried, in which she was accompanied by Laura, who declared it to be her firm opinion that Angelina had been once more intruding herself upon the haunts of the evil spirits in St. Mark's Abbey, and that they had borne her away to regions unknown, as a punishment for her presumption. In the meantime, Mr. Woodfield bent his way towards the ruins, thinking that she might, in spite of his strict injunction to the contrary, have been tempted once more to visit her favourite haunt, and that very likely some accident had happened to her from some of the falling ruins, or (and he trembled with apprehension at the bare idea) she might have been seen by some of the smugglers, whom he imagined infested this place, who had either removed her to some place of security, where she could not betray, or have quieted their doubts at once by her death! At all hazards, Mr. Woodfield determined to search every part of the ruins, until he was satisfied one way or the other; and nerved with fresh courage, when the probability of the truth of his conjectures more forcibly struck his mind, he redoubled his speed, and the black and ivy covered walls of the old abbey soon rose, like the dark shadow of a mountain, on his view.

Mr. Woodfield regretted that he had not brought with him two or three of the young men who had volunteered their services in the search, for should he be surprised by any of the ruffians whom he suspected inhabited the Abbey, what could he do to repel them, especially when he was quite unarmed, having nothing with him but a stout stick. However, he resolved to be cautious, and, in all probability, by that means, he might be enabled to avoid the danger he apprehended; besides he was not positive that the abbey was the retreat of smugglers, he only judging by the rumours that were afloat, and imagining it to be very likely, from the great facility it afforded for such purposes, being so near the sea, and having been for so many years shunned by the inhabitants of the surrounding town and villages with terror. But then one powerful circumstance was in favour of the idea that the rumour was erroneous, which was, Angelina being there so many times, and even nearly entirely over the ruins without encountering any danger of the sort.

It was very dark, but fortunately Mr. Woodfield had brought with him a lantern, it having been his intention when he left the cottage to have explored the adjacent wood. He ascended the rocky eminence on which the gothic Abbey stood, and finding nothing to obstruct him, he entered its dreary and desolated hall. The owl screeched dismally, as though disputing the right of any person to intrude upon a place of which he had long been the undisturbed occupant. The pavement was covered with the broken fragments of the crumbling ruins, and Mr. Woodfield was obliged to proceed with caution, for fear he should hurt himself; suddenly, however, he was startled by hearing a noise as of some person approaching, and, directly afterwards, an authoritative voice exclaimed —

" Who comes this way, and for what purpose do you wander in these dreary ruins at this hour of the night?"

Before Mr. Woodfield replied, he held the lantern above his head, and its light fell upon the tall figure of the mysterious woman of the ruins.

" Ah!" ejaculated she, when she recognised him, " Mr. Woodfield?—I know why you come, but it is too late I am afraid; even now the unfortunate damsel, of whom you come in search, is being borne away by wretches who would not shrink from perpetrating any crime, however monstrous. I sought to save her, but my arm failed in its purpose, although it was well directed."

" Good God! can this be true?" cried Mr. Woodfield in a tone which fully expressed his consternation.

" Think you I would tell you false?" demanded the woman, in a tone of dignity; " follow me, for there is not a moment to be lost."

" And who are you, mysterious woman," said Mr. Woodfield, " who appears to take so deep an interest in the fate of a girl who is an entire stranger to you?"

" A stranger to me," replied the woman,

with an ironical smile, "oh, little do you know how well I am acquainted with Angelina. But it is not a time to talk on such a subject; come, come, this way."

Trembling with anxiety at the probable fate of his niece, and a thousand times blaming her for having acted in disobedience to the warnings he had so frequently given her, Mr. Woodfield followed the woman, who bounded over the fragments of stone with which the Hall was

THE MYSTERIOUS WOMAN'S EXULTATION AT THE DEATH OF DARE-DEVIL WILL.

strewn, with an agility that astonished him, and descending the rock at the back, paused at the base.

"Open the lantern," she cried.

"Mr. Woodfield obeyed, and a flood of light streaming upon the earth, the corpse of the ruffian, Dare-devil Will, met his gaze.

"What means this?" he demanded, with astonishment; "who has done this?"

"I," replied the woman, "and could but

my arm have accomplished its purpose, Angelina would have been rescued from their power."

"Merciful powers!" ejaculated Mr. Woodfield, "what is to be done?—Tell me, I beg, have you any suspicion by whom these wretches were employed?"

"I have," was the answer; "nay, so positive am I, that I could almost venture to take an oath that my surmises are correct."

"Whom, then, do you suspect?" impatiently asked Mr. Woodfield.

"The Baron de Morton.'

"Impossible! the baron is away from his castle; besides, what motive could induce him to such an outrage?"

"Have you not before had a specimen of what he is capable of doing?" observed the woman; "I knew well his motives, and what should prompt him to do the deed; but we waste that time in useless words and conjectures which should be devoted in an effort to rescue the unfortunate maiden. This fellow may contain something about his person which might afford us a clue. Ah!" she continued, as she drew her hand from one of the coat pockets of the ruffian, "here is a paper. The hand writing is familiar to me. Let me peruse it.

"You will convey the girl to the Grey Tower, where I will be anon; use no more violence than necessary; unless she be obstinate, and then, sooner than run the hazard of a discovery, consign her to the deep."

"She is lost! She is lost!" exclaimed Mr. Woodfield, in a despairing tone, when he had heard this note read.

"She shall be saved if there is any possibility," said the mysterious woman; "there is no name to this note, but yet I am certain that my surmises are right, and that it is the villain De Morton who is at the head of all this; but his dark schemes shall yet be frustrated, and——"

She paused, and seemed wrapped in deep cogitation for a second or two, during which time the intense anxiety of Mr. Woodfield may be very readily imagined.

"It is unfortunate that *he* is not here," she murmured to herself.

"Of whom do you speak?" demanded Mr. Woodfield, hastily.

"No matter, no matter," replied the woman. "Can you be secret, when by so doing you may have the only opportunity afforded you of saving Angelina from the danger which now threatens her?"

"Oh, can you doubt me?" ejaculated Mr. Woodfield, eagerly.

"Will you swear, that if I exert myself to save this damsel, and restore her to your arms, that you will not disclose to any other person, without my permission, what I may have occasion to reveal to you?"

"I will—I do swear!" answered Mr. Woodfield, impatiently.

"Enough! Nothing can be done till tomorrow evening."

"To-morrow evening!" cried Mr. Woodfield; "so long; alas! it will be too late then—all hope will be at an end before that time."

"Nay, be not impatient," said the woman; "the only person that can render you any assistance will not be here till that time, and any attempt on your part without his aid would be entirely futile. Attend me."

Mr. Woodfield followed her with a heavy heart, and after winding among the rocks for a few minutes, she stopped before one at the base of which was a large stone. She beckoned Mr. Woodfield to assist her, and after considerable exertion they succeeded in rolling the stone away. A large opening in the rock then presented itself to the astonished eyes of Mr. Woodfield, and holding up the lantern, he perceived a flight of steps hewn out of the rock, which seemed to descend into a cavern below. The woman took the light from his hand, and beckoned him to follow her. She then began to descend the steps, and Mr. Woodfield, wondering how this adventure would terminate, followed the example she had set him.

They soon entered a spacious and lofty cavern, round which were piled an immense number of casks, chests, and apparently bales of goods, while arms and ammunition were there in abundance.

"Where am I?" demanded Mr. Woodfield, "and for what purpose have you brought me hither? This is evidently the secret retreat of some lawless gang——"

"It is the secret depository," interrupted the woman, "of as brave and worthy a set of fellows as ever run the hazard of their lives, to avoid paying an unjust and tyrannical impost."

"Smugglers?"

"Ay, so are they called," answered the woman; "but it matters not, they are your friends, and so you will find if you do not act unfairly by them; but you have sworn to be secret."

"I have," answered Mr. Woodfield, "and I will not break my oath. What would you have me do?"

"Meet me here to-morrow evening before sunset," answered the woman, "and prepare yourself to go some distance, for the Grey Tower stands far beyond the sea."

"But is there no hope before?"

"None; who can render you any assistance? Come, the word; will you meet me?"

"I will."

"Enough, yonder is your path, return home, and remember your oath."

As the woman thus spoke, having ascended from the smugglers' cavern, she pointed out the path among the rocks, which Mr. Woodfield must pursue, and stood watching him until he was out of sight.

CHAPTER XIV.

MR. WOODFIELD passed a restless night, for his mind was tormented with the thoughts of the dangerous situation of his niece, and the probability of his failing to rescue her from it. Yet did he place great confidence in the promises of the woman of the ruins, who so mysteriously seemed to take a deep interest in the fate of Angelina. The determined persecution of the Baron De Morton filled him with surprise and indignation; but there were certain circumstances connected with the private interview he had had with that nobleman, which excited strange suspicions in his mind, and which at a future period of this narrative will be unravelled.

To the earnest inquiries of Mrs. Woodfield and Laura (the latter of whom was most ardently attached to her fair cousin), he only returned evasive answers, until towards evening, when he informed them that he had gained a clue to Angelina's retreat, and was about to depart to liberate her from the power of those who unlawfully detained her, and that if he was gone some time they must not be alarmed, for he would return as soon as possible, and they might rest assured that he would not be in any danger.

He found it no easy task to quiet the fears of his wife and daughter, which the mystery he maintained as to the place of his destination and what was the clue he had obtained, served to increase; he felt, however, that he had acted prudently in keeping it a secret, for had he made them acquainted with what had occurred to him at the ruins, he would not only be breaking the promise he had made to the woman, but should very likely be the cause of frustrating all the plans she had devised to save Angelina.

No sooner had the first grey shadows of evening fallen upon the earth, than Mr. Woodfield, having first taken the precaution to have a brace of loaded pistols with him, in case he should happen to fall into any danger, bade his wife and daughter an affectionate adieu, and quitted the cottage. He took a circuitous way to the Abbey ruins, in order that they might not have any idea of the right direction in which way he was going, and having crossed a corner of the wood, soon came in sight of the venerable fabric.

The evening was very mild, and the sea was barely rippled by a light and refreshing breeze. The moon seemed to rest calmly on the bosom of the deep, and the screech of the owl from the ruins, and the melancholy wailing of the sea-mew, were the only sounds that disturbed the stillness which reigned around.

It wanted yet full half an hour to the time he had appointed to meet the woman, but he walked round the Suicide's Rock to go to the place where he was to await her arrival. The corpse of the ruffian was gone, and had probably been consigned to the deep, but the marks of blood were still visible. Having stood to gaze upon this and other things for a few moments, Mr. Woodfield passed on amid the chain of rocks, until he reached the place of appointment. He had no difficulty in finding it, but there was no person present, and the stone was covered over the entrance to the cavern exactly in the same manner as it had been left the night before. He tried to remove it, but found that it was more than his strength could accomplish ; so in order to pass the time away unti, the woman should arrive, he walked back, and ascending the rock, entered the abbey.

The rays of the moon beamed full in at the several apertures which time had made in the roof and wall, so that Mr. Woodfield was enabled to distinguish the surrounding objects as clearly as if it had been noonday. He walked through the cloisters, and was about to ascend a flight of steps at the extremity, when his progress was suddenly arrested by hearing the sound of music.

He listened attentively : he was convinced that he was not mistaken, it was a guitar, and was touched by a masterly hand. A short symphony was played, and then a female voice of the most bewitching melody, singing an air of plaintive sweetness, vibrated on his ears. Astonished and delighted, Mr. Woodfield scarcely ventured to breathe, for fear he should lose a note sung by the accomplished vocalist and so entranced did he become by the strangeness of the event, and the melancholy stillness of the scene around him, that he was very near-

yielding to the vulgar superstitions of the neighbourhood, and thinking the ruins were inhabited by spirits. Suddenly, however, the voice ceased, and immediately afterwards Mr. Woodfield heard a door open from above, and the next moment the mysterious woman of the uins stood before him.

" Why do you loiter here?" she demanded, in a harsh and peremptory tone, "is this the place where we appointed to meet ?"

".It is not," answered Mr. Woodfield, " but having arrived too soon, I merely strolled into the ruins to pass away the time."

" And heard you anything?" inquired the woman eagerly.

Mr. Woodfield replied in the affirmative, and related what he had heard, and expressing at the same time his belief that the abbey was inhabited by some poor unfortunate, whom she was acquainted with.

The woman interrupted him hastily, and pressing her hand upon his arm, she looked earnestly in his face and said—

" Whatever may be your surmises, whether just or not, I charge you, as you value your own life, and that of one who is the victim of oppression and cruelty ; of one who may be nearer to those you love, than you can possibly form any idea of; I charge you, I repeat, never to mention what you have heard here, neither to seek to penetrate a mystery which cannot at present be unravelled."

" You may rely upon me," said Mr. Woodfield, ."but yet——"

" Enough," interrupted the woman, " we must not waste any more time here, follow me !"

Mr. Woodfield bowed his head in submission, and she led the way from the abbey. When they had reached that part of the eminence which commanded the most extensive view of the sea, she paused, and leaning against the long wand which she always carried with her, seemed to be watching the appearance of something with the greatest impatience.

The moon shone so clearly, that the eye could

discern the smallest object at a great distance, but Mr. Woodfield could behold nothing but the calm unruffled ocean beneath, and the pale silver moon sporting through the bright fleecy clouds above.

The woman seemed disappointed, and muttered some words to herself, which were quite inaudible to Mr. Woodfield; the following, however, which were spoken in a louder tone, he heard—

"'Tis yet too soon; and this bright moon is all against them;—they will not be here yet."

Mr. Woodfield imagined she was speaking of the smugglers, and every moment's delay caused him the most poignant anguish, for might he not be too late to save Angelina, if even the woman was able to procure him the assistance she had promised? The woman seemed to read what was passing in his mind, but she made no observation, and proceeded to descend the rock, followed by Mr. Woodfield. The woman motioned him to assist her, and by their joint exertions, they removed the stone from the entrance, and descended into the cavern. She went into a kind of recess, and presently returned with a lamp which she lighted, and then beckoning Mr. Woodfield to a seat, reascended from the cavern, and left him to himself.

Above an hour passed in this manner, and the patience of Mr. Woodfield was almost exhausted, when he heard the woman exclaim in a tone of satisfaction—

"Ah! they come!"

Immediately afterwards he heard a sound like that of oars in the water, at a distance. The sounds grew louder, and the boats evidently approached rapidly towards the cavern. Mr. Woodfield had not the slightest doubt but that these were the smugglers running their cargo, and he was all anxiety and doubt to know what would be the result of this adventure. He had not much time to think, for in a few minutes he heard a noise as of a number of men jumping ashore, and then a gruff voice exclaimed—

"Halloa! who the devil are you, a friend or foe?"

"Why, if you had not either lost your sight or your senses, Ned Stukely, you would know me," answered the woman.

"Oh, it is Kate of the Ruins," said the first speaker. "Well, I did not know you at first, for you stand there just for all the world as if you was some evil spirit. Now, lads, to work; we have not a minute to lose. Ah! who removed the stone from the entrance of the cavern?"

"I," answered Kate.

"By yourself?" enquired the man.

"With the aid of another," returned the woman.

"Ah! why you have not——"

"Never mind what I have done," interrupted Kate, "neither you or your companions will suffer anything by it. Your captain is on board, I suppose?"

"He is."

"When you return to the ship, tell him I would speak with him on particular business."

The man gave some sort of a sullen answer, and directly afterwards he appeared with two or three other men at the top of the rock-hewn steps, bearing upon their shoulders, each, a heavy cask. As Ned Stukely prepared to descend, the light from the lamp reflected full upon the person of Mr. Woodfield, and the former, starting back a few paces in astonishment, ejaculated—

"Hell and the devil! who is this? Are we betrayed?"

"Hold, Ned!" cried Kate, advancing towards him, "there is no cause for fear; this is a friend."

"A *friend!*" repeated the smuggler, in a tone of dissatisfaction, "friends are very scarce, mother, but——"

"There, there—trouble yourself no more about it," interrupted the woman, "but finish your business, and send the captain to me, as I before desired you."

The man muttered something, which was

unintelligible, and then descended into the cavern, followed by his companions. They scrutinised Mr. Woodfield from head to foot with doubtful looks, and having deposited their load, hastened from the cavern, and returning to their boats, the sound of their oars in the water convinced Mr. Woodfield that they had put off again to the vessel.

In a very short time the boats again returned, and the men brought a fresh load each into the cavern. Mr. Woodfield listening, heard some person conversing with Kate, whom he supposed to be the captain of the smugglers. Their conference was brief, and immediately afterwards Kate descended into the cavern, followed by a tall handsome young man, enveloped in a large mantle. We need not, however, describe him, as it was the stranger who had so deeply interested Angelina, and who had rescued her from the violence of the Baron de Morton.

He advanced towards Mr. Woodfield with a graceful air, and extending his hand towards him, said—

"I am very happy to see you, Mr. Woodfield, but wish it had been under different circumstances; however, do not despair, for if you will only rely upon me, I will either restore your fair niece to liberty, or perish in the attempt."

"And say, to whom will my gratitude be due for this generosity?" asked Mr. Woodfield, greatly prepossessed in favour of the noble-looking youth, upon whose brow sat intelligence and sincerity.

"It matters not," replied the young man, "my real name must not at present be divulged; but call me, if you like, Hugh Clifford. But come, we have no time to lose; will you trust yourself on board my craft?"

"With pleasure," replied Mr. Woodfield, pressing the young man's hand most cordially.

"Then let us be gone," said Hugh! "Kate, good Kate, a parting prayer from you for our success in this undertaking—a shake of the hand, and away we go."

Kate raised her hands towards heaven, implored its aid in earnest terms for the success

of their stratagem, then embracing Hugh, all three ascended from the cavern, and the stone was again rolled over the entrance.

Mr. Woodfield bade Kate farewell, and then entering a boat with Hugh, it was quickly rowed off towards the small swift-sailing smugglers' vessel, which was lying off at a short distance.

We will now return to Angelina

CHAPTER X

"THIS way," cried a man who stood in the low gothic-arched doorway of the Grey Tower, when Angelina was brought into the court-yard; "this way;—what ho! Bridget, why do you loiter there behind?"

Bridget hastened forward, apparently afraid, and Angelina was hurried into the Tower; and as she passed the man whom she supposed to be the husband of the former, and whose voice was familiar to her ear, the light from a lantern, carried by one of the ruffians, enabled her to have a full view of his features, ; and in them she recognised those of Rufus. She shuddered with horror when she saw him; and as she recalled to her memory the conversation she had heard between him and the baron in the vaults underneath the abbey, it at once convinced her that he was a villain who would not hesitate to perpetrate any crime for the sake of lucre. She fixed a look of supplication upon him, but he frowned, and motioned to the fellows who had the charge of her to hurry on. Finding, therefore, it was useless to appeal to men who were callous to all sense of pity, she resigned herself to her fate.

She was taken through a hall, dark and dreary: and after ascending a long flight of stairs, and traversing a gallery, they stopped at a heavy oaken door, strongly barred, and which had all the appearance of the entrance to a prison. Rufus unlocked it from a large bunch of keys which he had attached to his belt, and

wards the very place where she was concealed? She held her breath, and tried to crouch beneath the rubbish around her. Rufus walked past the column and almost touched her, but fortunately he saw her not; and after the lapse of two or three moments more, he returned to his trembling companion.

"We were deceived," said he; "it was only the wind that had blown some of the ruins down."

"Probably it was," replied the baron; "but I forgot—this abbey, as you are aware, was formerly in the possession of my family, and I have got the key of those gates with me. I will lock them, and that will secure us from being surprised that way, at any rate."

"Good God! what will become of me? I'm lost!" thought Angelina, as she heard the baron lock the gates.

They now resumed their conversation, but Angelina was in too great a state of agitation to listen to it. At length they prepared to depart by the way they had entered; and as the baron unlocked the ponderous gates, his companion said in a loud tone—

"Enough, my lord—you know you may depend upon me. I will keep a vigilant eye upon them; and should our suspicions be verified——"

"You know how to act," added the baron. "Get thee gone, it may not be prudent for us to depart together."

"Rufus bowed, and following the baron, the gates were locked on the outside, and our distracted heroine found herself a prisoner in the chapel of the abbey ruins.

CHAPTER V.

FOR a few moments Angelina stood and wrung her hands in despair, totally at a loss what to do. The wind whistled cold throughout the chapel, and she was so overcome by her fears and the chilliness of the place, that she could scarcely support herself. The words that she heard pass between the baron and his villanous colleague, and the allusions they had made to some deeds of darkness perpetrated by them in former days, were strongly impressed upon her memory, and the unintelligible threats they had held out to her and her uncle, brought to her recollection the warning she had before received from the mysterious woman in the ruins. These then were the parties she had to fear; and yet how could she or her uncle have incurred their enmity? She was unconscious of having wilfully deserved the hatred or persecution of anybody, much less the Baron de Morton, and therefore was she the more perplexed. But this was no time or place to reflect, for

the day was waning apace, and what would become of her if she was unable to escape from that dismal fabric, which her disordered imagination now filled with the most awful forms? Again lighting her lamp, she searched around the chapel, and more particularly inspected the altar; behind which she was positive she had seen the form that had alarmed her, vanish; but she looked in vain—no signs of an outlet met her eyes, and she clasped her forehead in despair.

Looking up above the place where she was standing, she perceived an aperture in the wall, large enough to admit of a human form, and which had been broken away by the ravages of time; but it was at such a height that she knew not how she could clamber up to it; and even if she succeeded in reaching it, she might be in the same dilemma, not knowing into what place it might open. Desperate situations suggest desperate measures, and accordingly Angelina determined to make an effort to reach it. She hastily collected some of the pieces of ruins, the largest she could lift, and piled them one on top of the other, until she thought she should be able to reach the opening, and then with cautious and trembling steps, prepared to ascend it. With much difficulty she reached the top of this pile, and then with a desperate effort the affrighted maiden clambered up to the aperture, and looking below, found that it opened into a gallery. To descend was a task of more danger than the ascent had been; but at last she accomplished it in safety, and pursued her way along the gallery to a gothic apartment at the end, the door of which was standing open. She entered it—it was lofty and spacious—and what was her surprise to find that it in every respect corresponded with the one she had seen in her dream! There were the portraits of the lady and gentleman; and what the more surprised her was, that the likenesses were complete. Thunderstruck at this remarkable coincidence, she stood and gazed around her, quite unconscious for the moment where she was. Casting her eyes above the arras on the western side of the apartment, she beheld the mouldering remains of a coat of arms, on which she was enabled to trace the devices of a *blood-stained shield and raven's nest.* Induced by these singular coincidences to search, she cast her eyes towards the oaken floor, and was horrorstruck to behold deep stains of what appeared to be human blood!—transfixed to the spot with terror, she continued for several moments to look upon these dreadful marks.

"Good Heavens!" she cried, "what deed of darkness has been perpetrated in this chamber? Alas! whither have my footsteps led me?"

She was startled by what seemed to be a dismal moan and to issue from the opposite side of the room. She trembled, the lamp and the light from a small window streaming full upon their persons and faces, Angelina's astonishment was not a little augmented, when she recognised in one of them the Baron de Morton, who lived near the spot, and in the other his repulsive domestic, Rufus !

Scarcely venturing to breathe, lest they should discover her, although she knew not why she should fear such a circumstance, she crouched down behind the column, and watched their actions.

"Well," exclaimed Rufus, "I suppose this spot will do for the communion ; you have no fear of listeners here."

"Right, good Rufus," replied the baron, "we need not indeed fear that the prying eye curiosity will watch our actions in this old abbey, and for that purpose did I resolve that our future secret consultations should be held here. We might have listeners in the castle, and already have I fancied that the baroness begins to——hark !—was not that a voice ?"

"Nonsense, 'twas only the wind," returned his servant, "come, to business."

"This is a gloomy place," said the baron, looking around him with something of fear in the expression of his countenance : "report has filled it with frightful forms, and——"

"Psha !" interrupted Rufus, "report is a common liar. Is it possible, my lord, that you can begin to feel qualmish and timid after all the daring deeds you have performed ?"

"Be silent, Rufus," returned the baron, in a tremulous voice, "would that those daring deeds of which you speak could be recalled—would that they had never been performed."

"And," rejoined Rufus, in a contemptuous voice, "that you might be the living model of virtue and integrity, and see another luxuriate in that rank and wealth which you now enjoy ! Bah !"

"Enjoy !" cried the baron, in a tone of bitterness ; "alas ! can there be any enjoyment in the fruits of crime—mur——hark !—again ! I could have sworn I heard a sigh !"

"Are you going mad ?" said Rufus ; "however I came not here to listen to a sermon, so, my lord, I'll e'en leave you till you are in a more fitting mood to talk upon the business in which you require my aid. 'Tis only fools who talk of conscience ! Psha ! the cant of priestcraft—the coward's bugaboo. What is the use of repenting of what has been done years ago, and which nothing can alter now ?"

"Well, well, be it so—perhaps I am weak—foolish, good Rufus," replied the baron, in a firmer tone ; "but enough, to business at once. Rufus, dost thou remember that dreadful night when, near this spot, thou didst, by my orders——"

Here a hollow gust of wind that swept through the chapel completely drowned the voice of De Morton, and Angelina in vain tried to catch the concluding sentence.

"Methought your lordship's *conscience* was ready enough to remind you of the events of that night, and two or three other circumstances," sarcastically replied Rufus, "but to prove to you that my memory is not in any way impaired, if it please you, I will recapitulate——"

"Nay, nay—hold, Rufus," hastily interposed De Morton, "I meant not that ; but I would ask you, are you certain that your arm was sure, and that——"

"Sure !" interrupted Rufus, in a savage voice, "what now ? Did not the disappearance of——did not my reeking dagger offer sufficient proofs how truly I had kept my word—how certain had been my aim ? Have you grown suspicious, my Lord de Morton ?" If so, the sooner we part the better."

"You mistake me, Rufus," said the baron, in an agitated tone, "I——"

Here the whistling of the wind again rendered the words of the baron inaudible, and it was several minutes ere Angelina could make out a syllable they were uttering ; she noticed the violence of the baron's gestures, who every now and then looked fearfully around the chapel, as though he was apprehensive that some one was watching them.

"Both, I tell you," at length Angelina heard Rufus say, "why should you doubt ?"

"'Tis strange," returned the baron, "and yet the astonishing likeness that rustic beauty bears to—— ; I was thunderstruck the moment I beheld her, and I felt a deadly chill run through my veins. Her uncle, too, I like him not ; there is a mystery about him that convinces me he is not what he wishes to appear to be !"

The conversation was now carried on in so low a tone, that not a word could be overheard. Angelina trembled with excessive terror, like an aspen leaf. The allusion to herself and her uncle filled her bosom with the most acute anguish ; and the warning of the mysterious woman of the ruins struck more forcibly on her recollection. In the agitation of her feelings, she disturbed some of the crumbling rubbish which lay around her, and it fell down with a rustling noise, that made both Rufus and the baron start.

"Did you not hear that ?" cried the latter.

"I did," returned Rufus, looking fiercely around.

"This time, I am certain I am not deceived," ejaculated the baron, "somebody is here besides ourselves."

"Then their lives shall answer for their curiosity," cried Rufus, drawing a dagger from underneath his mantle, and stalking hastily towards the spot from whence they imagined the noise had proceeded. Who shall attempt to describe the terror of Angelina, when she heard the villain's threat, and saw him advance to-wind which moaned dismally along the different passages and galleries of the tower, she listened with breathless attention, but all was as still as death.   Again she implored the protection of the Almighty, and arose from her knees more composedly and re-assured.' At length, completely worn out, she conquered her fears in some degree, and retiring to the chamber, secured the door as well as she could inside, and threw herself upon the bed.   An

THE VILLAIN RUFUS'S THREATS TO ANGELINA.

irresistible drowsiness suddenly stole over her senses, and she fell asleep.

How long she had slept she knew not, but she was suddenly aroused by feeling something like an icy pressure of a hand upon her arm. She started from the bed, her whole frame convulsed with terror, and drops of perspiration started from every pore.   The light was just dying away in the socket, and cast its last faint ray upon the portrait.   Good God! was it her imagination that wandered, or was she tormented by some wild dream? She fancied she saw the picture move, and then a low sigh seemed to issue from the place where it hung! Completely overcome with her terrors, she uttered a loud scream, and sunk insensible upon the floor.

When she recovered, the scorching rays of the morning sun were streaming full in at the chamber windows, she arose, and endeavoured for a short time, in vain, to recollect where she was. But soon the full misery of her situation, and the horrors of the night, recurred to her memory.

She was suddenly startled by hearing a strange noise, which seemed to proceed from the court-yard. She hastened into the next apartment, and getting upon one of the chairs, looked down upon the court below. A carriage had just driven up to the porch, and the next moment a gentleman alighted from it. He cast his eyes up towards the casement at which our heroine was standing, and she recognised the Baron De Morton. She staggered from the chair, and her frame trembled violently with fear and anguish. A few moments only elapsed, and she heard footsteps advancing along the gallery; they stopped at the door, and she heard the key turning in the lock, and the bolts being withdrawn. The door flew open, and the baron stood before her.

He walked towards the centre of the room, and folding his arms, gazed upon her with a smile of exultation. Acting upon a sudden impulse, the maiden fell on her knees at his feet, and with looks of the most impressive supplication, and eyes streaming with tears, implored his pity.

"Oh, my lord," ejaculated Angelina, as she clasped the knees of the baron, "how have I deserved this outrage?—In what have I offended you, that you should thus seek to break the hearts of my friends, tear me from my home, and make me a prisoner in this frightful place?—Surely, a poor, humble girl like me cannot be an object of——"

"Ah! the very tone of her voice! the very expression of her countenance!" interrupted the Baron De Morton, as he fixed his eyes sternly and intensely upon the kneeling damsel, "by Heaven I could almost fancy that she had sprang again from the grave, imbued with all her former youth and beauty!—Girl, thou hast come like a curse upon me, to arouse once more, with all their insupportable poignancy, the thoughts that I had partly succeeded in obliterating from my memory. Why did you cross my path?"

"My lord," exclaimed the terrified Angelina, who marked the strong emotion which raged in the baron's bosom, "what mean your mysterious words? Oh, in pity to my anguish, relieve me from this horrible state of suspense, and tell me in what way I can possibly have incurred your displeasure, and willingly will I make you all the reparation in my power. Restore me to liberty—promise me that you will cease to persecute me, and I am ready to vow that I will never disclose to any one what has taken place."

"Fool!" cried the baron fiercely, as a malignant smile passed over his features, "and think you I would be the idiot, tamely to resign my prey, after I have taken so much trouble to get it into my power? No; I have you securely now, and no power on earth shall release you; girl, until you have satisfied me that you are not the person I suspect you to be, you shall never quit these walls!"

In spite of the terror which beset her mind, conscious of her own innocence, and of the injustice of her haughty oppressor, indignation swelled the bosom of Angelina, and suddenly, arising from her supplicating posture, with a look of offended pride and dignity, which for a moment filled the mind of the baron with confusion and surprise, she said—

"And by what authority, proud Baron de Morton, do you dare to detain me? Humble and poor as I am, think not that your conduct will go unpunished, or that my wrongs will be undiscovered or unavenged. I have deigned to solicit that which I have a right to command, but I now insist upon you telling me why I am brought hither, and demand my instant restoration to liberty and to my friends."

Thunderstruck at the alteration in her manner, the baron stood for a few minutes, and gazed earnestly upon her without speaking. Every lineament of her countenance he seemed to scrutinize with the most mysterious earnestness, and it was very evident that his mind was undergoing the most powerful and conflicting sensations. Angelina watched him with the most poignant anxiety and suspense, and in spite of the firmness she had assumed, she felt her heart sink and her terrors every moment becoming stronger. At length he appeared to recover himself, and rushing suddenly towards her, he seized her arm with a vehemence that pained her, and demanded—

"Girl, seek no longer to deceive me; tell me your name, your real name?"

"You know it, my lord," answered Angelina, "why do you ask the question? I——"

"No evasion, girl," interrupted De Morton fiercely, "little do you know the man whom you seek to tamper with. Your real name, I say, and who and what are you?"

"Oh, why should you ask so ambiguous a question, my lord?"

"Beware—beware, if you arouse my wrath, your obstinacy shall cost you dear," ejaculated the baron, pressing her arm yet more violently, and fixing upon her a look which seemed to penetrate to her soul; who and what were your parents?"

"Alas! I knew them not," replied Angelina, as tears filled her eyes, and her bosom heaved with emotion, "they died ere I had arrived at years to know and appreciate their worth; the only parents I have ever known, are my kind uncle and aunt; but why do you ask the question?"

"Their names!" demanded De Morton, breathlessly.

"You know the name of my uncle," replied the maiden faintly, "the same belonged to them?"

"By hell, 'tis false!"

"Oh, my lord," exclaimed Angelina, who now began to think that the baron was suffering under an aberration of intellect, "what is the reason of this violence? For the love of Heaven, explain the mystery of your conduct."

"You would deceive me, girl," said the baron, "you have some reason for wishing to conceal the real name of your parents? But your uncle, as you call him, he has not always moved as a humble peasant?"

"I believe my uncle has been in better circumstances," answered Angelina, "but misfortunes, with which I am unacquainted, reduced him, and I was too young to remember him in his prosperity."

The baron remained silent for a short time, and stood with his eyes fixed upon her countenance; then folding his arms, he traversed the apartment for a few seconds with hasty and uneven steps, and murmured some incoherent sentences to himself, the only part of which that met her ears was the following—

"'Tis strange—should I be mistaken—but no—it cannot be—the likeness is too strong for me to doubt; curses on the weak arm which—but no matter; what have I to fear? Who can prove that—but I have her now securely in my power, and I am determined that nothing shall remain to threaten my safety."

Then turning suddenly round to Angelina, whom for a few minutes he seemed to have forgotten was in his presence, he said—

"For the present, girl, I leave you; but, remember, that from this place you can never escape, and your restoration to liberty depends entirely upon your speaking the truth. Any obstinacy or deceit on your part will be visited by my vengeance. Once more I warn you; beware! When we meet again, learn to be more communicative, or dread the consequences!"

"Oh, mercy! mercy! my lord! Do not leave me in this dreadful place!" screamed the distressed damsel, as the baron moved away, but he turned upon her an inexorable frown, and before she could reach him, he had left the apartment and locked and bolted the door as before. She threw herself upon her knees, and clasping her hands, burst into a torrent of tears and sobs at the utter hopelessness of her situation.

CHAPTER XVI.

THE horrors of the mysterious fate which attended her, each moment became more apparent to the mind of Angelina, and the recent behaviour of the Baron de Morton convinced her that so obstinately positive was he that she was the daughter of some persons whom he had cause to dread, that he might be urged into the perpetration of any horrible crime! And now the awful event of the previous night returned to her recollection, and she shuddered with horror. She was convinced that it had been no delusion; no wild chimera of her own imagination; she was positive that she felt the icy touch of the clammy fingers upon her arm; saw the picture move, and heard something like the rustling sound of a person passing by the bed. Good God! were these apartments really haunted by some troubled spirit, and she doomed to remain a prisoner in them? The thought was madness: she glanced fearfully around her, then placing her face on the cushion of the chair, she gave full vent to the violence of her grief.

She was aroused from this melancholy posture by the entrance of Bridget, who advanced towards her with a respectful and sympathizing air, and placing her hand upon her shoulder, said in a voice of compassion—

"Come, come, my dear miss, you must not give way to this violent sorrow; all may yet be better than you expect. Rufus and the baron have left the tower, and so I have come to pass an hour or two with you if it be agree-able. But, dear me, you have not eat anything, this is very foolish, for I am sure you will make yourself ill if you do not partake of some refreshment. Now, let me beg of you to try a little; it is very nice, for although I say it, that shouldn't say it, there are very few better cooks than I am."

Angelina shook her head, and made no immediate reply; but at length, seeing that Bridget was preparing to resume her importunities, she said—

"Alas! my good woman, my heart is too full to eat. Oh, how have I deserved a fate like this?"

"I pity you, miss," returned Bridget, "from my very soul, I do; and I'm sure it wrung my heart with grief to see what you suffered on the way to this place. I wish it was in my power to assist you, but it is not; and if Rufus or the baron were to know that I had spoken to you this much in kindness, I don't know what would be the consequence."

"But, why should they persecute me?—I, who am a stranger to them, and therefore cannot have given them any occasion for such conduct?" enquired Angelina.

"I cannot tell you, miss," replied Bridget; "but you may depend upon it, the baron has some motive or the other for his conduct, or he would not act so. Heaven pardon him; but I do believe he is a bad man, and will have much to answer for when he dies."

"And yet," said our heroine, hastily, "and yet you are in the service of him, and are the wife of his confidant?"

"Alas!" returned Bridget, with a sigh, "it is too true; more's the pity. Ah, you can form a very poor idea of what I suffered since I have been the wife of that man. But it is no use repining, it was to be my fate."

Here Bridget ceased speaking for a few minutes, and seemed to be ruminating upon some subject that gave her great pain, but at length Angelina interrupted her by saying—

"And did this place always belong to the Baron de Morton?"

"Oh, no," answered Bridget, "he purchased it some years since of the Marquis Delmaine, who, a very short time afterwards was found murdered near this spot."

Angelina shuddered.

"And how far is it from De Morton Castle?" she enquired.

"Oh, dear, miss, it is many, many miles," answered Bridget, "for we were two days and a night upon the water when you were brought here, most of which time you were insensible, and indeed I thought you would never recover again."

"Good God! and am I then so far from my friends—so far from all hope of rescue?" cried Angelina, wringing her hands. "But tell me, I conjure you," she continued, "do you not know what is the baron's design with me?"

"Indeed I do not," answered Bridget, "unless he is in love with you, and——"

"Impossible," interrupted Angelina, "has he not already got a wife?"

"And is it not possible too; miss, that he may have a wife, and yet not be insensible to the charms of another?" said Bridget shrewdly. "Ah! the baron has been a strange, wild gentleman in his time, or else report belies him; and they do say that if these walls could speak, they could tell sad stories."

"Ah! speak—tell me, what do you mean?" asked the damsel, eagerly, as the occurrences of the previous night darted across her mind.

"Oh, do not be alarmed, miss," replied Bridget, "they only say of this tower, as they do of all other old buildings, namely, that it is haunted; but for my part, I never believe in such foolish tales, and I'm sure no ghosts or noises have ever annoyed me since I have been here."

"Then it was not imagination," gasped forth Angelina; "it was not a wild dream that alarmed me."

"Goodness me!" cried Bridget, with an expression of astonishment, "what can you mean? Surely you have not seen or heard anything?"

Angelina trembled and looked fearfully around her, and then related, in as few words as possible, what had occurred to her on the night before.

"Well, miss," observed Bridget, when she had concluded, "if I had not heard a similar story before, I should imagine that you had only been labouring under some frightful delusion. But it is certainly very strange, to say the least of it, and makes one believe that the story of the poor young woman and her lover who were brought here, and never went out alive again, is not without foundation."

"Of whom do you speak?"

"I do not know what they called her," answered Bridget, "though they say she was a lovely young creature. But I am afraid of frightening you, or I would tell you all I know about it."

"Oh, no, indeed you will not frighten me," eagerly ejaculated Angelina, whose curiosity was excited in an extraordinary manner; "pray let me hear it."

"Very well, miss, I will do as you wish," said Bridget, "but you must promise me that you will never mention a word of it to anybody."

"You may depend upon me," said the impatient Angelina; "alas! perhaps if I had even the will to do so, I shall never have the opportunity."

"Oh, don't say so," remarked Bridget, "you must not give way to despair; and you don't know but this adventure may turn out for the best after all. But all is secure; no one is near to listen to me, and so now to make a beginning."

As Bridget spoke, she drew her chair closer to Angelina, and proceeded to relate the following awful and marvellous story:—

"Well, miss," began Bridget, "what I am going to relate, took place when this old tower was in the possession of the Marquis Delmaine. He was a nobleman who was very much disliked in the neighbourhood, for they say he was a stern, haughty, and savage-looking man, and that he treated all those who were under him in such a manner, that he could never get his servants to stay long with him. My poor mother—God rest her soul!—lived with his father for many years, but she did not remain long in the situation when the property came into the possession of the nobleman of whom I am speaking, for she could not submit to his tyrannical ways. The marquis was very fond of gambling, and nothing but the most dissipated noblemen ever associated with him. The tower was one continual scene of riot and debauchery, and was shunned by every respectable person in the neighbourhood. The Baron de Morton was at that time, I have heard, one of the most constant guests here, and he and the marquis were on terms of the most strict intimacy. Thus it went on for some time, and nothing particular occurred, when suddenly there was a singular alteration in the temper of the marquis, and he abandoned all his former associates, and kept himself almost entirely secluded in this gloomy tower, and never had any company. Two or three strange and savage-looking men had, however, been noticed by some of the inhabitants lurking about the neighbourhood, and more than once the marquis had been seen to walk forth in conference with them, which excited strong suspicion, and they were certain that he was meditating something of no good. But, dear me, how very faint you must feel, not having taken anything to eat for so long ;—now do let me prevail upon you, miss, to try a little bit; if it is only a mouthful."

"If you will proceed, I will try," replied Angelina, who was deeply interested with the story which Bridget was relating.

"Ah! that's right ; now you will do;" observed Bridget, as Angelina commenced tasting the viands, "you will find them very nice. Well, to continue my story. This part of it came from the lips of poor old Simon Barney, who lived with the marquis at the time, but who is now dead and gone, so that there certainly may be some reliance placed upon the veracity of it. 'One night,' he said; 'the domestics were all commanded to retire to rest at an early hour, and not, upon pain of his displeasure, to be seen up when he returned home, as he could let himself in. It was about midnight when old Simon was awoke by a terrible scuffling noise below, and soon afterwards he heard them ascending the stairs which led to the gallery on which was the chamber of the old man. As you may imagine, his curiosity was excited in no small degree, and he longed, yet feared, to watch them. His lamp was still burning, but, apprehensive that, if it was seen by the marquis or any of his friends, they might think that he was watching them, and would be sure to punish him, he concealed it as well as he could, and with his ear to the key-hole of the door, he listened with the greatest attention, thinking he might catch a word or two that would enable him to judge what was the matter. There seemed to be several persons, but the voice of the marquis might be heard high above the rest, as he gave directions to his companions.

"'Away with him,' Simon heard him say, 'we have him safe enough now, and he will find it rather a difficult matter to escape. The blue chamber in the north wing will be the most secure place.' "

"A noise like that of a person struggling violently, was now heard by Simon, and soon afterwards the tones of a man's voice exclaimed—

"'Cowardly ruffians, release me!—What would you with me?—Ah! the Marquis Delmaine!—I know you now!—For this outrage the vengeance of my——'"

"Curses on the mask!' interrupted Delmaine, passionately; 'but no matter, that discovery has sealed his fate. In with him ;—mind not his threats, they are but the frenzied ravings of a madman.'"

"Another violent struggle ensued, and then they seemed to have got past the door. Unable longer to endure the anxiety and suspense, notwithstanding the strict injunctions of the marquis, and the danger he knew he should run in disobeying them, he opened his chamber door without the slightest noise, and peeped out. At the further end of the gallery, by the light emitted from a couple of lamps, he beheld, though rather indistinctly, the dark shadows of several figures surrounding some object, which Simon judged to be the person upon whom the outrage was being committed; but he was unable to make out more, for whoever he was, he seemed to be enveloped in a large mantle, part of which was also thrown over his head, and entirely concealed his face from observation. He appeared to be very powerful and vigorous, for he was quite as much as those who held him could manage. The next moment they turned the corner of the gallery, and were hidden from the old man's view. He returned into his room, and shuddered with horror at what he had seen; for he could not doubt but that the design of the marquis was murder. The next morning the servants looked at one another with strange glances, for more than Simon had heard the noise of the night before, and strange winks and murmurings passed from one to the other; but Simon acted on the wisest plan, for he said not a word about what he had heard and seen, and pretended not to know what they were talking about.

"Many of the domestics would have been glad to have left the marquis's service, but they, knowing his suspicious temper, were afraid to give him warning, and among that number was Simon. There were several strange and ill-looking men now in the tower, who were no doubt the ruffians whom Delmaine had employed in his guilty transaction. In the course of that day, the marquis called all the domestics together, and in a voice which told them he would be obeyed, commanded them at their peril, not in future to attempt to approach the north wing of the tower, except the persons whom he had deputed to keep watch there, and who were the fellows before spoken of. He then departed from the tower, ac-

companied by two fierce-looking men, who seemed well calculated for the perpetration of any crime.

"The marquis did not return for three days, and during that time no one except the sentinels appointed, ventured near the north wing, in which was undoubtedly incarcerated some unhappy victim of the marquis's cruelty. No one saw him return, for it was late at night, and the inmates of the tower had long retired to their beds. The next morning, however, it was noticed by every one that he was ghastly pale and dreadfully agitated, and if any one spoke to him, he started, as though they had awoke him out of a dream, and stared vacantly around him. He was never absent from the presence of the men whom he had so lately introduced to the tower, and he was locked up in his study with them for hours. Towards evening three of the men went away from the tower, and the marquis kept himself secluded from the sight of every one; it was, however, well known, from the light being seen burning in his apartment, and he also being seen pacing it at a late hour, that he had not gone to rest.

"The servants had scarcely retired to bed, when they were aroused by hearing loud and and appalling shrieks, in a female voice, proceeding from the direction of the north wing of the tower, which gradually grew fainter, until they died away entirely, and all again was as silent as the grave. But, God bless me, what was that?"

Angelina started, and trembled at the same time, for she was almost positive she heard a sound like a stifled groan proceed from the chamber, and again the portrait seemed to tremble. She caught the arm of Bridget in great perturbation, and directed her attention to it, but was unable to say a word. Bridget at first looked very pale, and troubled a good deal, but she soon recovered her self-possession, and entering the room, examined the portraits and different parts of the chamber, and at last noticed that one of the windows was partially open.

"Oh, it was only the wind whistling among the ivy around the window, and shaking this grim portrait of one of the ancient possessors of the tower," she observed, smiling; "the dismal story I am telling makes our fears more ready than they usually are, and then the thoughts of these being the very apartments in which ——"

"Good Heavens!" exclaimed the alarmed Angelina, "you surely do not mean to say that these are the chambers in which the suspicious events to which you have just alluded took place? Alas! and am I fated to remain a solitary prisoner, without——"

"Hush!—pray do compose yourself," said Bridget, "it was really very silly of me to say anything about it; but it can't be helped now. Even supposing the restless spirits of those beings whom I have mentioned, do indeed haunt these chambers, what need you fear from them, when you never knew them, and consequently could not have done them any injury?"

Just as she ceased speaking there was a noise in the court-yard, and she hastened to the window to see what was the occasion of it.

"Dear me!" she exclaimed, "how vexing: it is Rufus returned; I shall not be able to finish the story till some other opportunity, for if he should catch me here, I don't know what would be the consequences. Good bye, for the present, miss; I will see you again this evening, if possible; but do not give way to useless fears. It will, no doubt, afford you some gratification to learn that the baron has not come back with my husband, and from what I heard the latter say, he will not be again at the tower for three or four days."

"Three or four days!" ejaculated Angelina, as Bridget left the room, and she heard her lock the door after her, "alas! never can I survive that time in this horrible place, and in the state of uncertainty in which I am. Alas! what a cruel fate is mine."

She sighed deeply, and tears filled her eyes, as she looked fearfully around; but still the absence of the baron did afford her a ray of consolation, although it was small indeed.

The tale which Bridget had told her, had filled the mind of Angelina with redoubled dread and uneasiness, and when she reflected that she occupied the same apartments in which the deed, whatever it was, was supposed to have been committed, she shuddered with horror, and looked fearfully around her, first at the portrait, and then upon the bed, with a sentiment of uncontrollable apprehension, expecting almost to see the ghastly phantoms of those who had probably there come by such a shocking and untimely death. And there was she doomed to pass her days and nights; but, alas! few indeed might be the days she would have to pass there; perhaps ere the morning's sun again should gild the eastern hills, her eyes would be closed in death; a violent death, with no one nigh, no friend, no relation to soothe her passage to the grave. And now the thoughts of the terrible anguish her uncle and aunt must be suffering at that moment recurred to her recollection more vividly than before, and her tears flowed afresh. She dreaded the approach of night, and wished anxiously for the return of Bridget, being resolved to endeavour to persuade her to sleep with her; but she waited in vain—hour after hour passed away, still the good-natured servant remained absent. She began to feel more and more uneasy—what could be the reason that Bridget did not come? Surely, Rufus must have learned the time they had been together, and had determined that she should no longer attend upon her. This idea filled her with the utmost terror. She arose from her chair, walked into the front room, and listened at the door, but not hearing any noise, she went back again into the room she had left, and looked from the window on the scenery beyond; but her mind was too distracted for her to view with anything like patience the wild and majestic works of Nature, which at any other time she would have contemplated with such delight and admiration, and she walked away from it again. Just at that moment she heard some one at the door, and her heart bounded with a momentary feeling of pleasure and renewed hope.

"It is her; it is Bridget!" she said.

The door presently opened, and the heart of Angelina again sunk with terror and disgust as her eyes fell upon the repulsive features of one of the ruffians who had brought her to the tower.

ANGELINA'S SURPRISE ON BEHOLDING THE PHANTOM.

He entered the room without saying a word, but cast a bold look upon our heroine, and then depositing a stone pitcher, containing water, on the table in the front room, a loaf, and other refreshments, together with a lamp, and means of procuring a light, he looked round, as if to ascertain that all was right, quitted the room and secured the door after him.

"Then," thought Angelina, wringing her hands, "my worst surmises were, alas! too true, and Bridget will no more be allowed to visit me ; thus have they deprived me of the only small ray of hope and consolation under this dreadful persecution."

Another thought also occured to her which was equally as painful as the rest that at that moment tormented her : perhaps the poor woman would have to suffer for her kindness, and thus she would be made the innocent cause of bringing misery to another as well as herself.

In a state of mind completely indescribable, she traversed both the rooms, and knew not what to do. The day seemed to pass unusually quick away ; and as the shades of evening began to gather fast around, so did her apprehensions increase. The least noise made her start and look fearfully around her ; and often did her disordered fancy conjure up the most frightful phantoms to her imagination, and she could almost believe she saw the hideous faces of fiends and ghosts grinning in at the casements upon her, and seeming to mock at, and glory in, her terrors and anguish.

It must not be imagined that, notwithstanding the mind of Angelina was so occupied with this painful and afflicting event, her thoughts never returned to the handsome stranger, and to the circumstances under which she had last seen him. She did think of it ; and when she remembered that it was proved beyond all possibility of a doubt that he with whom she had been so strongly prepossessed was the captain of a gang of smugglers, she felt a sentiment of disappointment and regret, for which she was quite unable to account.

"I wish I had had an opportunity of returning him the miniature," she sighed ; "for should he think that——"

She was unable to finish the sentence ; but taking the miniature from her bosom, where she had kept it ever since the fatal night on which she had been forcibly dragged away from her home, she gazed attentively upon it, and a tear involuntarily came to her eye. The expressive and handsome eyes seemed to look up into her countenance appealingly ; and in spite of what she had seen, she was ready enough to dismiss from her mind anything to his disparagement, and to admit the idea that he was the victim of circumstances, and was not following his present lawless life from choice, but necessity.

Night had now set in, and Angelina had lighted her lamp, and stirred up the fire in the grate, for the air was pretty keen, and the room would have had a miserable appearance without. She then once more carefully surveyed the apartments ; and after committing herself to the care of Omnipotence, she took up a book and tried to divert her thoughts from the gloomy subject which at present occupied them, by reading ; but this was a fruitless task, and she soon laid it down again, and walked to the window and looked out. It was a clear night, and she could see for a long distance over a large tract of hilly country. For a few minutes her mind was estranged from everything else in contemplation of this scene ; but at length, feeling the night air blowing rather too keenly upon her, she left the window, and returned to her seat. Encouraged by the stillness of all around, Angelina felt her mind gradually becoming more firm and calm, and she once more took up the book and began reading it. The subject was one of a deeply interesting nature, and it kept her attention wholly engrossed, until she heard the hour of eleven chime forth from the bell in the old tower ; and feeling sleepy and tired, she once more prayed to Heaven for protection ; and breathing a blessing on the heads of her dear friends, she threw herself on the bed without undressing, and was soon locked in the arms of sleep.

She could not form any conjecture of the time she had thus been sleeping, but she was suddenly aroused in a similar way to what she had been the night before, and was positive she was not this time dreaming. Once more she felt like the icy touch of the hand of a corpse upon her arm ; and as her blood curdled with horror, she jumped from the couch, and at that moment a piteous sigh seemed breathed close to her ear, and she just caught the glimpse of what appeared to be some light shadowy form, which seemed to flit past her with the speed of lightning.

Great God protect me!" exclaimed the terrified maiden, falling upon her knees, and covering her face with her hands : the moment after her senses left her.

When she recovered, she had but an indistinct recollection for a minute or two of what had occurred : but too soon it rushed upon her memory with all the full force of its horror, and the blood seemed to curdle in her veins. The light in the lamp shed but a feeble ray, and made the objects in the room appear more gloomy and indistinct. Oh! how Angelina regretted that she had not remained in the same state of unconsciousness till daylight! But her thoughts were soon directed to something else. Suddenly she imagined she heard a noise in the next room, the door of which she had closed, but could not fasten it on the inside, owing to some accident having occurred to the lock. She listened with breathless horror, and again was almost positive that she heard a sound, something like a person stealing gently across the floor. Her heart throbbed with the most intense terror, but she was completely paralized to the chair on which she had sunk. Again all was still ; and after the lapse of a few seconds, Angelina tried to imagine she had been deceived, and that the noises were only those created by her own perturbed imagination. She began to revive a little, and rising from her chair, almost took courage sufficient to walk to the room door. She did move a step or two forward, but started back with renewed alarm, when she again distinctly heard the tread of a foot in the adjoining room. Not a moment was given her for reflection, when the door of her chamber was gently and cautiously opened, and Angelina screamed with uncontrollable affright, when she saw Rufus, bearing in his hand a light, standing at the entrance. No

sooner did the ruffian behold her, than he muttered something between his teeth, extinguished his light, and hastily departed.

Angelina was so overcome by the force of her terrors, that she was unable to move or speak, but stood gazing into the next room with a vacant stare. It was evident now that her death was determined upon, and that the villain Rufus had gone to her chamber that morning for the very purpose of putting the dreadful deed into execution. She was about to give way to the most horrible feelings of despair, when suddenly she felt a strong current of wind blowing in upon her ; and looking towards the door of the front apartment, what was her astonishment to behold it standing wide open ! Rufus, in the confusion of the moment, had forgotten to close it after him.

CHAPTER XVIII.

IT was several minutes before Angelina could sufficiently recover herself to put her energies into action ; but when she did so, her first impulse was to hasten to the door, and to listen if she heard anybody stirring beyond it.

She stood by the door by which the villain Rufus had lately departed, but not a sound met her ears, save the hollow gusts of wind as they swept along the gallery upon which it opened, or the dismal screech of the owl who had taken up his abode in some of the chambers and the old turrets of that part of the edifice. She paused, uncertain how to act. What strange consternation or thoughtlessness could have occasioned Rufus to have left the door open, she was at a loss to imagine. He must, certainly, have been frightened ; and expecting to find her wrapt in the arms of sleep, had taken her for some apparition, which his guilty conscience conjured up She returned to the other room, and took up the lamp, and then looked out into the gallery with fearful eyes ; but not a single object did they encounter; and a perfect stillness seemed to reign throughout the building. Angelina cast her eyes upon the lock of the door, and found that Rufus had left the key (to which was attached a large bunch of others) in it. In a moment, a thought struck her — might not these keys open her way to liberty, and should she miss so favourable an opportunity to escape from her enemies?

But should she miss an opportunity which might never occur to her again, to escape from a fate which she could not look upon without the utmost horror? Might she not, if she could succeed in getting out of the tower, enlist the sympathies of some persons in her favour, who might not only protect her from the power of the Baron de Morton, but also assist her to return to her friends?

"Yes, I will make the attempt," she exclaimed; "Almighty Father, who knowest how unjustly I am persecuted, to your care and protection I commit myself."

As she thus spoke, she felt still more assured and prepared to put her design into execution. First of all, she locked the outward door to prevent her being suddenly surprised; and having ascertained that all remained quiet, she prepared for her departure. The clothes which she had worn when she was brought to the tower had, fortunately, not been taken away from her, and she proceeded hastily to envelope herself in her cloak and bonnet; and then once more briefly soliciting the protection of Providence, with a trembling step she took up the lamp and prepared to leave the room. The door, on the instant she had emerged from the room, was blown to with a loud bang, which made the place re-echo again, and caused the utmost terror in the breast of our heroine, as she was afraid it would arouse the inmates of the tower, and that her flight would be speedily intercepted. The noise, however, having died away, all was again still as the grave, and Angelina gained more courage. She now bethought herself which way she should proceed, and held the

lamp above her head; but its feeble rays only permitted her to penetrate for a very short distance. She, however, determined to take the same way by which she had been brought into the tower; and, accordingly, she cautiously passed along the gallery, often timidly looking back, as the murmuring of the wind made her imagine that it was the voices of persons in pursuit. She had just reached the end of the gallery, and was about to descend the stairs, when she started with terror, as she thought she heard the closing of a door at the other end; and, looking towards it, she was almost positive that she saw the glimmering of a light; but in an instant it was gone, and all remained the same as before.

Apprehensive that her flight was discovered, she leant against the bannisters, uncertain how to act; but hearing no further noise, she somewhat regained her composure, and proceeded to descend the stairs. First, however, she looked down to be certain that there was no one watching her. All was safe; so she descended with silent steps, and scarcely dared to breathe, so fearful was she that she might be overheard. She reached the hall, which she traversed with the same caution, and at length she gained the hall door. First, looking fearfully around her, she tried the various keys attached to the bunch, and at last found one which turned in the lock. Her heart throbbed eagerly with hope; but the bolts, which were very heavy, resisted all her efforts to pull them back, and she gave up the attempt in despair.

Disappointed, Angelina now stood uncertain which way to act. She must return to her prison—all hope of her escape was at an end. She sighed heavily as she thought of this, and was about to re-ascend the stairs, when, looking round, she perceived, to the left, a low archway, towards which she hastened. The rays emitted by her lamp showed her an oaken door; but fearful that it might open into apartments occupied by some of the family, she placed her ear to the key-hole and listened attentively, but all was quite still; and placing her lamp upon the pavement, she tried the different keys, and at last found one which opened it. The moment the door flew back, a thick cloud of dust was blown around her, and it was a second or two before Angelina could perceive anything; but when she did, she found herself in a small closet, which did not contain any furniture, and seemed as if it had not been used for some time.

A door on one side of this closet, which was standing open, showed to our heroine a dark staircase; to the bottom of which the light from the lamp could not penetrate.

She had to step with caution, for the stairs were very rotten, and several had crumbled away altogether. At length she reached the bottom, and a rush of unwholesome air curled around her, and made her tremble with cold. She shielded the lamp as well as she could until it had passed away, and then found herself in a long subterraneous passage, the walls of which were of stone, but green with age and damp, and it was evidently older than the other part of the building.

The termination of the passage she could not see, for there were many windings. While she thus stood, suddenly she heard a loud and confused noise from above, followed by the opening and closing of doors. Alarmed beyond description (for she did not doubt but that her flight was discovered, and that the ruffians were in pursuit of her), the agitated maiden fled along the passage with more speed than could have been expected in such a moment of terror, until, having proceeded for some distance, she was compelled to pause to take breath. No sooner had she done so than the voices of men vibrated in her ears, and they had evidently entered the closet, and were about to descend the stairs.

"Good God!" she mentally uttered, "protect me! All hope of escape is now at an end; and should they find me, what may not their rage tempt the wretches to do?"

"It is very evident, from the hall-door being closed, that she has fled this way," at that moment ejaculated a gruff voice, which Angelina, with horror, recognized directly to be that of Rufas. "The jade cannot escape us unless she reaches the iron door which stands open. Two of you take the passage to the right, and two to the left, and she will be in our power again—that's certain. What a fool I must be to leave the room-door open!"

We need not attempt to describe the terror of our heroine when she found herself in the grasp of the ruffians; her blood seemed to be frozen in her veins, and her heart to lose its pulsation. In that dreadful moment, despair seized upon her mind, and took possession of all her faculties, and she gave herself up for lost;—she could not doubt but that her life was sought, and that the villains would not miss so excellent an opportunity, and such a convenient spot as that gloomy place, to perpetrate their sanguinary deed. Oh, how terrible was her anguish as these thoughts rose in a moment to her mind!—to die so young—and by such cruel means—to be plunged into eternity in the midst of all her youth and vigour, with the blossoms of hope springing in her path, was awful indeed to think upon. She would have implored the mercy of the ruffians who held her, flinty-hearted and callous to humanity and pity as she had no doubt they were; but, although her lips moved, her tongue refused to perform its office. The men, however, seemed to read her thoughts, for one of them said—

"Oh, no, young lady, no running away again;—you have giving us a pretty good hunt this time, all through the stupidity and carelessness of Rufas; but you may depend upon it you will be taken proper care of in future, until you are disposed of as my lord, the baron, may think fit."

"Disposed of as the baron may think fit?" thought Angelina, with a shudder. Alas! that seemed to confirm her most dreadful apprehensions, and she could scarcely save herself from swooning with terror. The ruffians hurried her along, and were soon afterwards joined by the villain Rufus, the appearance of whom filled the bosom of our heroine with disgust and consternation. Rufus looked at her with an expression of countenance that was truly fiendish, as he said—

"So, you are caught, are you? Fool! and then did you think to escape from this tower?—If you had even gained the exterior of the building, nothing could have saved you from again falling into our clutches. However, I will take good care that you shall not have a chance of making such an attempt again. Bring her along to her old quarters."

"If one spark of pity inhabits your bosom," said Angelina, for the first time being able to speak, since they had re-taken her, "for the love of Heaven, spare me; I know not, I cannot conceive what motive can prompt you to persecute me in this manner, unconscious as I am of ever doing anything to excite the baron's vengeance."

"It's of no use your talking to me," answered Rufus. "I only know that it is the will of my lord, the baron, that you should be here detained, and it is my duty to obey him. This way, this way!"

Finding that all her supplications were useless, Angelina, with a mental prayer to Omnipotence, resigned herself to her fate, and was led, by a different way to that which she had come, once more to those apartments she had so recently quitted.

Having seen her securely in, Rufus and his companions left the place, and having safely locked and bolted the door, Angelina found herself once more too safely a prisoner to entertain the least hope of escaping.

With insupportable agony the unfortunate girl wrung her hands, and sobbed convulsively, as she fixed her eyes upon the confined limits of her prison, and thought upon the probability that she was never more fated to leave that place alive.

"Oh, God!" she ejaculated, "what a strange, yet terrable fate is mine; thus to be deprived of my liberty, and threatened with a violent death, by a person whom I scarcely know, and for what reason I am also ignorant. But, surely the Almighty, who knows my innocence, will watch over and protect me. Yes, to Him will I trust, and patiently endeavour to await the result of this terrible adventure."

The latter thought served in a great measure to abate the anguish of her feelings, and she endeavoured to reflect calmly upon her situation. The circumstance of the persecution of the baron and the hints he had thrown out, served to recall many observations that at different times had been made use of by her uncle inadvertantly, which at the time she had considered strange, but being unable to form any conception of the meaning of them, she had soon forgotten;—now, however, they were all restored to her memory, and, combined with other events, induced her to believe that there really was some mystery attached to her birth which her uncle had particular reasons for concealing. Of her parents, she had not the least recollection, and she now remembered the agitation Mr. Woodfield had ever betrayed whenever she happened to mention her father and mother, and the anxiety he evinced to evade the subject. Then again she thought upon her several adventures with Kate of the ruins, and the statement she had made upon their first meeting, "*that she was not what she seemed to be;*" and all these circumstances combined served to confirm her the more in her surmises. But what could be the mystery of her birth? was not Mr. Woodfield really related to her? who were her parents? —did they still live? or what had been their fate? These perplexing thoughts harassed her mind, and she in vain endeavoured to come to some satisfactory conclusion.

Tired at length with rumination, and being not at all disposed to seek her couch, she arose and walked to the window. It was now quite daylight, and the morning breeze breathed refreshingly in upon her from between the iron bars, the window being up. It was a lovely morning, and the scenery, which the window commanded a full view of, was brilliant with the first effulgent beams of the morning's sun. Angelina, in the contemplation of the wild but picturesque beauties around, lost for awhile the remembrance of her own troubles, and the critical situation in which she was placed ; and being an enthusiastic admirer of nature in all its phases, she dwelt with a feeling of delight upon the objects that met her view, and which momentarily expanded into more loveliness, as the radiance of the sun increased. The birds were carolling forth their sweetest songs, and the flowers breathed their most delicious perfume ; and as Angelina inhaled their odour' her mind felt composed and refreshed.

While she still stood at the window, she imagined she beheld the figure of a man in the distance, which seemed to be approaching in the direction of the tower. Another second convinced her that she had not been deceived, for the man hastily advanced, until she was enabled more narrowly to trace his person, and as she did so, it struck her as being familiar to her. Her heart throbbed with an indefinable sensation as this idea crossed her mind, which was not a little increased as the form came nearer. At length it was hid from her view by the wall which separated the gardens from the country beyond. But it was not long ere it was once more presented to her observation, and she was not a little surprised when she beheld it scaling the wall, and the next instant it alighted in the grounds ; and after looking cautiously around him, as if to ascertain whether any person was observing him, he approached along the path upon which the window where our heroine was standing immediately looked. As he advanced, Angelina was the more confident that she had seen him before ; and a strange trembling came over her, which she in vain tried to vanquish.

At length he came almost immediately beneath the window, and after reconnoitring for a while, raised his head ; and what was the astonishment and agitation of Angelia, when she recognised in his expressive features those of the stranger, the smuggler captain, from whom she had already received such services.

The maiden's heart leaped with a mingled sensation of surprise and delight. What could have brought him to that spot ? Was it possible that he could have heard where she was confined, and had come to release her? But in a moment she discarded this idea as preposterous. How was he to discover where she was, and why should he take such an interest in what befel her, after the manner in which she had repulsed his advances ? She sighed ; and never did she feel more severely the pain of her confinement. Would that he could see her, but that was impossible, or that she could adopt any method of letting him know in what part of the building she was confined, but that was equally unavailable ; besides, if it were even in her power so to do, prudence would have forbidden her doing so to a stranger, and especially one who, from what she had see, she had a right to suspect was a man of questionable character. Quick again as lightning these thoughts evaporated and made room for others of a contrary description ; had he not promised to protect her, and was not any situation than the one in which she was now placed, and the danger which threatened her, preferable ? Yes !—But in what way could she apprise him that she was confined in the tower, and direct his attention to the exact part of the fabric she inhabited? She looked anxiously in both apartments, but in neither could she perceive a pen and ink ; and she did not dare venture to call, for fear that some of the creatures of the Baron de Morton would be listening, and the action should not only immediately decide her fate, but consign him to punishment. In this state of mind, the feelings of the hapless maiden may be very readily imagined ; but she knew not how to act. Oh, that she could attract his attention to the window at which she was standing, then would hope revive in her bosom ; but, as if to mock her wishes, he seemed to examine every casement but the right one. Having apparently walked round the building returned to the same spot again, and after the lapse of a second, seemed about to quit the place, which Angelina perceiving, was wound up to a pitch of agony and impatience quite intolerable; and once more casting her eyes around the room, she beheld a small piece of wood, which had been broken off one of the legs of the table. Thinking to attract his attention, she picked it up and threw it from the window, and it fell just by his feet. It had the desired effect; Hugh Clifford (as he had denominated himself to Mr. Woodfield) observed it, and immediately running forth a few yards from the tower, looked up, and directly observed our heroine.

We will not endeavour to describe the emotion evinced by Hugh Clifford upon recognising Angelina. He stood for a few seconds as if bewildered; then suddenly waving his hand, and bowing with infinite grace, he turned and left the place with much precipitation. When he had got but a short distance from the spot, he again turned round, and waved his hand to Angelina; then leaping over the wall, was soon hid from the sight. Our heroine, in a transport of joy and gratitude, left the window; and throwing herself on her knees, poured forth her thanks to Providence for the circumstance which again inspired her heart with hope.

She arose from her knees, and then began to question herself what reason she had to rejoice so much at seeing the stranger? How could he assist her, and why should he trouble himself to do so? But then again, what had brought him to the tower at such a singular hour? Again did her most sanguine hopes revive; yes, he had by some means elicited in whose power she was, and where she was confined, and had come with a determination to restore her to liberty. Already did her heart overflow with gratitude towards the handsome stranger, and she involuntarily breathed a sigh as she thought upon him. She took forth the miniature she had dropped from her bosom, and then she discovered that a

small locket which she always had suspended from her neck was missing. The locket was a very curious one, and her uncle had always enjoined her to take particular care of it, as he said it was one which had belonged to her parents. She knew that she had it in her possession when she left the place of her incarceration to attempt the escape from the tower, and consequently, she must have dropped it on the way.

This discovery caused our heroine considerable uneasiness and vexation, for she had no means of recovering it; and should it fall into the power of any of the ruffians, she knew not what might be the consequences.

The adventure of the morning had, however, somewhat revived her hopes, and she endeavoured to tranquilise her mind; but this was a much more difficult task than she had apprehended, for she was surrounded by so many dangers, that before any assistance could be rendered her, if such indeed were intended, her fate might be decided.

Nothing particular occurred to her that morning, and she continued to sit at the window and watch the expanding beauties of the young morn, until she was aroused by hearing the key turn in the outer door of her apartments; then the bolts were withdrawn; and just as her heart was beating with apprehension, her astonishment and gratification were not a little excited, when the door opened, and Bridget entered, bringing with her her morning's repast.

Angelina could not help expressing by her looks the pleasure she felt at again seeing the good-natured domestic, who, for her part, plainly showed that she experienced the same feelings.

"I was fearful that you had been subjected to some species of cruelty for your kindness to me," observed Angelina.

"As for that matter, Miss," replied Bridget, "I have been harshly enough treated by Rufus; but that is nothing new to me. But I am fearful almost to speak, for I know not who may be watching me, and listening to what I say."

Bridget now closed the door, and preceded our heroine to the inner apartment, where she spread the repast on a table, and requested her to partake of it. Angelina could not help remarking that Bridget appeared agitated, and that she wanted to say something, but was yet afraid to speak. After a pause, however, and having looked carefully into

THE BARON DE MORTON RECEIVING THE LOCKET FROM RUFUS.

the front room, and gone to the door and listened, she returned to the room in which she had left our heroine, and said in a low voice :—

"How foolish you were, Miss, to take ad-vantage of the neglect and forgetfulness of Rufus last night, and to try to effect your escape from this place. Why, it would be a matter of impossibility for any one to do so who was not thoroughly acquainted with the tower, for there are so many intricate windings. Besides, what could you have done alone, if even you had got outside this building, so far away from home as you are, amid strangers, and in a place where the emissaries of the baron are in every hole and corner?"

Angelina sighed.

"Alas!" she exclaimed, "I did no more than what any other person would have done under similar circumstances. What a terrible fate is mine; and the uncertainty of it renders it still more fearful."

"I can but repeat what I have before assured you," said Bridget, "namely, that I pity you from the bottom of my heart; and God knows, if it were in my power—but—I fear, Miss, that the attempt you made will but exasperate the baron the more, when he comes to hear of it!"

"Was it not all through the carelessness of your husband?" said Angelina, hastily; "and do you not think it is far from probable that he will make the baron acquainted with it?"

"He cannot help doing so," answered Bridget; "a circumstance has occurred which will compel him to reveal every particular, otherwise he might have been induced to have hidden it from his knowledge for fear of his displeasure!"

"Ah!" ejaculated the maiden, eagerly, "to what circumstance do you allude?"

Bridget once more went on tip-toe to the door of the front room, and listened a minute or two; then returning to the chamber, she said in a whisper to Angelina—

"Did you not lose something last night, when endeavouring to escape from the tower?"

"I did," hastily answered our heroine; "what of that?"

"It was a locket, was it not?"

"True, true," replied the maiden, "and one that I prized more than anything else I possessed in the world, for it was the only sad memento I possessed of my poor parents."

"'Tis strange!" observed Bridget thoughtfully; "what could be the cause of his violent emotion?"

"Of whom do you speak?" demanded Angelina, with much agitation, "oh, pray inform me!"

"I speak of Rufus," answered Bridget. "One of the ruffians who seized you in the vaults beneath the tower found the locket you had dropped (which I suppose got disengaged from your neck in the struggle), and brought it to him; and no sooner did he behold it than he became very pale, and looked at it so wildly, that I thought he would have gone mad. ''Tis—'tis the same,' he murmured, unable to remove his eyes from it, 'though so many years have elapsed, I cannot be mistaken. The baron must be made acquainted with this discovery without delay.' Then perceiving me in the room, he gave me some gruff salute in his usual way, and hastily quitted the place, and soon afterwards the tower to go to the baron, I have no doubt; who will, I dare say, return to the tower with him before long."·

Angelina shuddered.

"Good God!" she cried, "where will this mystery end—for what am I destined?"

"You say the locket was the gift of your parents?" said Bridget, after a pause. "Pardon me, Miss, but who might they be?"

"I never knew them," answered Angelina, "they died when I was an infant, and I was left to the protection of my uncle, Mr. Woodfield."

"And was Woodfield the name of your father and mother, Miss?" inquired Bridget. Angelina answered in the affirmative, and added—

"Why the locket should cause your husband so much apparent emotion I cannot imagine; would that the Almighty would solve this painful mystery, and release me from this state of doubt and apprehension; certainty would not be half so terrible as this suspense."

"I wish I could assist you—indeed I do," said Bridget, earnestly; "alas! much I fear the baron intends you no good, and——"

"Oh, do not hesitate, for God's sake do not!" supplicated our heroine, in a tone bordering on distraction; "if you know anything—suspect anything, in pity do not conceal it from me."

"I know nothing," replied Bridget, looking fearfully around her; "what should I know, but——"

"What, ho! Bridget," at that moment exclaimed a coarse voice, "are you going to stand there all the day?"

"It is the voice of Martin," said Bridget, with terror, "the man who always has the charge of the tower when my husband is absent. I hope he has not overheard what I have been talking about, or—but I must go;—I will come again by and by, if possible."

As the domestic thus spoke, she was about to leave the room, but perceiving the earnest looks of supplication which Angelina fixed upon her, she turned back, and in a whisper scarcely audible, she said—

"Examine the portrait."

She then, without uttering another word, quitted the apartments, and left our heroine in a state of perplexity and astonishment, which we feel at a loss properly to describe.

CHAPTER XIX.

FOR a few seconds after Bridget had quitted the room, Angelina was so overcome by the mystery of her words and manners, that she was quite incapable of moving; but to the danger of her situation she was too sensibly alive. But how was she to escape from it? Who was there to assist her?

True, she had seen the handsome stranger who had two or three times before been her preserver; but had he the power, even if he had the will, to rescue her? He might, to be sure, by letting her friends know of her situation, enable them to demand in court of justice her delivery to them, and bring him to punishment for the outrage he had committed; but alas! long before that could be accomplished, her doom might be sealed. She thought upon the alarm, the trepidation evinced by Bridget; and then the words she had made use of at parting, recurred to her:—"Examine the portrait," and she became still more lost in bewilderment. In situations of danger, however, the most trifling circumstance which creates hope is seized upon with avidity, and Angelina experienced these feelings, and was about to do as Bridget had desired her, and had walked towards the portrait, when her footsteps were suddenly arrested by hearing the sound of the rumbling of carriage-wheels in the court-yard. She therefore hastened to the casement, and beheld the Baron De Morton alight, followed by his faithful myrmidon, the villain Rufus, and immediately hurried into the tower. A cold sweat came over our heroine when she again saw the baron, and recalled to her memory what had taken place on their last interview, and the threats he had then held out. She stood for awhile immoveable; then finding that all remained quiet in the tower, she became more composed; and as every moment, she imagined, might be precious, she hastened towards the portrait. She paused as she stood before it, and could not, in spite of the state of distraction her mind was in, help admiring the beauty of the painting. So great had been the talent the artist had displayed upon it, that it almost appeared to be imbued with life, and the eyes, in particular, seemed to beam upon the maiden an expression of encouragement. Hope again suddenly took possession of her bosom, and she proceeded in her search with greater spirit than could have been expected. She scrutinised the painting minutely, examined every part of it, the canvass, the frame, but still she saw nothing to gratify her curiosity; and she was about to give it up in despair, when suddenly her hand fell upon some cold and hard substance in the side of the frame, and upon looking more closely into it, she perceived what appeared to be a small brass spring. She pressed with all her might upon it, and in an instant the painting, frame and all, glided back without the slightest noise; and Angelina was completely thunderstruck when a spacious apartment met her view.

Filled with astonishment, Angelina stepped into the apartment and gazed around her. It was very handsomely furnished, and seemed to have been but recently occupied. The wainscot was of oak, panelled and richly carved, and several portraits and views, executed in the most skilful style, were hung around. The floor was richly carpeted, the tables were of highly polished mahogany, inlaid with mother-of-pearl ; the chairs and sofa were covered with rich crimson damask ; and arranged on shelves on one side of the apartment, were a number of books in elegant bindings.

Angelina could scarcely believe the evidence of her eyes, and stood for a few moments in utter amazement. For what purpose could she have been placed so near this room, and who had been its occupant or occupants, she was at a loss to conjecture. The discovery, however, by no means displeased her, for if she was doomed to remain a prisoner within these gloomy walls, here was a change, and something to lighten the tediousness and melancholy of her incarceration. But then she remembered the peculiar emphasis with which Bridget had uttered the words, "Examine the portrait," and at the same time the deep solemnity of her countenance, which seemed to imply that she had everything to dread ; besides, she had told her that "she feared the baron intended her no good," and, consequently, she concluded that she had directed her attention to the apartment for some purpose which she could not at present fathom ; but it was evident that it was not as a means of escape, for here she was as much confined as in the adjoining rooms ; true, she saw a door on the other side of the apartment, but it was locked, and therefore she had no means of effecting an escape that way.

In vain endeavouring to fathom this mystery, our heroine advanced towards the library, and was about to take a book from the shelf, when she was startled by hearing a loud noise like the banging of a door, which seemed to proceed from no great distance from her. She trembled and looked around her, expecting to see some one in the apartment ; but all was the same as when she entered it. That she was not mistaken, she was certain ; and shortly afterwards, as she listened with breathless anxiety and curiosity, she could plainly distinguish the murmuring of voices, which evidently proceeded from that side of the apartment on which the door was. Our heroine, more surprised than ever, approached on tip-toe the door, and, with an emotion almost insupportable, she stooped and peeped through the key-hole. For a second or so she could not clearly distinguish any particular objects ; but at length she observed that the room beyond was very small, and apparently entirely of stone, and contained but little furniture. But her attention was soon wholly engrossed by two objects that had at first been hidden from her view, and who now advanced towards the table. It was the Baron de Morton and Rufus ; the former held something in his hand, upon which he was intently gazing, and, by the colour of the ribbon which hung from it, Angelina had not the least doubt but that it was the locket which she had lost.

The baron at length raised his head, and she could perceive an expression of unusual agitation in his strongly-lined features. He folded his arms a moment, and traversed the room hastily, as if buried in deep and painful reflection ; then he returned to the table again, at which his faithful myrmidon was standing, and once more fixed his eyes earnestly on the locket.

"Rufus," at length he uttered, "it is the same ; and this at once confirms our suspicions—this is the very locket I have seen worn by Algernon! The truth is now evident ; and this pretended peasant's brat—this girl whose beauty has caused such a sensation among the young men in the neighbourhood where she has resided—is her whom I thought was long since mouldered to dust, the hated offspring off——"

"True," interrupted Rufus, "I knew this locket in a moment, and there cannot any longer be a doubt but that she is the girl we suspect."

"Curses light upon the arm that failed in its office!" exclaimed the baron, gnashing his teeth, and stamping on the floor with rage; "no wonder my heart throbbed and my blood froze to ice, when I first beheld her!—When I gazed upon her features, an ocean of blood seemed to roll at my feet, and the screams of the murdered to ring in my ears! But by what strange means could she have escaped the death to which she was doomed, and which I believed to have been accomplished?"

"I cannot imagine," replied the ruffian, "for I could swear that——"

Angelina could not catch the remainder of the sentence; and presently the baron exclaimed,—

"Feelings, horrors that had long lain dormant, are by this discovery once more aroused; and conscience——"

"Psha! my lord," cried Rufus, "conscience is a bugbear that none but fanatics and old women will encourage."

"Think you, Rufus," returned the baron—"think you that I can look upon this girl, whose likeness to my victim is so powerful, that I could scarcely believe but that she once more stood before me, and not feel that I am a wretch, a villain, a——"

"The cant of priestcraft," sneered the ruffian, "unworthy the Baron de Morton. Come, come, no more of this; is not the girl in your power, and the arm which has once failed may at last be successful?"

"But yet so young, so lovely too!" uttered the baron, as he once more gazed upon the locket, and sighed deeply.

"How long is it since compassion before found a place in the breast of the Baron de Morton?" scornfully and sarcastically observed Rufus; "but this is only a waste of time; it is necessary for the safety of us both that the girl should die!"

"But should her friends discover who are her murderers?" said the baron.

"Friends!" repeated Rufus, "what friend has she but Woodfield?—and he is too poor, too powerless, to cause you any apprehension; it is not improbable that he will be too glad to get rid of the incumbrance to take much trouble about it."

"I know not that," observed the baron, "and indeed I like not that same Woodfield; there is something in his air and behaviour that convinces me he was not born in the humble station he now occupies. The answers he gave at the interview I had with him were bold and independent; and there was a nobleness in his bearing, which seemed to sink me into insignificance. He obstinately refused to gratify my curiosity on the subject of Angelina when I pressed him to do so; and as he fixed his eye upon me with an expression of hatred and contempt, there was something in his glance which made me tremble, and which I was confident was familiar to me. I would that this business could be accomplished without the shedding of more blood; would not all fear be at an end if we were to keep her closely confined within this tower for the remainder of her days?"

"Her death would be the surest and safest way of preventing any accidents occurring," answered Rufus; "and for my part, I cannot see why you should hesitate. I will myself perform the deed, and suspicion cannot light upon us. No one knows, except ourselves, that she is in our power; and what motive could they imagine you could have for committing such an outrage? No person would ever know whether she was living or dead; for, after the deed is accomplished, let her body be consigned to the deep, and then——"

The terrified Angelina could not listen to any more that passed, for the agony of her feelings overcame her, and she sunk insensible in a chair.

When she again became conscious, it was several moments before she could collect her thoughts sufficiently to recall the conversation she had overheard, or remember where she was; but when she did, to what a state of horror was she awakened! It was evident now that her fate was sealed, and she had no means of evading it. She looked around her, clasped her burning temples, then wrung her hands in despair! Was there no way for her to avoid a fate so terrible? And must she, so young, fall beneath the murderer's knife?

"Oh, merciful God!" she exclaimed in a paroxysm of anguish, "in Thee alone is my trust; oh, do not forsake me in the hour of need!"

She again listened at the door—but all was still. She looked through the key-hole, but the baron and the wretch Rufus had left the room. She threw herself upon her knees, and covering her face with her hands, for awhile, in the intensity of her sufferings, became lost to everything around her.

At length she arose, and returned to her chamber, closing the secret door after her. Such were the multiplicity of racking ideas that crowded upon her imagination, that she could with difficulty arrange them into anything like order, so as to ruminate on her perilous situation. One moment she gave herself up to the most violent despair, and the next a ray of hope would dart across her mind, when she remembered that the baron seemed to relent. Oh, yes; he might spare her—he would—he never could take away the life of one so young, who even if she was the daughter of the person he seemed to suspect, had never injured him. Villain, as she really thought him to be, she could never believe that he would be monster enough to perpetrate such a crime. Then the circumstance of her seeing the handsome young stranger returned to her recollection. "He saw me—he bowed to me," she said; "he will assist me—I feel assured he will. Oh, I will not yet despair!" Again she threw herself upon her knees, and implored the protection of Heaven; but she was suddenly aroused, by hearing a noise from the apartment she had just quitted; and she had only just time to spring upon her feet, when the portrait was slid back, and the Baron de Morton entered, his eyes darting fury, and his cheeks flushed, evidently from the effects of wine.

"Mercy! mercy!" screamed Angelina, in tones of the utmost agony, as she threw herself on her knees, and looked up piteously and imploringly in his face—"Oh, spare me, my lord!"

The baron seemed startled by her words, and gazed upon her earnestly for a moment, without speaking; but then, as a fearful expression overspread his features, he exclaimed, in a hoarse voice—

"Ah! 'twas thus *she* spoke; those were her last words, her very tones! and as I gaze upon this girl, the—but fool that I am, it was not for this I came here. Girl, answer me; no deceit—remember, your life is in my hands, and I will learn the truth! Know you this locket?" Holding before her eyes the one she had lost.

"Oh, my lord!" ejaculated our heroine, tears of terror chasing each other rapidly down her cheeks, "of what——"

"No, hesitation girl, this locket——"

"Belongs to me, my lord," answered the alarmed maiden, still clasping her hands, and looking up in his face with the most earnest supplication; "the locket is mine."

"Ah! your own is it?" cried the baron his eyes seeming to flash fire and his whole frame violently agitated; "and from whom did you receive it?"

Angelina tried to answer, but her feelings overpowered her, and she could not.

"Obstinate wretch!" exclaimed the baron in a voice of vehement passion, at the same time clasping her arm savagely; "will you persist in not answering me?"

" It was the gift of my parents ; but oh, for the love of Heaven——"

" The gifts of your parents !" cried De Morton, his body dreadfully convulsed with rage ; " ah ! then it is true—yes, the certainty flashes upon my brain ! Fiends of hell surround me, and urge me on to the bloody deed ! Die detested offspring of——"

The baron held a dagger in his hand, which, as he thus spoke, was raised in the air to strike the fatal blow, when suddenly Rufus rushed in from the secret entrance, and arresting his arm, exclaimed—

" Hold, my lord ! Not now ! not now !"

" Slave !" shouted the enraged baron, " why am I interrupted ?"

" Danger threatens us from without," was the answer of Rufus ; " do not delay, my lord." And without saying another word, the ruffian drew the dagger from his master's hand, and forcibly led him away, and Angelina overcome with terror, fell prostrate on the floor, and became insensible.

Overpowered by what she had suffered from terror and despair, Angelina, for some time after the baron and his creature had quitted the room, remained in a state of unconsciousness ; and when she did recover her senses, she found herself reclining on the couch, and Bridget standing by her bedside, anxiously watching her.

" Ah !" she exclaimed, looking wildly round the apartment, as if she expected to encounter some dreadful form, " where am I ?—am I still alive !—where is *he*, the murderer, the——"

" Hush, for goodness' sake, Miss," said Bridget, " pray endeavour to compose yourself ; for the present you have nothing to fear."

" For the *present*," returned our heroine, " for the present you say, but oh, who shall save me from his future wrath ?"

Bridget did not answer directly, but seemed to be hesitating whether or not she should divulge something of which she was the depository.

" If you would only endeavour to calm your feelings, Miss," she at length said, in tones that scarcely amounted to more than a whisper, " if you would only endeavour to calm your feelings, I could tell something which would show you that you still have some cause to hope to rescue yourself from the power of the Baron de Morton !"

" Ah ! say you so ?" eagerly demanded Angelina ; " oh, do not deceive me ;—do not play with my feelings, but tell me at once what——"

" For Heaven's sake, Miss," said Bridget, looking fearfully around her, " do be more cautious in what you say, for should we be overheard, not only would all chance of your enlargement be at an end, but both our lives would be sure to be sacrificed.—If you will abide by what I shall advise, and do not act rashly, before the morning, I have no doubt you will be at liberty."

" Delightful words !" said Angelina in a voice of ecstasy ;—" but can you speak seriously, or are you only——"

" What interest could it be for me to deceive you, Miss ?" interrupted Bridget reproachfully ; " but you will soon be convinced of the sincerity of my words. Listen—I have something to relate to you which it is necessary you should know, in order that you may understand the circumstances that have led to what I am commissioned to inform you of."

Our heroine descended from the bed, drew a chair close to where Bridget was about to sit, and prepared to listen to her with the greatest anxiety and impatience. Bridget first closed the outer door, and having looked into the secret apartment, to be certain that no one was concealed there, returned to Angelina ; and taking a seat by her side, began as follows—

" You must know, Miss, or perhaps you do know, that there is a celebrated smuggler about these parts, called Captain Clifford, or Hugh Clifford, which is the name he chooses to go by, though I have heard that it is not his right one; however, that's nothing at all to do with my present subject."

"Is the person of whom you speak a young man?" interrupted Angelina, eagerly.

"Yes, indeed he is," replied Bridget; "and a handsome young man, too; with features so mild yet dignified; eyes so bright, and enough to pierce you through; and a form so tall, and so graceful, that I do not wonder he should have made so many conquests over the young damsels' hearts."

"It must be him," observed our heroine.

"Oh, then, you do know him," said Bridget, inquiringly, "and, therefore, he did not deceive me?"

"I think I have seen the individual of whom you speak," returned Angelina, with a blush, and a confused manner.

"Think—ah, there is no thinking in the matter," remarked Bridget; "the whole of it is, that you need not be ashamed to acknowledge that you know Captain Clifford, for, although he is a smuggler, there is not a more noble man in existence; and, for my part, I do not see any particular crime in what he does, as he has been driven to it by misfortune and not by choice. He is one of the most generous benefactors to the poor (whom he considers deserving of relief) that ever existed."

"At any rate, you seem to know him," said Angelina.

"Ah, Miss, you are right there," replied Bridget. "When Rufus gained the consent of my parents to make me his wife, a young man, to whom I had been fondly attached, and who loved me sincerely in return, was so cut up at the circumstance, that he left his regular employment, and joined the crew belonging to one of Captain Clifford's vessels. Poor Jerome! it was a cruel thing on the part of my parents to force me to marry a man against my will; but then they were deceived by him; for, in spite of his habitual black looks, Rufus knows how to dissemble."

"And have you never heard who this Hugh Clifford, as he is called, actually is?" inquired our heroine, whose heart was so deeply interested in the account Bridget was giving, that she forgot for a while the more important information which she was so eager to gain.

"Why, there are various reports upon that subject," answered the servant; "but it is the general belief that he is the son of some great gentleman, who, for particular reasons, has discarded him;—but no one that I have ever heard of has ever yet questioned him upon, or hinted at, such a subject.

"He is very rich, and is supposed to have wealth secreted in all parts of the country; and he manages matters so cleverly, that he has never yet been detected, and may be said to carry on his illegal traffic with impunity. They do say, that the principal portion of his property is deposited in some secret place in or near the ruins of St. Mark's Abbey, from the neighbourhood of which you were taken; and they say also that *Kate of the Ruins* (who is a particular friend of the captain's, and is said to be possessed of supernatural powers) has put a spell upon the place; for, although the ruins have been searched by the officers several times, and not a corner been left unexplored, they have never been able to find out the smuggler's retreat, although they are certain it is on that spot."

"Kate of the Ruins?" repeated our heroine; "and is that what they call the mysterious woman, who has made those ancient ruins her place of abode?"

"It is," answered Bridget; "and there is as much mystery attached to her as to the smuggler Captain. She has been known to inhabit that place for many years. I have been told that every person in the neighbourhood is afraid of her, although she has never been known to do any harm to anybody. Some look upon her as a supernatural being, and others as a wretched maniac; but I think that she is in some way or other connected with Clifford, or she would not take such a deep interest in his fate as she does. But, dear me; I am straying from my subject. Well, Miss, as I was going to say, early this morning I took a walk down to the cliffs, and on my way, who should I meet but poor Jerome! Then I knew that Clifford was in the neighbourhood, and (I don't know what could put such a thought into my head) I began to think that there might yet be some chance of saving you from the fate which threatened you ; and in spite of the risk I should run in so doing, I was determined to do all that lay in my power to assist you ; for

ANGELINA SUPPLICATING DE MORTON FOR HER LIBERTY.

I could view but with horror and abhorrence the persecution to which you are so unjustly subjected. I need not describe my meeting with Jerome ; but I was not a little surprised when he informed me that he was about to lurk in the vicinity of the tower, for the very purpose of seeing me. He requested that I would accompany him to the vessel, as Hugh Clifford wished to see me on a matter of the utmost importance. At first I refused, for I considered

I should be acting imprudently; but Jerome so strongly urged me to comply with his request, that I could no longer resist; and accordingly went on board, where I saw the captain, and another person with him, who, I was informed, was your uncle, Miss."

"My uncle!" reiterated Angelina, with astonishment.

"Yes, Miss; your uncle," said Bridget. "I feel positive it was him, because he spoke so affectionately of you, and seemed to be in such a violent state of agitation. Well, Miss, to make as short of my stay as possible, I was soon made acquainted that the object of Captain Clifford in wishing to see me was, to endeavour to prevail upon me to aid them in effecting your liberation from the tower; for they said they were well aware that you was there confined. Notwithstanding the danger I should run, it did not take many minutes to gain my acquaintance. The stratagem was as quickly contrived; and then your uncle wrote this note, which I promised to deliver to you."

Angelina eagerly snatched the note from Bridget's hand, and opening it, read, in the well-known characters of Mr. Woodfield, the following words:—

"Dearest Angelina, do not despair, your liberation is at hand. Bridget will inform you of the plot we have formed, and you will be pleased to abide entirely by her directions. At midnight, you will meet me and a strager, but a sincere friend, till which time, my dear child, Heaven protect and bless you, is the fervent prayer of your affectionate uncle."

In a transport of ecstasy Angelina pressed the note to her lips, and tears of joy chased each other down her cheeks; then turning to Bridget, she said—

"But what is the stratagem you have devised?"

"It is simply this," answered Bridget; "I shall have to attend upon you, and when we think that all is secure in the tower, you are to change clothes with me, and pass out by the way I shall direct you; and, taking a secret passage which is well known to me, you will find your uncle and Clifford waiting for you, who will immediately conduct you to the vessel; and before daylight, you will be far enough away from this hated place. Once on board the smuggler's vessel, you need not be under any apprehension, for his power is as much dreaded as if he were a most formidable enemy."

"But how know you that before the time you speak of, it may not be too late; and that the baron may not have accomplished his inhuman purpose?"

"Neither the baron nor Rufus are at present in the tower," said Bridget, in reply, "and I am certain they will not return before to-morrow. When I returned from the vessel, I observed Rufus, who had come by another way, and had evidently been watching the vessels. He did not perceive me, and I secreted myself until after I had seen him depart from the spot some time, and to take the direction to return home, when I followed him. On my arrival here, I found Rufus and the baron in a state of great excitement, which was no doubt occasioned by what the latter had seen. Soon afterwards they both left together, after having first laid the strictest injunctions on me and the fellows left behind, to look narrowly after the security of the prisoner. But now I have explained everthing, and I must beg of you, Miss, to endeavour to act with as much firmness and caution as you possibly can. I must leave you for the present, in case the suspicions of the ruffians below should be aroused from my long absence; at night I will see you again."

"But, my dear, good creature," ejaculated Angelina, "what will become of you? will not all the blame——"

"Oh, fear not for me, I pray," interrupted Bridget; "great as will be the risk I know I shall run, the Almighty, who knows the justice of my intentions, will watch over and protect me from any harm that may threaten me."

"Kind hearted woman, never, never shall I

be able to repay you for this," said Angelina; but Bridget heard it not, for she had hastily quitted the room, and our heroine was once more left alone.

CHAPTER XX.

UNUSUALLY long and tedious seemed to be the hours that intervened between the time that the kind-hearted Bridget had quitted the apartment of our heroine, and the hours she had promised to return to her once more, to open to her the gates of liberty! Liberty! oh, what heavenly music did that sound seem to impart to her ear; should she then once more breathe the pure air unrestrained, unconfined? Should she again be restored to her dear friends? Oh, how bitterly they must have suffered during her absence, and what pains, what untiring pains, they must have used to discover the place of her concealment. Then her thoughts reverted to the handsome stranger, Hugh Clifford, as Bridget had described him; and she could not help feeling a strong sentiment of gratitude towards him, for it was evident that he felt a deep interest in her fate, and was doubtless instrumental in the attempt to release her; but how her father and he had become acquainted, she was totally unable to imagine. As her thoughts were thus occupied, she unconsciously took forth from her bosom the miniature of Hugh, and fixing her eyes earnestly upon it, sighed deeply, as she observed—

"It is a pity that one so young, so generous, and so—so handsome, should follow such a lawless course!"

A deep blush suffused the maiden's cheeks, as she found herself dwelling upon this subject, and she mentally asked herself why a thought as to Hugh's circumstances or pleasure, should enter her mind? Oh, Love, almighty power, how soon you gain the stronghold of the heart's affections!

Many were the prayers that Angelina offered up to Heaven that afternoon for success in the stratagem which had been formed to release her from incarceration, and that no harm might befal those who were attempting to rescue her; and her mind fluctuated painfully between hope and fear. She counted every stroke that fell upon the bell of the old tower clock; and oftentimes listened in the secret closet, thinking she heard voices, or that some one was pacing the apartments beyond; but all remained still, and at length darkness fell upon the earth, and the wind howled dismally along the different avenues of the building. Angelina stirred her fire, and re-trimmed the lamp, and she then took up a book to endeavour to dissipate the tediousness of waiting for the return of Bridget; but her mind was too much harassed for her to fix her attention upon the contents.

As hour after hour passed away, and still Bridget did not make her appearance, the heart of Angelina sunk with disappointment and impatience, and she began to think that she had deceived her, and had only been sporting with her feelings; but the next moment she banished the thought, and reproached herself for having entertained such a suspicion; and she had scarcely done so, when she heard the key turning in the lock of the outer door; bolt after bolt was withdrawn, and directly afterwards, while the heart of our heroine was throbbing violently in her bosom, with mingled feelings of hope and doubt, the door flew back on its hinges, and Bridget entered, bearing a tray on which were wine and provisions. She first placed the latter on the table, after motioning Angelina to silence, and then fastening the door again, in a whisper requested her to follow her to the inner apartment.

"No doubt you thought I was never a-coming," said she, in a low voice, "but I could not help it; the fellows below would detain me, and I dared not raise any objection lest I should excite their suspicions. I think we are right enough now: for they have both been drinking so freely, that they have fallen off into a deep sleep, from which I do not think it would be a trifle that would arouse them. But I hope, Miss, you are quite firm, for the task will require all your courage and presence of mind."

"I feel fully competent for the undertaking," answered our heroine; "but I am afraid you will run too great a risk; and dreadful even as my fate might be, I would never consent to purchase my escape from it, by the sacrifice of another."

"Oh, do not fear for me, Miss," said Bridget; "I have contrived everything for my security, and I feel assured that Providence will assist me in the performance of a good action, and protect me from the malice and revenge of the wretches who would imbrue their hands in innocent blood. But come, Miss, we have no time to lose, for should the ruffians below awake, our schemes might be entirely thwarted. Will you not partake of some refreshment? and then you had better exchange clothes with me directly."

"Oh, no, my mind is too much occupied with other things to suffer me to eat," replied Angelina. "Dear Bridget, how shall I ever be able to repay this unexampled kindness?"

"There now, my dear girl," said Bridget hastily, "I do not want to hear any more of that; I seek no other reward for what I am going to do, than that which my own conscience will afford me. Now then, it is past ten o'clock, and the captain and your uncle expected to see you before this, and will either think that our stratagem has failed, or that I have deceived them."

With trembling haste Angelina now proceeded to equip herself in the clothes of Bridget; and when all was completed, both she and the good-natured servant fell on their knees, and prayed for the protection of Providence; after which, having arose, Bridget put into our heroine's hand a bunch of keys, with instructions which way to proceed, placed the lamp in her hand, embraced her affectionately, and they separated, the latter following her to the door, and watching her until a turn in the

gallery hid her from her further observation, and she then returned to the apartments which Angelina had so recently occupied, thinking it not at all prudent to leave the place immediately.

In the meantime our heroine, with noiseless footsteps and palpitating heart, proceeded on the way which Bridget had pointed out, and trembled at the slightest noise, fearing that her flight had been discovered, and that they were in pursuit of her. Frequently as the wind moaned hollowly through the gallery, her affrighted fancy made her believe it to be the voices of men; and at such times her trepidation was so great, that she was frequently compelled to stop and lean against one of the pillars that supported the roof of the gallery, almost ready to sink with terror. She reached the end of the gallery, and descended into the hall without interruption, and she gradually gained courage. But her greatest trial was yet to come; she had to pass through the room in which the two ruffians mentioned by Bridget were sleeping, and should they be aroused, her death would be certain. When she reached the door she paused to listen, and her agitation was almost insupportable. The loud snoring of the fellows, however, re-assured her, and she ventured to open the room door gently and peep in. One was lolling back in his chair with his legs stretched towards the fire-place, and the other had placed his head on the table, and appeared totally unconscious of all that was passing around him.

Emboldened by these observations, Angelina stepped lightly into the room, and made towards the door on the opposite side; but in doing so, she was compelled to pass the table. Her foot came in contact with something on the floor, and stumbling against the table, she knocked down the lamp, and immediately the fellow who had been snoring there raised his head, and rubbing his eyes, demanded—

"Hollo! who the devil's that?"

"It's me—Bridget," answered our heroine, feigning her voice as well as she was able; "I have upset your lamp."

"Ah! I see you have ," returned the fellow, yawning; "but never mind, it's light enough by the fire to see to sleep."

With these words, the man again laid his head upon the table, and his loud snoring soon convinced our heroine that he once more slept. Thankful to the Almighty who had given her the presence of mind to reply in the manner she had done to the ruffian's questions, Angelina stepped softly to the door which was open, and passing out, bolted it on the other side, so that the men could not pursue her that way until she had sufficient time to effect her escape. Many underground apartments and passages did our heroine traverse, to the walls of which hung unwholesome damps, and which struck a deadly chill of terror to her heart as she gazed upon them ; but at length she paused, and concealed her light, as the glimmering of another at a short distance met her sight. She trembled violently, and hid herself in a small recess in the wall, to watch whether they were friends or enemies. They advanced nearer and nearer, and then our heroine could perceive the dark shadows of several persons, but she could not distinctly recognise them.

"Surely the woman has deceived us," said one: "it is getting late, and yet there are no signs of her."

"Uncle—dear, dear uncle, I am here !" ejaculated the frantic damsel, who knew his voice in a minute ; and rushing from the place where she had concealed herself, they were quickly locked fondly in each other's arms.

During the brief interval allowed to this, Hugh Clifford, with folded arms, and eyes sparkling with admiration, had been contemplating the beauteous and sylph-like form of our heroine, as she threw herself gracefully into the arms of her uncle and benefactor. But he did not suffer them to indulge long in this, but gently reminding them of the danger by which they were surrounded while they remained there, he took the arm of Angelina in his, and in a few seconds afterwards they emerged from the hollow in the rock, which formed the secret entrance to the Grey Tower, and were standing on the sea-beach.

* * * * *

Contrary to the opinion of Bridget, at midnight Rufus returned to the tower, and made his entrance unknown to any one. His brow was gloomy, and it was evident he contemplated the perpetration of some dark deed. He made his way to his own room, where he hastily swallowed off two glasses of wine; and taking the lamp in his hand, began to ascend the stairs towards the northern wing of the tower, in which our heroine had so lately been confined. As he proceeded, no sound interrupted the death-like stillness which reigned throughout the building, save the dreary screech of the owl, which seemed like the harbinger of some approaching event of horror.

The ruffian reached the door which opened into the apartments wherein our heroine had been incarcerated: it was all secure. He paused and listened. Everything was still; and with as little noise as possible, he proceeded to withdraw the bolts. He entered the room on tip-toe, and advanced towards the chamber. There he once more paused, and drawing a dagger from his vest, listened at the door. A low breathing sound vibrated on his ears.

"She sleeps," he muttered ; "it will be a long one to her; a moment longer and all will be over. And yet do I feel a secret dread upon me, which I never felt before ! 'Psha ! have I grown a coward ?"

As the villain spoke, he entered the chamber. A form was stretched upon it—it was that of a female. Rufus again paused, shuddered, and then, as if ashamed of his weakness, hastily stepped up to the couch, and averting his head, raised his arm. But a second, and one piercing cry was heard. The murderer started, and the rays of the lamp fell full upon the distorted features of his unhappy victim. A convulsive shivering shook his limbs; a livid hue overspread his countenance; he dropped the dagger, and in a voice of terror, exclaimed—

"Demons of darkness! whose features are

these? Bridget! Horror! horror! I have murdered my wife!"

CHAPTER XXI.

A BOAT was waiting under the rock the approach of Hugh Clifford and his companions, into which they stepped; and the men quickly plying their oars, it scudded over the vast deep with the speed of lightning, and they soon were all safe on board the smuggler's vessel.

Angelina felt timid at first when she found herself surrounded by the rough and hardy smugglers; but a look from Hugh Clifford, and the respect with which they all treated her, soon re-assured her, and with a heart overflowing with gratitude to her deliverer, she suffered herself to be conducted by the captain, followed by her uncle, to a very handsomely fitted-up cabin, in which refreshments were already prepared. Hitherto, our heroine had had very little opportunity to express her joy at her restoration to liberty, and her thanks to those who had been the cause of it; but unable any longer to restrain her feelings, she now threw herself into her uncle's arms, and, in a transport of delight, wept upon his bosom.

"Oh! my dear uncle," she cried, "what bitter anguish you must have suffered at my mysterious disappearance! My poor aunt, too, and Laura, were they not in a dreadful state of alarm? Oh! yes, I know they must have been. I shall never—never be able to repay you for rescuing me from the terrible fate with which I was threatened."

"Nay, my love, to this gentleman, and to the mysterious woman of St. Mark's Abbey, your gratitude is principally due," observed Mr. Woodfield; "for without them, I might still have remained in ignorance of your concealment, and even after I had obtained that knowledge, I should have lacked the power to release you."

Angelina turned her eyes, beaming with sensibility and thankfulness, upon the handsome countenance of the smuggler captain, and while deep blushes of maiden modesty dyed her cheeks, she said, in a tone of sweetness which went immediately to the heart, and seemed to hold it captive in its fascination—

"I do, indeed, thank this gentleman; and I trust that he will do me the justice to believe that I entertain a full sense of his kindness, not only upon this occasion, but once before when he saved me from the power of the Baron de Morton."

The fine expressive eyes of Hugh Clifford sparkled with more than usual brilliancy, and he appeared to hang upon every word which escaped the lips of Angelina with ecstasy; at the same time an indefinable feeling came over her heart, and she trembled with agitation, as Hugh gracefully bent one knee, and respectfully pressing her hand to his lips, thus ejaculated—

"Fair lady, Hugh Clifford considers these the happiest moments of his life, in which he has been rendered instrumental in saving you from danger. Your smile more than repays him, and he trusts that time will prove that he is not undeserving of a continuance of your friendship."

Angelina could not make any reply, but her looks spoke more than words could possibly have done. Never had she gazed upon a more handsome or noble-looking man; never had she listened to sweeter words, or expressed with greater delicacy. Could it be possible that he had always been used to the lawless life he was then in? Oh, no, she could not believe that he had been; some heavy misfortunes had driven him to it; and in this opinion the account of Bridget confirmed her. Involuntarily she sighed, and turned towards Mr. Woodfield.

The vessel had been got under weigh immediately after they had gone on board, and as she rapidly pursued her course from the Grey Tower, Angelina began to feel more composed, and partook of the refreshments provided; after which, at the request of Mr. Woodfield, she gave a minute detail of all that had happened to her since her abduction. The indignation of her uncle at the recital of the baron's villany, may be readily imagined, and he dwelt with breathless impatience upon every word she uttered. The narrative no less excited his astonishment than his wrath, and he frequently interrupted her by giving utterance to an expression of his wonder and perplexity. When she related the particulars of her losing the locket, and the conversation she had overheard betwenn Rufus and De Morton in the secret chamber, he evinced considerable emotion, and for some minutes paced the cabin with hasty and uneven steps, as if buried in deep meditation; at intervals muttering incoherent sentences to himself; at length, turning to our heroine, he said—

"I am perfectly at a loss to conceive what can be the baron's motives for such extraordinary and violent conduct;—he must be labouring under some singular delusion, and his behaviour looks more like that of a madman than anything else; at any rate, I am determined to have a full explanation of it, and to take such measures as shall secure you in future from his fury."

"But, my dearest uncle," observed Angeline, "after the repeated circumstances that I have encountered—the conduct of the baron, and the words that have been told me by—by another party, I cannot help thinking that there is some mistery attached to my birth, which you have particular reasons for concealing."

"Mystery?" repeated Mr. Woodfield, in a confused manner; "what mean you—what mystery should there be?—'Psha!—You are talking absurd, my love. And pray, what have you been told by some other party, and who is the said party, whose name you seem so fearful of disclosing?"

Angelina mentioned the warning she had received from Kate of the Ruins, the first time she had encountered her; but concealed her name, and likewise where it had taken place.

"Nay," said her uncle, "this is not like my Angelina; why should you be so fearful of revealing to me the name of the person who gave you this *important* information"?

"Pardon me, my dear uncle," remarked our heroine; "but I must not."

Mr. Woodfield seemed vexed and dissatisfied, and remained still for a short time.

"This is ridiculous, 'tis childish," at length he said.—"You have been perusing some old romances, until—but let us change the subject."

They now walked upon the deck. It was a beautiful starlight night, and the moon shed her bread beams upon the undulating mirror, reflecting a myriad of dazzling beauties. The light sails fluttered gently in the breeze, which came pure and refreshing across the expansive ocean, while the vessel smoothly glided on her way, skimming the waves with the lightness of a zephyr. As her eye fell upon the sturdy, figure of some old smuggler, standing in the reflection of the moonbeams, and smokink his short black pipe—with his huge dark whiskers and strongly lined features—Angelina could not help feeling powerfully the novelty ot her situation; and then her thoughts would immediately revert to Hugh Clifford, and the degrading life in which one so well calculated to adorn society, was placed by some untoward fate; and to say that these thoughts were not accompanied by a feeling of deep regret, would be concealing the truth.

Soon after our heroine and her uncle had been upon the deck, they were joined by Hugh, and they entered into a discourse upon different topics, in each of which he displayed intellectual and conversational powers of the highest order, and Angelina listened with the most uncontrolable pleasure to all that he said.

"Yours must be a precarious life, sir," remarked Mr. Woodfield, "and it is one which is surrounded by danger; pardon me, I wish not to appear inquisitive, but I cannot help thinking that it must have been some very strange and unfortunate circumstances that could have driven a person like you to such a calling."

"Ay," replied Hugh, with a sigh, "young as I am, I have had my share of trouble; but no matter—it is all over now, and the secret belongs to my own breast alone. As for this life, which you seem to entertain but such an indifferent opinion of, sir—it suits my nature; I am wedded to it—I love it as a patriot loves his country; and my gallant barque here dearly as a parent loves his child. Many a rough gale has she borne me safely through; and many—many a golden harvest has she conveyed me to shore. She and I will never part company till one or the other of us is laid low."

There was a fine manly energy and sincerity in the smuggler's tone and general demeanour, which could not but create the deepest interest and admiration, and Angelina marked all he said with the strictest attention. Mr. Woodfield seemed to be no less pleased with his companion than was our heroine, and they continued to converse together, heedless of the flight of time.

In the course of the evening, a circumstance took place, which confused Angelina greatly, and occasioned her considerable uneasiness. The miniature, which belonged to Hugh, and which she had ever since, for safety, continued to wear in her bosom, accidentally fell out, and the smuggler observed it. In a moment an expression of pleasure illumined his features, which the blushing Angelina could not but understand, and she hastily concealed it from his view. She would have restored it to him, but she was restrained by motives of delicacy, for she did not wish her uncle to become acquainted with the event which had placed it in her possession.

Time passed quickly away, and the conversation was kept up between Hugh Clifford and Mr. Woodfield with unabated animation. Hugh was eloquent upon every subject, and each sentence he uttered evinced a fine and highly-cultivated taste. When Angelina ventured to put forth an opinion, he seemed enraptured, and if by chance their eyes met, there was a warmth,

an intensity in his glances, which plainly showed the interest she had excited in his bosom.

Often as their eyes met, the expressive look of admiration which he fixed upon the maiden's countenance, called the blush of embarrassment to her cheeks, and imparted a sensation to her breast which she had never experienced before.

It was late when they separated for the night, and Angelina was not then at all disposed to rest. She recalled to her memory every word Hugh Clifford had spoken, and pondered over them with feelings of delight and admiration; and two hours after they had separated, she was found looking with earnest attention upon the miniature which traced with such admirable correctness his handsome features.

No sounds now met or heroine's ear, save the heavy tread of the smuggler who was keeping watch upon the deck, or the dashing of the waves against the sides of the vessel, and she was about to retire to repose, when the tones of a guitar, touched by a masterly hand, met her attention. A short, but brilliant symphony was played, and then a rich and melodious voice, which she immediately knew to be that of the smuggler captain, sung the following words, to which she listened with unbounded gratification:—

Sweet maid of the blue and the mild beaming
    eye,
Oh, why for the cot in the valley still sigh?
Haste with thy lover, across the blue sea,
And who then so cheerful, so joyous as we?—
There is not a damsel 'mid fashion and pride,
That shall happier be than the smuggler's
    bride.

Oh, 'tis sweet, with a fav'ring breeze,
To glide o'er the bright expansive seas;
But greater the pleasures I then should share,
When thou, my own beauteous one, wert
    near.

Thou should'st reign the queen of the ambient
    tide,
And many should bow to to the smuggler's
    bride.

In my bonny barque we would stem the wave,
And there is not a joy thou should'st not have,
And thy radiant smile would have the powers
To nerve my arm in danger's hour.
Then come, o'er the ocean we'll gaily ride,
And no care shall e'er sadden the smuggler's bride.

The voice ceased, but our heroine continued to listen in imagination to its melodious tones, so delighted was she with the sweetness of the air, and the exquisite manner it was sung. All, however, was now again quiet, and at length Angelina retired to rest, and soon sunk into

RUFUS MURDERING HIS WIFE, IN MISTAKE FOR ANGELINA.

sleep, pleasing visions flitting before her fancy until the morning dawned.

All the following day were they upon the ocean, and time but increased the admiration of Mr. Woodfield and Angelina towards Hugh Clifford. He most studiously attended to their comforts, and seemed to possess no greater pleasure than that which could be found in their society. To Angelina he behaved with the strictest attention, and she, in spite of her efforts to think to the contrary, felt, as they approached nearer and nearer towards the place of their destination, and the hour drew nigh that they must separate, that Hugh Clifford was to her not an object of indifference.

It was night, and the moon had risen, when the distant and moss-covered ruins of St. Mark's Abbey rose dimly upon their sight. The vessel swiftly stemmed the waves, until the old abbey burst full upon their view, illumined by the broad moonbeams.

The vessel was now anchored within a short distance of the shore, and under shelter of the rocks to screen her from observation ; Hugh Clifford then ordered the long-boat to be lowered over her side, and having assisted our heroine into it, he quickly followed himself, as did also Mr. Woodfield, and several of the crew. The boat soon reached the point of landing, but scarcely had Hugh Clifford stepped on the shore, when two men darted upon him, and seizing him violently, ordered him not to resist at the peril of his life.

"Ah !—the lubbers are on to us," he exclaimed ; " courage lads, to shore with ye, and let us see if we cannot soon teach these fellows better manners ;—off, off, with ye, ye land sharks !"

With these words Hugh Clifford, although they were very powerful men, hurled them to the earth as though they had been children, then drawing his cutlass, he stood upon the defensive.   Half-a-dozen shots immediately whizzed passed him, and several revenue officers darted from the different apertures in the rocks, where they had been lying in ambush, and surrounded Hugh.

"Down with the d—d swabs !" cried the smugglers in a breath, as they leapt, sword and pistol in hand, upon the beach, and desperately cut their way to the side of their captain, who was fiercely engaged with a host of the assailants, and fighting with a bravery which nothing could surpass.

The clashing of swords—the firing of pistols—the shouts of the smugglers—the curses and groans of the wounded—now rendered the scene truly awful, while the brightness of the moon rendered it clearly visible.

Mr. Woodfield and Agelina were left alone in the boat ; and the latter, completely overcome with terror, screamed aloud, which attracted the attention of Hugh, who exclaimed—

"Back, back, to the ship again !—Some of you hasten to their aid ; a handful of us is enough to chastise these fellows !"—

In a moment one of the smugglers jumped into the boat, and prepared to take the oars, but scarcely had he attempted to do so, when a pistol was discharged at him from the shore, the contents of which lodged in his breast ;—he gave a yell of agony, and bounding in the air, dropt lifeless into the ocean, and sunk to rise no more.

Angelina screamed and fainted, and Mr. Woodfield, finding it would be impossible for him to reach the smuggler's vessel without assistance, laid his niece down at the bottom of the boat, to escape the shots that might be fired after them, and once more took the oars, and using all his strength, he endeavoured to wind round to the back of the rock, thinking there he might effect a landing in safety, and seek a shelter in St. Mark's Abbey, until the conflict was at an end.   He had scarcely, however, taken a dozen strokes, when the boat dashed with impetuous violence against a point of rock, which abutted into the sea, and which he had not observed, and immediately upset, and Mr. Woodfield and his niece were both immersed in the water.

Mr. Woodfield immediately arose again to the surface, and with frantic haste looked round him in search of our heroine ; the bright moonbeams immediately pointed out her light dress to him floating on the waves, and with desperate haste, he made towards her, and succeeded in clasping her round the waist. Mr. Woodfield was an excellent swimmer, but the alarm and exertions he had undergone had almost exhausted him, and it was with extreme difficulty he gained the shore, where, with the senseless form of Angelina over his shoulder, he rushed towards the rock, upon the summit of which stood the ruins of St. Mark's Abbey; but not many paces had he advanced, when a man, armed with a cutlass, and by his dress, one of the officers, rushed out upon him and not only impeded his progress, but was in the act of aiming a violent blow at him, when a determined voice from the rock above, and which seemed to make the whole place resound again, exclaimed—

"Hold! cowardly knave!"

Before he had an opportunity to turn to see who it was that uttered the mandate, the report of a pistol was heard, and the man dropped a corpse at the foot of him he was about to attack.

Mr. Woodfield looked up, and standing at the very edge of the rock, which overhung the beach, was Kate of the Ruins, holding in each hand a pistol.

She did not, however, remain in that attitude long, but dashing down the rock, with astonishing precipitation, she snatched the form of our heroine from him, and with a strength which seemed almost superhuman, threw her over her shoulder, and retraced her steps up the side of the steep rock, calling upon Mr. Woodfield to follow.

Completely thunderstruck, Mr. Woodfield obeyed her; but he had the utmost difficulty to keep pace with her; and when she entered the abbey ruins, she was entirely hidden from his view, until the moonbeams, streaming in at one of the apertures time and decay had caused in the roof of the aisle, revealed to him her white robes, as she flew along with increased swiftness even, and looked more like some spirit of the grave than a human being.

Mr. Woodfield quickened his speed, and followed his strange conductor up several spiral and winding staircases, the steps of which tottered beneath his feet, but over which she flew with unabated rapidity, until they stopped at a door concealed in the wall, and which no one who was not acquainted with the secret,

would have thought was anything else than part of the stone-work, which Kate desired him to press against with his back with all his strength. He complied, and instantly the door fell back on its hinges, and disclosed to his astonished eyes a comfortable, well-furnished apartment, in which was a bed, and a fire blazed cheerfully in the grate.

Kate gently laid her senseless burthen on the rock, and taking from her bosom a phial applied it to her nostrils, then poured a portion of the contents into the palm of her hand, and chafed her temples.

The mysterious woman then pointed to a small ante-room, to which she requested that Mr. Woodfield would retire for a few minutes, and having complied; she closed the door upon him. He had not been there long, before Kate again opened the door, and beckoned him to return into the room again, which having done, he perceived that Kate had changed the wet clothes of his niece, and having placed her in an arm-chair by the fire-side, she was fast recovering under the influence of its genial glow.

"She is out of danger now, poor girl," said the mysterious woman, in gentle tones, and gazing upon our heroine with looks of the deepest interest; "I must leave her for a few minutes,—but I will return to you again, and —rest contented that no harm can reach you here."

"Kind, generous, noble-hearted woman," exclaimed Mr. Woodfield, as he arose from his chair and advanced towards her; but Kate waved her hand, and darting instantaneously from the room, closed the door upon him, and he was left to the reflections which the strange adventure he had met with, and Kate's more singular conduct had given rise to.

His first care was, however, to see to the recovery of his niece; and it was not long ere he had the pleasure to find that his efforts were crowned with success. Angelina opened her eyes, and then looking around the apartment, exclaimed, in tones of amazement and perplexity—

"My uncle, dear uncle, is that you? Methought we were swallowed up in the ocean—and that he—oh, tell me where are we?"

"Be calm, my love," replied her uncle; "you are in a place of safety;—this is St. Mark's Abbey."

"St. Mark's Abbey!" replied the astonished damsel.—"Ah! I remember now; it was near the abbey where that terrible conflict began, and I saw *him* surrounded and closed in by the glittering weapons of his antagonists; oh, my uncle, surely his fate—" then suddenly recollecting herself, and blushing deeply, she added—"but why should I hesitate?—Is it not natural that I should feel anxious to know the fate of him who saved my life, when twice threatened by——"

"Compose yourself, my love," said her uncle; "all may yet be well; Kate, the kind, though the mysterious, woman of these ruins, to whom we are indebted for our safety, will soon return, and then we shall doubtless know the result of the combat; and but from the un-exampled bravery displayed by the smugglers there is very little doubt but that they were triumphant."

"*Smugglers?*" repeated Angelina, with peculiar emphasis and expression of countenance which Mr. Woodfield could not help noticing.

Before they could make any further observations the door opened, and Kate entered. She advanced towards Angelina with the utmost kindness depicted in ther countenance, and taking her hand, said:—

"My poor girl, it joys me to see you restored;—it will not, however, be safe for you to leave the abbey to-night, for there are those lurking about the neighbourhood who might do you harm. In this place you may rest with the greatest security, and I will be your companion. I have also prepared a chamber for you—your—Mr. Woodfield, I mean; and as soon as you like in the morning you may depart, and I will conduct you by a secret avenue from hence."

"Ah, tell me," eagerly ejaculated Angelina, "the smugglers; they——"

"Have defeated the land sharks, and left few of them to give an account of it," rejoined Kate;—"and Hugh Clifford and his companions regained their vessel in safety, and are now far away from hence."

"Heaven be praised!" exclaimed our heroine, fervently, and clasping her hands, unable to restrain the full expression of the feelings that animated her bosom.

Kate looked upon her with the deepest interest as she thus expressed herself, and more than once a sigh escaped her bosom. Mr. Woodfield watched her with mingled feelings of awe and astonishment; but suddenly recollecting himself, he said:—

"To you, strange but kind-hearted woman, how shall I express my thanks, my—"

"Enough," interrupted the woman. "Kate of the Ruins needs not any such expressions as those; that she has been able to do what she has done, affords her more satisfaction than she can express;—Heaven above only knows the gratification, the gratitude which now fills my breast;—poor girl, had you in whom I have reason to feel so deep an interest, met with such a fate as that to which you were exposed, what else would Kate then have to live for? what besides her who——"

She suddenly paused, and checked herself, as though she considered she had said too much, and then continued in a different tone:—

"But you must be tired, after the fatigue you have undergone; so, if you will follow me, I will conduct you to the chamber allotted to your repose."

"Mysterious woman," cried Mr. Woodfield, "your words fill me with amazement; why should you feel so deep an interest in one who is almost a stranger to you?"

"Stranger!" reiterated Kate, with a melancholy smile—"—but no matter;—seek not to know that which time only can unravel. Follow me!"

Finding that it would be useless to question her further, Mr. Woodfield affectionately embraced his niece, and obeyed.

CHAPTER XXII.

KATE of the Ruins led Mr. Woodfield to a comfortable-looking apartment not far from the chamber in which she had left our heroine, and there placing a lamp upon the table, she was about to bid him good night, when, just as she reached the door, a sudden thought seemed to strike her, and turning back, she said:—

" Whatever noises you may hear in the night, which may sound strange to you, I must beg that you will take no notice of, as you may rest confident that no harm shall come to either you or the beauteous maiden who is under my protection for the night. There are many mysterious circumstances connected with this old abbey, which time may perhaps unravel, and which must work their own course. Be cautioned by what I say, and be silent about all that you may see or hear."

Without giving Mr Woodfield time to make any reply to this speech, Kate of the Ruins waived her hand, and left the former to his conjectures.

The more he reflected on the behaviour and words of Kate, the more was he struck with the singularity of her character, and at a loss to fathom it. At first he had, notwithstanding his disbelief in the supernatural, been half-tempted to imagine that she had some knowledge of the black art; but that idea was now entirely altered, and he was inclined to form a better opinion of the motives of her conduct, which seemed kind and gentle, although she thought proper to involve them it such a garb of ambiguity. The frequent warnings she had given him as regarded the safety of Angelina; the mysterious words she had uttered to him in the wood; the deep interest she seemed to take in her fate, and various other facts, combined to astonish and bewilder the mind of Mr. Woodfield; and the more he reflected, the deeper did he become entangled and lost in the maze of wonder, doubt, and perplexity. What could make her take to that singular life, and how was it that she seemed to be so intimately acquainted with the affairs of other persons? Hugh Clifford, about whom there was as much mystery as Kate, seemed to be well acquainted with her, and yet he most studiously avoided talking about her; and notwithstanding that Mr. Woodfield had frequently thrown out hints upon the subject, he had never been able to elicit anything from him which was at all calculated to gratify his curiosity. Often as he looked narrowly into her countenance, he could not help thinking that there was something in it which was remarkably familiar to him, and the tones of her voice struck him as being like those he had often heard before, under different circumstances and in far happier scenes; but yet did he rack his brain in vain to endeavour to recal to his memory the original of the likeness he had some slight idea he had discovered.

Tired of dwelling upon this subject, in which he only became involved in still deeper perplexity, his thoughts reverted to Hugh Clifford, who had excited in his mind the greatest interest and admiration, mingled with feelings of suspicion, regret, and uneasiness. His admiration and gratitude were excited by the many personal and intellectual qualifications which he possessed: his suspicion, from having noticed his conduct during the voyage, the observations he had frequently made before their arrival at the Grey Tower, and his behaviour to Angelina after her rescue; from all of which circumstances he was led to believe that the beauty of our heroine had made a deep and lasting impression upon his mind, which caused him considerable uneasiness, for though he placed the utmost confidence in the prudence of his niece, he knew how ready the heart is to imbibe an attachment for one possessed of the all-powerful recommendations of Hugh Clifford, and what misery too often accrues to those who love an object they can never possess. He had watched Angelina narrowly on the voyage back, and he could not help remarking the modest but admiring eyes with which she seemed to observe the handsome young smuggler, and the evident delight with which she listened to him, while he so eloquently harangued upon every topic that was broached; and he felt a sentiment of regret that fate had placed him under an obligation to one from whom so much misery might spring.

Had not Hugh Clifford have belonged to the lawless profession to which he did, there were other circumstances which would have presented an insurmountable barrier to any union between him and Angelina; which, for reasons that will probably be known in the sequel, he kept confined to his own breast.

Filled with these reflections, and amused at the novelty of his situation, Mr. Woodfield did not feel inclined to retire to rest for some time after Kate had left him. The apartment he was in, seemed of a date coeval with the original structure, but it was in capital repair and was furnished, if not with elegance, with the most sedulous attention to comfort, which was greatly added to by the cheerful blazing of a wood-fire, that cast a red glare upon the oaken wainscot; and as its beams danced upon the carved figures with which it was covered, it gave them a variety of grotesque appearances, that would not only amuse but suggest a variety of conceptions to the beholder.

The apartment was in the south wing of the building, and commanded a view over a wide extent of woodland scenery, which now, dimly lighted by the moon, had a particular solemn appearance; the trees looking, with their dark foliage waving in the breeze, like the gaunt phantoms of another world, or the giant supporters of a vast quantity of funeral palls.

While Mr. Woodfield still stood at the casement watching this scene, a piercing shriek, more terrific than he ever remembered to have heard before, ran through the place, and seemed sufficient to arouse the dead. His first impulse was to start to the door, thinking it was Angelina, and that she needed his protection; but what was his astonishment to discover that it was quite fast, and evidently closed with a spring, which could only be opened on the out-

side? He next called aloud, but the echo of his own voice was the only answer he received. Next he kicked violently at the door, but all to no purpose: no person replied to him. Then he remembered the warning which Kate had given him, to take no notice of any noises that he might hear, and he paused and remained silent for a few moments. It was not long, however, before he was again startled by hearing a shriek still louder than the preceding one, and which was immediately followed by deep groans as if from a number of persons in extreme agony. Scarcely had these subsided, when the plaintive tones of a guitar, touched with such sweetness, that it brought forth sounds

"Which might create a soul under the ribs of death,"

sounded in his ears, and kept him in wonder and inexpressible delight. For full five minutes did this lovely melody continue, and the instrument seemed to be played by no earthly hand, while Mr. Woodfield listened with the most breathless attention, fearful of losing even the slighest note. Gradually it died away and all was again silent as the grave.

Lost in astonishment at what he had heard, and scarcely crediting his senses, Mr. Woodfield remained for a few minutes buried in fruitless conjecture. He was not a timid man, neither was he, as we have before observed, superstitious; but there was something so very out of the range of common occurrences in what had lately taken place, that he scarcely knew what to think, nor to what to attribute them. Here were the wild reports he had so often heard about the abbey ruins all but verified.—What construction, too, could he put upon the singular and superstitious conduct of Kate, in fastening him in the chamber? At one time he was half inclined to suspect her of some treachery, and trembled for the safety of his niece; but the next moment he rejected such surmises as absurd, after the proofs she had given of her friendship to Angelina, and the trouble she had taken to rescue her from danger.

Having taken another survey of the room in which he was, Mr. Woodfield once more walked to the casement. The dark clouds that had before nearly concealed the moon's bright face, had now passed over, and objects without, therefore, were rendered more visible.

Mr. Woodfield continued to watch for several minutes, without observing anything to particularly excite his curiosity; but presently he heard a sound as if some person was moaning under the window where he stood, and almost immediately afterwards, a spectral-looking figure in white flowing robes seemed to glide from some portion of the ruins, and as she darted into the darkness beneath, again the terrific shrieks rent the air, followed by groans and loud laughter, which seemed to proceed from the bowels of the earth, and had a particularly solemn and appalling effect.

Completely thunderstruck by what he had seen and heard, Mr. Woodfield stood for some time transfixed to the spot, and still continued to gaze into the dark vista of trees, where the form vanished, and left him quite at a loss what to think or do. Then he left the casement, and listened at the room door, but not the slightest sounds met his ear, save the moaning of the wind, as it swept along the different avenues and apertures in the abbey ruins.

"Some awful mystery is in this, which it is out of my power to unravel or to guess at," he exclaimed, as he walked towards the fire, which he stirred, and seated himself beside it; "alas! what dreadful crimes may not have been perpetrated within these ancient and mouldering walls; how many poor wretches——"

A hollow moan, which appeared to issue from the wainscot immediately behind, interrupted him. He started round hastily;—but no object met his view, and all again was quiet.

"It was only the wind," he said; "these strange events have unnerved me."

Feeling tired, but not sleepy, he threw himself on the bed, without undressing himself;

but not many minutes had he done so, when he was once more startled by a loud crash, which sounded like the falling of something ponderous, and appeared to be in an adjacent room.

We will now return to Angelina.

During the temporary absence of Kate of the Ruins, Angelina could not help reflecting on the events that had recently occurred to her, and wondering for what she was now reserved. The conflict which had taken place with the smugglers and the revenue officers, was impressed upon her recollection in the most vivid colours, and she shuddered when she reflected upon the imminent danger in which Hugh Clifford had been placed.

"Oh, that he would abandon this life of peril," she soliloquized; "surely with such qualifications as he possesses——"

She checked herself, and blushed deeply to find her mind wandering upon such a subject; and asked herself why she should take so deep an interest in the fate of the smuggler captain? She tried to persuade herself that it was excited merely by gratitude for the services he had rendered her; but yet reason, in spite of all her efforts, would convince her, that the sentiment deserved a much more tender name. She tried to divert her thoughts from him, but in vain; the handsome countenance of Hugh Clifford seemed to be continually before her eyes, and his words to ring in her ears. Every sentence he had uttered was treasured in her memory, and she pondered over them with feelings of the most exquisite delight :—

"He is noble, he is generous," she ejaculated. "Oh, Hugh Clifford, to you my gratitude is for ever due!"

As she thus spoke, she had unconsciously taken the miniature from her bosom, and with a feeling of the most intense admiration, she gazed upon each lineament of a countenance which the artist had so skilfully pencilled. She sighed as she did so, and pressed the miniature fervently to her heart.

She was aroused from this state of meditation by hearing a deep sigh from behind where she was sitting, and on looking round, what was her surprise and confusion to behold Kate of the Ruins contemplating her with a mingled expression of pity and admiration. She hastily thrust the miniature in her bosom, and cast her eyes towards the floor, abashed that the mysterious woman should have observed her.

"Poor girl, poor girl," said Kate, as if communing with herself;—"already has love's potent power taken possession of her heart, and with maiden diffidence she rejects the truth, and would fain assure herself that the passion she feels does not merit so warm a title. But it must not be," she continued in a louder tone, "but it must not be; maiden, you must crush that passion in the bud; the encouragement of it is fraught with danger, with destruction."

Angelina started, and looked at the woman with amazement, while the wild rolling of her eyes, and the peculiar expression of her countenance, impressed our heroine with an idea that her senses were disordered.

"Nay," resumed Kate, in a mild voice, and with a softened look, "do not deceive yourself, maiden; you love Hugh Clifford; yes, love him, and it is natural, for he is formed to captivate and to—— but I warn you, Angelina, and believe me your friend while I do so, I warn you, I say once more, to endeavour to erase him from your thoughts, until you can think of him only as a friend."

"As such only do I think of him," replied Angelina, regaining her composure, and feeling vexed at the words of Kate, and the construction she had put upon her conduct; "as the saviour of my life, surely Hugh Clifford is entitled to that name?"

"He is, he is," returned Kate, "but as such only think of him; indulge no other sentiment, for a barrier is placed between you which is insurmountable."

Our heroine felt a deadly chill at her heart as Kate uttered these words, and she looked at her with the most undisguised astonishment. Kate seated herself opposite to her, and fixing her eyes upon her countenance, seemed to be wholly absorbed in the contemplation of her features. A silence of several minutes ensued, during which interval Kate never once removed her eyes from Angelina, or altered her position.

"How like her," at length she murmured, as if talking to herself; "the very eyes, the very features, the very expression!"

"What mean you? of whom do you speak? And why do you gaze upon me so earnestly?" demanded the astonished maiden.

"Ah! there! more like her still," observed the mysterious woman;—"but no matter;—let me not be too premature in— maiden, heed me not;—I was but looking back through the long vista of time, and it brought back recollections that were accompanied with many a pang. You do not fear me, Angelina?" she continued, in a softened tone; "I am a mysterious being, at least my conduct may appear so,—but, believe me, thou dost not possess a dearer, or more faithful friend, than wild Kate of the Ruins."

"Your conduct is indeed to me mysterious," answered our heroine; "you seem to take so deep an interest in my fate, and yet till lately, I never beheld you, and even now we are almost strangers to one another."

"Thou art no stranger to me, maiden," said Kate, emphatically, "and so time will prove; the period when concealment will be no longer necessary, has not yet arrived;—the secret must not yet be divulged."

"What secret?" eagerly inquired Angelina; "what secret can you be acquainted with, which is connected with me?"

"Ask me not," said Kate; "for awhile it must be locked within my own breast; but the time will come, when that shall be divulged which will strike horror into the minds of some and astonishment to others."

Here Kate once more relapsed into silence

and seemed to be ruminating upon something of the most painful interest.   Angelina continued to look upon her for some moments with surprise ; then taking courage, observed—

"Surely it must have been some heavy sorrow, some terrible affliction, which could tempt you to take to this wild and singular life, and to seclude yourself in this manner from the world?"

"The world?" repeated Kate, with a bit-

MR. WOODFIELD FINDS CLIFFORD AT THE FEET OF ANGELINA.

ter smile ; "name it not ; it is disgusting to me !—The world and I have long been divided ; —I think upon it with the same shuddering horror, as the wretched sinner anticipates the torments of perdition.   The world !—It is a

hell ; treachery lurks in every street ;—and ——but it is enough that I have experienced sufficient to make me hate it ; as for the rest, it is a secret which must be confined to my own breast.—Come, child, it waxes late ; retire to rest ; I will remain where I am ; my busy thoughts will keep me fully employed till the morning dawns.''

Angelina hesitated, and looked round the Gothic apartment.

"Nay, girl, why do you pause ?'' interrogated Kate, angrily ; ' do you doubt me ?'

"Oh, no, you wrong me by such a supposition,'' said our heroine, eagerly ; "I must indeed be ungenerous to doubt one, who has already so often proved herself to be my friend.''

"Enough, enough,'' said Kate, affectionately, and embracing her ; "the pallid hue of fatigue his on your cheek ; retire, my child, and Kate will watch over your slumbers with all a mother's care ; no harm can visit you here while I am present.''

Angelina obeyed. Kate stirred the fire into a bright cheerful blaze ; then taking her seat in one corner of the fire-place, she placed her elbows on her knees, rested her chin on her hands, and became buried in deep rumination. Our heroine watched her for several minutes, until, completely worn out with the unusual exertion she had undergone, sleep pressed heavy upon her eyelids, and she soon became unconscious of all around.

She had not, however, slept long, when she was awakened by feeling the warm pressure of some person's lips upon her cheek, and opening her eyes, to her inexpressible astonishment, she beheld, as well as the light of the fire would permit her, the figure of a female clad in black, and whose countenance, though pale, was exquisitely beautiful, standing over her in an attitude of affection, and with her hands raised towards Heaven, as if she was invoking a blessing upon her head. The instant she beheld that Angelina had awoke she uttered a faint cry, darted from the side of the bed with the rapidity of lightning, and passed out at the room door, which our heroine now beheld was open.

"Stay, mysterious being, phantom, mortal, or whatever you are,'' cried Angelina, springing from the couch, and rushing towards the door ; "what would you with me ? Why do you visit me at this nocturnal hour ?''

But the form, whatever it was, had vanished, and Angelina returned to the room. Kate was not there, and as she looked around the apartment, but dimly lighted now by the red glare of the dying embers, she felt an irresistible sensation of horror stealing over her, and she clung to the back of a chair completely paralysed by what she had seen.

While she thus stood, the piercing screams which her uncle had heard, vibrated in her ears, and made her almost sink with terror. Her blood began to run cold, and she trembled violently in every limb. At this moment the door leading to the ante-room was thrown open, and Kate appeared. She seemed surprised and confused when she beheld Angelina had arisen, and hurrying towards her, said—

"What has alarmed you, maiden ?—I have not long been absent, and now I return, your cheek is blanched with terror, and the trembling of your limbs, and your quivering lips express the utmost alarm.''

"What mysterious being have you allowed to have access to this chamber, and for what purpose came she hither ?'' demanded Angelina, in a tremulous voice.

"What mean you ?'' said Kate, apparently astonished at her questions, but evidently confused. "What strange delusion are you labouring under ?''

"Oh, no—it was no delusion,'' said our heroine, earnestly ; "I saw her as plainly as I see you now ; she hung over me—she pressed her lips to my cheek ; she surely was mortal, and yet——''

"Indeed, my child,'' said Kate, in a persuasive tone, "you must have been dreaming ; —no person could have visited this room since I left it.''

"You would deceive me,'' said our heroine ; "I am positive of the truth of what I have asserted. I marked her features well as she hung over me, and there was something in her expression which I shall never forget. Tell me, for I am convinced you know, who she was and for what purpose came she to me?"

Kate returned no answer, but walked to the other end of the chamber, and stood for a few seconds apparently deeply wrapped in thought.

"It was imprudent," she murmured to herself, in a low tone, but sufficiently loud for Angelina to hear her, "'twas folly—twas madness."

"Ah! you do know," uttered our heroine, "yet you refuse to satisfy me? Tell me—this abbey is inhabited by more than yourself."

"Seek not to know that which I am not at present permitted to reveal," said Kate, solemnly;—"by maintaining a profound silence upon all you see and hear within these ancient walls, you can only hope to escape that trouble which would otherwise attend you. Be satis- that all who reside here are your friends.

Kate uttered these last words with an earnestness of expression that particularly struck Angelina; but still was her mind anxious and uneasy about the mysterious event which had lately occurred to her. That she had not been deceived she was confident; she had distinctly seen the female form leaning over her—she had, in the brief space of time that she was permitted to gaze upon them, marked well her features, and she was certain that it was no phantom, the creation of her dis- ordered imagination, but a tangible object—a human being, and who she had not the slightest doubt, for some particular reasons, known only to herself and Kate, sought a refuge in the abbey ruins. The strange behaviour of the latter more and more surprised her, and she was completely bewildered in endeavouring to imagine what could be her motives for her conduct, and why she should take so deep an interest in her fate; but she was unable to form even the most remote idea upon the subject.

"Girl," said Kate, after a pause, "girl, I see that your curiosity is excited to a great de- gree to know who I really am, and why I should preserve such a mystery in my general conduct; and I am not surprised that it should be; but

some time or other, when I shall be enabled to explain myself, trust me you will perceive that I have been justified in the course I have pursued, and that cruel necessity left me no other alternative. You will then be grateful to me for——But enough of this, I must not explain more for the present—be satisfied, and above all, be secret as to what you may see or hear within these walls, for on that probably the life of more than one individual depends. If you should have occasion to speak of me to any one, appear to place credit in my superna- tural powers, for it is by assuming that character I keep the simple persons in the neighbourhood in awe, and render my retreat secure."

Deeply impressed by the tone in which Kate spoke, our heroine promised implicit obedience to her wishes, and could not help scrutinizing her features more narrowly than she had pre- viously done, and was forcibly struck with their remarkable beauty, although age and sorrow had made sad inroads upon them. At times there was a wildness in her eye, and her gene- ral demeanour, which gave a supernatural effect to her appearance, and was sufficient to fill the mind of a stranger with a secret dread; but when she addressed herself to our heroine, her tones were gentle, and the expression of her countenance was redolent of affection. Once or twice Angelina beheld her gazing intently upon her, and observed tears trembling in her eyes; but if she noticed her, she would hastily withdraw her looks from her, apparently with much confusion.

"Prithee go to rest, my girl," said Kate, after a short interval of silence, "you must need repose: and rest assured that no one will again interrupt your slumbers, but that you are perfectly safe here while I am near you."

Angelina could not refuse to comply with this request, but her thoughts were too much occu- pied with the occurrences of the evening to suffer her to sleep; she, however, closed her eyes, and gave herself up to the free indulgence of rumination till the morning. She then arose, and shortly afterwards her uncle knocked at the door, and was admitted. Kate greeted him with much cordiality, but she looked astonished and perplexed, which indeed she was, with the singular events which had occurred to him in the night. Kate's piercing eye seemed to penetrate to his thoughts in an instant, and seeing him about to speak, she said—

"Remember my caution, and be silent."

"You are, indeed, a strange woman," said Mr. Woodfield, "and I have tried in vain to unravel your real character. I like not so much mystery and secrecy."

"In this case it is absolutely necessary, and I beg of you to do as I have requested you," replied Kate; "were you to disobey me, you would have reason bitterly to repent it when it would be too late, and it would entail perpetual misery on yourself, and on her who is perhaps dearer to you than even your own life."

Mr. Woodfield looked at her earnestly for a few minutes, and then said—

"Rest assured that I will attend to your request, since I believe you to be guided by no bad motives, and as circumstances have convinced me that you are my friend."

"You but do me justice by the opinion you entertain of me," answered Kate; "but the Baron de Morton——"

"Is a villain! and that I will tell him," exclaimed Mr. Woodfield, "and demand satisfaction for the outrage he has committed."

"For some time you will not see him," said Kate; "he has left this part of the country; but oh, beware of him! Be cautious how you approach him—and be wary and watchful of him, for you little know his craft and cunning, and no one has more cause to be your enemy than he has."

"I fear him not," said Mr. Woodfield. "Although he may think that his rank and power may shield him, he shall learn that while there is justice in the country, that a person is not to commit so daring an outrage, and hold the life of a fellow-creature in jeopardy, with impunity."

Kate returned no answer to this, but she shook her head, and after a short pause, expressed by her manner that she was anxious they should depart. Mr. Woodfield took the hint, and rising from his chair, took the arm of his niece, and followed Kate to the entrance of the ruins, where, after once more enjoining them to secrecy, and having uttered a benediction on the head of our heroine, she hastened from the spot, and left them to pursue their way home.

Mr. Woodfield, notwithstanding the caution which had been given to him by Kate, felt it a very difficult matter to conceal from Angelina the strange events of the night, and he could plainly perceive by the paleness of her countenance, and the agitation of her manner, that something had also occurred to her, which she had been warned not to divulge. They talked but little on their way home, and then t was evident that the subjects they spoke upon were entirely barren of any interest to them. The remarkable concatenation of events connected with Kate and the ruins of St. Mark, conspired to fill both their minds with vague ideas, doubts, and perplexities, and their neat and handsome cottage burst upon their view before they had bestowed a thought upon it, or the anxious beings that were so impatiently awaiting their arrival.

The agitation of Mrs. Woodfield and Laura during the absence of Mr. Woodfield may be easily imagined; and when day after day passed away without their hearing any tidings of either him or Angelina, their minds were racked almost to distraction, and they began to think that not only had the latter perished, but that Mr. Woodfield had also lost his life in attempting to rescue her from the power of the villain who had borne her away from them. Their suspicions still lighted upon the Baron de Morton; and unable longer to endure their fears and anxiety, they determined to obtain an interview of the baroness, and to demand an explanation. With this design in view, Laura and her mother had left their cottage, and were proceeding to the castle, when Kate crossed their path, and commanded them to abandon their project, and to return home, assuring them that both Mr. Woodfield and his niece were safe, and would, in a few days, be restored to them.

Fearful of disobeying her, and seriously believing that Kate possessed some supernatural power, they did turn back, and endeavoured to reconcile themselves, and to place full reliance in the promises of the woman of the ruins. Need we describe their ecstasy, when, as they were seated on the bench underneath their cottage-window, they beheld Mr. Woodfield and Angelina approaching? At first they could scarcely believe their eyes, but when they came nearer, and they were certain they were not mistaken, a scream of joy escaped from each of their bosoms, and rushing towards them, they became locked fondly in each other's arms.

The first emotions of their restoration having subsided, they eagerly demanded an explanation of the whole affair—who had borne Angelina away—how Mr. Woodfield had found her out—and by what means he had been enabled to rescue her. These questions Mr. Woodfield answered as briefly as possible, taking care at the same time, not to disclose anything that Kate had enjoined him too keep secret. They both heard the account with much astonishment, particularly when they were informed that to Kate they were indebted for the life of Angelina.

"Well," observed Laura, after they had been discoursing for some time upon the subject, "it is very clear that the wild woman of the ruins is a witch, or she never could act in the manner she does."

"I am decidedly of your opinion," coincided her mother; "but, at any rate, she is the best sort of a witch I ever heard of, for, unlike others, instead of doing all she can to annoy and perplex we poor mortals, she seems to take delight in thwarting the designs of the guilty, and in assisting the oppressed."

Mr. Woodfield did endeavour to remove this absurd and superstitious idea, which was favourable to the wishes and designs of Kate. But they listened apparently with even deeper interest to the eulogies which Mr. Woodfield bestowed upon Hugh Clifford, who had so generously and willingly given them his assistance, without which he could not have succeeded in his object.

"Bless my soul!" ejaculated Laura, smiling, "what a romantic adventure—old Gothic ruins—a haunted tower—a stolen damsel—and a knight-errant in the shape of a gallant young man who, of course, must be very handsome—is he not, Angelina?"

Angelina blushed deeply, and faltered out some confused answer; and the tantalizing Laura observing the effect her question had upon her, seemed inclined to persist in following up the subject.

"Ah!" said she, smiling archly at her cousin, "I see I have guessed right. Your knight-errant has charms and graces to recommend him; but then the idea of a smuggler captain——"

"Enough of this, Laura," interrupted her father, impatiently; "his situation in life is his misfortune; but to him we owe a debt of gratitude which we shall not be able easily to repay."

Laura became silent, and our heroine felt great relief. They then entered upon the subject of Angelina's seizure, and Mr. Woodfield expressed his indignation against the Baron de Morton in no very measured terms, and mentioned his determination to seek redress, and to gain the protection of the law against any future attempts that the baron might make.

"The baron is wealthy and powerful," said Mrs. Woodfield; "and I think it would be much better to avoid any contention with him, by leaving the neighbourhood altogether, by which we shall escape his persecution, which is the most singular and unaccountable that I ever heard of."

"Think you then that his wealth or power will intimidate me from seeking that redress which the law entitles me to?" said Mr. Woodfield: "No, indeed, it shall not; but for the present we will drop the subject, and wait till the baron returns to the castle. In the meantime, Angelina must use the utmost caution in her behaviour, and not be away from home any more than she can possibly help; for, doubtless, the villain will have some of his myrmidons lurking about the neighbourhood."

The conversation was now dropped, and they separated.

Grateful to heaven for her providential rescue from the fate with which the Baron de Morton had threatened her, every time her thoughts adverted to the subject, so did the image of Hugh Clifford rise upon her mind, pictured in all the glowing colours which her warmest admiration could suggest. For hours she would contemplate his likeness, and recal to her memory the expressive looks he had bestowed upon her, the sentiments of evident regard which his tongue had given utterance to; and reflection but stamped his form more indelibly on her mind, and convinced her that she had admitted a passion to her heart, which she had known alone by name, before she saw him. Wrong as she knew she was in retaining possession of the miniature, she could not make up her mind to part with it, neither had she the means of returning it, not knowing where to find Hugh Clifford, or when they might meet again.

Several days elapsed, and nothing particular occurred; our heroine, in obedience to her uncle's injunctions, had not left the cottage to any distance, and the baron was still absent from the castle. Angelina had several times thought upon the adventure she had met with in the abbey ruins—the form she had seen, and the awful noises she had heard—and she in vain tried to solve the mystery. The words which Kate had spoken to her, and the caution she had given her, with regard to Hugh Clifford, also frequently tormented her thoughts, and her mind might be said to be in a continual state of restlesness.

It was about a week after her return home, that Angelina, Laura, and Mrs. Woodfield were sitting in the cottage parlour one evening, when they were suddenly alarmed by hearing a groan which seemed to proceed from some person immediately outside the cottage. They were terribly frightened, and for a second or two were uncertain how to act. Mr. Woodfield had been from home since the morning, and as a sudden thought darted across Mrs. Woodfield's mind, she jumped from her chair, and exclaimed—

"Good God! surely it cannot be your uncle, Angelina;—should any harm have happened to him——"

The groan was at that moment repeated, and the three females rushed simultaneously to the door and threw it open. Angelina started back with a scream, when she beheld Hugh Clifford leaning against the door-post, and bleeding profusely from a wound in his breast.

It would be impossible to describe the consternation of all three when they beheld the smuggler captain, and prompted as they were by motives of humanity, still did neither Mrs. Woodfield nor Laura offer to render any assistance, they were so astonished and alarmed. But the extreme agitation evinced by our heroine, the more surprised them, and especially when she exclaimed in a voice of deep emotion!—

"Good God! he is murdered! alas! who has done this?"

Hugh Clifford looked up in her face and there was an expression in his eyes which showed how much her words delighted him, and more than compensated him for any pain he might endure. In those few words he discovered that which he was so anxious to know, namely, that he was not indifferent to her; that she felt for him already, although probably unconscious of it hereslf, the dawning of a passion which would shortly expand into all the extent and ardour of woman's most fervent love. At that moment, even in the midst of the pain he then endured, he experienced a sensation of delight which he had seldom felt before.

"Sweet maiden," he uttered, in feeble tones, "be not alarmed;—some miscreant has fired at me, near this cottage,—I am faint with the loss of blood, but I do not think I am dangerously wounded;—I cannot proceed further, and—

Hugh Clifford could not say another word; but completely exhausted, would have sunk to the earth, had not Angelina and Laura (who appeared to be completly struck either with the singularity of the circumstance, or the beauty of the smuggler captain, but probably from both causes, supported him.

"Pray assist me to lead him into the cottage, and I will then go for the assistance of a doctor; do not hesitate, I beseech you, or he will die,' urged Angelina, fervently. Mrs. Woodfield looked astonished at the earnestness of her manner, but prompted by feelings of humanity, she did as she was desired, and placing him in a chair, endeavoured to stop the wound, from which the blood flowed profusely.

"It is the preserver of my life," said our heroine, in reply to the inquiring looks of her aunt and Laura; "oh, God, what murderous hand has done this; alas! should he die!—"

Hugh Clifford, who had at that moment recovered, and overheard the observations she made use of, looked up, and smiling gratefully upon her, said, in a faint voice :—

"I thank you, from my heart I thank you, for the anxiety you express, fair damsel;—but I require the immediate attendance of—"

"I will hasten for a doctor," cried Angelina, eagerly, and unable to conceal the deep anguish which filled her breast at the situation of Hugh. As she made a motion to go towards the door, however, he, by a significant expression, recalled her, and beckoning her to come nearer, he observed—

"No, no, sweet damsel, that must not be;— a stranger might—but, you understand me?"

"I do," replied Angelina, "but what is to be done?—you must not be left to die!"

Hugh Clifford once more thanked the agitated maiden with his looks, and said—

"Your uncle,—is he not within?"

"He is not," replied Angelina.

"That is unfortunate," said the wounded man; "I would send to Saint Mark's Abbey, and let Kate know what has happened, and she would hasten to my assistance."

"Endeavour to stop the flowing of the blood," returned Angelina, "and I will myself hasten to the abbey."

"You, child! and at such a time?" said Mrs. Woodfield, in astonishment; but Angelina heard her not, for before she had finished the sentence, she had hastily snatched her bonnet and cloak from behind the door, and was on her way to the abbey ruins.

Filled with the utmost alarm, the maiden fled with precipitation, and in a very short time reached the ruins, which she entered, but was at a loss which way to proceed, or how to obtain an interview with Kate. It was completely dark, and the solemn silence which reigned around filled her bosom with dread but the perilous situation of Hugh Clifford quickly banished every other thought, and after after a pause, she endeavoured to find out the staircase which led to the apartment whither Kate had conducted her and her uncle, on their escape from the coast-guard. She had just succeeded in gaining the foot of the stairs, when she suddenly heard a door close to, and a light from the gallery above streamed upon her. She looked up, thinking it was Kate, and to her astonishment beheld the same figure which she had seen leaning over her on the night she had slept at the abbey. She carried a lamp in her hand, and was just in the act of descending the stairs. When she beheld our heroine, she fixed upon her an earnest look of surprise, emotion, and affection; then suddenly darted back into the room from which she had just before emerged, and Angelina was left in darkness.

There was no time for delay; even now it might be too late to save the life of Cliffodr, and with a resolution which the circumstances engendered, she ascended the stairs, and was about to knock at the door through which the form had vanished, when she beheld a light at the other end of the gallery, and the next moment Kate stood before her.

" How now, maiden," she exclaimed; " what brings you here at this hour, and in such a state of trepidation? What seek you?"

In a few words, Angelina informed her.

" Good God! wounded, say you?" she exclaimed, and her counsenance and demeanour betrayed the greatest consternation and agitation; " oh, let me fly to his assistance. Angelian, hasten back to the cottage; it would not be well for us to be seen together; I shall be there as soon as you are."

Angelina obeyed her, and on the way back to the cottage, she reflected with the most intense anxiety upon the situation of Hugh Clifford, and mentally offered up a prayer to Heaven for his preservation. In that moment, for the first time, the real situation of her heart became evident to her, and in spite of every struggle, every obstacle which might present itself, she was convinced and mentally acknowledged that she loved him.

When she reached the cottage, she found that Kate, attended by a man—whom our heroine remembered to have seen on board the smuggler's vessel, and who acted in the capacity of surgeon to any of the crew that were ill, or happened to get wounded—had already arrived there, having gone by a nearer route than she was acquainted with. Mr. Woodfield had also returned home, and was up stairs with the wounded man, who had been removed to bed. Hugh Clifford's wounds, upon examination, were pronounced by the doctor not to be dangerous, but he said it would be impossible to remove him for the present, and that he must be kept as still as possible. With the most motherly care and affection, Kate hung over him, and more than once she pressed her lips to his, and gave utterance to words of love and tenderness. Hugh could

give no further account of the affair, than in passing near the cottage, on his way to the abbey, some person, who seemed to be lying in ambush, fired at him, and the darkness would not permit him to see the wretch who had attempted his life. That their object was not robbery, was quite certain, and he could not form any idea who the intended assassin could be.

Kate listened to him eagerly, then paused, and bit her lips; but she made no answer.

Mr. Woodfield could not help noticing the eagerness with which Angelina inquired after Hugh, when he returned to the parlour; and the warmth with which she exclaimed "Thank God!" when she was informed that the wound was not dangerous. Her uncle looked earnestly for a minute, then walking to the other side of the room, muttered some words which were unintelligible to any one but himself. He plainly saw the impression which the smuggler captain had made upon her, and he regretted more than ever the circumstance which had brought him to the cottage.

There was another thing which troubled Mr. Woodfield; this was, how to accomodate him. The chamber he was now in was the one in which Angelina and Laura slept, and he had no other convenience for them; but at length it was decided that they should intrude upon the kindness of their neighbour, Dame Gertrude, until Hugh Clifford had recovered and was able to quit the cottage. This arrangement being made, they departed for the cottage of the old woman, attended by Mr. Woodfield. He informed Gertrude that having not long before received an unexpected guest in the person of a male relation, from a distant part of the country, he requested that she would endeavour to accommodate his daughter and niece by suffering them to lodge with her while he (the said relative) remained with him.

Gertrude was very ready to consent to this, for she was much attached to Laura and our heroine, and besides, it would afford her company, her cottage being lonely, no one living in it but herself; and she had another excellent bed, which her son, who was now away from home, used to sleep in. As soon as Mr. Woodfield had taken his departure, old Gertrude, having forced them to partake of the humble repast which she had spread before them on their entrance, would have entered into a long conversation, and have asked a multiplicity of questions about the guest at Mr. Woodfield's

MR. WOODFIELD FORBIDDING CLIFFORD'S ADDRESSES TO ANGELINA.

cottage, but Angelina evaded her questions as much as possible; but she had considerable difficulty in preventing the garrulous tongue of the thoughtless Laura from relating all the particulars and betraying who it was, notwithstanding her father had particularly cautioned her upon the subject on their way thither. Soon after they had had supper, Angelina having pleaded a head-ache, and Laura being anxious to have some conversation

No. 12.

with her cousin upon the strange event of the night, they requested Gertrude to excuse them, and she conducted them to the clean room in which they were to sleep.

"We'l," observed Laura, "I wonder how Mr. Clifford is now. I must confess, Angelina, that he has one of the handsomest faces that I ever saw before; and then his manners are so elegant. Who would think he was a smuggler? But yet I do not wonder after all, though I couldn't help noticing it at first, that you should express such violent emotion when you saw him, and the glances of affection that—"

"Laura," interrupted our heroine, hastily, while crimson blushes suffused her cheeks, "what mean you? Glances of affection?"

"I repeat it—affection," said Laura, pertinaciously. "Ah, coz., looks sometimes express more than words; and when a handsome young man like this Hugh Clifford (bless me! what a romantic name!)—I say, when a handsome young man like Hugh Clifford, considering that you are indebted to him for your liberty and your life, is the object, there are very few girls that would be able to resist him. I must say that I have no such adamantine heart, and I am so captivated with him, that I am half inclined to become your rival, and to set my cap at him."

"Laura," said our heroine, who was vexed at her cousin's observations, or rather chagrined that she should have discovered that which she had barely been able to acknowledge herself yet, "you are always forming some erroneous and preposterous conjectures."

"But my conjectures are not unfrequently verified," returned Laura, smiling; "and particularly in these love affairs: why, I reckon myself as good as a witch. Ah! that sigh more than confirms the truth of my ideas. Your heart is gone, cousin, irrecoverably gone, and indeed if he was only anything else but a smuggler, I feel certain that he is in every way worthy to be its keeper."

"What nonsense you do talk, Laura," returned Angelina; "indeed I shall be vexed if you persist in speaking to me upon the subject."

"Well, then, I am fearful that I must incur you anger, rather than cease to talk upon a subject, which has so taken my fancy, that I cannot get it out of my thoughts," said the imperturbable Laura. "But now, my dear cousin, why should you be so cross, when I am only endeavouring to pay a very high compliment to you taste; I never saw such a charming man, both as regards his person and manners. What beautiful eyes he has got; and then his hair is so dark and so glossy, and—— but let me see; now I think of it, surely I have seen him before? Where was it?—I have it. This is the very young man whom I saw some few months back waiting in the meadows. Ah! you blush, Angelina; I see I am right; and I perfectly well remember how confused and bewildered you were when I mentioned it to you!"

Angelina blushed more deeply at this, and her confusion and mortification were much excited by the manner in which her cousin continued to tantalise her.

"Come, come, Angelina," she resumed, "do not continue to deny you sentiments; it is no use to me;—and——ah! as I live, a miniature too, and exactly like him; well, this does indeed astonish me!"

Our heroine hastily endeavoured to conceal the miniature which had escaped from her bosom, but it was to late—Laura had seen quite enough of it to satisfy her that her conjectures were true.

Never did Angelina feel more confused and mortified than she did upon this occasion; but the more she tried to conceal the real state of her heart, the more did her blushes reveal it to the inquisite Laura, who, in spite of the emotion which her cousin betrayed, seemed to enjoy the discovery she had made vastly, and appeared determined to persevere in her raillery, until she had made her confess the truth, with the most provoking obstinacy.

"Well, Angelina," she exclaimed, "I must

confess that I never imagined you were so sly; why, you are a perfect intriguer; carrying on a secret correspondence with a young man, and accepting miniatures from him, and goodness knows what; by-and-by I should not at all be surprised if we hear of an elopement. Dear me! I really should delight to hear of such a circumstance, if it were only for the romantic character of the affair."

"Laura," said our heroine, seriously, " this levity is cruel, and I am astonished that you will persist in it. Besides, such insinuations as you have just uttered, throw a doubt upon my want of prudence, which you must be confident is quite groundless. I will never act in any way which may not meet the approbation of my friends or my own conscience!"

"Heigho!" ejaculated Laura, "what serious mortals this love makes of us poor girls, at least of some of us; but, for my part, I cannot see that there is anything at all serious in the matter, and if I thought there was, I would forswear matrimony, and live in single blessedness all my days. Now, my dear coz., do not look so solemn, I pray! I have no doubt you think me a very wicked, provoking, little girl; but you mistake me I assure you. I am not going to be jealous of you, neither am I going to upbraid you for that which I am liable to be guilty of myself; for love, I take it, is a very natural thing, and has been established ever since the world began; and it is one which I hope will be as long as creation lasts, for what poor mortals should we be without it, but now, my dear girl, all that I wish you to do is to confide in me, and you will find me, I will answer for it, a sincere friend, and a good adviser in spite of my many frivolities."

Angelina turned away her head and sighed.

"My dear cousin," resumed Laura, "can you look me seriously in the face, and deny that you love this Hugh Clifford?"

Our heroine again sighed, but returned no answer.

"Ah! I see how it is," ejaculated Laura, taking her cousin's hand, and looking tenderly in her face; "I have guessed right; your heart acknowledges Hugh Clifford for its lord, and yet you would fain persuade yourself to the contrary. Nay, it is useless to deny it; rather tell me the truth, and relate to me all the interviews you have had with him; all the sweet things he has uttered to you, and the affectionate responses you have made; let me know all ——"

"Laura, dear Laura, for Heaven's sake,"—interrupted our heroine; "indeed you are wrong; never have I had any secret interviews with him; never have I uttered a word that could give encouragement to his views or ——"

"Oh, then you will acknowledge that *he* has confessed?" eagerly added Laura, smiling archly. "and yet your heart could be so obdurate as to resist him! But I cannot believe it was so; besides, is there not proof sufficient that you did not discourage his vows, or why accept of him the miniature which you now wear?"

Angelina felt more confused than before; she had no alternative but to relate the whole truth, or Laura would still retain the wrong impression her mind had received, and she might then, very justly, not only accuse her of imprudence, but hypocrisy; she therefore request her cousin's patient attention for a few moments, and then, in as few words as possible, related the manner in which the miniature had fallen into her possession, and the circumstances that had prevented her having an opportunity of returning it. Laura listened to her with much apparent interest; and when she had concluded, turned to her and said—

"But after all, Angelina, tell me, and that candidly; does not your heart feel a different sensation to that it never did before, since you and Clifford have met?"

"It would be ingratitude in me not to esteem the preserver of my life, Laura," answered our heroine.

"I like not that cold word, esteem, cousin," returned Laura; "and indeed your tone, your looks, your emotion, convinces me that your heart dictates the word love in its place! Come, come, cousin, it is so, I see it is, and there is an end of the matter."

Angelina looked in her cousin's face; a tear trembled in her eye; she saw a sympathising one sparkling in that of the artless, but excellent-hearted girl; and throwing herself on her neck, she gave free indulgence to her long-confined feelings.

Great was this relief to our heroine's bosom; it was what she had long wanted—a sympathizing heart, in which she could repose those thoughts, those wishes, which she had scarcely yet dared to acknowledge herself, and she felt at that moment happier than she had been for many months. Laura, although a giddy, was a sensible girl, and very fond of her cousin; and she, therefore, expressed the warmest interest in her situation, and offered her all the advice that her knowledge and mature deliberation on the circumstances suggested.

"But alas!" observed Angelina, after they had been conversing for some time, "what is the use of my encouraging a passion which can never be gratified? It is only putting the cankerworm of care and misery to both our hearts."

"And why so, my melancholy cez.?" asked Laura; "what are the wonderful, the insurmountable obstacles which present themselves to your imagination?"

"Is he not a smuggler?" returned Angelina; "besides, he is unknown to us, and he maintains a secrecy over his real name that——"

"Nonsense," interrupted Laura; "if he really loves you, he will soon remove the latter difficulty, and satisfy yourself and my father that his intentions are honourable; as for his being a smuggler, I confess I do not see anything very objectionable, for he only retaliates upon the revenue which plunders us of millions. However, may he not abandon that course of life?"

Angelina sighed and shook her head doubtfully. She then remembered the serious injunctions of Kate of the Ruins, and the positive manner in which she had declared that she and Hugh must never love one another but as friends; and her heart once more became the abode of melancholy and despair. Tired of talking, the fair cousins retired to bed, and in a few minutes sleep closed their eyelids.

CHAPTER XXIII.

HUGH CLIFFORD's recovery, notwithstanding the skill of the medical man who attended him, was very slow; a circumstance which caused Mr. Woodfield considerable uneasiness; for, during his illness, his suspicions as to the affection which Angelina had imbibed for him, were considerably strengthened, not only by the many and earnest inquiries which she made concerning his health, but the pleasure she evinced upon receiving a favourable answer; while, on the contrary, any change for the worse was always received by her with the deepest melancholy and expressions of fear. These circumstances left no doubt upon Mr. Woodfield's mind, that his niece loved the smuggler captain; and if he was convinced of her affection, no less so was he of Hugh Clifford's experiencing a reciprocal attachment; for whenever the name of Angelina was mentioned, his eyes would brighten up, and he would evince other symptoms of violent emotion, which plainly showed that she was the object on whom his thoughts were continually fixed.

Many hours of misery did this idea cause Mr. Woodfield, and he was extremely glad when the doctor pronounced that Hugh was well enough to be removed; and Kate of the Ruins urged his quick departure to the abbey, for fear that some of his enemies might discover his present retreat, and not only bring him into some trouble, but place Mr. Woodfield and his family in rather au awkward position for having given shelter to him.— The morning intended for the departure of Hugh Clifford, all the family met at breakfast. I was the first time the former and our heroine had seen each other since the evening of the accident, and the pleasure they felt at meeting, and their sorrow at the thoughts of being so soon compelled to separate again, were too apparent to escape the observation of Mr. Woodfield. At parting, Hugh Clifford, after having in the most warm and enthusiastic manner expressed his thanks for the kindness he had received at the hands of Mr. Woodfield and his family, hoped he might be permitted to pay them an occasional visit when he was in the neighbourhood. Angelina's eyes sparkled when he made this request, and she watched eagerly the countenance of her uncle. He observed her; but although he replied in a less cordial manner than was his custom to Hugh Clifford, he felt bound, after what the latter had done to serve him, not to refuse, and the smuggler captain quitted the cottage, accompanied by Kate, who had come there early in the morning for that purpose.

Several days passed away, and Mr. Woodfield had in vain endeavoured to think of some plan to put an end to the evil he apprehended. Angelina he had observed to be more that usually melancholy, and, of course, he was at no loss to imagine the cause.

It was on the fourth day after Hugh Clifford had quitted the cottage, that Mr. Woodfield had just returned from his afternoon's walk, and was crossing the garden, when just as he had reached a small alcove, he heard the voices of two persons talking in tones which induced him to listen. At first he could not distinguish what was said, but at length the following words, in a female voice, caught his ear:—

"Alas! why should I conceal it? Surely, there cannot be anyting culpable in acknowledging those affections that spring from virtue alone, and which the heart declares it would be hyprocrisy to deny?"

"Heavenly sounds! blest words!" replied the voice of a man, in enraptured accents, "am I then so happy, or is it a delusion too sweet to be true? You love me then, dearest, best of girls, ardent as that affection which dwells within my heart for you? Oh, let me seal the dear acknowledgment with a thousand kisses!"

The patience of Mr. Woodfield could endure no more; he rushed round to the front of the alcove, and beheld Hugh Clifford with one knee bent to the earth, while he pressed the hand of the blushing, but willing Angelina with the fondest transport to his lips.

For a few minutes Mr. Woodfield was so astonished that he was unable to speak, and stood gazing upon the bewildered lovers with mingled expressions of anger and pity. Hugh Clifford hastily arose from the ground, while Angelina, covered with blushes, and trembling with emotion, averted her head, and waited in terrible suspense for those reproaches which she expected her uncle would give utterance to. Hugh Clifford was the first who recovered himself, and seeing the indignation which mantled the countenance of Mr. Woodfield, he looked supplicatingly towards Angelina, and made an effort to address him; but Mr. Woodfield, waving his hand with a serious aspect, prevented him.

"Not a word, sir," said he; "you cannot offer a word in extenuation of your conduct. I regret that the good opinion I formed of you should be thus changed; an honourable man, would not have chosen such a method of——"

"Mr. Woodfield," interrupted Hugh Clifford, "hear me, I beseech you; but one word."

"Not a syllable," said Mr. Woodfield, peremptorily. "I should at all times have been happy to meet you as a friend;—but henceforth, I must decline your visits altogether · believe me, I shall never forget how much I owe to you for your services. Angelina, follow me."

A momentary glow of indignation and offended pride mantled the cheeks of Hugh Clifford, at the haughtiness of Mr. Woodfield's demeanour; but our heroine fixed upon him an expressive look, and it vanished in an instant, and turning to her uncle, as he was about to lead her into the cottage, he said, in an earnest and urgent tone—

"Mr. Woodfield, I must beg of you not to leave me without affording me an opportunity of explaining myself. However severely my heart may feel it, I will be ready to submit to your will. Grant me only a few moments conversation."

Mr. Woodfield hesitated for a short time, but seeing the earnestness of Clifford's manner, and probably remembering that gratitude for the service he had done him demanded some little consideration, he relented, and made the following answer—

"I will yield to your request.—Angelina, retire."

With a trembling step, and without venturing to give a glance towards Hugh Clifford our heroine obeyed, and her uncle having watched her safely into the cottage, turned to the former, and said—

"Now, sir, what have you to say in excuse for your conduct?"

"Love, ardent, pure, and sincere love," answered Hugh Clifford, fervently; "oh, my dear sir, surely I may be excused for imbibing an affection for a damsel, whose intrinsic and personal charms would e'en kindle love in a stoic's heart? By Heaven! I——"

"Nay, sir," interrupted Mr. Woodfield, "I wish not to hear any vows; they will all be useless; fate has placed an inseperable barrier between you, and you must meet no more."

"Surely this decision is cruel, is harsh," said Hugh, reproachfully; "but I can easily conjecture your reason—you scorn me, because I am a smuggler! But lawless as you will say I am, Hugh Clifford cannot reproach himself with the performance of a single action which could call the blush of shame into his face, or which he would not readily perform again. But enough of that. I love—I adore your beauteous niece, and this day I have received an assurance from her sweet lips——"

"I heard it," interrupted Mr. Woodfield, impatiently; "it was, doubtless, extorted from her, and therefore——"

"By Heaven you wrong me!" exclaimed Hugh

"Then why meet in a clandestine manner?" demanded the other, "why not seek my consent in the first instance?"

"It was my intention to have thrown myself at your feet this very day, and acknowledging our mutual passion, request of you to suffer me to pay my addressess to Angelina," replied Clifford.

"That would have been useless," returned Mr. Woodfield. "I repeat, that you must forget each other."

"Impossible!"

"It must be so—fate ordains it," added Mr. Woodfield; "but believe me, Mr. Clifford, harsh and tyrannical although you may think me, I entertain a due sense of your merits, and shall always be happy to meet you as a friend; but, until you can conquer your unfortunate passion, you and my niece must be strangers to one another. It is useless to seek to alter this determination; it is irrevocable."

"If my occupation is the objection," said Hugh, "dear as my brave associates are to me, and warmly attached as I am to the life of liberty, here at once will I renounce it."

"Forget that ever you saw Angelina," exclaimed Mr. Woodfield, in a tone of pity, but decision; "erase her image from your heart, for she can never be yours."

"Never; by——"

"Hold!" interrupted Mr. Woodfield; "again I tell you vows are useless; and, Mr. Clifford, I caution you, nay, I entreat of you, as you value your own peace and the future happiness of her you have acknowledged you love, do not persist in urging your passion; do not seek to strengthen an affection in her heart, which, as it is without the least chance of being gratified, might cause that heart to break."

"And what can be this strange, this mighty obstacle you mention?" demanded Clifford, in a state of great agitation.

"It is a secret none must be acquainted with at present," answered Mr. Woodfield; "but let it suffice that it is so, and that my wishes must be obeyed."

"They must!" exclaimed a loud voice; and the next moment Kate of the Ruins darted from behind the alcove, and stood before them, fixing her eyes sternly upon the smuggler captain, who seemed astonished and bewildered at her sudden and unexpected appearance, and turned away his head in evident confusion. "Rash boy!" she continued, after a brief pause, "seek not to disobey, as you value your own peace, and that of her who has ever been your dearest friend. Alas! you know not the dreadful consequences that the indulgence of this unhappy love may be productive of—I shudder to contemplate them."

"By my soul, this mystery is insupportable," cried Hugh Clifford, passionately; "are all my hopes to be blighted by an accursed fate, over which it appears I have no control, but which I cannot fathom?—Why do you not solve this painful riddle?"

"At present it must not be," answered Kate; "but it is the will of a Power we dare not question, and you must submit to it. Follow me, Hugh!"

Kate spoke this in an authoritative tone, and by her manners showed that she could command obedience. Clifford at first hesitated, and turned a look of entreaty upon Mr. Woodfield; but the latter averted his head, and Kate having repeated her mandate, he reluctantly obeyed, and slowly left the spot, followed by that mysterious woman—

and Mr. Woodfield hastened into the cottage.

Angelina had retired to her own apartment; but her uncle did not inquire for her, although it was evident that his mind was greatly agitated, and he frequently strode hastily across the room, and seemed to be absorbed in the most painful thought.

Mrs. Woodfield and Laura (the latter of whom was with her cousin up stairs) were perfectly aware of what had happened, and being prepossessed in favour of Hugh Clifford, who, during the time he had been at the cottage, had completely charmed them by the sweetness and urbanity of his manners, sincerely sympathised with them in their affection, and would have felt glad had no obstacle presented itself to their union; though why Mr. Woodfield should be opposed to it, unless it was on account of Clifford being a smuggler, they could not conjecture.

Many were the tears of bitter anguish our heroine shed when she retired to her room. Just at the moment when she felt the full effervescence of that flame which had for some time been gathering in her bosom—when she had listened with extatic delight to the ardent asseverations of Clifford—when her lips had acknowledged a reciprocal attachment, and at that moment she felt that he was dearer to her than her own life, that he was, as it were, interwoven with her very existence —her uncle had appeared; and his looks were sufficient, if his words had not been, to convince her that despair was at hand to darken all those bright hopes she would not many minutes before have ventured to indulge in. The time which elapsed during the interview between her lover and her uncle, seemed an age to her, and her suspense was almost insupportable. Yet did she dread to hear the footsteps of the latter, for she expected he would summon her into his presence, and she trembled at the thoughts of the lecture he would probably read her. But in this idea she was agreeably disappointed; Mr. Woodfield did not offer to disturb her; and after listening for hours to the exhortations of the affectionate Laura, she became considerably more composed, and retired to rest, where her busy imagination recalled in dreams the image of her lover, and every word to which he had given utterance.

In the morning, Laura arose before her cousin, and the latter, on descending the small flight of stairs which led into the parlour, in which they always took their meals, timid and dreading to meet her uncle, as if she had been committing some heinous crime, she paused at the door, which was partially open, to give herself time to compose her agitation, when the voices of Mr. and Mrs. Woodfield, speaking in loud tones, excited her curiosity, and she could not help pausing to listen. They were seated at the further end of the room, and their backs were towards her. Laura was busying herself at the breakfast table, and did not appear to take any notice of what they were conversing about.

"It is cruel," observed Mrs. Woodfield, reproachfully, "it is very cruel thus to blight the hopes of the poor girl (who I know really loves him), and those of Hugh Clifford, who, in spite of his being a smuggler, I am certain is a worthy youth, and would make her a good husband. He has money, and, as you say, he has offered to abandon his present calling—what, in the name of all that is wonderful, can be your objection to——"

"Dame, I tell you now, as I have often told you before," interrupted Mr. Woodfield, "that I cannot countenance the affection of any one for Angelina. Did not circumstances, which it behoves me not to divulge at present, form an insurmountable barrier to their union; even during the short time I have known him, and, notwithstanding the peculiar circumstances in which he is placed, I confess that there is not a man to whom I would sooner give the hand of my niece than this same Hugh Clifford. I am much deceived if he does

not possess a noble, a generous, and a virtuous heart."

"Ah! that I am sure he does," returned Mrs. Woodfield, warmly—"have we not had sufficient proof of that?—Has he not twice saved the life of her he loves? and who, then, possesses a greater claim upon her hand and heart than he does?"

"That is all very true, Dame," replied her husband; "I respect the young man's virtues, and esteem his friendship—but as to his marrying Angelina, I can never give my consent."

"Why, goodness me, Arthur!" ejaculated the old woman, "how strangely you talk; who but *you can* consent to their nuptials? Are you not the only protector Angelina has in the world; and who can question your conduct?"

"Of that I am not certain," said Mr. Woodfield, in an ambiguous manner; "but enough of this—I like not the subject, as I have often told you; my mind is made up; and once for all I say, that for the present, I cannot—I will not—ever give my consent to the union of Angelina."

"Then you will certainly break her heart, and have her death to answer for," said the dame; "for I am confident by what Laura has told me, what I have myself observed of her conduct, and the excessive violence of her grief last night, that her heart is immovably fixed upon him. As for poor Hugh, although our acquaintance has been short, I have watched him narrowly—I have noticed the admiration with which he viewed our neice, and I am, therefore, certain, that without her his life will be for ever miserable. Indeed, it is too bad thus to blight the happiness of one so young."

"I am sorry to be the cause of grief to him," replied Mr. Woodfield, "but I cannot change my mind. Did you but know all, you would not blame me."

"And what is the reason I am not considered worthy of your confidence, Arthur?" inquired his wife—"this is not well. What secret of such importance can there be attached to——"

"Ask no more questions," interrupted her husband; "you know that such inquires always vex me. Some day or other I may think proper to tell you something which will convince you I have acted right in what I have done; till then be satisfied in knowing that it is my will, and that I have powerful reasons for the incongruity of my conduct."

ANGELINA MUSING ON THE CLIFF.

Angelina, during the time this dialogue was going on between her uncle and aunt, had seated herself at the breakfast-table, unobserved by all but Laura, who, at a significant nod from her cousin, did not offer to speak, although she had paid so little attention that she did not understand the tenor of the conversation.

At this part of the discourse, Mr. Woodfield turned round, and beheld that Angelina was present.

No. 13,

"Ah! Angelina," he exclaimed, with more kindness in his tone than she had expected, "are you here? How long have you been in the room?"

Angelina, whose mind revolted at the bare idea of a falsehood, in a tremulous voice informed him.

"Then you, probably, overheard the conversation between me and your aunt?" observed Mr. Woodfield.

Angelina, in a low voice, answered in the affirmative, and her cheeks suffused with blushes, she turned away her head, and sighed. Her uncle watched her steadfastly for some time, but said nothing; he could see from the sunken eyes and pallid cheeks of his niece, the deep emotion she had suffered, and from his heart he sincerely pitied her. He approached her at length, and taking her hand, pressed it affectionately as he said—

"Angelina, after what took place yesterday, it would be folly in me to deny that I know the fatal passion which has unfortunately gained possession of your heart. Nay, my love, do not weep—I am not going to reproach you for having imbibed that sentiment which is inherent in all our natures; but I wish to warn you—to adjure you to exert all your woman's fortitude, and stifle it in its infancy, to suffer not the ardour and impetuosity of youth to lead you to encourage an affection for that object which can never be yours."

Our heroine gently raised her head; the tears were streaming from her eyes; she tried to speak, but could not, and once more covering her face with her handkerchief, she sobbed convulsively.

"Come, my dear girl," said her uncle, in the tenderest accents, "do not give way to this violent grief; it distracts me to see it. Would that it were in my power to accede to your wishes; but as it is not, nay, more, as you would save yourself and me from future misery, promise me that you will endeavour to conquer your unfortunate passion, and that you will

give no further encouragement to the advance of Hugh Clifford."

It was some minutes before Angelina could make any reply to these observations, but at length, ashamed of the weakness she displayed, she made a powerful effort to regain her equanimity, and succeeded sufficiently to answer as follows, in a tone of comparative firmness:—

"My dear uncle, I trust that you have hitherto never found me disobedient; and in the present instance, sooner than cause you a moment's uneasiness, although my heart break in the effort, I will endeavour to do as you desire."

"Dear, excellent girl!" ejaculated Mr. Woodfield, kissing the tear-moistened cheek of his neice with the utmost fervour, "I ought to have known that you would not act in opposition to my will, even at the sacrifice of your own peace of mind. Rest assured, strange and ambiguous as my conduct may appear at present, it is prompted only by an earnest desire for your future peace and welfare. The object who has inspired this passion in your bosom is, I am sure, too noble, too generous, when he finds that circumstances conspire to place an insuperable barrier to his love, not to endeavour to vanquish it, and try to place his affections on another woman not less worthy of him."

"He can never do it, I am certain," remarked Mrs. Woodfield, warmly; "Hugh Clifford, or I have most egregiously mistaken his real character, is not of that fickle-minded temper, so easily to eradicate from his memory the only girl upon whom he has placed his warmest affections. He may appear to obey you, but in secret he will indulge his ardent love, until it preys upon his health, and probably may bring him to a premature grave. Indeed, I like not such unnecessary cruelty."

Angelina shuddered with horror at the picture which Mrs. Woodfield drew.

"Dame," said her husband, angrily, "will you obstinately persist in urging me to that which I have already told you could only be productive of the most unhappy consequences to us all? Have I not told you that it is necessity, and not my will, which compels me to reject the young man's suit? Let me again desire, nay, command you to mention the subject no more to me, unless you would make me wretched, and bring down the greatest misery upon those whom you love. Angelina, remember!"

Having thus spoken, Mr. Woodfield hastened from the room to attend to his duties in the field, and the three females were left to themselves.

When Mr. Woodfield had left the cottage, the grief occasioned by his words, in spite of all her efforts to restrain it, found vent in a copious flood of tears. Mrs. Woodfield expressed by her looks and her manner the deep sympathy she felt for her, and Laura, whose hilarity was seldom interrupted, now evinced a seriousness of demeanour which was in her very remarkable. The efforts of she and her mother were combined in an attempt to sooth her.

"Nay, my poor child," said her kind-hearted aunt, "do not give way to this violent grief; your uncle may relent; he surely will, for well do you know the affection he bears you, and I am certain he cannot long see you unhappy."

"Oh, no, I'm sure he cannot," observed Laura, "my father possesses too affectionate a heart to remain long inflexible. So come, my dear cousin, dry your tears, and live in hopes."

Our heroine shook her head and sighed.

"Alas!" she replied, "what hope is there for me? Has not my uncle commanded me to forget him? Have I not promised that I will endeavour to obey him, and has he not told me that any dereliction on my part will only be productive of misery to us all? No, no—there is nothing but despair for me."

Neither Mrs. Woodfield nor her daughter made any reply to these observations; and after a pause, Angelina continued:—

"Would to Heaven we had never met; what hours of anguish it would have saved us both; yes, both I say, for I am certain—my heart tells me—that Clifford's sentiments are as ardent and sincere as my own. Oh, he is too noble, too generous, to deceive me; and why should I be ashamed to acknowledge a virtuous passion? For a long time did I seek to deny my affection, even to myself; but I can no longer do do so. Hugh Clifford, though fate may divide us, my heart must ever be united to yours while it shall throb with the pulsation of life!"

This was the first time that Angelina had ever so openly divulged the sentiments that filled her bosom, and she felt relief from it.

"From my very soul, dearest child," said her aunt, "from my very soul do I pity you, and would that the power rested with me to make you happy, how readily—how joyfully would I do it; for there is something in the countenance and behaviour of Hugh Clifford, which convinces me that he is worthy of you, in spite of his situation, and the mystery which hangs over him. Nevertheless, there is no knowing what time may affect; so endeavour to compose your feelings, and rest assured that——"

"Oh, no, no," interrupted Angelina, "I must not hope, for to do so would be to disobey my uncle, and to break the promise I have made to him. I will seek to think upon him only as a *dear* friend; and though my heart should break in the painful struggle with my feelings, I will not do anything contrary to the wishes of my benefactor."

"You are a good girl," said the dame, "and deserve a better fate; but I cannot help thinking that your uncle is too mysterious and too cruel——"

"You wrong him, dear aunt—indeed you do," fervently ejaculated Angelina; "my uncle has certainly some powerful motives for his conduct, and acts not by his own will or inclination. He has ever been kind, indulgent—all that a father could be towards his child. But now I think of it, there certainly is a mystery in his conduct and his words that surprises me, and which I am at a loss to unravel. From what he said to you, and which I overheard, there appears to be some secret attached to my birth, which he must not for the present divulge! What, in the name of Heaven, can it be, and for what am I reserved? The woman of the ruins, too, has repeatedly told me that I am not what I seem to be, and has taken an interest in me, which adds to the mystery by which I am surrounded."

Mrs. Woodfield seemed greatly surprised and agitated, but she made no immediate reply.

"It is indeed strange and unaccountable," at length she said; "but believe me I know no more about it than yourself, My husband and his brother had not been friends for many years, and I never saw either him or his wife. They lived at some distance from us. At length, however, your uncle received a letter, informing him that his brother was at the point of death, and begging that he would hasten to him, so that he might receive his forgiveness before he died. Of course my husband did not refuse, and was absent several days, when he returned in a state of great anguish, and informed me that two days after the demise of his brother, his sister, having caught the fever of him, expired also. He brought you with him —being then a child about two years old—who, he gave me to understand, was the only child of his unfortunate brother and sister, who being quite unprovided for, it was his intention to protect and bring up. This is all that I have ever been able to elicit concerning you, and your uncle has always most sedulously avoided speaking to me upon the subject, and showed much emotion whenever my curiosity prompted me to refer to it."

Our heroine remained wrapt in thought for a few moments after her aunt had given the above account, and appeared to be suffering the most acute mental agony; but, at last, turning towards Mrs. Woodfield, in a melancholy tone, she remarked—

"It is indeed strange—every strange; but the Almighty, in His own infinite wisdom, will some time or other unravel the mystery; into His hands I resign my fate, and am prepared to abide by His will."

Having given utterance to these pious ejaculations, she felt more tranquillized; and after conversing with her aunt and Laura for a few minutes longer on different subjects, she arose and left the room, with an intention of paying a visit to old Dame Gertrude, merely to pass the time away, and hoping, in conversing with her, to divert her thoughts to some less painful subject.

The morning was extremely fine, and the sun shone with uncommon brilliancy upon the delightful scenery by which that romantic spot was surrounded; but it failed to produce any effect on our heroine's mind; and in spite of all her endeavours, she found it utterly impossible for her to banish from her bosom the gloomy thoughts which the recent events had excited. It seemed as though a blight had fallen upon her heart, and scattered before its influence all the joys, the hopes, and the wishes that had before occupied it. She was awakened to a full certainty of her ardent passion, but to be overwhelmed by all the oppressive weight of dark despair. Alas! what is more torturing to the human mind than the imbibing of a hopeless love? It is the cankerworm that too often preys upon the vitals of youth; destroys all its buoyant hopes—lays waste its jocund pleasures— renders life a hell—and ultimately brings its victim to an untimely grave. And Angelina was doomed to feel all the misery in the fullest extent; and now that the tongue of her uncle had forbidden her to love, she felt the full certainty of the fate which awaited her, and not only her, but he to whom her whole soul was devoted.

She walked slowly on, almost unconscious whither she wandered; the bright rays of the sun spread a broad, an interminable expanse of gold before her;—the fields, the meadows, the hills, the valleys, were clothed in their richest verdure; but she noticed them not. The birds sang sweetly upon every spray, but her ear was deaf to their mellifluous notes; her thoughts were entirely absorbed in that one all-engrossing subject, in which her very existence seemed rivetted and bound up; and how much farther she might have wandered in this state of unconsciousness is quite uncertain, had she not suddenly been aroused by the barking of a dog, and, looking up, what was her astonishment to behold herself standing near the rock which was surmounted by the moss-covered ruins of Saint Mark's Abbey.

It was the first time she had been near the venerable pile since the adventure which she and her uncle had met with after their return from the old Grey Tower. She viewed the ruins now with a double interest, for it was near them she had first beheld Hugh Clifford; and from also knowing how closely he was connected with them, and their mysterious occupant. Acting upon the impulse of the moment, she ascended the rock, and looked down upon the broad expanse of water, which was glittering in the golden beams of the morning sun. Here and there a fisherman's boat glided over its surface, and the song of the contented fisherman, and the whistle of the hardy-looking fisher-boy, vibrated on her ears. Angelina sighed when she brought to her recollection the night when she had first seen Hugh Clifford with the smugglers, and when her heart might be said to have received its earliest impression. Then came upon her memory, in the most vivid colours, his noble conduct in rescuing her from the power of the Baron de Morton, when he had first threatened her life; and the danger and hazards he had run to release her from her imprisonment in the old Grey Tower. Her bosom swelled with anguish as she thus reflected, and knew that the object who, by such deeds, and the accomplishments of his mind, had kindled her heart's affection, could never be her's.

"And must we never meet again?" she sighed, "must I no more listen to the honied accents that fell from his lips? Alas! no; it is forbidden, unless we can meet only as friends; friends—how cold the word, how inadequate to express the intensity of a passion which, in spite of all my endeavours, I feel must continue to hold possession of my heart, until death shall release me from my misery."

"Angelina," at that moment exclaimed a well-known voice, immediately behind her, and looking round, to her confusion, she beheld standing at her elbow, and with her eyes fixed seriously upon her, Kate of the Ruins.

"Angelina," repeated Kate, in a yet more solemn tone, and pointing significantly towards the old abbey porch, "follow me!"

Angelina trembled, and shrunk beneath the sternness of her glance.

"What would you with me, Kate?" she demanded, in a faint voice; "accident, and not design, brought me hither, and——"

"Follow me, girl, I say," interrupted Kate, in still more peremptory tones, as she advanced towards the abbey, to which she pointed the wand that she always carried with her.

Our heroine obeyed, and her mysterious conductor having entered the ruins, proceeded until she came to the old aisle, and passed on to the altar at the extremity. Here she paused, and appeared to be feeling for something at the side. Presently, to the infinite astonishment of Angelina, a secret door flew open, and discovered a flight of steps beneath the altar, which Kate instantly began to descend, having taken a lamp in her hand, which had been standing lighted on the altar.

"This way, Angelina," she said, beckoning impatiently to our heroine; "come—quick—quick."

"Why is all this mystery, and for what purpose do you want me?" once more asked Angelina, with considerable doubt and alarm depicted in her countenance.

Kate frowned.

"No matter, girl," she replied, "no harm is intended thee; do as I command thee."

Angelina always felt that unaccountable awe in the presence of Kate, that she feared to disobey her, and mentally praying for the protection of Heaven, she followed as the latter desired.

Kate continued to descend, followed by our heroine, for some time, and at length alighted in a square stone chamber, upon which opened different ranges of vaults and cemeteries, in which were deposited the remains of the monks, who many ages before had inhabited the abbey. A sickly vapour encircled the lamp which Kate carried on their entrance, and almost extinguished the light; the walls were streaming with water, and as Angelina cast her eyes forward, she beheld the different piles of stone coffins in which were deposited the ashes of the dead. She shuddered with a feeling of irresistible horror, and turned to Kate for an explanation. The latter, however, received her inquiring glances with a look of total indifference, and without saying a word, advanced towards a low archway, and beckoned Angelina to follow.

"What strange and awful place have you led me to," said Angelina, shrinking back, "and what is your purpose with me? I will not follow you farther without you explain yourself to me."

"Beware, maiden—beware, I say," ejaculated Kate, in solemn accents, "you little deem the danger you run by disobedience; your own life, and the lives of those who are dear to you, depend upon your doing as I desire. Attend me without further hesitation."

Again, fearful of refusing to do as Kate bade her, Angelina followed her beneath the low archway, trembling with apprehension as to what would be the result of this singular adventure. To her horror she now found herself in the interior of a cemetery, and on either side were piled coffins, while on the damp stone pavement, were to be seen several ghastly relics of the dead, such as human bones and skulls, &c. The rays from the lamp, which Kate carried, only rendered these objects partially visible;—but Angelina saw sufficient to, make her terrors increase, especially when Kate, grasping rather forcibly hold of her arm, pulled her towards one of the piles of coffins, and after looking at her with a piercing glance for a short interval exclaimed—

"So, girl, after the caution you received from me, after the solemn assurance I gave you that your love was forbidden by the laws of nature, and your declaration to me that you, looked upon Hugh Clifford with no other sentiment than friendship, you have rashly encouraged a passion, which has gained such strength in your bosom, that nothing will be able to eradicate it?"

Angelina, unable to return any answer buried her face in her hands, and sobbed with emotion—

"It is useless for you to attempt to deny it," continued Kate, "your looks, your words sufficiently prove it. Oh, maiden, you cannot have any conception of the misery this unfortunate passion, if encouraged, will entail upon you and yours. Be warned in time, and here, in this awful place, the abode of the dead register an oath that you will never encourage the vows of Hugh Clifford, and that you will endeavour by every means in your power, to erase him from your memory!—Do not hesitate;—here, over the ashes of those whose souls are now in Heaven, swear the oath I will administer to you!"

The agitation of our heroine at the earnestness and energy of the woman's manner, and the dismal place to which she had conducted her, was almost more than she could support, but as Kate pointed to the coffin, upon the lid of which a ghastly skull and cross-bones were placed, and repeated her demand, fresh resolution seemed to take possession of her soul, and in a firmer tone than she had hitherto spoken, she ejaculated—

"My heart revolts at the idea of an oath administered under such awful, such unnatural circumstances, I will not take it unless you explain to me who you are, and by what authority you seek to extort it from me?"

"By the authority, girl, of those who gave thee being, and whose spirits are now watching over us," answered Kate, in deep, solemn accents, at the same time fixing her expressive eyes yet more steadily upon the countenance of our heroine. "Oh, pause before you refuse to do my bidding; remain obstinate, and disgrace, sorrow, and every care will be yours, and that of those under whose protection you are; my curse, and the curse of the dead will also fall upon your head, and all the horrors——"

"Oh, forbear! forbear!" cried the distracted girl, shuddering at the thoughts of what Kate was describing; and her limb trembled violently.

"Take the oath!" exclaimed at that instant a hollow, sepulchral voice, which seemed to proceed from the interior of one of the coffins. Cold drops of perspiration stood upon our heroine's temples, and gasping for breath, she clung to the arm of Kate for support, while her looks were expressive of the most indescribable horror.

"Hark! the voice of the dead commands thee to obey," said Kate, solemnly; "the spirit of her who bore thee, speaks to thee; wilt thou scorn its sacred warning?"

Angelina tried to speak, but her tongue refused its office. But an instant, and a peal of heavenly music seemed to float around the place, a loud crash smote her ears, a thin form in robes of the purest white, arose from behind one of the piles of coffins, and, standing before the maiden's horror-struck gaze, was the ghostly phantom she had on a former occasion, pursued through the vaults of the abbey.

The heavenly music still floated on the air, and filled the breast of the paralyzed Angelina with sacred awe, while the spectre fixed upon her a look of solemnity, mingled with pity and love, and stood for a few seconds fixed as a marble statue. Kate of the ruins bent low before it, and seemed to await with anxiety and eagerness the words she appeared to anticipate the spirit would give utterance to. It was an awful interval; the supernatural light still illumed the frightful place, and gave a tenfold horror to the ghastly objects by which it was on every side surrounded, and indeed it was a fitting scene for the abode of the dead. Cold drops of perspiration stood upon the temples of our heroine, and her heart seemed to lose all pulsation, as with distended eyelids, she gazed upon the unearthly visitant. At length the music ceased, a dead silence reigned around;—the lips of the spectre moved, and in sweet, but solemn tones, it thus spoke—

"Angelina! Angelina! Angelina! the spirit of thine injured mother speaks to thee and commands thee to take the oath;—obey!"

"Blessed shade of her who bore me, if such thou art, at thy feet let me prostrate myself, and crave thy blessing!" exclaimed Angelina, rushing frantically forward towards the spot on which the phantom stood. In an instant, however, a sound like a clap of thunder shook the vault, the place became involved in utter darkness, and completely overpowered by her terrors, Angelina sank upon the earth, and became insensible.

When she recovered, she found herself stretched upon the bed on which she had reposed, on the night that she and her uncle remained at the abbey, but there was no person in the room. The dreadful recollection of all that had past in the the abode of the dead rushed upon her brain, and filled her bosom with terror and agony. Raising herself on the bed, and clasping her aching temples, she glanced hastily around the chamber, expecting to behold some appalling object, and in phrenzied accents ejaculated—

"Good God! and could it be reality? Did my eyes indeed behold the vision of her who bore me?—Sainted spirit of my mother, oh, where art thou? Why do youo not again appear to me and unravel the dark mystery which envelopes my fate?"

All remained still as death in the apartment, and after a pause, our heroine continued—

"Those words, those horrible words, did she not command me to take the oath, the dreadful oath which the mysterious woman, of the ruins sought to extort from me, and which would consign me to everlasting misery? Oh, Clifford, why did we ever meet, since fate commands that we must not think upon each other? and yet to think of you, forms the chief delight of my existence, deprived of which, life would become a burthen too heavy for me to bear. But shall I disobey the spirit of my mother? Am I not commanded by her to take those vows which will make you, dear Clifford, and myself no more than strangers?—Oh horror! let me not think upon it,—my brain is racked to madness!"

She threw herself back on the bed, covered her face with her hands, and scalding tears came to her relief. In this manner she remained for several minutes, and during that interval nothing occurred to disturb the silence which reigned in the room, and, indeed, throughout the whole abbey. At length, surprised and alarmed at her situation, she started from the couch, thinking to find herself a prisoner, but much to her relief and astonishment the door was standing wide open, and nothing appeared to obstruct her egress from the abbey.

While Angelina thus stood and contemplated with eager eyes everything in the room, the awful events that had occurred to her when she was before there, came to her recollection, and smote her heart with terror. It was here she had before seen the phantom which had recently appeared to her, it was there she was aroused from sleep, to behold her spirit standing over her, and gazing at her with looks of solemn and intense affection. She looked

towards that side of the apartment, where, on that occasion, the spectre had seemed to vanish, and beheld traced upon the wainscot the following words—

"Angelina, depart; remember the injunctions of thy mother's shade, and when next we meet, learn to obey.—KATE."

With trembling steps Angelina quitted the room, and after some difficulty in finding her way, gained the exterior of the abbey ruins. The agitation of her mind we shall not seek to describe, for after the exciting events that had occurred, an idea of it may be very easily formed. She had not proceeded any great distance from the abbey, when looking up, she beheld her uncle hastening towards her. She rushed forward, and throwing her head upon his shoulder, the power of her emotions overcame her, and she burst into tears.

"Nay, my love," said Mr. Woodfield, kindly, "calm your agitated feelings, I pray. I know all that has befallen you, Kate has been to me, and made me acquainted with everything, but for the present, endeavour to banish the subject from your thoughts, and let us make the best of our way towards home."

"Oh, my dear uncle, if such indeed you are," sobbed our heroine, as he took her arm and led her away, at the same time she looked imploringly in his face, "why keep me in this painful state of mystery and ignorance? why withhold from me who were my actual parents, what their fate, and your motives for concealing it so long from my knowledge? Surely it is cruel to torture me thus."

"Angelina," answered Mr. Woodfield, emphatically, and he seemed violently agitated, "as you love me, pursue this subject no further for the present; I cannot, must not answer your questions."

"Am I then the child of shame, that you fear to mention the names of those to whom I am indebted for being?" demanded Angelina, while a blush of wounded pride suffused her cheek, and her heart swelled with the anguish which that thought excited.

Mr. Woodfield looked at her with apparent surprise for a moment or two, and then in tones expressive of enthusiastic pride, he answered—

"Angelina, the child of shame, oh, no! no! virtue and——but I dare not trust myself to say more, and oh, Angelina, however strange and inconsistent my conduct may appear at present, do not, I intreat you, do not interrogate me further. Fear not, there will be a time come when you shall know all."

HUGH CLIFFORD ON THE SEA SHORE.

Our heroine sighed deeply, and clasping her hands vehemently together, raised her eyes towards Heaven, as if praying that the words of her uncle might be realized. She said no more, but absorbed entirely in her own agonizing thoughts, leaning on Mr. Woodfield's arm, walked slowly towards the cottage.

What pangs, what racking torments filled the bosom of Angelina, as alone in her chamber, she reflected upon the awful occurrences of the day, and upon the inscrutable mystery by which she was surrounded.

"Oh, God!" she cried, "what a terrible fate is mine; thus to be perpetually tormented with doubts, fears, and perplexing surmises. Alas! why was I not always kept in ignorance of my being any other than the poor cottager's niece? Why partially withdraw the veil from before my eyes, merely as it would seem to make me wretched?—Clifford too, he whom my heart acknowledges its master; he, my first, my only love, even he am I forbidden to think upon, save with the cold sentiment of friendship!—Oh, the horror of that thought! Forget you, Clifford !—There is death in the idea !—But it must be ;—I am commanded from the grave to do so ;—I am told that nature forbids our union, and shall I dare to disobey? dear Clifford ;—for in spite of all, ever dear must you be to me ;—we must meet no more !"

While sobs choked her utterance, the poor girl took from her bosom the treasured miniature, and gazed with a feeling of the most intense sorrow and rapture upon it.

"Dear, dear resemblance," she ejaculated, "you seem to reproach me for that decision, but oh, could you read my heart, then would you know the torture I am enduring; how strongly your image is engraven there !—But am I not doing wrong by retaining this bauble, which so vividly brings to my recollection the object I am commanded to forget?—Alas! can I part from it—it is the only memento I have of one who—No, no, I cannot, I will not resign it!

She sobbed convulsively, as she raised the miniature to her lips and kissed it vehemently again and again, then sinking on her knees, with clasped hands, and upraised eyes, she added :—

"Almighty Father, into thy hands I commit myself; be thou my guide, and direct me to do that of which my own conscience may afterwards approve.'

The entrance of Laura aroused her, and arising from her knees, she listened with grati-

tude to the words of consolation which the former endeavoured to impart to her. But alas! the good intentions of the affectionate Laura were entirely without having the desired effect; the grief of Angelina was too powerful to be easily removed, and time alone, if anything, could effect that object.

"Well, I always said that gloomy old abbey was haunted," observed Laura, for a moment forgetting that any allusion of the kind was the very thing which was most likely to increase the alarm and emotion she was so anxious to remove ; "I was certain that it was the abode of evil spirits, hobgoblins, and all such like, and so I told you, but you wouldn't believe me, and now you see how correct I was in my surmises. Ye may mark my words, that Kate, as she calls herself, is no earthly being, although she——"

A significant look from our heroine, silenced the thoughtless girl, and she said no more, but endeavoured to divert the thoughts of her cousin into some other channel, an attempt, however, in which she signally failed.

———

CHAPTER XXIV.

SEVERAL days elapsed, and Angelina continued in much the same state, or, if anything, her melancholy became more intense, and she seemed to shrink from consolation or advice.—Mr. Woodfield was, as may be expected, deeply grieved to see this, and he scarcely knew how to act. He saw how strongly the image of Hugh Clifford was engrafted in her heart, and how even a sense of duty, and all the expostulations of himself, had hitherto failed to have the least effect towards eradicating it ; and he was thrown into a complete state of perplexity as to what plan it would be most advisable to adopt, to remove her poignant grief, and to effect the object he had in view.

Mrs. Woodfield still, in spite of her husband's displeasure, gave free expression to her opinions upon the subject, and she did not hesitate to designate the whole affair as most cruel and unjust.

" Ah ! poor girl," she observed, " hers is, indeed, a cruel fate, to be thus continually tormented, and disappointed in all her hopes, and frustrated in all her wishes, just merely to please the whims of two or three persons, who must have some interested motives for their conduct. I do not like that Kate of the Ruins; who is she, I should like to know ? How has she became acquainted with the mystery attending Angelina, and why should she take such a prominent part in the affair ?—Surely, it cannot be any business of hers ; and, for my part, although I do not doubt but that the old abbey ruins are haunted, I am inclined to believe that this ghost which the poor girl thought she saw, was nothing more than the work of Kate, to terrify her into a compliance with her wishes, and to further some sinister design with which I am not acquainted."

" Will you hold your peace, dame ?" said Mr. Woodfield, angrily ; " how many more times am I to tell you that your foolish ideas, and your obstinate curiosity, can have no other effect than making things worse, and yet you will persist ? Once for all, I tell you that I will not be spoken to on the subject, neither will I have my conduct questioned—conduct which is only prompted by affection for Angelina, and a wish to save her from sorrow."

With these words, Mr. Woodfield quitted the cottage.

At length, after the most harassing thoughts, Mr. Woodfield came to the conclusion that the only hope of alleviating the grief of his niece, was by change of scene; by removing her from that spot, where there were so many things to keep the image of her lover in her memory, and where the imprudent observations of his wife continually tended to thwart all his designs.

Of putting this plan into execution, he had every opportunity, as he had a distant relation living near Scarborough ; a widow, with one daughter, about the same age as Angelina, and who had some years back been on the most intimate terms with him, and had shewn a great partiality towards our heroine ; and, only a few months before, he had received a letter from her, and requested that Mr. Woodfield would suffer her to go on a visit of a few months to her house. This, Mr. Woodfield had, at the time, declined, for he could not bear the thought of a separation from his niece, but now, when he saw in it the only means of accomplishing his wishes, he determined to make a sacrifice of his feelings to necessity.

Mrs. Montmorency, the person alluded to above, was the widow of a naval officer, who had greatly distinguished himself in the cause of his country, and who, when he died, left her sufficient property to keep her and her daughter in comfortable, if not affluent, circumstances. She took up her residence near Scarborough for the benefit of the sea-breeze, as her health had been for some time past in a very delicate state; and she kept up a regular correspondence with Mr. Woodfield, for whom she felt much respect.

Mrs. Montmorency was a very accomplished and amiable woman, and it was therefore with a degree of confidence he could make up his mind to entrust Angelina to her care, stating the circumstances under which she came, and not doubting but that, by the advice of Mrs. Montmorency, and the change of scene and society, the experiment would be attended with the most beneficial results.

It was with the greatest reluctance Mr. Woodfield broke his design to Angelina, and her anguish at the thoughts of even a temporary separation from those dear friends with whom she had been from childhood, may be better imagined than language could pourtray it.

Angelina had never been, even for the shortest time, away from home, and the idea of a separation at present, although she knew enough of the amiable character of Mrs. Montmorency, (from what she remembered herself and what had been told her by Mr. Woodfield)

filled her bosom with the utmost melancholy.—
She could not also help thinking that there was
something cruel in the determination Mr. Woodfield had come to, and notwithstanding he assured her that he did it all for her good, and
that they would meet again in a very short
time, she could not persuade herself but that
some heavy calamity was in store for her,
which would render that circumstance abortive.
Laura was almost as much affected as our
heroine, for she was most ardently attached to
her; she entreated her father to suffer her to
accompany her cousin, but this he objected to,
alledging, as a reason, that he could not dispense
with her domestic services, against which argument Laura, of course, could not urge the
least objection, But there were more reasons
than one why the latter was so anxious to
accompany Angelina on her visit to Scarborough, she deeply sympathized with her in her
affection for Hugh Clifford, and she was anxious
to be with her, and to offer her all the consolation in her power.

We will pass over the morning of separation,
(which was, indeed, to Angelina and her friends,
a most melancholy one) and place the former
in the vehicle which was to bear her to the residence of Mrs. Montmorency. Nothing particular occurred to her on the journey, and we will
therefore pass hastily over it, and bring her at
once to the place of her destination.

Mrs. Montmorency received her visitor with
the utmost cordiality, and Charlotte, her
daughter, who was a warm-hearted girl, evinced
by her manners how highly delighted she was
at having such a companion. If anything
could have alleviated the grief of Angelina,
it must have been the enthusiastic manner in
which she was received by Mrs. Montmorency
and her daughter, and she did, indeed, feel a
transitory relief from the heavy sorrow that
oppressed her.

Mrs Montmorency was still a very good-
looking woman, and had evidently, in her
youthful days, been exceedingly handsome;
her manners showed that she possessed a highly
accomplished mind, and to which was united
every good quality that can render woman
charming. Of Angelina, she seemed to possess
a most affectionate opinion, and entering with
sympathy into her sorrows, she endeavoured,
by every means in her power, to divert her
thoughts from the subject which occupied her
heart, and did all that she possibly could to
render her comfortable.

Charlotte Montmorency was a pretty, intelligent, and vivacious girl; and Angelina
felt a deep and sincere friendship for her the
moment she beheld her. Her manners were
candid and fervent; and brought up under
the care of her mother, it may be expected
that she imbibed all her virtues and intrinsic
perfections. If Charlotte possessed one weakness
it was in being a little too vain of her personal
charms, but that was a fault of which her
mother had not the slightest doubt, she could
divest her in time, by advice; or, which she
felt confident, her own natural good sense
(when her mind had become more staid and
mature,) would destroy.

Charlotte was just seventeen, and her
numerous graces, and her personal beauties
had already gained her many admirers, who,
in the warmth of their anxiety to gain favour
in her eyes, had flattered her profusely; therefore, in one so young, and of so volatile a
temper, it is not at all surprising that her
vanity, (a weakness inherent in all the human
race, to a greater or smaller degree,) should be
excited. But she had never encouraged any
of their addresses, and, in fact, she had not
seen one whom she could more than regard as
a friend.

In this lovely girl, Angelina found an excellent companion, and her separation from
her friends was soon felt by her with only
half the severity; while her melancholy was
greatly alleviated by the uninterrupted gaiety
of Charlotte, and her irresistible sweetness of
disposition. To say that she had forgotten
Clifford, would not only be false, but preposterous; no, he was too powerfully imprinted

on her heart, for her ever to do that; but then her anguish was softened, and she was enabled to submit with calmness to her fate, and to patiently humble to the will of Heaven.

Charlotte was a most accomplished musician, and our heroine had always possessed an extraordinary talent that way, which Mr. Woodfield, when he had been in more prosperous circumstances, had taken great pains to cultivate; the former was also very clever in drawing, and in that beautiful art, too, Angelina had shown considerable taste, so that in practising together, they not only found an excellent source of amusement, but improvement to each other. When tired of these amusements, Angelina and Charlotte would wander among the beautiful marine scenery of the place; and in the contemplation of the charms of nature, they found the most unbounded means of gratification and instruction. Rambling on the cliffs, they would watch the proud vessels as they skimmed majestically the deep blue waves, and gaze upon the beauties of the setting sun, as he sunk from his daily course in the western horizon. At such times, Angelina would picture to her mind's eye Hugh Clifford, and form various conjectures of where he was, and if he ever thought of her, and as her heart felt confident that the ardour of his love was equal to her own, and that neither time, distance, nor circumstances could change it, she thought more of the unhappiness he was enduring than that she was suffering herself. Many times did fancy picture to her his gallant vessel, and often did she, in imagination, view it gaily flying over the ambient tide; but from such illusions she was always awakened to disappointment, and more poignant sorrow than she had previously experienced.

The mystery attendant upon her, also frequently occupied and harassed her mind, and the more she reflected upon it, the more did she become involved in doubt and perplexity. The opposition which her uncle and Kate of the Ruins had shown to the love of her and Hugh Clifford, was perfectly inexplicable to her, and why they should so carefully conceal their motives for the same from her, was also equally mysterious. Then the awful circumstance which had occurred to her in the vault, was continually recurring to her memory, and the words of the supposed spectre she had seen, still rung in her ears, and excited in her bosom sentiments of awe, terror, and uncertainty. That she had not been deceived by her own disordered imagination, she felt confident; and the recollection of the event never failed to make her bosom the abode of the most profound sorrow and anguish.

Thus passed away a month, and in that time Angelina had received two or three letters from her uncle and Laura, which she read with delight, couched as they were in language of affection and consolation. Both Mr. Woodfield and his daughter, however, most carefully avoided mentioning the name of Hugh Clifford, neither did they make any allusion to him. Of course, Angelina saw at once their reasons for doing so, and could not help applauding that which showed that they wished to avoid a subject which they knew would only cause her pain. Charlotte and our heroine had now become as much attached to each other as if they had been constant companions from childhood, and the disposition of the former was so much like that of Laura, that it in some measure made up for the deprivation of her society.

Mrs. Montmorency saw but little company, and what she did, was of the most select description, and such as was calculated to improve the mind of her daughter, and we need not, therefore, say that Angelina was delighted with them, and that the little parties that were frequently formed at the house of Mrs. Montmorency, were genuine parties of pleasure, and had the most beneficial effects upon her spirits and disposition.

One evening, Angelina and Charlotte were seated at the drawing-room window, which commanded a view over the sea, and were watching, with sentiments of unbounded admiration and delight, the setting of the golden orb of day, when the former suddenly beheld the figure of a man emerge from behind one of the rocks, and walk on at a quick pace towards the house. There was something in the appearance of the man which struck Angelina immediately as being familiar to her, and her heart beat violently against her side. As he approached nearer, she was the more certain that she had seen him before; but when he raised his head, and she recognised Hugh Clifford, the reader will be able to judge her excessive astonishment and agitation. She could not repress an exclamation of surprise, and turned very pale, which Charlotte observing, eagerly inquired what was the matter. Our heroine, fearful of betraying the truth, replied with as little confusion as possible, that she left suddenly indisposed, and retired from the window; but her emotion was so powerful that Charlotte was not satisfied with the answer she had given her, and again urged her to inform her what had happened to occasion her such evident alarm; but Angelina evaded her questions, and still pleaded indisposition as the cause.

The nature of our heroine's thoughts upon this occasion, may be imagined without much difficulty. Had Clifford become acquainted with the place in which she was located, and come there purposely to obtain an interview with her? or had he come there by accident, and knew not that she was in the neighbourhood? She was more inclined to think the former, and her heart trembled with fear as she thought so, lest he should come to the house, and demand an interview with her. Still, however, upon more mature reflection, she could not believe that he would act so imprudently, and she became more easy upon that point. But oh, how her heart panted for an interview with the dear object of her heart's warmest affections; how she longed to tell him the place he still held, and always must hold, in her love; and that, although cruel

Fate had apparently ordained that they should never come together, yet, while she had life, to him alone her heart would be devoted.

Fearful of exciting the suspicions of Charlotte, she did not venture to look from the window again, so that she might ascertain whether Hugh Clifford was still there; and the state of anxiety and doubt she was plunged into, was almost insupportable. A quarter of an hour elapsed, and as Angelina did not hear any knock at the door, or receive any summons from Mrs. Montmorency, she concluded that Clifford knew not of her being there, and that he had only come by mere chance, and would leave the place without knowing she was there on whom his affections were irrevocably fixed. Conscious as she was that obedience to the wishes of her uncle rendered it imperative on her to shun a meeting with Hugh, she could not indulge these thoughts without considerable pain, and the ardour of her passion had a powerful struggle with her sense of duty and propriety.

Unable to restrain the power of her agitation, and apprehensive that Charlotte would suspect what was the cause of it, she, at length, made an excuse, and retired to her chamber, where she could, unobserved, give free indulgence to the tumult of thoughts which crowded on her brain.

"Alas!" she soliloquised, "my fate is a most tormenting one. Why was he again brought before my sight, but to remind me of the hopelessness of my love, and the cruel destiny which tells us we must never hope to be united? Little does he imagine, I dare say, that she who feels that she still loves him with all the fervour which it is possible for the human heart to entertain, is so near him; for if he did, well am I convinced that no impediments would prevent him from rushing into my presence. Oh! Clifford, absence from you, I feel, has only increased the passion you have created in my bosom."

Angelina, not being in proper spirits to endure the society of her friends, did not leave her chamber again that evening, and she went to bed at an early hour, and long before Charlotte (who slept in the same apartment with her) joined her. But sleep was a stranger to her eyelids; her mind was too busy to admit of that respite from care; and even after Charlotte had been in bed for some time, and had sunk into a deep slumber, Angelina continued to toss restlessly on the pillow, and the unexpected appearance of Hugh Clifford harassed and bewildered her mind.

It was about eleven o'clock when Angelina was suddenly aroused from this state of rumination, by hearing the tones of a guitar, played by a masterly hand, and which seemed to proceed from immediately underneath her chamber window. She listened with breathless attention. The air was a very plaintive one, and she was almost certain that she had heard it before; and, after awhile, a voice, whose tones could never be erased from her recollection, sang the following words, every syllable of which was listened to by her with the most enthusiastic delight and admiration—

"The heart which throbs with passion true,
　　Though fate may interpose,
Nor time nor distance can subdue;
　　Each day more fierce it glows!—
Oh, who can stop its secret moves,
　　Or its fond links dissever?
The heart that truly, fondly loves,
　　Must faithful beat for ever!
　　　　　　　　For ever!
'Till its pulsation cease in death,
　　That heart must love for ever!"

It was the voice of Clifford, and the reader may easily judge with what emotion she listened to the words of the song, to every one of which her heart so faithfully responded; but, at the same time, her agitation was still greater when she found that Charlotte was awake, and was apparently listening with much surprise and pleasure to the nocturnal serenader.

"Well, I declare," she exclaimed, when Hugh Clifford had ceased, "this is an event worthy of a romance—a serenade at midnight! Dear me! I wonder who the poor love-sick swain is?—No doubt, however, it is one of my numerous admirers. Poor fellow! what a pity it is that he should break his rest, and exert his lungs in such a hopeless case."

Angelina felt a great relief when she heard Charlotte express this conjecture, and she made some slight reply to her observations, which affected to coincide with her opinion, and then relapsed once more into silence, listening anxiously to hear whether Clifford would again sing.

But the tones which had so charmed her no more vibrated on her ears; and with a feeling of regret and disappointment, she turned to her companion, who, notwithstanding the words she made use of, seemed to be as much surprised and delighted as Angelina.

It was now evident to our heroine that Hugh Clifford had found out the place of her retreat; and with this certainty, was mingled a feeling of pleasure, which, in spite of the injunctions of Mr. Woodfield and Kate of the Ruins, she could not resist. Oh, no, let whatever circumstances there might arise, even though she should incur the greatest misery through the same, his image was too strongly engraven on her heart for her ever to efface him from her memory; and something whispered to her that, notwithstanding the untoward aspect of affairs at present, it was their fate, some time or the other, to come together. How she longed that she could have revealed herself to him, and by a look, a glance, assure him of the continuance of her love, and convince him that no earthly power could ever make her forget him.

And what must be his sufferings? Too well could she tell the sentiments of his heart, and she was convinced that his breast was the abode of the most agonizing grief; and to know that he was wretched, at the same time that it imparted to her a feeling of ecstacy, as it convinced her of the reciprocity of his love, made her feel more miserable than any other occasion could have made her.

A brief silence now ensued, and both she and Charlotte appeared to be listening with the hope of once more hearing the melodious tones of the mysterious minstrel, and to be equally disappointed when their wishes were not gratified.

"I wonder who it could be," observed Charlotte; "I never remember to have heard the voice before, although it is one I should not have the slightest objection to hear again. Do you not think his voice, and the manner in which he executed the serenade, were very beautiful, Angelina?"

The question confused our heroine for a moment; but, recollecting herself, she replied with assumed composure—

"He certainly sang very sweetly, Charlotte, and evidently possesses no ordinary musical taste."

"You are perfectly of my opinion," replied the latter; "but I wish I had been up and dressed, to have seen who it was. I can't, for the life of me, guess, for I have such a multiplicity of admirers, that I might, positively, if I liked, have a fresh beau for every day in the year. Heigho!—what a thing it is to be a little pretty, Angelina; the men do tease the very life-time out of you."

Although her mind was so fully occupied with that one engrossing subject, Angelina could not refrain from smiling at the vanity of her companion, and said—

"Why, Charlotte, as you say you have so many lovers, and that you do not deign to smile upon any of them, you will, certainly, have a deal to answer for, owing to the number of hearts you will be the cause of breaking."

"All that may be very true, my dear," observed Charlotte, smiling; "but then I sometimes do give one or two of the poor fellows a smile, which relieves my conscience greatly."

"But I am afraid, my dear Charlotte," returned Angelina, "that if you act in that manner you will gain the name of a coquette, which is no easy title to get rid of again."

"Well, they may e'en call me what they please," said Charlotte, "it will not effect me much; for, in fact, I scarcely know what I am myself. However, our serenader seems to have got tired of his job, and, therefore, let us e'en go to sleep again, Angelina."

But it was very little sleep that our heroine could obtain that night; and when she did, it was only to dream of Hugh Clifford.

She longed, yet dreaded to meet him; her affection urged her on to endeavour to do so, but then her duty to the commands of Mr. Woodfield, and the spirit of her mother, forbade her. It was, indeed, a painful struggle with her feelings, and many a severe pang did it cost her, before she could make up her mind to obey the dictates of duty. How he had become acquainted with the place she was staying at, she could not imagine, for it was very evident that Mr. Woodfield would not inform him, and if Kate of the Ruins was aware of it, she would be equally careful in not divulging it to him.

She could not imagine that Clifford would act so imprudently as to endeavour to seek an interview with her at the house, but she had no doubt that he would wait about in the neighbourhood, in the hope of seeing her; but anxious as she was once more to behold him, she was fearful of doing so in the company of Charlotte, and she, therefore, declined their accustomed walks on the following day, on the plea of indisposition, and remained at home in the society of Mrs. Montmorency, whose lively and intelligent discourse succeeded in partially estranging her thoughts from the subject which had before so fully occupied them.

Two days passed away in this manner, and Angelina neither heard nor saw any thing more of Hugh Clifford. She became restless, and her melancholy increased; for the idea of his having quitted the place without having made an effort to see her, afflicted her more than all, and it was some time before she could banish it from her thoughts.

It was on the third day after the circumstance we have mentioned had taken place, that Ann, the servant girl of Mrs. Montmorency, came running into Angelina's apartment, where she was alone, and had been engaged in reading, with curiosity depicted in her countenance, and in breathless haste said—

"Lor', my dear mistress, what do you think?"

ANGELINA BROUGHT T WHERE THE WRETCHED BRIDGET IS CONFINED.

"What's the matter, Ann?" inquired our heroine; "you seem all in a flurry."

"You may say that, Miss," answered the simple girl;—oh! such an adventure."

"An adventure!" repeated Angelina—"what mean you?"

"Why, Miss," replied Ann, "I'll tell you all about it as soon as I can get my breath;—it's all concerning you, though."

"Concerning me!" ejaculated Angelina with astonishment;—"I cannot understand you, so pray explain yourself."

"Ler, Miss, you are so very impatient," said the tiresome girl; "I have run all the way home on purpose to tell you, and I am ready to drop, so you must allow me a minute or two to recover myself."

Our heroine saw that it would be useless to seek to lead her out of her regular course, so she walked to the other side of the room with some impatience, until such time as Ann thought proper to find herself in a fit condition to impart the important secret.

"Well, Miss, you must know," at length she said, "that when I went out of this house about an hour ago, what should the first object be that I clapt my eyes upon but a man!"

"A man, you silly girl," said Angelina, laughing; "and pray is there anything so remarkable in that?"

"Why, no, Miss," replied Ann, "there is nothing *pertickler*, as I knows on, in that, to be sure; but then this man behaved in such a curious way, and that's what I want to tell you."

"In what way do you mean?" asked our heroine, her curiosity being now somewhat excited.

"Why, when I went out," returned Ann, "he was walking backwards and forwards past the house, and looking up at the windows of your apartments, Miss, as if he was anxious to see somebody."

Angelina blushed deeply, as the idea of Hugh Clifford occurred to her mind, and she eagerly inquired—

"What kind of a man was he, Ann?"

"Why, Miss, he was a tall, middle-aged, surly-looking man, with very large eyebrows," answered Ann.

"It certainly was not Hugh Clifford, then," thought Angelina; "but is that all you have to relate of him, Ann?" she inquired.

"Oh, no, Miss," returned the girl, "that is not all. As I said before, when I first went out, he was watching the windows, apparently to ascertain whether there was somebody there hat he knew. But when he saw me, he at

first walked away, but afterwards turned back, and stepping up to me, with a smile, which I could not help thinking sat very badly upon his savage-looking features, he said—

"'Good morning to you, my pretty lass,— yes, he said *pretty* lass," added Ann.

"Well, well," ejaculated our heroine, impatiently, "go on—what else did he say?"

"Why, as I said before, Miss——"

"Oh, never mind what you said before," interrupted Angelina, impatiently, "but let me know what the man said."

"That's just what I was going to do, Miss, only you interrupted me," observed the girl;— "well, the man touched me under the chin, and said, 'Good morning to you, my pretty lass; you are the servant here, I presume.' Well, Miss, I must say that I thought this was rather *impartinent*, hows'ever I answered, 'I don't see what difference it can make to you whether I am a *sarvant* here or not; sarvants is as good as other people, if not better, for anything I know.' 'Well, well,' said the man, 'don't you go to be cross, my dear, I didn't mean to offend you. I suppose you have something more to do now you have a visiter?'

"'And how do you know that we have got a visiter?' said I, with no small astonishment, as you may guess, Miss.

"'Oh, I know Miss Angelina well,' replied the man."

"Know me!" cried our heroine, with the utmost amazement, and turning very pale.

"Yes, that was what he said, Miss," continued Ann, "and so I said to him, 'what if you do know Miss Angelina, I am sure you know no harm of her, for she is as amiable a——'

"'Oh, oh, then *it is* Angelina who is your visiter here?' interrupted the man, with a laugh, and away he walked, without saying another word."

"Singular!" ejaculated our heroine, when Ann had concluded; "who could it be?—I know no person answering that description, and —Ann, I must beg that you will not mention this circumstance to any other person, and if you again see the man, avoid him, if possible, but above all, do not answer his interrogatories."

" That I will not, Miss, you may depend upon it," said the girl, " for I do not like the looks of him, although he did call me a pretty lass. But wasn't it very remarkable ?"

" It was, indeed," replied Angelina, " and I cannot help thinking that there must have been some mistake."

" There could not have been any mistake on my part, Miss," returned Ann, "for I'm sure he mentioned your name as plainly as I have told you."

After a little more conversation, from which our heroine could not elicit anything more than what had been related to her, Ann left her, after pepeating her promises to keep what had happened a secret.

This adventure created the utmost astonishment in the mind of Angelina, but she was quite incapable of solving the mystery by which it was surrounded. Who could this man be, of whom Ann gave such an unprepossessing account. How had he become acquainted with her name and residence, and why should he seem to be so curious about her? She was completely bewildered, and could arrive at no reasonable conclusion. At one time, she thought he might be one of the men belonging to the smuggler's vessel, and that he had been employed by Hugh Clifford to endeavour to ascertain for certain, whether or not she was an inmate of Mrs. Montmorency's house. But this idea she rejected almost as soon as she had formed it, and she could not believe that Clifford would have behaved so imprudently as to have made a confidant of one of his crew, and to have employed him on such an errand; and she, therefore, became quite at a loss what to think of the mysterious affair.

After racking her brain to no purpose, she gave up the attempt, and in the society of Charlotte and her mother endeavoured to banish the recollection of it from her memory.

The following day, Angelina walked out alone, Charlotte having an engagement with one of her female acquaintances. The fineness of the weather induced her to wander farther than she had at first intended, and she was returning hastily towards home, thinking that Mrs. Montmorency would be surprised at her lengthened absence, when she was astonished to hear her name repeated by some one behind, and turning round, her amazement and confusion may be easily guessed, when she beheld Hugh Clifford running towards her.

Completely paralized, she could not move a step, and the next moment Hugh Clifford was pressing her rapturously to his bosom.

" Oh, Angelina, dearest girl," he exclaimed, in accents of indescribable tenderness, " do we then again meet—do I once more embrace you? Alas! that we should ever part, that anything should occur to place a barrier between the union of two fond hearts so ardently devoted to each other. Speak to me, my love, in those accents of affection I have listened to with such rapturous delight, say that you still love me ; say that you have not forgotten me, or——"

" Oh, Clifford," interrupted Angelina, "too truly do I feel I love you, and that with all the effervesence of woman's fondest passion ; but we are forbidden to love each other ; cruel destiny ordains that we should be no more than as friends, and we must submit. Alas ! that we ever met, since it must be so !"

" Oh, no—no, say not so, my sweetest," ejaculated Clifford, " it must not, shall not be ; surely Heaven sanctions our love, or why inspire our hearts with such an intense, such a mutual passion ? Yes—yes, believe me, dear girl, this opposition is only the offspring of caprice, or to further the designs of——"

" Clifford," said Angelina, withdrawing herself from his embrace with a look of surprise, "and can you venture to impugn the character of my excellent uncle, by attributing to him motives which I am sure his nature would despise? You surprise me, Clifford, indeed you do."

"Oh, pardon me, my dearest Angelina," cried Clifford, "the impetuosity of my love hurries me into the expression of sentiments I can only afterwards regret. Heaven forbid that I should do your uncle an injustice, but surely it is cruel to seek to divide two hearts so truly formed to meet."

"It is indeed hard, Clifford," returned Angelina, in accents of melancholy regret; "but I am certain that my uncle does it for the best, and however it may, and will wring my heart, I must obey. Leave me, Clifford, I implore you; this is only adding fresh agony to a bosom already the residence of such acute anguish; leave me, Clifford, and in the society of other females, forget that you ever beheld Angelina."

"Forget you, Angelina," cried Hugh Clifford, fervently; "never, by Heaven! nay, I feel it is impossible! You are so interwoven with my nature, that you have, as it were, become a portion of myself—and nothing but death can divide the union. But can you wish me, Angelina, to leave you? Alas! did you love with the fervour of the passion which inhabits my bosom, never could you utter such a wish!"

"Oh, Clifford!" ejaculated our heroine, in a voice of extreme agitation, "in pity to my sufferings do not——"

"Down with him!" at that moment exclaimed a coarse voice, which proceeded from immediately behind them; the next instant Hugh Clifford was felled to the earth by a violent blow from a cudgel, and Angelina, to her horror, found herself forced away towards the cliffs by the villain Ruthven, and several other ruffians, and the moment she attempted to scream, a gag was thrust into her mouth, and she was forced into a boat, which was lying beneath the rocks.

Terror completely paralized the faculties of our heroine on finding herself to be once more in the power of the myrmidon of her bitterest, her most dreaded enemy, and she was totally incapable of making the least attempt at resistance, (although that would have been useless) and could not even give utterance to the slightest outcry, as the ruffians forced her away towards the boat, while some stayed behind with Hugh Clifford, who, with a feeling of horror, too powerful for us to describe, she had not the least doubt they intended to murder.

"See to that fellow, Evans," cried Ruthven, as they hastened away, addressing himself to one of the wretches who was leaning over him; "you know how to dispose of him."

"Ay—ay," replied the man, "that is all right; I'll warrant he does not slip through my fingers."

"Mind he does not," returned Ruthven. The next moment they had reached the boat, into which they hurried Angelina, and the men plied stoutly at the oars, making towards a vessel, which she perceived lying at a distance; she also observed another boat fastened beneath the rocks, but she did not know whether it belonged to Ruthven and his party, or to Hugh Clifford.

They soon came to the ship, and went on board, and our heroine was convinced that it was the same vessel in which she had been conveyed to the Grey Tower, for she recognised several of the crew among the fellows upon deck.

She was taken into a small but comfortable cabin, where she was left in the charge of an old woman of shrivelled and waspish aspect, and who looked upon her with the most forbidding gestures.

Angelina's heart was almost broken, but the uncertainty of the fate of Cliffor agonised her more, even than the danger in which she was placed, and her bosom was the abode of the greatest horror and apprehension. Knowing, however, how useless it would be to make any complaint, and turning with disgust from the revolting old woman, she remained silent, and with clasped hands and upraised eyes, she mentally breathed a prayer to Heaven for its protection, and then seating herself in one corner of the cabin, she covered her face with her handkerchief, and gave herself up to the dismal feelings her situation gave rise to.

"What a terrible fate is mine," reflected the poor girl. "I am truly unfortunate; there is always something occurring to render me miserable. I am completely the sport of fortune, and yet never do I do anything to deserve such misfortune. Alas! Angelina, what little cause you have to wish to live, since it seems that you are doomed to continual misery,"

At this moment, a noise upon the deck attracted her attention, and she listened carefully, thinking to be able to ascertain the cause of it, but she could distinguish only a murmuring of many voices, and the heavy stamping of feet over her head, and once imagined she heard the groans of some person as if in the greatest agony. A thought in a moment darted across her brain :—it was her lover they had brought on board ;—it was Hugh Clifford, and this idea, while it gave her some assurance that he still lived, filled her with the most poignant anguish, for in the power of the baron, (who had reason enough to hate him), she trembled at the fate to which he would, in all probability, be exposed, and at the almost utter hopelessness of her being again rescued, since he was rendered unable to assist her, and all knowledge of whither she had gone, and in whose power she was, would not reach the ears of her friends. What anguish would they endure when they heard of her disappearance, the mystery of which would be greatly increased by the disappearance of Hugh Clifford also. Whichever way she directed her thoughts, she saw not the least thing which could inspire hope in her bosom. The baron, no doubt, greatly incensed at the manner in which his nefarious designs had been foiled, would treat her with increased severity, and she might dread the worst from his savage temper, and the strange hatred he seemed to bear towards her. Upon Hugh Clifford, too, who had rescued her from his power, she had not

the least doubt but that his deadliest vengeance would fall, and that thought caused her more pain than the idea of any torture she might be subjected to herself.

She also felt greatly for the awkward and disagreeable situation in which Mrs. Montmorency was placed by the circumstance; for Mr. Woodfield had entrusted her to her care, thinking she would be perfectly safe, and there was no knowing what construction his suspicions might put upon the event, or whether he might not surmise that Mrs. Montmorency was accessary to it. That thought, however, she did not suffer to remain on her mind many minutes for she considered that her uncle could never be so unjust, or so unreasonable as to suppose that Mrs. Montmorency, (whose unimpeachable character he so well knew), would be guilty of such a crime, in which she could not possibly have the slightest interest.

The vessel got under weigh immediately, and Angelina now felt that they were skimming over the sea at a most rapid rate, and she had not the least doubt but that it was their intention to convey her once more to the old Grey Tower.

The Baron de Morton, she reflected, must have some very powerful reason for [thus so resolutely pursuing his persecution towards her, but what that reason could be, she had not the means of forming even the most vague conjecture. That he would use such means as would effectually prevent her from again escaping from him, she had not the slightest doubt; and, therefore, whichever way she directed her thoughts, they were met only by dark despair.

"Alas! dear Clifford," she reflected, "to what a dreadful fate has your unhappy passion for me exposed you ;—it is my greatest misfortune to make those who are my best friends partakers of the troubles that are continually falling to my lot."

The old woman, who continued in the cabin with our heroine, and employed herself in knitting, several times gave utterance to a monosyllabic expression, and seemed anxious to elicit a reply from her, but finding that all her efforts were ineffectual, she abandoned it, and shortly afterwards she quitted the cabin, and Angelina (much to her relief) was left to herself.

She traversed the narrow confines of the cabin with hasty and agitated steps, and wrung her hands with the most intense agony; then scalding tears rushed to her eyes, and partially relieved her overcharged bosom. She tried the cabin door, but it was fast. Oh, that she could only have made her way to the deck, she felt that she could more freely have rushed upon death, rather than continue to endure the bitter suffering she was now undergoing, and that which she apprehended she had yet to undergo.

The dashing of the waves against the sides of the vessel, came with a melancholy sound upon her ears ; and every now and then, the boisterous laughter of the ruffians, who seemed to be carousing and enjoying themselves, alarmed her, while her ears were frequently shocked by their blackguard expressions and oaths.

Thus passed away several weary, dull, and monotonous hours, and Angelina experienced no change, and no relief from the anguish of her bosom. It was night, and a dead silence reigned o'er everything around, save at intervals, when the wind, which blew pretty fresh, howled through the different parts of the ship, and the sea-mew uttered its pitiful wailing cry. None of the men offered to intrude upon her, but the old woman came into the cabin again, and it appeared that it was her intention to stay there all the night. This circumstance Angelina much regretted, for the very looks of the old woman were sufficient to inspire her with disgust and horror, and she could not for the life of her, find courage sufficient to address a word to her, or even to glance towards her.

We shall not take the trouble to enter into a minute detail of the voyage, as nothing occurred worthy of any particular attention, and the following day, the vessel arrived at the place of its destination, which our heroine found to be, as she had anticipated, the old Grey Tower, in which she had before suffered such a painful incarceration. How she shuddered with terror as she gazed upon its blackened walls, which seemed to frown despair upon her, and thought how probable it was that she might never more emerge from them ; and as the ponderous doors closed upon her, her heart sank as though she had, at that moment, been enclosed in a tomb.

She was hurried across several lower apartments, but in quite a contrary direction to that in which they had taken her when she had been brought there before ; and at length, she was much alarmed, when raising a trap-door which discovered a flight of steps beneath, and which was very dark, they began to descend the stairs, and she was forced to follow. These steps she had no doubt, led to some of the dismal under-ground apartments, and her terror may be well imagined, when she thought upon this, and conjectured that in all probability, they were going to confine her in one of the dungeons under-ground.

"Oh! for God sake, inform me whither you are taking me?" exclaimed Angelina, addressing herself to Ruthven, in the most piteous accents.

"To a place from which you will find it rather difficult to escape, methinks," replied Ruthven, with a savage grin of exultation ; "you was not contented when you were indulged with handsome apartments, and now we must try what a little more rigorous confinement will do."

"Father of mercy, look down upon me, and protect me !" exclaimed Angelina, in accents of terror and despair ; and, Ruthven seizing hold of her arm, hurried her on; until having descended the stairs, they entered upon a subterraneous passage, which was so dark that the objects beyond could not be distinguished. Ruthven kindled a light in a small lantern which he had with him, and our heroine then discovered that they were in one of the passages she had traversed when she had made her escape from the tower. At length, Ruthven stopped before an iron door, and applying a large key, from a bunch which he carried by his side, after some difficulty he unlocked it, and revealed to the horror-struck Angelina, a gloomy dungeon, in one corner of which was a mattress, in the centre, an old deal table, and a chair. It seemed as if it had been recently inhabited by some unfortunate being, who had probably sunk beneath the cruelty and oppression under which it was most likely her fate to suffer.

"This is your apartment, young lady," said the villain Ruthven, with a sarcastic grin; "it certainly is not a very splendid one, but admirably adapted for the breaking of certain refractory tempers. In with you."

"Oh, for the love of heaven, if you have one spark of humanity in your breast, do not leave me in this terrible place," cried our heroine in frantic tones; "oh, mercy! mercy! Rather kill me at once than leave me here."

"Oh, you will get used to it in time," said the heartless wretch; "there, don't stand listening to her, nurse."

"Oh, save me, save me from this awful doom!" shrieked Angelina: but the next instant Ruthven rudely thrust her into the dungeon, and having left the lantern on the table, he and his companion quitted the place, and, closing it upon her, secured it by locking and bolting it.

Left in this awful place, no language could do adequate justice to the severity of our heroine's emotions; she wrung her hands, and beat her breast in despair, and made the place re-echo with her cries of anguish. The dungeon was deadly cold, and its black and flinty walls seemed to frown dismally upon her, as, when her agitation had became less violent, see prayed for the interposition of Omnipotence. Her idea of being confined all night in that horrible place, made her blood freeze in her veins, and her brain was racked to distraction. It now seemed certain to her that her assassination was determined, and here the dreadful crime could be perpetrated without even the slightest chance of its being frustrated.

But to reflect on a fate so shocking, and which now appeared also to be so inevitable, in one so young, was particularly awful, and as she did so, her despair almost amounted to madness. At length, completely worn out with her cries and lamentations, she became more calm, and sinking on a seat, she covered her face with her hands, as if to shut out the terror of the place, and rocked herself to and fro, in a state of great mental agony. Suddenly, however, she started from her seat, and gazed around her with a mixture of alarm and astonishment, as a deep groan, which seemed to proceed from no great distance, smote her ears.

With breathless attention she listened, while a great feeling of dread came over her, which the horrors of the place were quite sufficient to inspire, independent of everything else; but for a short time all again became as silent as the grave, and Angelina actually feared almost to look around, lest her eyes should encounter some terrific object or other. Again, the deep moaning of a person, apparently in great pain, smote her ears, and was followed by a sound resembling the clanking of heavy fetters, and it now appeared so near that she could almost have imagined it was in the dungeon in which she was confined. Her terrors increased, and her curiosity was excited to an almost insupportable degree, to know from whom the sounds proceeded. Were they the solemn wailings of some restless spirit, or were they the cries of anguish emanating from the bosom of some poor suffering being, who, like herself, was held a prisoner in these awful dungeons? She was unable to come to any satisfactory conclusion; and in a minute or two afterwards the sounds were repeated, followed by some words which she could not, at first, catch. At last, however, placing her ear close to the wall, she plainly overheard these expressions, uttered in accents of the most poignant agony—

"Holy father! look down with pity upon me, and in mercy put an end to my sufferings;

—this state of perpetual horror and anguish is worse than ten thousand deaths!"

Our heroine was now convinced that it was some poor suffering fellow-creature, and she felt also certain that she was confined in the adjoining dungeon. Her voice, too, was perfectly familiar to her, but she tried in vain to recollect where she had heard it before.

Although this circumstance afforded her a melancholy satisfaction to think that she should have one near her to whom she could communicate her thoughts, and who would, doubtless, sympathise with her in the misery she seemed fated to endure; the idea that there was another being as wretched as herself, and the dreadful state to which she seemed to be reduced (for the voice was that of a female) filled her bosom with sincere pain; and even amidst all her distresses, she felt if she could only alleviate the sorrows of the wretched prisoner, it would be some relief to her bosom.

Again Angelina heard the voice of the female giving utterance to some expressions of agony, but it was in so low a tone that they were rendered quite inaudible. She, however, determined to speak to her, and, therefore, after waiting for a few moments, in order that she might recover herself from the confusion and agitation into which such an unexpected adventure had thrown her, she, in as firm a voice as possible, exclaimed—

"Unhappy being, tell, I beseech you, a fellow-unfortunate who you are, and if there is anything that she, by words, can offer you to ameliorate your distress most willingly will she do it."

A loud rattling of chains, and a lumbering noise, as if something had fallen heavily upon the earth, followed this speech, and Angelina imagined that the wretched prisoner, to whom her sympathies were directed, had fainted, probably from exhaution.

"Poor creature!" she cried, "she either hears me not, or else she has become insensible. My God! what a monster must this Baron de Mort n be, thus to delight in inflict-ing unmerited torture upon his fellow-creatures. And must I remain in this horrible place," she continued, "the very aspect of which is sufficient to fill the stoutest heart with fear; and from whose damp and noisome walls, a chill, like that of death, freezes the blood within my veins, and palsies my limbs? Alas! what motives can induce the baron to this unprecedented cruelty?"

Once more she raised her voice, and addressed the prisoner; there was no answer returned, and the awful silence which prevailed seemed more impressive than as if it had not been interrupted.

"Great God!" ejaculated the trembling damsel, as a sudden thought flashed across her brain, "perhaps she is dead!—perhaps the Almighty has listened to her prayers, and terminated her sufferings, and here am I confined in the immediate proximity of a corpse!"

A cold sweat bedewed her temples, as this thought occurred to her, and it was with the utmost difficulty she could sustain herself; then the idea of what might be her own fate, tormented and distracted her imagination; probably left to starve, as the unfortunate being incarcerated in the next dungeon to her had very likely been? This idea was more than she could endure, and she groaned aloud.

More than an hour elapsed in this manner, and all remained still; Angelina had thrown herself on her wretched pallet, and covering her face with her hands, to shut out the horrors which her gloomy dungeon presented, gave herself up to feelings of the most intense anguish and despair. From the silence which continued, it now seemed not at all improbable but that her conjecture as to the death of the prisoner was correct; and many were the tears she gave to her untimely fate, which she could so sincerely commiserate, although she was not aware that she was at all acquainted with the unfortunate woman, notwithstanding the familiarity of her voice, which had so forcibly struck her, still haunted her recollection.

The light in her lamp was now beginning to burn very dim, and seemed as if it would shortly expire, and this added to our heroine's terrors tenfold, for to be left in this horrible place in total darkness, was too dreadful even to think upon. Were the spirits of the dead permitted to wander this earth, which she now firmly believed they were, since the awful adventure she had met with in the vaults of Saint Mark's Abbey, what more fitting place

ANGELINA EXPRESSES HER DISGUST AT THE BARON'S SUIT.

could they have for their dreary wanderings than this subterraneous prison?—How many wretched beings had, perhaps, there ended their days in confinement;—how many had there groaned beneath the cruelty of their oppressors, and had ultimately fallen by their hands? The dark deeds of ages seemed to arise to her imagination, and fancy clothed them in all the various garbs of horror which a fevered brain could impart to them, and she almost feared to look up, lest she should behold those ghastly forms which only existed in her own imagination.

And now the light was but just faintly glimmering in the socket, and in a minute or two longer it must have expired, when, to her astonishment and fear, she heard the key turning in the lock, after which the bolts were withdrawn, the door flew back on its hinges, and Ruthven stood before her.

He carried a light in his hand, which he held above his head when he entered the dungeon, to accelerate his view, and after standing for a minute or two, and contemplating our heroine with a look of apparent satisfaction and exultation, he walked closer to her, and placed the lamp upon the table.

Wound up to a pitch of the most overwhelming distraction, and imagining that Ruthven had come to perpetrate the horrible crime for which purpose it appeared she had been brought there, Angelina started from the mattress, and throwing herself at the villain's feet, with clasped hands and supplicating looks, she implored his mercy.

"Why, what are you making all this fuss about?" demanded the man, in a cold and unfeeling tone;—"what have you got to be alarmed at? If the knife was at your throat you could not do more. You do not seem to fancy your new place of confinement, then?"

The violence of Angelina's emotions prevented her from returning any answer to this brutal speech, and the ruffian continued—

"There, there, no more of this squeamishness; I thought I could soon find a way to cure you of your obstinacy; get up and follow me."

"Oh! whither would you take me?" ejaculated our heroine, as a terrible presentiment crossed her mind that he was about to commit the shocking deed with the perpetration of which he had probably been entrusted. "Tell me, I implore you: and oh! take pity on my sufferings—take pity on one who never injured you or he by whom you are employed!"

"There, I want no whining," said Ruthven, pointing towards the door of the dungeon;— "obey me, or I must use force."

"But, surely, cruel as you are, you will not leave the unfortunate woman in the next dungeon to die, if she is not dead already?" ejaculated Angelina, with increased vehemence, and, at the same time, thinking by that means to be able to elicit who the prisoner was, and for what purpose she was confined.

"Ah!" cried Ruthven, as a strange and indescribable expression passed over his savage features, "you have heard *her*, then? 'Tis well: you shall also have the pleasure of beholding her, and you will then see what those may expect who accede not to the wishes, or oppose the will of the Baron de Morton or his confidant. This way, girl!"

Wondering how all this would terminate, trembling with apprehension, and yet anxious to have her curiosity gratified, Angelina did as the ruffian commanded her; and Ruthven led the way from the dungeon, through a short narrow passage, until they came to an iron door, to the lock of which Ruthven applied a key, and after some difficulty the door was opened, and revealed a dungeon similar to the one they had just quitted, only it was larger, and if possible, more wretched. The place was involved in utter darkness when Ruthven opened the door; and our heroine terrified at the sight, started back a few paces, until Ruthven scowled upon her; when, with trembling steps, she entered the place, and stared aghast at the appalling spectacle which met her view. At first, the rays emitted by the lamp were so faint that she was unable to distinguish anything but a black void; but at length she was horror-struck at beholding, in one corner of the dungeon, crouched up on some straw, a form, which was so squalid and emaciated, that she could not at first imagine it was anything human. It was chained to the wall, and in a sitting posture, with the arms resting upon its knees, and its head reclining on its hands, apparently in a state of insensibility, while its dishevelled hair, which was very long, completely concealed its features from observation; by its side stood a stone pitcher, and there was not a single article of furniture in the loathsome cell.

Angelina's feelings were harrowed up to complete horror at the sight of this revolting and pitiable object. It was a woman, and it was evident that from her had proceeded those cries which had so much alarmed her. She never offered to move or alter her position in the least when they entered, and seemed to be either dead, or unconscious of all around her.

"Good God," cried Angelina, "the work of cruelty is accomplished—the unfortunate being is no more."

Ruthven watched the countenance of our heroine narrowly; and when he saw the emotion she evinced, a savage grin of gratified revenge and brutal exultation, passed over his features; and, at last, pointing to the miserable wretch, who still remained inanimate, he said—

"Behold! this is one who is justly punished for daring to betray the trust reposed in her; and who, by her treachery, thwarted the schemes of those it was her duty to obey; but you have not gazed upon her features. Probably that may gratify you, especially if you should happen to recognise those of one whom you knew."

The ruffian, as he spoke, advanced to the unfortunate woman, and shaking her violently, exclaimed—

"Come, come, no more of this nonsense, but look up, and pay a proper respect to your visiter. Arouse yourself, I say."

The woman, at first, did not offer to move, and Angelina then began to think that the conjecture she had formed of her being dead, was correct; but at length the ruffian shaking her more fiercely than before, she slowly lifted up her head, and fixing her eyes upon Ruthven, she uttered a terrific scream, and falling at his feet, in hollow and piteous accents, cried—

"Mercy, mercy, Ruthven: has not your vengeance yet been satisfied, but that you must keep me in this state of lingering torment? For the love of Christ, end at once my sufferings and stab me to the heart."

"Good God!" exclaimed the horror-struck Angelina; "that voice—those tones so familiar to mine ears; where, oh, where have I heard them before?"

"Come forward and satisfy yourself," said the wretch Ruthven, with a sardonic grin; and as he pulled our heroine towards him, he held the light close to the features of the unfortunate victim of his cruelty.

"Bridget! oh, horror! horror!" gasped forth Angelina, as she recognised that ill-fated woman, and overcome with the horror of her feelings, she uttered a loud shriek, and sinking on the earth became unconscious of everything around her.

———

CHAPTER XXV.

WHEN Angelina regained her senses, the scene was so changed in which she found herself, that although the horrors she had lately experienced quickly came to her recollection, they only appeared to her as some terrific dream; in fact, they were too dreadful for her at first to dare to place any reliance upon their reality. She found herself reclining upon a sofa, in an elegant apartment, the furniture of which was very handsome, and everything was arranged with corresponding taste. It was morning, and the sun was darting his scorching beams in at the gothic casements, of which there were two; there was no person in the room, but it was evident, from the bottles and different things on the table, that her recovery had been attended to. She arose from the sofa, and passing her hand across her temples, endeavoured to recal to her memory what had happened to her, and how she had come thither; and soon all the horrors of the truth flashed upon her recollection, and she trembled with the violence of her emotion. With the most indescribable feelings of terror she reflected upon the dreadful spectacle which the wretched Bridget had presented; and the awful sufferings to which she was still subjected, unless death had mercifully released her from her agonies. Gracious Heaven! she ruminated, could it be possible that there could be such monsters in existence, as to take an apparent delight in practising such unparalled cruelties upon a fellow-creature; cruelties, which so closely resembled those which had been perpetrated with impunity in the feudal ages? Had they no fear of the retributive arm of justice overtaking them? And what could Bridget have done to bring down upon her head the vengeance of the baron and her ruffian husband? The next moment the whole truth of the circumstance rushed upon her mind, and added to the bitter anguish which filled her bosom; she remembered the words which Ruthven had made use of, viz., to the effect that Bridget was punished "for thwarting the schemes of those whom it was her duty to obey;" and she could not doubt but that for the part which she had taken in assisting her (Angelina) to escape from the tower, she had been doomed to the awful fate she was then, if living, enduring. The blood in her veins ran icy cold, when this idea occurred to her; and she groaned with agony to think that she should be the cause of bringing the kind-hearted Bridget to such a barbarous destiny, filled her bosom with the most unspeakable grief, and her sufferings were as grate as those of she for whom her commiseration was so powerfully excited.

In situations like that in which Angelina was now placed, and after the dreaful scene she had just witnessed, which convinced her to what a terrible extent the cruelty of her oppressors would lead them, there was nothing to alleviate her anguish, or to give the least cause for hope. There was no one at hand to help her, no one who could interpose between her and the singular and unaccountable vengeance of the Baron de Morton, and deep and immovable was her despair. Her doom appeared now to be inevitable, for had she not, in her previous incarceration in this awful place, been exposed to the most implacable revenge of the baron? and had she not escaped from the shocking fate to which he had condemned her only in the most miraculous way? and therefore it was not now to be supposed that he would lose taking the opportunity which was placed in his hands.

"Alas! my dearest friends," exclaimed the poor girl, "you will never again behold your unfortunate Angelina. Ere you will be able to interpose in her behalf, the fell assassin will will have done his cruel work, and she, in whom your fondest affections are placed, will have ceased to be. Not for myself do I so tremble (although it is hard for one so young to exchange the sunny spring of life, for the icy winter of death) but for the endless agony you will experience, should my dreadful fate ever reach your ears. Oh, God! grant me fortitude to support this awful trial, for much indeed do I now need Thine Omnipotent aid; and, if it is Thy will that I should perish by the hand of a murderer, by the hand of one whom I am unconscious of having offended, and whom my conscience acquits me entirely of injuring—grant thy protecting aid to those I shall leave behind me, and teach them to support the dreadful event with resignation."

She clasped her hands as she gave utterance to these ejaculations, and traversed the chamber with hasty and disordered steps, and the violence of her emotions for a while completely choked her utterance.

"Clifford, too!" she exclaimed, with frantic agony at length, and a deadly chill ran through her heart when she thought of his name; "alas! what is your fate!—What has become of you?—Have you fallen by the hands of the wretches?—Oh, Heaven! this thought is madness! Dear, dear youth, had it not been for me, you would have been spared this dreadful fate; but sorrow and suffering seem to be the lot of all who take any interest in my misfortunes, and endeavour to rescue me from heartless and unmerited cruelty. Oh, Clifford! never, in this world, shall we meet again, and cruel destiny, which forbade us to love each other, will thus be satisfied."

Once more did her tears flow more copiously than ever, but they were shed for Hugh Clifford, whose fate was so uncertain, and not for herself. She remembered all the tender asseverations he had given utterance to at their different interviews; the earnest and fervent vows of unutterable affection he had spoken, and the soft eloquence with which his tongue had spoken the language of love; his generous interposition when danger threatened her, and his agony, his intense agony, when told by her uncle and Kate of the Ruins, that they must love no more. There was not the most trifling circumstance connected with him and the ardent passion which they had imbibed for one another, which did not at that moment rush to her memory, and increased the bitter anguish of her soul.

But what was the fate of Hugh Clifford?— This was a question which racked her brain to madness, and which she had no means of satisfactorily answering. At first, she dreaded that he had fallen by the hands of the ruffians on the spot where her seizure had taken place: but when she remembered the words which Ruthven had spoken, and the orders he had given to the villains who had him in their charge, this idea was banished from her mind, although she had not the least doubt but that he was still held in confinement; and when she reflected upon the dreadful tortures to which his enemies would put him, the terrors of her situation became more unendurable, and she wrung her hands, and smote her breast, with the intensity of her anguish.

She now recollected the noise and confusion she had heard soon after she had been brought into the old Grey Tower, and a thought struck her that her lover was confined in the same terrible place. This imagination was too probable for her easily to reject it, and again

did he groan aloud with the horror excited by the idea of the suffering he would there, doubtless, be fated to endure. From this, her thoughts once more reverted to the unfortunate Bridget, and nothing could exceed the power of her anguish, when she recalled to her memory the appalling spectacle she presented, and that it was, without doubt, her interference to release her from the power of the Baron de Morton, which had brought down upon her the shocking punishment to which our heroine had been a witness she was suffering,

"Oh, horror!" gasped forth the hapless damsel, "she will perish!—She cannot long survive, subjected to such insupportable sufferings, and I shall ever accuse myself of being the cause of her untimely death!—Merciful Heaven! look down upon me with compassion, and, at any rate, release those from misery who are suffering for my sake."

Her tears again flowed, and sinking into a chair, she covered her face with her hands, and gave way to the unrestrained intensity of her grief.

She remained in this state without any interruption for about two hours, and by degrees she became more resigned to her fate. She took a more minute survey of the apartment she was in, and observing a door, discovered that it was unfastened, and opened upon another handsome chamber, in which was a bedstead, hung round with elegant furniture, and every other article in the room was of the same costly description as the one she had just quitted, and in spite of the state of her mind, she could not but look upon everything around her with the utmost admiration and satisfaction.

But what particularly attracted her notice, and fixed her attention, was the full-length portrait of a lady, which was suspended from the wainscot, and the eyes of which seemed to be fixed with a melancholy, yet affectionate expression upon our heroine's countenance. With an emotion, too powerful for utterance, Angelina fixed her eyes upon this portrait, and was unable for some time to remove them, for the countenance struck her immediately as being exactly like that of the mysterious form which she had several times seen in Saint Mark's Abbey, and which Kate of the Ruins had informed her was the spectre of her mother. Indeed, the likeness was so great, that she could almost have imagined that the phantom stood before her. There was something in the mild, expressive, and melancholy countenance of the portrait, traced with such skill by the pencil of the artist, that insensibly drew the affections of Angelina towards it; and as she gazed upon it, her bosom throbbed with a feeling she never remembered to have experienced before, and she could almost have knelt down and worshipped the senseless canvas.

The protrait represented a lady of tall and dignified form, elegantly dressed in white; and her features were beautiful and regular in the extreme, forming a contour of face which could not fail to captivate the most insensible heart the moment it was seen.

Completely overpowered by the indefinite feeling which took possession of her bosom, she fell upon her knees before it, and with up-raised hands, uttered a prayer to the spirit of her the portrait represented for protection and fortitude under the heavy trials by which she was now visited.

While she was still in this positition, the door of the outer room was opened, and a woman entered, whom she had not seen before, carrying a tray, which she placed on the table, and just casting a glance towards the chamber in which our heroine was, probably to ascertain whether or not she was safe, she retired again without uttering a word.

Our heroine returned to the outer room, but she turned with disgust from the wine and the other refreshments which the woman had brought, as the idea of poison entered her mind, and did not offer to touch them. She sat herself on the sofa, and endeavoured to calm her ruffled feelings, which having, after some time, partly succeeded in doing, she arose,

and standing upon a chair, was enabled to gaze from the window on to the scene beneath. She was now confined in a different wing of the tower, and it commanded a beautiful marine view, romantically diversified by little isles which shot out into the ocean. She beheld in the distance several vessels, proudly stemming the waves, and light skiffs ever and anon shot past the rock upon which the Grey Tower stood with the rapidity of an arrow. Oh, what would not the poor damsel have given to have been the inmate of one of these vessels! Alas! it was hard to gaze upon liberty without the means of enjoying its sweets, and with only the prospect of a terrible death before her eyes; and to know that she had done nothing to deserve so shocking a fate. Many were the sighs that escaped her over-charged bosom, and nothing could assuage the violence of her grief.

She was interrupted in her meditations by hearing a voice behind her repeat her name, and turning hastily round, her terror and surprise were excessive, when she discovered the Baron de Morton standing, and gazing upon her with such altered looks, that she could scarcely believe the evidence of her senses. Instead of the savage expressions of revenge with which she had expected he would meet her, she saw him gazing at her with mingled looks of admiration and delight, and his countenance, which was still handsome, was softened into an expression of kindness and gentleness which she had never imagined it was in his power to assume or experience. Surprised, incredulous, yet revived by hope, our heroine knelt at the baron's feet, and with the most supplicating looks, and a voice choked by sobs, implored his pity and forbearance.

De Morton seemed to gaze at her with the deepest interest, and for a few moments he made no reply; but at length, in a voice of softness, he ejaculated—

"Rise, fair maiden, and fear not; I will not harm you—no, sweetest, believe me, the sentiments I once entertained towards you, are now entirely changed, and if I have acted with apparent severity, it has only been occasioned by the ardour of the love I have imbibed for you, and the utter impossibility I felt of existing out of your presence. Nay, start not fair Angelina, nor turn that look of scorn and indifference upon me; believe me, I speak the pure sentiments of my soul, and upon you alone depends my happiness or misery. I love you, Angelina, ay, love you to madness and——"

"My lord," exclaimed the astonished maiden, turning from him with a look of the utmost indignation and aversion, "this from you, the only cause of all my misery and the sufferings of my friends; this from he who threatened and employed his myrmidon to attempt my life;—this from the man who has doomed that poor woman to a horrible and lingering death, merely because her humanity prompted her to assist me to escape from that confinement in which you unjustly then, and now, hold me?—This from the husband of the Baroness de Morton, from him who, but for the interference of Providence, would long ere now have plunged his poniard to my heart?—Away, and mock me not; disgust not mine ears with your revolting words!"

The baron stood for a minute or two, apparently astonished and bewildered at her words, and the resolution with which she gave utterance to them, and did not return any answer; at length, once more endeavouring to take her hand, and to press it to his lips, he ejaculated—

"I will admit that my conduct was harsh, that it was cruel, sweet damsel; but I was urged on to it by some accursed spell—I laboured under a strange, an unhappy delusion, and——"

The baron here again paused, and looking n the countenance of our heroine with greater intensity than before, added—

"And yet the likeness is so great, so powerful, that even now—— but, 'psha!—I am growing foolish again!—It cannot be. Pardon me, Angelina, for this digression;—you have accused me of behaving cruel to you, I admit it, and now would make you reparation, by the

most unbounded kindness and love. You have taxed me with undue severity towards she who, in disobedience to my orders, and the commands of her husband, assisted you to escape, when you was before confined here; I acknowledge it' but it is in your power to release her, and I promise you, faithfully promise you, that I will make her all the amends in my power, by the most unlimited kindness. You speak of the Baroness de Morton? True, she possesses my hand, but my heart is yours, and yours only! —You tell me I have sought your life?—I cannot tell what could cause me to do so, only the strange, the lamentable infatuation, which I have before mentioned. Thus do not, beauteous, all-captivating girl, suffer these painful circumstances to prejudice you against he who loves you to madness!—Here, on my knees behold me bow my adoration for your beauteous, your all-powerful person, and on this fair hand to seal——"

"Hold! sir," cried the indignant damsel, forcibly tearing her hand from the baron's grasp, while her cheeks turned alternately red and ghastly pale, "your words are as revolting to me as your person; away, and rather let me endure the horrors of the dungeon to which your myrmidon consigned me when he brought me hither."

The baron seemed abashed for a few moments at the boldness of the maiden's manner, and made no answer. He bit his lips, his brow became contracted, and it was very evident that he had a violent struggle to stifle those expressions of anger, which the impetuosity of his disposition excited.

At length, chasing all looks of displeasure from his countenance, he turned upon Angelina an expression of affection, and said:—

"Beauteous girl, let me beg of you to endeavour to vanquish this repugnance, which I own is only natural, after the pain I have unfortunately been the cause of inflicting upon you; let me entreat that you will cease to look upon me with the jaundiced eye of prejudice, and that you will view me only as one who loves you as ardently as ever man could love a woman, and who is ready to make any sacrifice to contribute to your happiness."

" Happiness !" repeated Angelina, with a look of scorn; " and think you the way to make me happy, is to clandestinely tear me from my friends, and leave them in a state of uncertainty as to my fate ?—To hold me in confinement in this horrible place, where every chamber seems to trace a crime of horror ?— To insult mine ears with the expression of your disgusting passion ? Leave me, sir ; your sight fills my bosom with horror and abhorrence."

" 'Tis well, young lady," observed the baron, in a voice of wrath; " you may, probably, repent this cold disdain. For the present, I will leave you ; but, remember, that you are now in my power, without any chance of being rescued, without the least prospect of any of your friends ascertaining where you are confined, and that if you persist in rejecting my suit, and not acceeding to my desires, force shall speedily make you !"

As he thus spoke, he turned upon our heroine a threatening look, and quitted the room.

Our heroine now felt, if anything, more wretched than before, for the passion of the baron she seemed to dread even more than his vengeance. But in the midst of her trouble she could not help reflecting with astonishment upon the change which had suddenly taken place in the baron's behaviour. What could have had the power to change his most deadly wrath to love, if the passion which he had avowed was deserving of that title ? This was a problem which she was quite at a loss to solve ; and after racking her brain for some time to no purpose, she gave up the attempt. Her heart revolted from the bare idea of the odious sentiments which De Morton had expressed, and when she reflected how securely she was in his power, she gave herself up for lost, and wrung her hands in despair. In fact, the last words the baron had given utterance to, convinced her that he was determined to gain his sinful desires by some means, and of his relenting she

had nothing to hope. Such a fate would be even more horrible than a violent death.

For more than an hour after the baron had quitted her, Angelina remained completely absorbed in the melancholy cogitations which the interview had given rise to, and did not offer to move from the seat in which she had placed herself prior to his departure from the room. Oh, how severe would be the misery, the agony of her friends, even greater than that which they now endured, did they but know the danger in which she was actually placed ! What, too, was the fate of her lover, the unfortunate Hugh Clifford ? Had he fallen by the hands of the ruffians, or had he been brought to the Tower and placed in confinement in these horrible dungeons, of which she had seen so dreadful a sample, in order that his tortures might be rendered still more exquisite ? The bare idea of this caused her more poignant agony than anything else ; for after what she had witnessed of the barbarous manner in which the wretched Bridget had been treated, she could not help thinking the Baron de Morton and his heartless creatures capable of any atrocity. With this thought, too, was recalled to her memory the appalling sufferings which Bridget was enduring through the assistance she had rendered her, and she could not but feel herself truly wretched. Yet a ray of hope darted across her mind, from what the baron had said, that she would be released from her confinement, and the miseries to which she had been subjected, if death had not already performed that task. He surely would no longer keep the unfortunate woman in that dreadful state of incarceration, after what she had said to him.—No, he could not expect to make any other impression on her (Angelina's) mind, but the most inexpressible horror, by such conduct ; and yet his chief object now, apparently, was to make an impression upon her heart, notwithstanding that the very idea of such a thing was preposterous. Oh, no, Bridget would be liberated, and by proper care and attention she might be restored to the same state of health and strength she enjoyed previous to the cruelties that had been lately inflicted upon her.

As this thought gained firmer possession of her mind, Angelina became more composed, and resolved to encounter any danger with becoming fortitude, and to lose her life rather than yield to the importunities of her persecutor.

At this moment her eyes rested upon the portrait, which had already so deeply interested her, and she could almost imagine that it smiled

CLIFFORD AND ANGELINA ASSAILED BY RUTHVEN AND OTHERS.

upon her and appeared to encourage her to hope. So completely infatuated was she by this imagination, that it was several minutes before she could remove her gaze from the portrait, but while she looked, a strange feeling came over her, and she felt tranquillised and resigned to her fate, whatever it might be.

That day passed away without anything particular occurring to our heroine. The old woman who had brought her refreshments in the morning, came once or twice into the room; but although Angelina put several questions to her, she maintained the most obstinate silence, and did not remain in the room any longer than was absolutely necessary.

As night approached, the fears of our heroine increased, and the thought of being left alone, and at the mercy of the Baron de Morton, made her tremble with apprehension for the consequences. Hitherto all had remained perfectly quiet in the tower, and she had been in hopes that the baron had quitted it, and would not return for the present; but she was soon convinced that this idea was erroneous, by hearing De Morton calling loudly to one of his domestics in the gallery. She trembled when she heard his voice, and listened with breathless anxiety, fearful that he might be coming to her apartments; but the sound of his receding footsteps soon convinced her that her terrors were for the present, at any rate, unfounded, and she endeavoured to become more composed.

Darkness at length fell upon the earth, and all was again silent in the Old Grey Tower; but Angelina could hear the dashing of the waves as they rolled against the rock on which the ancient building stood. It was a melancholy sound, and accorded with the feelings that at present occupied her mind. She looked forth from the casement on to the ocean beyond; it was but faintly illumined by the moon, which was partially hidden behind a cloud. At a short distance, however, she could discover the shadows of several vessels that were lying at anchor; and sometimes she would observe a boat skim lightly over the surface of the deep, but they could not approach near enough to the rock for her to make the persons who were in them hear her; and had it been in her power, it would, in all probability, have been unavailing, as they might neither have the power nor the will to render her any assistance.

She was aroused from the contemplation of these objects by hearing the bolts of the front room-door withdrawn, and filled with the utmost horror, as the idea of the Baron de Morton occurred to her, she remained standing upon the chair (which she had been forced to do to enable her to reach the casement) completely petrified, and incapable of moving.

Her alarm was, however, in some measure dispersed when the door opened, and the old woman entered. She seemed to be rather surprised at the situation in which she beheld our heroine; but Angelina having quickly recovered herself when she saw who the intruder was, stepped from the chair, and awaited to hear what the woman's business might be with her.

Having placed a fresh-trimmed lamp upon the table, and some supper, which she had brought in with her on a tray, she seated herself in the chimney-corner, and, making a sign to our heroine to come forward, she commenced without any further ceremony to eat heartily, and seemed resolved to make herself quite at home.

"You had better get your supper at once, young woman," she said, "and let us retire to rest, for it's quite late enough."

"Are you, then, going to sleep with me, my good woman?" inquired Angelina.

"Yes, I am going to sleep in the same room with you, if you have no objection," replied the woman. "The baron thought you might be dull in such a place by yourself, and so he very considerately ordered me to become your companion."

Angelina thought that if she rendered herself no more agreeable than she had hitherto done, or maintained the same taciturnity, she would make but a sorry companion; still, however, her presence afforded her some satisfaction, as it seemed to be a guarantee for her not being intruded upon by the Baron de Morton. She put several more questions to the woman, but she refused to answer them; and finding it was, therefore, a fruitless task to endeavour to elicit anything from her, she gave up the attempt; and, after parting slightly of the repast, she prepared to retire to rest.

The old woman, having wrapped herself in a huge cloak which she had brought with her, stretched her limbs upon the sofa, and was soon fast asleep; but not so Angelina—busy reflection long kept the drowsy god from her pillow; but at length, fatigued and careworn, sleep did come to her relief, and she found a temporary forgetfulness of her sorrows.

Angelina slept calmly until a late hour in the morning; and on opening her eyes, she found that the old woman was already up, and was preparing the breakfast. She mentally offered up a prayer of gratitude to Heaven for preserving her through the night, and she arose and dressed herself. The old woman seemed to be in rather a better disposition than she had been the night before, and began to be somewhat more garrulous. Angelina perceiving this, ventured to inquire of her whether Bridget was yet alive, and if she were still confined in the horrible dungeon underneath the tower.

"She is alive, and doubtless will be very soon restored to health," observed the old woman. "Yesterday morning the baron ordered her to be removed from the place where she was confined; and she has now proper attendance, and will continue to receive it until she has recovered."

"Thank Heaven!" ejaculated our heroine, fervently.

"To be sure, she has been very severely punished," said the woman; "but, upon the whole, and taking every thing into consideration, it is no more than she richly deserved; for what business had she to assist you to escape from the custody of her master?"

"And what authority had her master, either then or now, to hold me in custody?" demanded the indignant Angelina. "Why should he persist in exercising such unparalleled cruelty towards one who is almost an entire stranger to him?"

"As for the matter of that, I know nothing about," returned the woman; "and it is not my place to question the conduct of my master. I dare say he has some authority for doing what he has done; but if he has not, it is no business of mine."

Angelina could not help turning away from the unfeeling old woman with disgust; but, at length, deeming it more prudent to disguise her real thoughts, she inquired in what manner it was discovered that she had assisted her to escape from the Tower.

"Why there could not be any mistake in that," said the woman; "for had she not exchanged dresses with you, and remained behind in the apartments wherein you had been confined? Besides, the foolish woman, as though she were anxious to be discovered, had partaken of something out of a bottle, in which there was an opiate which she was aware of, and that steeped her senses, so that she fell into a deep sleep, and in that state she was found by Ruthven, who entered the chamber at midnight."

"Ah! for what purpose?" gasped forth Angelina, as a terrible idea of the truth darted across her imagination.

"No matter," answered the old woman, with some confusion; "she had to pay dear for her treachery—her husband stabbed her in a mistake——"

"In a mistake for me!" added our heroine, hastily. "Wretches, murderers, well do I now perceive what were their blood-thirsty designs, but which were so singularly frustrated. Alas! poor Bridget, what have you suffered to serve me!"

"Ruthven was at first terribly alarmed when he discovered what he had done," said the old woman, after a pause; "but the wound was not a dangerous one, and she soon recovered. When she had got well, she was most severely reproached by my lord and her husband, for the treacherous part she had acted; and, as a further punishment for the offence of which she had been guilty, she was confined in the dungeon, as you observed her, and, in my opinion, very justly too,"

"The villains!" exclaimed the horror-struck Angelina, when the woman concluded; and she could not help feeling the utmost abhorrence of one who could make use of such brutal observations as she had done, and was ashamed to think that they should emanate from one of her own sex.

"It's fortunate for you, young woman," said the woman, "that neither the baron, my master, or Ruthven, are present to hear the titles you bestow upon them. But, for my part, I consider that if I had been guilty of what she was, I should have merited the most severe punishment that could have been inflicted upon me. However, I must not remain here any longer—I have other business to attend to."

With these words the old woman quitted the room, and our heroine was left to the indulgence of her own reflections. Deeply did she lament the sufferings which the unfortunate Bridget had undergone for her sake; but unboundedly grateful she was that she had at last been liberated; and she earnestly hoped that she might speedily recover from the effects of the brutal treatment she had received, and be permitted again to see her.

This day passed away without anything taking place to call for any particular notice here; the baron did not visit her, and the night went over in much the same manner as the preceding one had done. On the third morning, however, after the old woman had left the room, the door was unfastened, and De Morton entered, and advanced with a look of eagerness and admiration towards Angelina.

The damsel felt a strange tremour seize her when he entered, but with a powerful effort she quickly recovered herself, and prepared to meet him with firmness and decision.

"Beauteous Angelina!" said the baron, in insinuating accents, "I hope that at our last interview I did not say anything that ought to have excited your displeasure; but if I did, I

pray you to attribute it to the impetuosity of my love, which hurries me on, and gives me no time to think. Should I have been so unfortunate, sweet maiden, most readily will I make you all the reparation in my power. Nay, do not frown, that brow was never formed for anything but smiles, and anger ne'er should choose it for a resting place. Again I come to offer you the homage of a heart, which, while the current of life circulates within my veins, must throb alone for you."

As he spoke, he bent one knee to the floor, and attempted to take the hand of our heroine, but she withdrew it with an expression of disgust and abhorrence, and in a voice of indignation, replied—

"Villain! is it thus you insult and wound the feelings of one whom you have already racked to torture?"

"Ah, maiden," said the baron, a flush of anger suffusing his cheeks, and his brow becoming slightly contracted, "you turn from me with scorn, and look upon me with hatred. What can I do to win but a smile from your sweet lips—to elicit one word of kindness? To gain your affections, there is no sacrifice that I would consider too great; then avert not your head in wrath, but say you pardon me for the step to which I have been driven only by love, and that you will listen to the vows of one who will abandon everything else for you."

It would be impossible to describe the emotion of Angelina during this speech. Her bosom swelled alternately with feelings of indignation, shame, and insulted virtue; and speech was almost denied her, until the baron once more attempted to take her hand; when, in tones of firmness and dignity, she ejaculated—

"Away, my lord—your language is a disgrace to your sex, and should call the blush of shame upon your cheeks!—Away, and no longer contaminate mine ears with the expression of sentiments which can only excite my disgust and hatred. Think you, because the humble Angelina is poor, that she is to be won to your base purposes?—Think you that you will triumph in your guilt with impunity? —No—be sure that justice will yet overtake you, and that you will be punished for the several outrages you have committed against a defenceless girl, who never gave you cause for enmity."

" I can submit to your reproaches, fair Angelina," returned the baron, stifling his passion as much as possible, " for I know that I deserve them. But I would make reparation, and——"

" If you would do that," interrupted our heroine, " restore me instantly to liberty—to my friends, from whom you have so unjustly torn me, and make all the atonement you can, by expressing your sorrow for the many hours of anguish you have caused both me and mine, and promise never to molest me again. Do this, and I will readily enter into a covenant to forgive and forget what has past."

The baron paused, and seemed at loss for some time what answer to make, and he was greatly abashed by the firmness and decision of her manner, but, at length, turning to her with an attempt to smile insinuatingly, he said—

" Suffer you to leave me, beauteous Angelina?—oh, never! never!—that cannot, must not be.—By Heaven I could not exist out of your presence; and to think you were likely to become the bride of another, would drive me to madness. Banish the mistaken sense of delicacy which now prompts your refusal to accede to my wishes, and live alone for love, and for one who will think nothing too dear to contribute to your happiness. Here you shall reign the mistress of my affections, and command whatever you desire; but liberty— that, repugnant as it is to my feelings, I must deny you; but I will provide for you such pleasures, such enjoyments, as will leave you nothing to regret."

" Base, heartless, unfeeling man," cried Angelina, in tones of anguish, " thus to tamper with the feelings of an unprotected female, and

to seek by shameless and disgusting sophistry, to win her to your infamous purposes. Were not the sufferings you before put me to, the hours of misery and anguish you have caused my friends, sufficient, but that you must add to it by again unjustly tearing me away from my home, and insulting my ears with the expression of your odious passion? Dare you to talk to me of love, and think upon her whom you swore at the altar to love and reverence? Why am I selected as a victim of your persecution and cruelty? Away—leave me; and if I must remain in confinement, let me not be tormented by your hated presence."

" 'Tis well, young lady," returned the baron, unable longer to suppress his wrath. " I know from whence springs this scorn, this hatred. Hugh Clifford, the smuggler, possesses those affections I aspire to. The lawless captain of a band of ruffians, has succeeded in gaining the heart of the gentle, the virtuous Angelina! Surely, every one must admire her choice."

At the mention of the name of her lover, deep blushes suffused the cheeks of our heroine, and when the uncertainty of his fate rushed upon her memory, a pang shot through her heart, which chilled the purple current that circulated in her veins, and she trembled violently, and was altogether so deeply, so powerfully affected, that for a few moments she could not give utterance to her feelings, until she was relieved by a copious flood of tears. Suddenly, however, she conquered her emotions, and assuming an air of dignity and fortitude which astonished and bewildered the baron, she fixed upon him a look of the most ineffable contempt, as she said—

" Hugh Clifford, the smuggler-captain, possesses virtues and noble qualities, the nature of the proud Baron de Morton has ever been a stranger to. He is good—he is generous— the ever-ready defender of the female sex, and one who would despise himself, could he by word or deed wound their feelings, or cause them a moment's unhappiness. The Baron de Morton would do well to follow the example set him by the lawless captain of a band of ruffians !"

The baron bit his lips, scowled fearfully, and folding his arms across his breast, paced the apartment to and fro, in a state of great excitement. At length, as a smile of secret exultation dwelt upon his features, he turned to Angelina, and in a tone of irony, observed—

"But yet this noble, this brave, this generous smuggler-captain, this robber, who is to set examples of virtue and integrity to his fellow-creatures, could not save himself from the power of his enemy !"

"My God !" ejaculated the alarmed damsel, "are then my worst surmises verified, and is the unfortunate Clifford, if he still lives, the prisoner of——"

"He who sues your affections," added De Morton, with a look of triumph, "but one word from you can restore him to liberty. Say that you will consent to reign the mistress of——"

"Hold, villain !" interrupted Angelina, "pollute not mine ears with a repetition of that with which you have already disgusted me. The Almighty will protect him from your malevolence, and I know he would sooner suffer all the horrors which your inhuman nature could invent, than he would purchase his liberty at the sacrifice of the virtue and happiness of her, upon whom his every thought, his every wish, his whole soul his fixed."

"And of what will avail his obstinacy or yours ?" said the baron; "are you not securely in my power; and could I not obtain that by force, which now I deign to sue for? Were it not my wish to win your love, and to prove to you the admiration and regard you have excited in my breast, I could this moment bask in those enjoyments I have taken so much trouble to obtain."

Angelina wrung her hands in despair, and gave utterance to a groan of intense agony.

"Come, come, lovely maiden," said the baron, in a milder tone, "you see the folly, the uselessness of remaining obstinate, and opposing me; banish all anger from your breast, endeavour to smile upon the vows of one who loves you to distraction, and the gates of liberty shall instantly be unbarred to Hugh Clifford."

"Never! never !" cried Angelina, energetically.

"Then your lover dies upon a scaffold !" answered the baron.

The maiden fixed upon him a look of contempt.

"Nay, proud beauty," continued De Morton, "you affect to treat my threats with scorn, but you may too soon, nevertheless, find them true. A price is set upon the life of Hugh Clifford, for crimes which render him amenable to the severest penalty, and to that fate it is in my power this minute to consign him."

A feeling of the most inexpressible horror fell upon the heart of Angelina, when the baron gave utterance to these words; her face became ghastly pale, her limbs trembled, and had she not dropped into a chair which was close by, she must have fallen to the floor. But in a very short time she recovered, so are as to be able to turn upon the baron a look which seemed as if it would penetrate to his soul, and then in a solemn voice ejaculated—

"Baron de Morton, you cannot speak the truth. Hugh Clifford cannot ever have been guilty of crimes that would render him liable to the punishment of death. It is only done to harrow up my feelings, and to exact from me a promise which virtue and every law, human and divine, forbids. But, surely, were it even true, cruel as you are, you could never be guilty of so barbarous a deed ?"

"I repeat that I have spoken the truth," said De Morton; "but," he added, in a softened tone, "why will you, sweet maiden, by your scorn and obstinacy, force me to behave in a manner from which my nature revolts? Why will you not endeavour to banish from your bosom the hatred and resentment you bear towards me, and make me your devoted slave, studious to promote your happiness, and anxious to banish from your memory all recollection of the past? Nay, do not frown so disdainfully upon me, but let this kiss end at once all ill feeling, and be the prelude to future joys."

As the baron spoke, he threw his arms around the waist of Angelina, and was about to put his words into execution, when, at that moment, he was arrested in his purpose by a sound resembling a deep sigh, or a hollow gust of wind, which seemed to proceed from the adjoining apartment, the door of which was standing wide open. The baron released our heroine, who trembled with terror, and looking towards the spot from whence the sound appeared to issue, his eyes became fixed on the portrait which had so particularly engaged the attention of Angelina, and which, at that moment, appeared, to his terrified imagination, to move, and the bosom to heave. His face became ghastly pale in an instant, his lips quivered, and, turning away from the contemplation of the portrait, with a shudder of horror, he said, as he hastily quitted the room,—

"I will see you again—anon, Angelina; for the present, farewell, and remember my words!"

As he spoke, he cast one more glance of terror towards the portrait, and left the apartment, while Angelina stood for a few minutes in a state of complete stupefaction, and could neither move nor utter the least exclamation.

When she did somewhat recover, the horror of her feelings was indiscribable. The determined persecution of the baron—the insults by which her ears had been contaminated—the confinement of Hugh Clifford, and the danger in which the baron had asserted he was placed —"a price set upon his life"—all—all rushed upon her memory at once, and nearly overwhelmed her; but, at length, sinking upon a chair, she found some relief in a torrent of tears.

When she could bring her mind to reflect more calmly and dispassionately upon her situation, she endeavoured to find out some means by which she could indulge in the hope of escaping from the power of the villain who detained her—but alas! there was none, unless it was in the liberation from confinement of Hugh Clifford; but the improbability of that was too deeply impressed upon her mind for her to give it any encouragement; for it was not likely that the baron would ever release him (although he had promised to do so, if she would accede to his wishes), as he would, of course, feel certain that Clifford would immediately avail himself of such an opportunity to make her situation known to her friends, and to adopt some scheme to enforce her release from incarceration.

When she thought of this, and imagined to herself what must now be the sufferings of Clifford, to know that she was in the power of the baron, her bitterest foe, and he without the means to render her any assistance, she wrung her hands, and paced the room with uneven steps, in a state of the greatest agony and despair.

She was interrupted in the midst of her grief by the entrance of the old woman, who brought with her the morning's repast, and having set it upon the table, turned to Angelina, and, in a tone of curiosity, said,—

"For goodness sake, young woman, what have you been saying to the baron, to put him into such a violent state of agitation? He has just left the Tower, accompanied by Ruthven, and he looked so pale, and he trembled so; lackaday! I could not help looking at him with wonder. Whatever can have been the matter?"

"The power of his own conscience has worked its terrors upon him," replied Angelina. "The guilty are sure to meet with an earthly punishment, in some way or the other."

"You talk very boldly, methinks, young woman," answered the old beldame, "but it is well the baron does not hear you. Conscience, indeed! But let me advise you not to remain obstinately blind to your own interest; if you readily assent to the baron's wishes, I know that he will make it his constant study to contribute to your happiness and enjoyment; but if, on the other hand, you incense him, you must take the consequences."

Angelina was so thoroughly disgusted with the coarse and revolting manners of the old woman, and the observations she made use of, that she averted her looks, and did not return her any answer; but, at length, thinking it would be much more politic to endeavour to make a friend of her than an enemy (if it were possible to excite friendship in such a flinty bosom), she made some observation of a conciliatory description, which seemed to have the effect desired. She inquired after Bridget.

"Oh, she is getting on very well," answered the old woman. "She will, no doubt, soon recover from the effects of the just punishment she has received."

"Pray God she may," ejaculated Angelina, with fervour.

"Ah, well, for my part," remarked the woman, "I do not see that she deserves the least pity; and I only hope that what she has suffered will bring her to her senses, and that she may henceforward know her duty better to her husband and her master."

Angelina made no reply to the observations of old Deborah (for such was the name of the woman), but, of course, she could not help feeling the utmost disgust at the inhumanity which she evinced.

"Take it altogether," continued the old woman, "I think she has been treated very leniently by those whom she has so grossly offended; and, after all, she may thank the clemency of the baron for pardoning her. However, it is no use talking about this matter—it is all over now, and Bridget will soon get over it, no doubt, though I do not think she will ever be on very good terms with her husband again."

"Friends with a miscreant!—a wretch like that!" exclaimed our heroine, with a shudder of disgust.

"Again I warn you, young lady," said Deborah, "to be a little more circumspect in your language, especially towards Rufus, for I would not stand in the situation of those who offend him for all the world. Even my lord, the baron, fears him."

"And why should he fear one who is his menial?" hastily inquired Angelina.

The old woman seemed confused, and at a loss what reply to make; but, at last, she said,—

"I do not mean to say that the baron lives in fear of Rufus, but that he would care not to—— But, pshaw! how I talk! What business is it of mine or yours? Only I would seriously advise you to alter your behaviour towards the baron as soon as possible, and you will find it to your advantage."

"But do you think they will suffer me to see Bridget again?" inquired our heroine, in an anxious tone.

"Why, as she will not have it in her power to aid you in any design which you might have to escape, and, probably, if she had, would not be inclined to run any risk, after the sufferings she has undergone, I do not see that my lord will have any objection—that is, if you do not continue obstinate in rejecting the suit of the baron."

"If, then, the only terms upon which I can hope to see her are by encouraging the base vows of one who is odious to me," said our heroine, "there is no hope."

"Well, miss, you know best," said old Deborah; "but I can only say that you are very silly, and that there are many females, in a far better station than yourself, and who could boast of more attractions, who would jump at the chance you have got. A poor peasant's niece, indeed, presuming to resist the offers of a nobleman! Well, to a certainty, the world has come to a very pretty pass, indeed."

"Old woman," exclaimed Angelina, solemnly, and unable any longer to restrain the expression of her disgust and indignation,— "old woman, tottering, as you are, on the verge of the grave, your hair silvered by age, are you not ashamed to talk thus, and to become the panderer to the vices of a villain, whom it would be wrong to call a man? Is your mind callous to all sense of feeling, to all sense of virtue and integrity?"

"Virtue!—integrity!" reiterated the old woman, fiercely, and looking spitefully upon

DEBORAH ADVISES ANGELINA TO YIELD TO THE BARON'S WISHES.

our heroine, " hoity, toity, and have I lived to all these years to be taken to task by a mere girl? Virtue, indeed! I tell you what it is; I have lived three-score years and ten in the world, and I never suffered a man so much as to press my lips."

If old Deborah had said that she had lived the number of years in the world which she had mentioned, and that not a man had ever deigned to look at her with any other feelings than those of disgust and detestation, she would have been nearer the truth. For she had never been remarkable for her beauty, or the sweetness of her disposition—unless a small pug nose, little piggish eyes, red blowsy cheeks, and a very large mouth, might be considered fascinating; and a sour, crabbed, envious, spiteful, and waspish temper might be thought amiable traits in a person's character.

Angelina, however, made no farther observation to her, but walked into the adjoining room, leaving the old woman muttering and grumbling to herself, at the same time that she was plying her needle.

Our heroine soon became abstracted from everything else in ruminating upon her present situation, and the words and importunities of the baron, which he seemed determined to follow up in the most indefatigable and resolute manner; and how to escape the dreadful fate impending over her she knew not. There was no one near to relieve her mind, or to impart to her bosom any hope or consolation. Then the idea of her lover, Hugh Clifford, being confined in the gloomy precincts of a dungeon, and left to the mercy of one who had every reason to him, recurred to her memory, and caused a sensation in her bosom which was almost insupportable; and then to know that his restoration to liberty was nearly hopeless, and the uncertainty of whether or not the baron had told the truth when he said that he was accused of crimes which rendered his life forfeited to the offended laws of his country caused more horror and agony in her breast than anything else. She was confident that Hugh Clifford's disposition rendered him incapable of being guilty of any crime for which he might merit such a punishment; but then she was aware that the nature of the life he led must make him numerous enemies, and that there were many who would not hesitate to trump up any charges against him, which might be the means of putting an end to his career.

Hugh Clifford had long been an eye-sore to the government, and the success which had invariably attended him made them anxious to get him and his comrades in their power; but hitherto all their endeavours to effect that object had signally failed, and it was, therefore, not at all unlikely that they would resort to any means which might ultimately place in their hands, and at their disposal, the much dreaded smuggler captain.

"Oh, that he would abandon the dangerous calling," said Angelina, "would to Heaven that he had never taken to it. Alas! what untoward circumstances could ever have driven him to such a hazardous and disreputable course of life? Had it not been for that, how happy might we both now have been, joined together in——"

She suddenly checked herself and added—

"Alas! no—that could not have been; our union is forbidden, and fate seems to have conspired against us, and to have ordained that we shall be for ever wretched."

Her eyes now accidentally fell upon the portrait, and in a moment the strange circumstance which had been the means of saving her from the insult which the Baron de Morton had offered her, rushed upon her recollection, and gave rise to a new train of reflections. Could the sounds both she and the baron imagined they had heard, be real, or mere phantasy? It might have been the wind, but yet the sound was so distinct, so hollow, and so impressive, that she felt unable to arrive at such a conclusion. She remained for several minutes with her eyes intently fixed upon the portrait, and as she did so, they filled with tears, and she felt a sensation dart through her bosom, and throb around her heart, she was at a loss to account for, but would not have banished it from her mind on any account.

The harsh and disagreeable voice of old Deborah calling her to dinner, broke in upon these melancholy meditations, and she re-entered the sitting-room.

To judge by the looks of the old harridan, which were a shade or two more unpleasant than usual, it would appear that she had not forgotten the remarks our heroine had made to her, and she determined to show all the spleen she could towards her. But Angelina was quite indifferent to her behaviour, and, in fact, took no notice of it; but thinking it was the best plan, she resumed the silence which she had at first assumed towards her.

Deborah never left the apartments the whole of that day, but that circumstance did not annoy Angelina, as she was too fully occupied with her own thoughts to take any notice of her.

That day and the next passed away, and the baron did not come near her, while Deborah remained constantly with her. Once Rufus looked in, but he did not remain many minutes; and after giving some instructions to the woman to be careful of her charge, he retired.

On the third morning, Rufus again made his appearance, and looking sternly upon Angelina, bade her follow him, at the same time pointing to the door. The maiden felt an irresistable sensation of horror creep through her veins whenever her eyes encountered this ruffian; and, wondering what could be the cause of his present behaviour, and what his intentions, she hesitated, and did not offer to do as he commanded her.

" Did you not hear me, young lady ?" said the wretch, scowling, " or are you disposed to treat my orders with disdain ?—Attend me, I repeat. As for you, old Mother Deborah, you can take your place among the other servants in the hall—your services are dispensed with for the present."

" Where would you take me, and what is your purpose ?" demanded the alarmed damsel.

" Bah !" coarsely exclaimed Rufus. " Why am I to be pestered with questions ? You have no occasion to fear; I do not intend any harm now."

Old Deborah had made her exit the instant she received the orders of Rufus; and Angelina, knowing it would be useless to offer to oppose his will, and committing herself to the protection of Providence,

followed the way which the ruffian conducted her.

He led her along the gallery, and across a corridor, until they arrived at another wing of the tower, and in a second gallery of less extent than that they had previously traversed, he stopped at a large oaken door, which he unlocked, and motioning Angelina to follow, he entered, and our heroine obeying him; found herself in a suite of apartments similar to the one she had just quitted, only they were hung round with tapestry of a dark purple, which gave them a sombre aspect, yet they were furnished in the same style of elegance, and they appeared to have been fitted up for her reception.

" It is the will of the Baron de Morton," observed Rufus, " that these should henceforth be your apartments, and doubtless you will not be worse pleased with them than those you have just quitted."

Before Angelina could make any reply, and the instant Rufus had finished these observations, a faint scream was heard from an adjoining apartment, the door in a moment was thrown back on its hinges, and a fragile form rushed in, as well as its strength would permit, to Angelina, and threw herself in her arms. It was Bridget, the faithful, the affectionate Bridget, who had risked and endured so much to serve Angelina, who at the time was comparatively a stranger,

The power of the most able pen must fail in attempting to do justice to the scene which followed this sudden and unexpected meeting. Neither Angelina nor Bridget could give utterance to their feelings any otherwise than by convulsive sobs, but they embraced each other with the fervent affection of sisters. Rufus, however, did not suffer this to continue long, and seemed to view it with feelings of the utmost impatience. Taking hold of the arm of his wife, he tore her rudely away from Angelina, and with a frown said—

" Remember what I have told you, and obey. Although unseen, I shall be constantly watching your behaviour, and will act as it dictates. You have experienced the consequences of disobedience to my will, so beware!"

Having thus spoke, Rufus quitted the room, and securing the door after him, Angelina and Bridget heard his heavy footfalls as he traversed the gallery.

For some minutes Angelina and Bridget embraced each other with the same fervour as if they were sisters; and their emotions at once more meeting after so long a separation, and under such circumstances, rendered them for some time unable to utter a word. At length tears gave relief to their bosoms, and they both gave unrestrained indulgence to their grief.

"Bridget, dear Bridget!" ejaculated our heroine, when she had become a little more composed, "oh, how glad am I to see you again, that I may have the opportunity of expressing the regard I feel for you, and my earnest regret at the horrible sufferings you have endured for my sake. Never shall I be able to repay the debt of gratitude I owe you."

"It is already repaid, Miss," returned Bridget, in a tone of sincerity—"it is already repaid, in the consciousness I have of having performed a virtuous action, and saved the life of a fellow-creature. As for my sufferings, dreadful, indeed, as they were, they are over now; and since we are permitted to meet again, and to be together, I will endeavour to forget them, or to remember them only with feelings of anything else but anguish."

"And are you, indeed, to be my companion, dear Bridget?" inquired Angelina, eagerly; "shall we be allowed to share the same apartments, and my sight no longer be offended, or mine ears disgusted, with that hateful old woman, Deborah?"

"Yes, Miss," replied the faithful Bridget, "the baron has told me that I am in future to be with you constantly, on condition that I never mention the past, and that I endeavour

all that is in my power to persuade you to receive his advances without abhorrence.— But his lordship must have thought very meanly of me, to have imagined that I could be capable of doing as he wished, and rather would I incur all that his utmost vengeance could inflict, and which, as I have experienced, he knows how to exercise with such severity, that I would even attempt to act in a manner so repugnant to my feelings."

"I know you would, my good, kind, affectionate Bridget," ejaculated Angelina, once more embracing her companion with the utmost ardour and sincerity. "Henceforth we are sisters, and nothing can ever estrange from my bosom the feelings of love and gratitude which I feel towards you. But what think you of the Baron de Morton's designs against me?"

"Alas! Miss Woodfield," replied Bridget, "I scarcely know how to answer you, for were I to endeavour to instil the sentiments of hope into your mind, I should not only be misleading you, but speaking in a manner contrary to my own opinions. The baron is a wicked man, and when he forms a design, there is nothing that he will shrink from performing to put it into execution. It is very certain that his former extraordinary hatred, and even dread of you, are changed into love, (if such a detestable passion as that he feels, deserves such a title,) and that he has formed a resolution, by some means or the other, to obtain the indulgence of his sinful desires. But I know that I need not beg of you to meet him with equal determination, and fear not but that Providence will protect you from the villain's wicked designs."

"I will, indeed, do as you say, Bridget," returned our heroine; "and the consciousness of the rectitude of my own heart will, I am confident, enable me to triumph. Yes, I will no longer despair, but meet my persecutor with firmness, and show him that virtue is as a coat of mail to its possessor, and may set at defiance all the evil machinations of the guilty."

"It delights me to hear you talk so," said

Bridget; "and I feel as certain as you yourself can, that your ideas will be realised. The baron is crafty and designing, and he will, doubtless, try every effort in his power to effect the gratification of his wishes. But a firm resistance, conducted with prudence, will frustrate his object, and distract him from his purposes, until such time as you may effect your liberation, and place yourself in a situation to defy his power, or wicked designs."

"Dear Bridget!" exclaimed Angelina, "how wisely you counsel; I feel renewed hope already, and have reason to bless the moment which has restored to me a companion so kind and attentive—one who feels such a deep interest in my fate, and can so well sympathise with my misfortunes. But you must not forget the warning of Rufus;—how I shudder when I think of it, and I am fearful, by thus so candidly and openly expressing your feelings towards me, you may be running yourself into danger. Should anything again happen to you, I should for ever upbraid myself."

"Oh, do not fear for me, my dear Miss," returned Bridget; "indeed, there is no cause for your apprehension."

"But did not your husband tell you that he should be constantly watching you, and should be sure to know if you disobeyed his mandates?" inquired Angelina.

"True, he did so," answered Bridget, "but I heeded not his threats; I know they are futile. Here we may give unrestrained expression to our sentiments without any fear of being overheard. Besides, of this I am convinced, that Rufus values his own neck too much to venture to go to extremities, when he would be certain that now, at any rate, there would be very little doubt of his being detected and brought to punishment."

"I feel satisfied by your confidence," said our heroine; "and henceforth I shall be able to meet my fate with a becoming firmness and resignation; indeed, could but Hugh Clifford regain his liberty, I should feel very little doubt of being speedily liberated."

"Hugh Clifford—Captain Clifford!" repeated Bridget, with an expression of astonishment, "is he confined here?"

"He is," replied Angelina, "and it is that which afflicts me more than my own sufferings. Oh, Bridget, in you I can confide, and I know that you will not only sympathise with me, but advise me how to act. I will, therefore, acknowledge to you that I love Mr. Clifford, and that with a passion which no earthly power can ever subdue."

"I do not wonder at it, miss," observed Bridget, "for Captain Clifford is a sweet young man, and, I am certain, is every way worthy of you. To be sure, he is a smuggler; but, after all, I do not see that there is any great deal of harm in that. Ah, many a time have I listened with pleasure to the details of the generous actions he has performed. But how knew you, miss, that Mr. Clifford is a prisoner in the tower?"

"If I may believe the assertions of the baron," answered Angelina, "I cannot entertain any doubt of it. He it was that told me Clifford was his prisoner; and, besides, I have but too good reason to suppose that the baron spoke the truth, since I was with the former when I was seized by Rufus and the other ruffians, who felled him to the earth, and as I imagined then, killed him. Besides, when I was brought into the tower, or, at least, shortly afterwards, I heard a strange noise, which led me to suppose that Clifford was brought a prisoner here. Alas! how unfortunate I am in thus bringing misery upon all those who are in any way connected with my fate, or who take the least interest in my affairs."

"From my very soul do I pity you, miss," observed Bridget, "and also regret that Mr. Clifford has fallen into such bad hands. Still, I do not think that the baron will venture to proceed to extremities with him, if it is only for your sake. Is he aware, miss, of the passion which you entertain for each other?"

"He is," replied our heroine, "at least he

suspects that such is the case, and has taunted me with it."

Bridget sat silent and in a musing mood, for a short time.

"Are your relations likewise acquainted with your love, Miss, if I may make so bold as to ask?" at length she said. "Surely they could not but approve of a passion which has for its object so worthy a being?"

Angelina sighed deeply, and shook her head. "Alas! you are mistaken, Bridget," she answered—"I am forbidden by my uncle to think of him with any other sentiment than that of friendship."

"On account of his being a smuggler, I suppose, Miss?" remarked Bridget—"your uncle could not have any other objection."

"What his reasons for so peremptorily forbidding our love are, I am at a loss to conceive; but of this I am certain, that he is determined, and, therefore, that I have no hope.—He has told me to forget him; but can I think of the many services he has rendered me—can I dwell upon the many noble qualities with which his mind is endowed, and obey?—Oh, never! In spite of everything, under whatever circumstances, Hugh Clifford must ever occupy a place in my heart."

"It is very hard that circumstances should thus occur to interrupt your happiness, and to crush your hopes," said Bridget, in a tone of pity; "but let us hope that things may not turn out so bad as you apprehend—that something may shortly take place to restore you and Mr. Clifford to liberty, and that your uncle will no longer oppose your union."

Angelina made no answer, but the expression of her countenance showed how little she partook of the hopes of Bridget. Our heroine then more particularly related to her what had happened to her since they had last met; and stated what De Morton had said regarding Hugh Clifford—that he had committed crimes which rendered him amenable to the severest penalty of the law, and that it was in his power to consign him to that punishment.

"I will never believe it," said Bridget.— "I will not believe that Mr. Clifford could ever have done anything to place him in danger of such a penalty. True, we know that he is transgressing against the laws, and that he is liable to punishment by fine and imprisonment, but anything more severe, he cannot have incurred; for I know he would not harm a fellow-being for the world. It is merely a fabrication of the baron's to frighten you, and to induce to purchase the freedom of Mr. Clifford, by yielding a compliance with his wishes."

"That is precisely the opinion I had formed," said Angelina; "but I will put my trust in the Supreme Being, who will not fail to frustrate the plans of the guilty, and to bring about the consummation of our wishes."

Bridget felt pleased to hear her make use of these observations, and encouraged her in those hopes, by every argument it was in her power to make use of. Angelina had received a brief detail of the sufferings of Bridget, and the terrible mistake made by Rufus, which had so nearly cost her her life; but, notwithstanding this, she was anxious to receive the account from her own lips, and, therefore, requested that Bridget would relate it to her.

"I would much rather not say anything more about it," replied Bridget, "but endeavour to forget it; however, as you request it, I will comply. You may also feel a curiosity to know by what means I became the wife of a man like Rufus, and I will, therefore, if you please, relate it."

Angelina having expressed her anxiety to hear these particulars, Bridget related them in the following words:—

"My troubles, I may say, Miss, began at a very early period, and no one can imagine what I have endured since. But yet was it a punishment to me for one act of indiscretion and disobedience to the will of my parents, of which I have ever since repented. My parents brought me up with the utmost attention, and bestowed upon me all the care which the greatest affection could suggest. In fact, I was their favorite child. There was a youth in the same village in which I was born, named Gilbert Merton, who had been one of my play-fellows in childhood, and between him and me a passion sprang up, as sincere as it was fervent, and we had no reason to suppose that our parents would raise any objection to our paying our addresses to one another, as Gilbert's character was irrepreachable—his circumstances in life were the same as my own—his parents had ever been on the most intimate terms with mine, and my father and mother always evinced a marked respect for the young man. He was always heartily welcomed to our house, and the attentions he paid to me were never noticed by my parents, although we could not but believe that they were aware of the love which we entertained for each other and were inclined to encourage it. But we were doomed to be disappointed. Hitherto we had only to one another confessed the affection which inhabited our bosoms; indeed, so perfectly did we imagine that our parents understood it, that it was unnecessary to say anything to them about it. It was shortly after the period I have just mentioned, that Rufus and his friends arrived in the village, after having been absent from it for several years. My parents, and those of Rufus, had always been particular friends, owing to some service which, I believe, the father of Rufus had formerly rendered my father, and the intimacy was renewed on their coming back to the village, with avidity. They were, in fact, at the house of my parents, or we were at theirs, at every possible opportunity.

"Rufus was at that time in the service of the Baron de Morton, who then bestowed particular marks of favour upon him. He had always looked upon me with eyes of admiration much to my annoyance; for I had never been able to feel for him any other sentiment than that of abhorrence: and I was very much vexed and disgusted when I found that the number of years we had not seen each other, had made no difference, unless it was to add to his

boldness, and to render him ten times more repugnant in my eyes. But what more surprised and perplexed me was, that my parents appeared to mark the attentions he paid me with satisfaction, and to be pleased when he paid me any particular compliment, or little gallantry.

"Gilbert beheld him with eyes of jealously; and it was only confidence in my fidelity which prevented him from immediately seeking an explanation; however, his conduct at last became so bold, that Gilbert resolved he would not remain in suspense any longer, but that he would at once throw himself at the feet of my father, and solicit of him my hand. This he did, and the result was a firm but cold denial, and a hint to the effect that the less he visited the house the more agreeable it would be to him. Poor Gilbert was distracted; he remonstrated with, and implored my father to relent, but it was all to no purpose, although he could not give any reason for his refusal, nor express any other sentiment than the warmest admiration of his character. But Gilbert guessed the real cause, and in a state of almost ungovernable rage and sorrow, he quitted the house, and sought me out to tell me the result of his interview with my father.

"I need not describe my feelings; you can, I know, Miss, well imagine and appreciate them. I could scarcely believe my ears, and yet, from what I had noticed in the conduct of my parents lately, had fully prepared me for such a result. I flew to my father—threw myself on my knees before him, and with tearful eyes implored him to recal his words; but he was deaf to my supplications, and, moreover, not only commanded me to forget Gilbert, but also to look upon Rufus as my intended husband, as he was the man he had fixed upon, and his mind being fully made up, nothing could alter his determination.

"My anguish upon receiving these peremptory and determined injunctions, may be easily magined by those who have experienced the pangs of disappointed love. I reproached my father for what I could not help thinking cruelty, and appealed to my mother; although she was likewise in favour of Rufus, yet she sympathised with my distresses, and promised me to endeavour to persuade my father to alter his resolution, and rather sacrifice his own wishes, than render me miserable for ever. She did as she said she would, and most earnestly do I firmly believe she pleaded my cause, but all her efforts were ineffectual. He could see no fault in Rufus, and attributed my objection to him to mere caprice, and from a want of a knowledge of the world. He said that his mind was made up, and that any future attempt to move him from his purpose, would have no other effect than that of making him hasten the union which seemed to be so repugnant to my feelings.

"I was distracted, and was quite at a loss to account for the behaviour of my father, who had ever before this evinced the most unbounded affection towards me, and had appeared to make it his constant study to contribute to my happiness. But certain it is that his resolute opposition to my wishes only rendered Rufus more hateful to me, and less careful of obeying the mandates of that parent, whose slightest word I had previously been used to consider as a law.

"The agitation into which this event threw me caused me to become seriously ill, and in the meantime my father took the opportunity of intimating to Gilbert that he could no longer be received at the house. The sufferings of the poor youth, who I knew sincerely loved me, it would be no difficult matter to imagine; and this he contrived to let me know, in spite of the caution used by my father, by means of a letter. In proportion as my father's opposition to our passion increased, so did our love for one another: and I was determined that I would sooner die than make a sacrifice of my hand, when my heart could not accompany it.

"Rufus knew well how to play the hypocrite, and that is the only means I can imagine by which he contrived to insinuate himself so firmly into the good opinion of my father. He behaved to me with the greatest apparent affection, and seemed to sympathise with me and Gilbert; but yet, he said, that the passion which inhabited his own bosom was too powerful to allow him to relinquish my hand. But he could not deceive me; and I, therefore, viewed him with that contempt and abhorrence which he merited; and whenever he was in my presence, my heart felt a certain dread, which I tried, but in vain, to conquer.

"Rufus was at this time the servant and confidant of the Baron de Morton, and report spoke in no very favourable terms of their connection, which naturally increased the dislike I felt towards him; added to which, in spite of the mask which he assumed, I could plainly perceive that he exulted in his triumph, and enjoyed the sufferings of myself and Gilbert.

"I was so ill, that for some days I was confined to my bed, which, in fact, was a relief to me; for when I was about, Rufus almost constantly intruded his society upon me, and annoyed and insulted my ears with his detestable passion. You may blame me, miss, for thus speaking of one who is now my husband, but when you hear the farther particulars of my history, you will not be inclined to wonder at these expressions.

"At length, my feelings became somewhat more tranquillised, and I was enabled to leave my chamber. My father behaved with kindness towards me, expostulated with me upon the folly of my seeking to oppose the plans he had formed for my future settlement, and in doing which, he had my happiness so closely at heart, pointed out to me the incompetency of Gilbert to keep a wife, and the advantages that were offered to me in a union with Rufus, who, independent of the situation he had with the Baron de Morton, had property of his own, and he was certain would make it his constant study to do all that was in his power to render me happy, for that he loved me, and with a passion ardent as it was sincere, he had not the least doubt. He also warmly eulogised his character to the utmost, and any one to have heard him would have thought Rufus was a perfect paragon of all that is amiable, virtuous, and affectionate. But I was not to be deluded: I had well read his real character, which any observing person might quickly do, and I knew him to

BRIDGET SUPPLICATES HER FATHER ON BEHALF OF GILBERT.

be a villain—one with whom my days would be passed in perpetual sorrow. Alas! how fatally have these prognostications been verified —how powerfully have been my sufferings since it has been my wretched fate to be his wife.

"I made no other answer to the words of my father, than by supplicating him for the present to spare my feelings; and seeing the very precarious situation in which, by illness, I was placed, he did as I desired, and desisted.

" By the same means which Gilbert and myself had managed to communicate with each other since he had been ordered not to visit the house, we contrived to do so, now I was able to quit my chamber: and this, indeed, was a blessing, if it only afforded us the opportunity of pouring our sorrows into each other's bosoms, without any prospect of our ever being able to avert the fate which seemed to be impending over us."

" As the time approached which my father had fixed upon for the union of me and Rufus, our unhappiness increased, and Gilbert reproached the cruel conduct of my father in no very measured terms, and I could not but reciprocate his sentiments. It was now two months since we had met, and, of course, I need not tell you, miss, how anxious we were once more to behold each other. Gilbert had frequently, in the letters which he had sent to me, urged me to contrive to meet him, and I was eager to comply with his request, but hitherto I had had no opportunity, in such restraint was I held by my father, and so perpetually was I annoyed by the presence of Rufus. At length, however, fortune did smile upon us; my father was called away a few miles in the country on particular business, and Rufus was compelled to attend his master on an excursion for a few days, so that I was thus left with no one but my mother, to whom my father left strict injunctions to watch closely after me; but he had no suspicion that Gilbert would attempt to come nigh the house, as it was so long since he had done so, and, ignorant of the correspondence which had been going on between us, he, doubtless, imagined that Gilbert had given up all thoughts of me, and fixed his affections on some other female. I, therefore, made my lover acquainted with these circumstances the day before, and appointed a place where I was resolved, by some means or the other, to contrive to meet him on the subsequent day.

" The morning arrived, and my father departed, which I never beheld with such feel-ings of satisfaction in my life before. I had previously devised the means of getting away from the house, and I did not suffer many minutes to elapse before I made the attempt. My mother was busily occupied with her domestic affairs, and I requested that she would permit me to walk in the adjacent fields for a while as it was a beautiful morning, and latterly I had been kept completely in doors, whereas the delicate state of my health much required such a recreation to restore me to convalescence.

" My mother was not at all suspicious of the truth, and readily assented, requesting, however, that I would not walk too far, in case I should be overcome by fatigue, and lay myself up again.

" This I promised to obey, and joyfully set forth, filled with expectation and anxiety. I soon reached the place where I had appointed to meet Gilbert, and found him already there. We rushed into each other's arms with a cry of frantic delight, and our meeting was of that extatic description, which language would fall short of in pourtraying. For some moments we were deprived of the power of speech, and could only mingle our tears of joy with each other.

" You may probably consider, miss, that I acted imprudently in thus making a secret assignation with a man, when my father had refused to encourage him; but when the impetuosity of my love is considered, and the unjust opposition which my father made to my union with the object of my choice, and who was every way deserving of me, I am confident that you will excuse me.

" I will not repeat all that passed at this brief interview—all the tender things we uttered—the mutual vows of constancy which we pledged to each other, and the resolution we formed to try, by every means we could suggest, to avert the union we dreaded—for were I to do so I should become tedious; suffice it to say, that before we parted, Gilbert had so far conquered my objections to do anything contrary to the wishes of my father, and had used such powerful arguments to prove that he was exercising an undue authority, that I yielded an assent to elope with him on the following evening, agreeing to become secretly married to him, and thus crushing at once the designs of Rufus. We arranged everything in a short time. Gilbert had saved a small sum of money, and it was therefore agreed that he should have a vehicle in readiness, at a short distance from the residence of my parents, in which he was to convey me to a female friend, with whom I might stay until the ceremony could be settled on the following morning. Having thus concocted ours plans, dusk the next evening was the time agreed upon for us to meet; and filled with impatience for it to arrive, and reiterating our vows of constancy, we parted.

"It was with the utmost difficulty I could conceal the agitation under which I suffered on my return home, from my mother. It sincerly grieved me to have to quit her roof for even a short time, and for her sake I hoped that all would turn out for the best, and that ultimately everything would be amicably arranged to the satisfaction of all parties. I made an excuse to retire to my chamber early, but I had but little rest that night. My time was fully occupied in getting together such little necessaries as I might want for my use, and in writing letters to my father and mother, in which I begged them to forgive me for the clandestine manner in which the power of my love and the opposition of my father had urged me to leave them, and to give my hand to the only man who ever had, or could possess my affections, and expressed a hope that they would receive us as their children.

"The next day appeared intolerably long to me, and my mind was violently agitated with doubt, fear, and anxiety, lest my schemes should be frustrated. At length, however, evening set in; I had been for about an hour in my own room, having complained of headache, and having listened to hear if all was

still below, I implored the protection of Providence, placed the letters on the table, and with cautious steps descended the stairs and left the house by the back-way, and hurriedly crossing the little garden, safely gained the fields beyond. I ran on with breathless haste, every now and then looking fearfully back to see whether I was pursued, and in a short time afterwards I reached the spot where me and Gilbert had agreed to meet.

"The pale moon was just riding in the heavens, and by the light which she shed upon the earth, I could distinguish the shadow of a form moving in the distance, and near the spot where we had appointed to meet. 'This must be Gilbert,' I ejaculated, and my heart beat high with expectation, and I quickened my pace. I came up to the figure I had seen; it was muffled up in a mantle, such as I had seen my lover wear, and his face was partially covered with the same. The figure was the same—it was, it must be he for whom I was hazarding so much. I rushed into his arms, and he pressed me rapturously to his heart. 'Gilbert, dear, dear Gilbert,' I exclaimed.

"'Hush, my love,' he whispered, in tones so low that I could scarcely hear them, 'be silent dear, we have not a moment to lose; come, come, let us away.'

"He took my arm, and led me hastily from the spot, and I did not offer to say another syllable, but my agitation was extreme, so great, that I had great difficulty in sustaining myself, and I felt that I was doing wrong, and repented that I had consented to leave my home in such a clandestine manner; my heart reproached me for my ingratitude to my parents. I also felt that Gilbert had not done as he ought to have done, in persuading me to elope with him.

"'Oh! Gilbert,' I cried, as we approached the vehicle, which was to convey us away, 'suffer me to return home; I cannot abandon my parents thus. I was to blame, very much to blame, to give my assent to this sinful step Let me return, and we will put trust in our

Providence, who will, doubtless, yet cause us to be united.

"To these solicitations, however, my lover made no reply; but hurried me towards the vehicle into which he assisted me, I being at the time almost unconscious of what was passing around me; and having followed himself, it drove off with the greatest rapidity, and we were soon far away from the neighbourhood in which I had been born, and where I had passed so many happy years of my youth.

"'Dear Gilbert,' I ejaculated, 'alas! why did you not accede to my wishes, and suffer me to return home; my parents will never forgive me for having thus acted.'

"A loud and coarse laugh was the only answer I received to this. I started, and my heart sank within me.

"'Good God!' I exclaimed, 'who is it with me? It cannot, it is not, Gilbert!'

"'No, proud, scornful girl, it is not he with whom you thought to elope; it is not the base knave who would have seduced you to ruin, and brought misery upon your parents, but your affianced husband —the man whom you have treated with such scorn and hatred, in spite of his affectionate attentions to you, and the claim he has upon your heart and hand. Look up, and behold yourself in the company of Rufus Baynard!'

"The wretch had uncovered his face as he spoke, and the moon shining in at the window of the coach, I recognised his features, now rendered more revolting to me than ever, by the expression of mingled rage and exultation which characterised them. Overcome with the power of my feelings, I uttered a loud scream and fainted.

"When I recovered my senses, I found myself in my own chamber, and my mother standing anxiously by my bed-side. She looked at me with mingled feelings of pity and reproach, but I could not bear to encounter her gaze, and averting my face, covered it with the bed-clothes, and burst into a flood of tears.

"'Nay, my poor child,' said my mother, 'do not weep; you have acted wrong, but I will not reproach you. Compose yourself, and endeavour to reconcile your thoughts to——

"'To Rufus! oh, never!' I cried vehemently 'rather let me die than be sacrificed to a being I so thoroughly detest.'

"'Disobedient girl!' ejaculated my father, (who at that moment entered the room,) in a stern voice, 'disobedient girl! are you still resolved to be obstinate? Was it not enough that you should assent to abandon your home and your parents, to fly with one who could never have sincerely loved you, or he would not have persuaded you to an act which must have made you miserable for ever after, but that you must still further add to your crime by continuing to oppose my will, instead of craving my forgiveness, and making all the reparation in your power, by immediately yielding your willing assent to my wishes?'

"'Oh! my father,' I sobbed, 'pray pardon me if I am acting otherwise than as a daughter ought to do; but I cannot, dare not think of becoming the wife of Rufus Baynard, without a shudder of horror.'

"'Why not?' demanded my father, sternly.

"'Because I cannot love him,' I replied. 'Oh, my father, there is something about that man which makes me view him with horror; but to think upon him in the character of a husband—oh! I dare not.'

"'Bah!' ejaculated my father, in a tone of resentment, 'let me hear no more of this nonsense; Rufus is a worthy, industrious, thrifty lad, and likely to do well in the world;—he is good-looking withal. I know he loves you, and, therefore, I cannot see what objection you ought to have to him, and to fix all your thoughts and affections upon that scrapegrace, Gilbert Merton, whose recent conduct shows that he is unworthy of you.'

"'Gilbert Merton unworthy of me?' I uttered, and I felt my cheeks glow with indignation as I spoke; 'father, you wrong him, indeed you do; Gilbert is good, is——"

" ' Psha!' hastily interrupted my farther, 'no more of this fulsome nonsense; I am not going to listen to a long harangue upon the merits of the man who would have seduced you from your duty, and probably have brought you to destruction. He shall never be yours, let that suffice; my mind is thoroughly made up, and in a week prepare to become the wife of Rufus Baynard.'

" He quitted the room as he uttered these words, and my mother, who had stood silently by all the time this brief dialogue was going on, endeavoured to calm the violence of my grief, but I was completely inconsolable. Whatever could have made my father so cruel?—he who had previous to this, ever been so kind and indulgent to me, I could not form the slightest conjecture as to the cause; but to become the wife of Rufus, I could not bear to think upon without the utmost feelings of disgust and horror.

" I did not leave my chamber the whole of that day and the next, for I felt really too ill, and during that time my mother was almost constantly with me, and did her utmost to endeavour to console me, and reconcile my mind to that circumstance which she said she was convinced my father was determined should take place. From her I learned that my father had had an interview with Gilbert after he was made acquainted by Rufus of our intended elopement; but what had taken place between them she could not inform me, although he had told her that 'he thought he had put a stop to the annoyance of Gilbert for the future, and that he did not think there was much fear of anything occurring to prevent my becoming the wife of Rufus Baynard.'

" On the evening when I and Gilbert met by appointment, Rufus, who happened to be passing by the spot where we were seated, had observed us, and concealing himself behind some trees, overheard the whole of the conversation which passed between us, and he thus was enabled to thwart the stratagem we had formed in the manner I have described. I have

often wondered since how he could restrain his rage sufficiently to prevent him from seeking a deadly vengeance upon his rival, either at that time or some future period; but he did not, and I have seen him several times since my unhappy marriage; and although I always endeavoured to avoid him, and have never entered into conversation, I could see from his pallid cheek and sunken eye, that the cankerworm of care was preying upon his heart. Alas! I can judge of his sufferings from what my own have been. But I am becoming tedious, I fear.

" I will not attempt to describe to you what I endured the few days only that intervened between me and future misery. My father remained inexorable. I was forced to the altar, and became the wife of Rufus Baynard—a man from whom I have experienced the treatment of a brute. For several weeks I was scarcely conscious of what was passing around me; and in my moments of sensibility, when the recollection that my fate was sealed rushed upon my memory, I prayed to Heaven that I might not survive to undergo the troubles which my mind foreboded were in store for me. I must, however, do my husband the justice to say, that he behaved to me with great kindness during this period, and paid me the utmost attention; but he was so abhorrent to my feelings that I shuddered with a feeling of dread whenever he approached me.

" In a few weeks the vehemence of my grief was, in some measure, abated, and I endeavoured to meet my fate with resignation, since I know it was sealed past recall. My sorrow had subsided into a calmed but settled melancholy, and I endeavoured to perform the duties of a wife in such a manner as my conscience could approve of. I succeeded in a way which has often surprised me to think upon. I endeavoured to forget Gilbert, since he could never be mine, and by dwelling upon him, my passion might increase to that ungovernable degree, that I might be tempted to swerve from my duty; and to my husband I behaved in such a manner as could not leave him or my parents cause to reproach me.

"I was still living with my parents, and Rufus—the Baron de Morton being at that time in London—was constantly with me, and he behaved to me with respect and kindness. However, in a few weeks, a letter arrived from the Baron, ordering Rufus to join him immediately in London, as it was uncertain how long he might remain there; and offering at the same time to take me into his service, so that my husband and me might be together. I need not say that Rufus gladly accepted of the offer; but the state of my mind, at the bare idea of my being separated from my parents, and being left to the entire control of my husband, whom in my heart I dreaded, may be imagined without much difficulty. But what excuse could I offer for wishing to remain behind? No, I dare not raise any objection; and I could see from the dark looks, and contracted brow of Rufus, that the grief I evinced at the thoughts of being about to leave home, caused a strong feeling of resentment in his mind.

"I will pass over the separation, which, as you may suppose, was an affecting one. On the way to London, I did not notice much change in the conduct of my husband. He behaved, in fact, occasionally with even more kindness than he had hitherto done, and endeavoured to reanimate my spirits; and, fearful of arousing his anger, I made a powerful effort to suppress the violence of my grief.

"We arrived in London, and here too soon did Rufus alter his behaviour towards me, and appeared in his true character—treating me more like a slave than a wife; and, indeed, without the least provocation, using me with the utmost brutality. He was continually upbraiding me for the preference I had given to Gilbert Merton, and he seemed resolved to gratify his revenge by incessantly tormenting me. This persecution was not confined to words alone, but more than once he struck me in the most savage manner; in fact, my life soon became almost endurable. I did not complain to my parents, for I wished not to make them unhappy, and I knew how truly wretched my father would be to hear of my sufferings, and to know that it was he who had consigned me to them. No, I kept my sorrows confined to my own breast, and prayed to heaven to give me fortitude to support them.

"The Baron de Morton filled me with disgust and dread the first time I had beheld him, and there were strange rumours afloat concerning him, which caused him to be looked upon by his tenants and dependents with terror, instead of esteem. These reports I will not repeat here, Miss, for, doubtless, you have heard them; but I strongly suspect that they are too well founded. And my husband was his confidant at this time, his myrmidon, his creature, ready to do his bidding, and had been his accomplice, it was said, in all the nefarious transactions that were attributed to him How dreadful were the pangs that racked my brain when I thought of this! and to this man was I united by the indissoluble bonds of matrimony. It was dreadful to reflect upon, and I shrunk from it with a shudder.

"I had only been married to Rufus a year, before I lost both my parents, and I was left entirely to the mercy of my husband, whose cruelty increased every day; but I was fated to endure much more. However, I was for several years released from his society altogether; the baron went on the continent, and Rufus accompanied him, but for some reasons which they did not state, I was left behind, and was sent as a domestic to this tower.

"Need I tell you how rejoiced I was at this providential circumstance? From what a weight of care was I released! It was like entering into heaven, and I felt quite a new being. My spirits were gradually restored to me, and my health, which had suffered much from the constant ill-treatment I received, speedily became recruited. How often did I pray that we might never meet again. We but seldom corresponded, and when he did write to me, the tone of his letters was all that I might have expected from the treatment I had experienced from him.

"Years had passed away in this manner, and still they did not return to England, and as I had not received a letter from him for some time, I began to think that my husband was no more; but he still lived to be the cause of future misery to me. You recollect, Miss, the return of the Baron de Morton, therefore I will pass over that and the subsequent events, and come at once to that dreadful night when you escaped from this tower, and I nearly fell beneath the dagger of my husband.

"When I recovered my senses," resumed Bridget, "on the night upon which the wound had been inflicted by my husband, I found myself stretched upon a rude pallet, in a small, dismal-looking room, and the disagreeable old woman who lately attended you, sitting by my side. My wound was very painful, but I soon ascertained that it was not dangerous.

"'Where am I?' I exclaimed, trying to raise myself in the bed, and forgetting what had taken place, 'where am I, and for what am I brought hither?'

"'That you will soon learn,' answered Deborah, 'if your memory is so imperfect; I can only say that you ought to be very thankful to your husband and my lord, that they have spared your life!'"

"The whole truth flashed upon my recollection in a moment.

"'Ah!' I cried eagerly, 'has she then escaped?'

"'Oh, then,' said Deborah, and a sardonic grin passed over her ugly features, 'then you do acknowledge that it was you who assisted her to escape?'

"'I do,' replied I, fearlessly, 'and I trust to Heaven that she has not be foiled.'

"'Very pretty—very pretty, indeed,' observed Deborah, 'so then you not only acknowledge your offence, but actually exult in the perpetration of it?'

"'I do rejoice to think,' I returned, 'that the designs of the guilty have been frustrated, and that I have been the lucky instrument in the hands of Providence to accomplish that task, and to restore that much wronged and persecuted female to the liberty of which she ought never to have been deprived.'

"'Well, I never heard such boldness and effrontery in my life,' ejaculated the old woman, turning up her eyes in apparent astonishment and incredulity.

"'And what have those who are conscious of having only done their duty to a suffering fellow-creature to fear?' I demanded.

"'It strikes me very forcibly, that you will find you have more cause for fear than you seem to imagine,' returned Deborah; 'a wholesome punishment will prevent you playing such tricks again, and break that obstinate, stubborn temper you possess; and were I in your husband's or the baron's place, I would take good care that you should not escape it.'

"I turned from the hateful old woman with disgust; I could scarcely believe she was one of my own sex. I must confess though, that I could not think upon my situation without a sensation of the deepest horror, notwithstanding I affected such indifference and courage. Too often had I experienced the terrors of my husband's vengeance, not to feel assured, that in the present instance there would scarcely be any bounds to the extent of cruelty to which he would not hesitate to proceed, more especially as he would be urged on to it by the baron, whose rage at your escape I anticipated would be of the most violent description. Indeed, when I came to reflect upon it, I expected nothing less than death; and I would have preferred it to the dreadful state of lingering agony to which I was doomed. One circumstance, however, brought temporary relief to my mind, and that was, I ascertained from Deborah that neither Rufus nor the baron were at present in the tower, and it was uncertain when they would return, as they had left the place almost immediately after your flight was discovered, and had, doubtless, gone in pursuit of you.

"The place in which I was confined was a very miserable room, the walls were damp, and it was evident that it had not been inhabited for some. Old Deborah did not stay with me any longer at each time than to apply such remedies to the wound as her knowledge of surgery suggested; and I was left alone, the door being securely locked, barred, and bolted upon. I was too weak to be able to rise off my pallet, which was very hard, and my bones were sore with lying.

"The nature of my thoughts in this dismal place may be imagined. That I should never leave there alive was my firm belief, and I endeavoured to prepare myself for the worst. I dreaded the return of Rufus and the baron, and I could not think upon it without the utmost horror.

"A fortnight passed away in this manner, and my husband and the baron still remained away from the tower. Deborah was more skilful than I had given her credit for at first, and my wound had nearly healed, and I was enabled to walk about the narrow confines of my prison. At length, however, the dreadful moment arrived—Deborah had been absent from me the whole of the day, when, suddenly' I heard the bolts being withdrawn, and the key turning in the lock. My heart sunk with a fearful foreboding in a minute, and it was very soon verified; the door was thrown back on its hinges, and Rufus and the baron rushed into the place, their countenances exhibiting the utmost fury. Overcome with my terrors, I threw myself on my knees, and, clasping my hands, I gazed up with supplicating looks at those whose vengeance I expected to feel.

"'Wretch! traitress!' cried Rufus, ferociously, and spurning me from him, 'dare you expect any mercy from me? If you can, what must be your expectations, as regards my lord the baron?'

"'Ay,' cried De Morton, fiercely, 'what clemency can you expect from me, woman? Have you not shamefully betrayed the trust reposed in you? Did you not assist Angelina to escape? It is useless to deny it. Every circumstance connected with that accursed event confirms it.'

"'Do you deny your crime?' asked Rufus, in a savage tone.

"I made no answer, for I could not.

"'Ah! you acknowledge it, then?' said my husband; 'you acknowledge that it is by your means the girl escaped, and severely shall you suffer for it.'

"'And was there any crime in assisting a fellow creature, and one of my own sex, in effecting her escape from that imprisonment in which she was so unjustly held?' demanded I, with more firmness; 'was it a crime to save an innocent person from that state of suffering to which she was so cruelly subjected; nay, more, from mur——'

"'Ah, wretch! dare you?' cried Rufus, before I could finish the sentence, and raising his hand, he seemed about to strike me to the earth, had not the baron arrested his arm.

"'Nay, we have another punishment in store for her,' said the Baron de Morton, 'far more severe than that you would now inflict. Away with her to one of the dungeons under the tower, and there let her linger out her days in such misery, that death would be considered a blessing. Away with her, Rufus; recollect it is my will, and if you disobey me, it will be worse for you.'

"At the mention of the dungeons under the tower I shrieked aloud with terror. Horrible were the stories I had heard related of them, and in spite of all the firmness I had at first assumed, it now vanished and gave place to feelings of the utmost consternation.

"'Oh, for the love of Heaven, spare me—save me!' I screamed; 'you cannot, you surely will not consign me to so horrible a fate. Rufus, am I not your wife? Has every spark of feeling or humanity become extinguished in your bosom? Rather kill me at once—put an end to my existence—than doom me to a fate I cannot contemplate without the most inde-scribable terror.'

"'Away with her, I say,' commanded De Morton; 'heed not her cries! It is too late to repent now, and she richly merits all that she may have to endure.'

"Once more in frenzied tones I shrieked for mercy, but Rufus heeded me not ; and seizing me by the hair of my head, he dragged me violently from the room, and, in spite of my piercing cries, conveyed me down the steps, until we reached the dismal vaults beneath the

RUFUS BIDS ANGELINA AND BRIDGET PREPARE FOR THE VOYAGE.

tower, the bare sight of which was sufficient to strike the beholder with the most unbounded feelings of horror. The dampness of the place struck a deadly chill to my heart the moment

we entered it ; and the foul air gathered around the lamp which Rufus carried in one hand, and nearly extinguished the light.

"He stopped before the iron door of the

No. 20.

dungeon in which you saw me, and throwing it open, thrust me in, at the same time exclaiming,—

"'This is your future apartment! Here learn obedience to the will of your husband, and your master.'

"'Oh, God!' I cried, wringing my hands with distraction, 'you cannot be the monster to leave me in this horrible place! Oh, reflect—relent; and rather plunge a knife into my heart, than consign me to a fate so terrible!'

"'You plead in vain, woman,' said the baron; 'there is your pallet,' pointing to a heap of straw in one corner of the wretched cell, 'and I hope you may enjoy a comfortable night's repose.'

"As the baron thus spoke, an ironical and demoniac grin overspread his features; and, beckoning to Rufus, they both hurried away, leaving me in the dungeon without a light. With a frenzied shriek, I sank upon the heap of straw; and, as their last foot-falls sounded hollowly in my ears, I fainted away.

"What a shocking night of suffering would it have saved me, had I remained in that happy state of insensibility; but it was not long—at least, so far as I could judge—ere I was aroused to a full consciousness of my situation. The place was so dark that I could not see the least thing in it, and so dreadfully cold with the damps that clung to the walls of the dungeon, that my limbs shivered as though I were troubled with the ague. All around was as still as death, save when the wind whistled along the subterranean passages, and sounded like the agonised wailings of fiends in purgatory. What a terrible situation was I placed in, and how preferable did I imagine death would have been to it. I was ready to dash my head against the flinty walls, and at once end my misery; but some inscrutable power seemed to withhold my arm. I wrung my hands, and then groaned aloud with the power of my anguish. I threw myself on my knees, and prayed fervently to Heaven to give

me fortitude to support my miseries. Then I crouched down in the corner of the dungeon, on my pallet of straw, and endeavoured to get some warmth into my shivering limbs, but in vain.

"I cannot describe all the horrors I endured on this, the first night of my incarceration in this frightful cell;—sleep I had none. In the morning (at least, so I judged it to be, for it was always dark in that awful place) I heard the door being opened, and Rufus entered, bearing in his hand a pitcher of water and a small brown loaf, and having placed them before me, he scowled frightfully upon me, and was about once more to quit the dungeon, when I again threw myself at his feet, and in piteous accents implored him either to release me from my present confinement, or end at once my sufferings by death.

"He made no reply, but tearing himself away from my hold, spurned me from him, and again left me in total darkness.

"I will not harrow up your feelings, Angelina, by detailing minutely all the horrors I endured in that awful cell. They were almost past credit; and it is wonderful that nature did not sink under them. On the night when you first saw me, no one had visited me for two days; and I verily believe it was their intention to starve me to death. It is evident that I could not have survived many hours more. With what has since occurred to me you are thoroughly acquainted, and, therefore, there is no necessity to repeat it."

CHAPTER XXVI.

"AND have you, then, endured all these sufferings for my sake?" said our heroine, when Bridget had finished her narrative. "How shall I ever be able to repay you?—how sufficiently express the gratitude I feel towards you? How few are there in the world who would have done as much for a fellow-creature, and one who is almost a stranger to you?"

"Oh, miss," replied Bridget, "do not mention it; it is over now; and the only thought which sustained me under sufferings that were enough to shake much stouter frames than mine, was the conviction that I had done my duty, and had, probably, saved one of my own sex from a fate, which, to the lover of virtue, would be far more dreadful than death. What I principally regret is, the unfortunate circumstance which has again placed you in the power of the Baron de Morton."

"It is an unfortunate circumstance," said Angelina; "but now that you are my companion, dear Bridget, I shall be released from half the misery I before suffered. I hope, too, that something will ere long transpire to defeat the evil purposes of the baron, and to restore me again to liberty."

"Heaven send that your predictions may be verified, miss," ejaculated Bridget, fervently. "It is a terrible job that Mr. Clifford is also the prisoner of the baron; for were he at liberty, he would soon contrive some scheme to obtain your enlargement."

"Alas! you speak but too truly, Bridget," said Angelina, sighing deeply, as she reflected upon the misery Hugh Clifford was very likely enduring: "and when I think of that circumstance, my heart again sinks with despair. But, why do you look so earnestly at me, Bridget?"

Bridget had been for the last few minutes looking most steadfastly in the countenance of our heroine, and then she would remove her gaze from her, and fix it on the portrait which had so deeply interested Angelina.

"Pardon me, Miss," she observed, in answer to the interrogatory that had been put to her by Angelina; "but I cannot help noticing the extraordinary likeness there is between you and the portrait. Any person, I'm sure, might take it for the likeness of your sister. Do you not think so?"

Angelina felt a strange and indefinite feeling come over her when Bridget put this question to her, and she could not at first return any answer.

"I cannot say that I have observed this," at length she replied; "but I have noticed a particular resemblance which it bears to——" Angelina could not finish the sentence; but she meant to have said, the phantom which she had seen in the vaults of St. Mark's Abbey. "I confess, Bridget," she continued, "that the painting has much interested me:—whom is it supposed to represent?"

"Ah! Miss," replied Bridget, "that portrait represents one of whom I have heard my mother speak in the most unbounded terms of affection, and about whose fate there hangs a mystery, which, probably, time may solve."

"And who may that be, dear Bridget?" inquired Angelina, eagerly.

"It is the portrait of Lady Ophelia de Morton," answered Bridget; "a lady no less famed for her beauty than her numerous virtues."

"Was she not the wife of Lord de Morton, the brother of the present baron?" asked Angelina, whose interest was greatly excited, and who was curious to learn all the particulars she could.

"It was: and much to the astonishment of every one, when her husband died, she became the wife of his brother, a short time afterwards," answered Bridget. "This was the more surprising, as the baron had always been looked upon by her, during the lifetime of his brother, with a repugnance amounting to abhorrence; and, notwithstanding the many strange rumours that were propogated concerning the mysterious disappearance of Lord Algernon, and the subsequent discovery of his death, but which was never properly explained."

"It is very strange—quite unaccountable," observed Angelina. "And was not the lady in the family way at the time she accepted the hand of the baron?"

"She was; and was soon afterwards delivered."

"And shortly afterwards died suddenly; was it not so?" asked our heroine.

"True," answered Bridget; "but there

was much mystery attendant upon her death, also; and I have often heard my poor mother say, with a shake of the head, that she was afraid that she had not come fairly to her end. It is very clear that some sinister means must have been adopted by the Baron de Morton to induce her to become his bride; and it is said that he used the poor lady in a most cruel manner."

"And what became of the child?"

"It was said to be still-born," replied Bridget; "but its sex was never known; and there are some doubts as to whether it was born alive or not. However, it was never seen by any one. About the same time that this event took place, there was brought to this tower one night, in a most secret manner at midnight, a female, who was closely confined by the orders of the baron, and no one suffered to hold any communication with her. My mother, however, did once contrive to catch a glimpse of her, and from what she stated, it appeared that the lady was extremely beautiful, tall, and graceful; and there could not be any doubt that she was not of common rank. Her countenance was stamped with the deepest sorrow; and she did not appear to be more than twenty-two years of age. Soon after her arrival and confinement in the tower, the most melancholy, but beautiful strains of music used to be nightly heard to issue from that wing of the ancient fabric in which she was kept a prisoner, accompanied by a voice of such sorrowful sweetness, that it moved every one to tears when they heard it. Suddenly, however, they ceased altogether; and it was soon made known that the White Lady (for so she was called) was no longer confined in the tower; but when or how she was gone, and whither, was a secret which was not known to any of the domestics; and there were many fruitless conjectures formed upon the subject—none of them, you may be sure, much to the credit of the Baron de Morton, who was frequently at the tower during the time the White Lady was confined there."

"It is very strange, indeed," said Angelina; "but was it never discovered who and what she was?"

"Never!" answered Bridget, "although curiosity was much excited upon the subject —so much so, that it was expected that a public investigation into the conduct of the baron would be demanded by some influential persons, whose interest was excited by the singularity and mystery of the circumstance."

"And why was the resolution, which I think was a very proper one, abandoned?"

"That I know not, miss," returned Bridget; "but it is said that it very suddenly was dropped, and little more said about it afterwards."

"And did it never transpire from whence the unfortunate lady came, previous to her being brought to the Grey Tower?" asked Angelina.

"Why, it is believed that she had been for a short time before confined in Saint Mark's Abbey; and it was from her being seen at the window of a night in her robes of white, and the melancholy strains of music that were constantly heard to issue from the abbey ruins, that they were first reported to be haunted."

"Well, this is certainly a most singular narrative," observed Angelina, who had listened most attentively to all that Bridget had related; "but I am quite at a loss to unravel the mystery—Heaven send that the baron may not be the guilty wretch that circumstances of a suspicious nature make him appear to be; but I much fear me he has a deal to answer for; and when the day of disclosure comes, which there doubtless will be, there will be many facts brought to light that will strike terror into the breasts of those who hear them."

"I am exactly of your opinion, miss," said Bridget, "and all that I hope is, that the guilty may be brought to that punishment and disgrace which their foul crimes may deserve; and that the innocent objects of their cruelty and oppression may have ample justice done to them."

"Amen!" ejaculated our heroine, sincerely. "But was Rufus in the service of the baron at the time these mysterious events took place?"

"He was," replied Bridget; "and, indeed, the baron and he were seldom apart. Rufus is several years older than me, and at that period I was quite a girl, and it was before the fatal time that he pressed his suit with my father. I have heard the old domestics speak of him often; and there was not one but viewed him with an eye of aversion and suspicion. Whatever the crimes of the Baron de Morton may have been, depend upon it, that Rufus is equally guilty."

"I fear that your surmises are but too just," remarked Angelina; "but I hope Heaven will pardon him, and bring him to a sense of his guilt, inducing him to make all the atonement in his power, by unravelling those secrets that are now involved in such impenetrable mystery. But alas! left to the mercy of the Baron de Morton, what have I not to dread?"

"Do not despair, miss, I beg," said Bridget; "your liberation from his power may be nearer at hand than you imagine. But hark!—what noise is that?"

They both listened, and a strange bustling noise from below sounded in their ears.

"Something has happened," observed Bridget; "there would not be such an uproar as that in the tower, if something unusual had not occurred. What can it be, I wonder?—Ah! some one is coming along the gallery."

The heavy tread of some person in the gallery was distinctly heard, as Bridget thus spoke; and, whoever it was, they stopped at the door which opened into the apartments they occupied. The door was quickly opened, and Rufus entered the room. At the sight of him, both Bridget and our heroine

trembled and turned very pale, while the ruffian seemed to be in an unusually surly disposition, and, scowling frightfully upon them, said—

"Put on your cloaks, and attend me directly."

"What is the meaning of this?" inquired our heroine, in astonishment. "Are we going to leave the tower?"

"You are," replied Rufus; "but ask no questions—be quick, or the patience of the baron will be exhausted."

"It is getting late," said Angelina, with some agitation depicted in her manner; "and for what reason are we going to leave here in so abrupt a manner?—It looks not well."

"It may not," said Rufus, with a malignant grin; "at any rate, it is the baron's will, and you will do well not to attempt to oppose it.—Do you hear me, woman?" he added, turning fiercely to his wife, who had been too much take by surprise to offer to do as he commanded; "prepare yourself for a voyage."

"A voyage!" reiterated Angelina, her alarm increasing.

"Ay," returned the ruffian; "but once more I tell you to ask no questions, but to get ready to follow me, unless you would prefer going as you are, which is quite immaterial to me."

Finding it would be perfectly useless to remonstrate with, or to question Rufus any more, Angelina and Bridget hastily did as he commanded them, and then followed him from the apartment, and along the gallery. Just before they began to descend the stairs, the Baron de Morton met them, and seemed to be in a state of considerable agitation—so much so, that he took but little notice of our heroine, only urging Rufus to quicken his pace with his charge. He then descended the stairs again, and preceded them through a low door in the wall of the tower, which seemed as if it were but seldom opened. They almost immeliately found themselves on the beach, where there was a boat waiting, apparently to receive them. The baron entered first, and was followed by the other three. The boat was then put off, the baron himself and Rufus plying at the oars. Having turned the corner of a rock, our heroine beheld a ship lying at anchor. In two or three minutes they were alongside of her, and immediately afterwards were on board.

CHAPTER XXVII.

WE will now return to Mrs. Montmorency, and her daughter, Charlotte, who, on the day of Angelina's mysterious disappearance, awaited her return home, when her absence had been prolonged beyond her usual time, with the utmost anxiety and uneasiness. Hour after hour elapsed—the sun sank to rest in the bosom of the ocean, but still she came not, and the uneasiness of Mrs. Montmorency increased to such a degree, that she was worked up to a state of complete distraction.

"Good God! what can detain the poor girl?" exclaimed she, in tones of the deepest distress. "Some accident must surely have befallen her, or she would not have been absent so long as this, when she would be aware what alarm it would cause us."

"I really do not know what to think of it," ejaculated Charlotte, who was as much frightened as her mother, for she had become as fondly attached to our heroine, as if she had been her sister; "but, indeed, I am fearful that your surmises, my dear mother, are too true, and that something must have happened to the poor girl."

"This state of suspense is insupportable," said her mother. "Send for Peter, and, accompanied by him, I will instantly go forth, and see if I can discover any traces of her.— If anything should have happened to her, Mr. Woodfield will ever blame me for what he must consider neglect on my part."

"I will also attend you," observed Char-

lotte, rising from her chair immediately, and slipping on her cloak; "I cannot remain behind, in a state of fear and uncertainty.— Probably, she is only detained by the beauty of the evening—you know how fond she is of watching the sun, as his last red streaks fade away on the western horizon."

"I hope it may be as you have imagined," said her mother; "but I have a foreboding that all is not right."

"Ah! and so have I ma'am," remarked Ann, who, at this juncture, entered the room, in obedience to the summons of her mistress; "and I think I have pretty good reasons for my fears, too."

"What do you mean, Ann?" demanded Mrs. Montmorency, impatiently.

"What do I mean, ma'am?" repeated the girl; "why, didn't I see a strange, ugly-looking, cross, middle-aged man, lurking about the house, only yesterday—and wasn't he looking up and watching all the windows?— And didn't he speak to me, and say to me, 'Good morning to you, my *pretty* lass?'—Yes, *pretty* lass, he said. And didn't he question me about having a visitor here?—And didn't he say that he knew Miss Angelina well?— And didn't he, when he had learnt from me that Miss Angelina was a visitor here, walk away, laughing, as much as to say——"

"Silly girl," exclaimed Mrs. Montmorency, with much agitation, "why did you not make me acquainted with this circumstance immediately?"

"Why, lor', ma'am," said Ann, "I did not think there was any danger to be feared from it. Besides, I did tell Miss Angelina all about it."

"Good God! this circumstance confirms my worst fears," ejaculated Mrs. Montmorency; "the unfortunate girl has again fallen into the power of her enemies!"

Charlotte now recollected the circumstance of the serenade which she and Angelina had heard, and an idea in a moment flashed across her mind.

"My dear mother," she suddenly observed, "I have just recalled to my recollection an event which leads me rather to imagine that Angelina has been carried away by her lover, Hugh Clifford, than the emissaries of the Baron de Morton."

Mrs. Montmorency, with much eagerness, inquired of her daughter to what event she alluded; and Charlotte related all that had occurred on the night in question, and the conversation which she and Angelina had upon the subject.

A ray of hope for a moment darted upon the mind of Mrs. Montmorency.

"And yet," she remarked, "should it even be as you surmise, it will be almost as bad; for, although Angelina would not be placed in the danger that she would had she again fallen into the clutches of the baron, yet, should she have had the weakness to yield to the persuasions of the young man, and become his wife, will she not incur the displeasure of her uncle? Yes, I am certain, he would never countenance her again; and there is no knowing what misery it might be productive of; for who can tell what are the secret motives that prompt Mr. Woodfield so determinedly to oppose their union?"

Charlotte could not deny the justness of her mother's observations; but she still urged the propriety of their taking immediate steps to ascertain the truth. Peter was, therefore, summoned to attend them, and Charlotte and her mother set forth in the direction which Angelina had stated it was her intention to take.

They walked on towards the rocks—they searched every spot which they knew she was found of traversing, but, of course, without success; and after inquiring at every fisherman's hut, if they had seen a female answering the description of our heroine, or heard any particular noise, and being answered in the negative, in a state of much grief and alarm, they returned home.

The next day came, and Mrs. Montmorency and her daughter renewed their inquiries, after having first despatched a letter to Mr. Woodfield, making him acquainted with all that had taken place. For sometime all their endeavours to gain the least clue to what they were so anxious to ascertain were completely fruitless, and they were again about to return home in despair, when they reached the spot where Angelina had been seized by the villain Rufus and his companions, and, to their horror, beheld the earth stained with blood (which had issued from the wound that the ruffians had inflicted upon Clifford, when they felled him to the earth), and at a short distance from the place, they found a bracelet, which they recognised in a moment as belonging to Angelina.

"Good God! The poor unfortunate girl is murdered!" cried the distracted Mrs. Montmorency, as she looked at the clotted blood upon the earth, and picked up this convincing proof that Angelina had fallen the victim of some dreadful outrage; "her enemies have gained their ends at last; and having performed their fiendish task, have, probably, thrown the body of their victim into the sea. How shall I impart this dreadful intelligence to Mr. Woodfield? Will he not accuse me of neglecting the trust he placed in my hands—and, perhaps, suspect me even of having connived at the destruction of his niece?"

"Nay, my dearest mother," said Charlotte, who was herself most violently agitated, but still more collected than the former, "pray do not thus afflict yourself. Dreadfully suspicious as it seems, it may not be so bad as your terrors suggest; and if it should even turn out to be so, surely Mr. Woodfield possesses too much good sense to entertain the horrible surmises you speak of. You, at any rate, he cannot blame for what has happened."

"Oh, yes, he will have every reason for blaming me," said Mrs. Montmorency; "for, was not the poor girl entrusted to my care?—and, ought I to have permitted her to walk out unattended? I feel myself that I have acted very imprudently."

What involved the circumstance in still greater mystery was, that no person had heard any outcry on the evening that Angelina had disappeared—not even those who resided immediately on the spot; neither had any parties been seen to lurk about the neighbourhood, whose appearance was in the least degree calculated to excite suspicion.

Charlotte, having with considerable difficulty somewhat composed the anguish of her mother's feelings, and persuaded her to return home, despatched Peter to the different authorities of the place, to make them acquainted with the circumstance, in order that every inquiry might be instituted, to endeavour to ascertain what had become of our heroine, and who were the parties that had committed the outrage. Her mother being too violently agitated, Charlotte then sat down to write to Mr. Woodfield the particulars of what had transpired since the first letter had been despatched to him—but at the same time, she endeavoured to soften the affair as much as possible, although, of course, she could not conceal from him the circumstance of the bracelet belonging to Angelina being found, and the blood which stained the spot.

It would be impossible for us to do adequate justice to the feelings of Mr. Woodfield upon the receipt of the first letter from Mrs. Montmorency. He was in a complete state of phrensy, and now reproached himself for having sent Angelina away from his home, and entrusting her to the protection of a female.

But it was done with the best of motives—he was urged on to it with what he considered to be the most praiseworthy intentions, and, therefore, why was he to blame?

"She has fallen into the power of the villain de Morton!" he exclaimed, in accents of despair, "and her fate may be sealed before the strong arm of the law can interpose to avert it. But where shall I seek him? How shall I discover the place where he has concealed her? It seems that nothing can save her from his vengeance. I will immediately away to the castle, and demand an interview with the baroness!"

Instantly he seized his hat, and left the cottage, bending his way with hasty steps towards the castle of De Montford. Having gained admittance to the hall, he demanded an audience of the Baroness Orillia.

"Her ladyship is engaged, and cannot see you," replied the porter, eyeing the person, and noticing the perturbed manner of Mr. Woodfield with much curiosity.

"But I tell you, I must and will see her," said the latter, in a determined tone, "unless your master is in the way, then would I insist upon seeing him."

"My lord is on the continent," answered the man, "and, as I told you before, my lady is at present engaged; but if you will state the nature of your business with her, I will deliver your message."

"My business is with her, and her alone—to no other will I communicate it," said Mr. Woodfield, growing impatient; "and I will not leave this place until I have seen her."

"Humph!" returned the old porter, "methinks you are rather bold, master. However, I will deliver your message, although I know beforehand, that it will be utterly useless."

"That we will see," said Mr. Woodfield, as the man turned away; and, without any further ceremony, he followed him up the stairs, much to the porter's astonishment, and only waited for him to enter the apartment, and to hear the baroness, in reply to his message, say peremptorily, that she could not be seen by anybody, when he forced himself into her presence, to her evident confusion and indignation.

When Mr. Woodfield entered the splendid apartment, the Baroness Orillia was seated upon a sofa, and by her side lolled a gaily dressed young man, of handsome features, and well-made form, who removed his arm from around her ladyship's waist, as she arose on the appearance of Mr. Woodfield.

We have before stated, that the Baroness Orillia was an Italian by birth, and her large eyes sparkled with resentment, and blushes of shame and confusion overspread her still beauteous countenance, as she gazed upon the intruder.

"Insolent!" she at length ejaculated, in a voice almost choked with rage, "what mean you by this bold intrusion?"

"I come to demand justice," replied Mr. Woodfield, with firmness, and looking with the most perfect composure and indifference

ANGELINA AND BRIDGET CONDUCTED FROM THE GREY TOWER.

upon the baroness and the gay gallant, who still lounged upon the sofa, and every now and then darted a look, which he meant to be dignified and awe-striking, upon Mr. Wood-field,—"I demand the present residence of the Baron de Morton!"

"Can it be possible that the fellow dare to address me thus!" ejaculated the baroness with increased wrath. "My Lord Ravensford, surely you will not hear me thus insulted by a menial knave?"

"'Tis well for your ladyship that you are a woman," returned Mr. Woodfield, with calm dignity, and looking contemptuously upon Lord Ravensford, who partially arose upon her ladyship's appeal to him, but, seeming to take a second thought, he sat down again, and crossing one leg over the other and shaking his foot, commenced picking his teeth. "It is well for you, madam," repeated Mr. Woodfield, "that you are a woman, or you might, perhaps, repent using such language to one who boasts as noble, or, perhaps, more noble blood than that which flows within your ladyship's veins. But I treat your words only as the wild ebullitions of a weak-minded woman; and as such they merit only my contempt and pity. But I have not time to argue with you. The Baron de Morton has again, with the villany which is natural to his base character, forcibly taken my niece away from those friends under whose protection I had placed her. You must be well aware of the place of his retreat; and, unless you connive at his nefarious actions, you will not hesitate a moment in giving me all the information in your power."

"So then," said the baroness, while her bosom heaved with rage, and an expression overspread her features, which rendered them very forbidding, "you are the uncle of that abandoned girl, who has contrived to wean the affections of the Baron de Morton from his wife, and who——"

"Hold! woman!" exclaimed Mr. Woodfield, and his eyes flashed with indignation, at the base aspersions which the baroness had uttered against Angelina. "Speak not that which you know is as false as the tongue that could give utterance to the foul calumny! But those who are themselves fallen, are always ready to defame the character of the innocent and the virtuous."

The baroness was almost choked with passion; her eyes beamed with a lustre which seemed as if it would penetrate to the soul. Her bosom heaved; her features were distorted with rage, her lips livid; and her limbs were perfectly convulsed. For a short time she tried to speak, but in vain; and when she did, she once more appealed to the booby foppling, Lord Ravensford, who arose slowly upon his feet, advanced in a menacing attitude towards Mr. Woodfield; but receiving a look from him, which told him that he was a man not to be alarmed at trifles, he contented himself by indulging in a damn, and several, what were meant to be, appalling gestures, and then returned to the sofa, and resumed his old attitude.

"Do you mean to tell me the place where your husband is at present concealed?" again demanded Mr. Woodfield, in a determined manner. The baroness tried, but in vain, to return an answer, but her tongue refused its office; and, seizing the bell, she rang it violently for the attendance of her domestics.

"Nay, then," said Mr. Woodfield, preparing to leave the apartment, "you refuse to grant my request, and I must, therefore, take other steps to compel you. High as may be your rank, there is law and justice for the poor as well as the rich, and that will I immediately seek."

With these words, Mr. Woodfield quitted the apartment, leaving the baroness and her senseless paramour in a state of astonishment and confusion, which was almost past conception.

———

CHAPTER XXVIII.

THE Baroness de Morton was a woman who, we have before stated, possessed passions of the most powerful nature, and being still very handsome, and with manners sufficiently fascinating to ensnare the affections of many men, it is not at all remarkable that, cold, morose, stern, unsociable, and even forbidding and repulsive in his manners, as the baron had lately become—seldom in her society but for a very short time—that she should gradually become indifferent to him; which indifference by degrees strengthened into dislike, and added to by feelings of jealously which crept into her breast, at several facts that had come to her ears, more especially the interest he took in Angelina, aroused all those strong and ungovernable feelings of revenge that had not been destroyed, although they had for some time lain dormant in her breast. His frequent absence from De Morton Castle, and various other circumstances, tended to increase her suspicions, and to add to the fire which raged in her bosom; and when she was, therefore, made acquainted with the disappearance of Angelina, and of the continued absence of her husband, where she was not exactly certain, but, as she believed, on the continent; her surmises were confirmed, and her passions of hatred, jealously and revenge, were inflamed to an almost insupportable degree. She felt at that moment that she would willingly have plunged a dagger into the baron's heart, and that no torture which she could inflict upon " the presumptuous beggar's brat," as she called our heroine, could be half severe enough. That she would gratify the implacable resentment which now raged within her bosom, she was fully determined; and soon after Mr. Woodfield had quitted the castle, she excused herself to Lord Ravensford, and retired to her private apartment, where she immediately sat down, and wrote in great haste a letter to the Marquis Florendos, in which she requested him to meet her with as little delay as possible at the castle, as she had something of importance to impart to him, which must be communicated immediately. This done, she traversed the room with uneven steps, and her compressed lips, and stern brow, showed the excited feelings under which she was labouring.

"And think you, Baron de Morton, that Orillia will suffer another—and that one, a bold and plebeian girl—to share those passions and embraces that belong to her alone? Think you that the blood of an injured woman, once aroused, will ever be quelled until she has had ample vengeance for her wrongs? No! by Heaven, I swear that you shall severely pay for this, and that I will not rest until you and this girl—this Angelina—have been made to feel what it is to arouse the indignation of Orillia, Baroness de Morton. Oh, how I now hate and despise that title, and curse the hour when I, weak fool that I was, assented to become the bride of one who has ever been insensible to the value of the treasure he possesses! The proudest, the noblest, and the wealthiest of Rome, paid adulation to my charms, and vied with each other to become the happy possessor of my hand and heart; and yet—strange infatuation —I rejected them all with disdain, for that man who is now playing me false, and treats me with cold and brutal neglect. But if my schemes succeded aright, this state of thraldom shall not last long. I will soon burst the chains that now confine me, and indulge without restraint in the gratification of those desires which others have inspired in my bosom."

As the guilty woman thus spoke, a look of fierce determination distorted her otherwise handsome features, and she again paced the apartment with hasty and disordered steps. The boldness of Mr. Woodfield, and the threats he had held out, had wounded her pride, and raised her indignation to the utmost degree; and she was chagrined beyond measure, also, to think that he should have forced his way into her presence, at the very time of her interview with Lord Ravensford.

This young nobleman had been a constant visitor at De Morton Castle, and it was there that the irresistible wiles which the baroness, (who saw in him a worthy conquest, being very rich,) made use of to allure, led him into the snare that she had so artfully spread for him; but, although she pretended to return the sentiments of the ignorant lord, while he continued to pander to her cupidity, she despised and laughed at him in her heart, and had it not been for the fear she entertained of his making their secret amours known to her husband, and thus render himself the means of frustrating the schemes of vengeance she had formed against the baron, she would have speedily contrived to abandon all further connection with him.

The Marquis Florendos, however, held a most paramount sway over her, although she had hitherto resisted all his importunities, and she now determined to make him the instrument to effect the revenge she basely contemplated against her husband.

The Marquis Florendos, as his name will imply, was a foreign nobleman, with whom Orillia had first become acquainted with in Italy, and his person and manners had immediately made a deep and lasting impression upon that weak and guilty-disposed woman's heart. The marquis was a man about her own age—tall, handsome, and particularly gallant. But his breast little corresponded with his exterior;—it was the receptacle of every vice, and there was nothing which he would not hesitate to perform for the gratification of his desires. He had wealth in abundance, and, therefore, his amours were generally attended with success. He no sooner saw the Baroness de Morton, than she inspired in him all those powerful passions of lust and desire, which had often driven him to such desperate extremities, and had rendered his name proverbial as a libertine and debauchee, all over Italy.

The Baron de Morton had ever seemed to view the Marquis Florendos with an eye of suspicion, and it was that which made Orillia so resolutely resist all the advances which the latter made towards her, although she had frequently admitted to him, that he held the entire possession of her heart. More than once had the marquis endeavoured to persuade her to elope with him, promising to remain constant to her while life should last—and a thousand times declaring that no other woman besides herself ever had, or could hold possession of his affections; but still the baroness remained firm to her first resolution, which was never to yield to the wishes of Florendos, until such time as the behaviour of De Morton became so as to be insupportable, when she would contrive some means to rid herself of him altogether, and to reinstate the former in his place, only on the condition that he undertook to accomplish whatever she might require of him.

The Marquis Florendos received the epistle from Orillia with mingled feelings of astonishment and hope; and he had he sooner read the contents, than he started to the castle with all the expedition that he could make use of; and on his arrival there, was ushered into the apartment in which the baroness was seated, impatiently awaiting his arrival. She smiled graciously on his entrance, and beckoned him to approach. Florendos advanced to the splendid ottoman on which Orillia was reclining, and taking her hand, pressed it fervently to his lips. She did not offer to repulse him; and surprised at this sudden change in her conduct, he awaited with impatience to hear her speak, but finding she did not offer to do so, he said—

"You sent for me, Orillia, for by that familiar name I must be permitted to call you."

"I did send for you, marquis," replied Orillia, exhibiting some slight confusion, which, however, soon vanished; "you are punctual."

"And think you, dearest woman," cried the hypocrite, "that Florendos would delay a moment, when Orillia needed his advice or assistance?"

"Florendos," observed Orillia, "my business with you can be told in a few words; but you will promise not to betray me, if even you think proper to decline being put to the test I shall require of you?"

"Betray you!" repeated the marquis,

warmly, and in a tone of reproach: "you wrong me by such a supposition.—Betray you! oh, sooner would I suffer unheard-of tortures than e'er so debase myself."

"You love me, Florendos?"

"Love you, most beautiful woman!" cried the libertine, throwing himself on his knee before her, and again pressing her hand in a more passionate manner than before to his lips; "by Heaven, there is not a term powerful enough to express the adoration I feel for you—tell me what is there that you can command of me that I would refuse to perform, to convince you of the sincerity and ardour of the sentiments with which you have inspired me? It matters not, however difficult it is, I swear to accomplish it, or to perish in the attempt."

The eyes of the baroness for a few moments sparkled with more than usual lustre, and she fixed upon Florendos a look of admiration.

"'Tis well, marquis," returned she; "we shall soon see what dependence there is to be placed on your word. My husband——"

"Ah! what of him?"

"Of him it is I would speak. What think you of him, marquis?"

"That he is unworthy of you," replied Florendos, energetically; "that he is a man who knows not how to appreciate the happiness with which Fate has supplied him. Excuse me, lady, if I be too bold, but you asked my opinion, and——"

"You have drawn but a faithful likeness of De Morton," interrupted Orillia, "and I now despise and hate him. Florendos, he has played me false, and is even now basking in the arms of a peasant girl, whom he holds within his power."

"Ah! say you so, lady?" ejaculated Florendos, and his countenance became lighted up with an expression of exultation; "nay, then, retaliation is but fair, and——"

"Hold, marquis," exclaimed Orillia, seriously, "do not mistake me. I tell you the baron has deceived me; he has disgraced my name, and I have vowed to have vengeance.

Say, what think you he deserves for the wrongs he has done me?"

Florendos looked around the room cautiously, and then placing his lips close to the ear of Orillia, in a deep, hollow tone, answered—

"Death!"

The marquis and Orillia both paused, and looked at each other earnestly for a few moments, and in that brief time the tumult of passions that raged within their breasts may be easily conceived.

"I see we understand each other, lady," said Florendos, at length;—"the Baron de Morton's doom is sealed—he dies!"

"Hush!" whispered the guilty woman, in fearful accents, and looking around the apartment, alarmed lest any one should be listening, "and you will undertake to accomplish it, then?"

"I will," replied the marquis; "but my reward?"

"The possession of her whom you have so long vowed to love so passionately," answered Orillia.

"Ah! that is enough," ejaculated Florendos, joyfully;—"to possess you, most lovely of women, I would readily run any danger, were it even death itself. But the joy is too great, scarcely to be credited;—say, tell me that you will not deceive me."

"Florendos," returned Orillia, in a reproachful tone, "and can you doubt me? If so, decline the task you have promised me to perform, and let another live to possess that form you have so often vowed to run any risk to obtain possession of."

"By Heaven! never!" cried Florendos; "pardon me, Orillia, if the strength of my love, and the fear that something might occur to render my possession of such a treasure abortive, hurried me into an expression which I meant not. Your wishes shall, rest assured, be complied with. But where shall I find the baron?"

"I am not certain," answered Orillia; "he left here under the pretext of going to the

Old Grey Tower, but whether that was merely a subterfuge to deceive me, I know not. However, you will be there able to ascertain what direction he has taken; wherever he is, the girl is his companion, for her uncle has but this day been here, demanding the place of the baron's concealment, and accusing him of having clandestinely borne her away from her friends."

"Her name?"

"Angelina Woodfield."

"And what would you I should do with her?" demanded Florendos.

"What are the limits, think you, to an injured woman's vengeance, marquis?" replied the baroness, in a deep, hollow tone, and with a ghastly expression of countenance, which made even Florendos shudder.

"I understand you, Orillia," he said, "and on your beauteous lips let me seal the oath which binds me to your service."

The marquis embraced the fallen woman, and pressed his lips to her cheek with fervour; then moving towards the door, he said—

"Farewell, Orillia; when next we meet, those who have injured you will be no more."

Thus saying, he kissed his hand to the guilty Orilia, and quitted the castle.

———

CHAPTER XXIX.

THE heart of Mr. Woodfield swelled with almost ungovernable rage as he quitted De Morton Castle; yet did a feeling of pity and contempt intermingle with the other passions that predominated in his bosom, for the weakness and depravity of the baroness. He could now plainly see that if Angelina escaped from the power of De Morton, (who, at that time, he firmly believed detained her a prisoner,) that she was sure to meet with a most implacable enemy in the baroness, whose jealousy being excited, he felt convinced that there was no length to which her revenge would not lead

her; for who shall pretend to conquer the jealous feelings of a woman, or who can guard against the secret and malignant designs of one incited to vengeance by the violence of the most irritable passions? He, therefore, was certain that he must adopt some determined plan or the other, to bring the baron to justice, and to prevent any of the dangers which he apprehended.

He walked slowly from the castle, and as he preceeded on the way, he reflected maturely upon the different circumstances, as they had occurred, and in spite of all that had transpired, and the doubtful manner ⬤ which the baroness had expressed herself, and which gave him every reason to suspect that his niece was in the baron's power, an idea darted across his mind, that, urged on by the impetuosity of his passion, Hugh Clifford had, by some means or other, discovered the place where he had sent Angelina, and had persuaded her to enlope with him, or otherwise had forcibly borne her away. In fact, he now recollected, for the first time, that Mrs. Montmorency, in the letter she had sent to him, had hinted at such a suspicion, and had related the circumstance of the serenader, and what Anna had stated about the person whom she had met, and who had questioned her so particularly about the visitor that was at Mrs. Montmorency's house.

"By Heaven!" he exclaimed, as this thought occurred to him and racked his brain; "by Heaven, it must be so! Hugh Clifford has become a villain, and destroyed my peace for ever. Never, I am certain, would Angelina have consented to have acted in so clandestine a manner; he must have used force to obtain her. Fool that I was, not to be able to penetrate through his specious mask before, and have resolutely forbidden his attentions to her, long ere I did. How could I be so deceived? —How could I be so easily duped, especially by one whose lawless avocation should have made me suspicious of him? Kate of the Ruins, too, she who pretended to be my friend, and that of Angelina, and seemed to take such pains to warn Clifford and her against encouraging a passion for one another—she must have been aware of the whole circumstance, and being in colleague with the smuggler captain, has acted the hypocritical part for the purpose of giving him a better opportunity of putting his designs into execution. Ah! I see it all now;—I have been basely, cruelly deceived, and my unfortunate Angelina has fallen a victim to the deep-laid scheme which has been so long formed to trepan her. If it is as my fears suggest, may the curse of the Almighty descend upon the heads of those who have deceived me! But I will instantly to the Abbey, and having sought an interview of Kate, demand a full explanation of the truth. If my suspicions are verified, I will not rest until I have had ample retribution upon the heads of those who have done me so irreparable and injury!"

As he thus spoke, his bosom swelled with agitation, and he quickened his pace towards the Abbey of Saint Mark's, so strong was this impression upon his mind, and so eager was he to have a thorough explanation of the whole affair.

The shades of evening had fallen upon the earth by the time Mr. Woodfield had quitted De Morton Castle; but, nevertheless, so impatient was he to have his ideas confirmed or dissipated, that he was determined not to postpone his visit till the morning. He soon reached the Abbey, and having ascended the rock on which it stood, he paused a few moments, and gazed down upon the deep blue ocean, upon which the moonbeams were shining brightly. The water was scarcely disturbed by a single ripple, and all around was as silent as death. Suddenly, however, Mr. Woodfield observed a white speck upon the distant horizon, which gradually expanded, until he could clearly perceive that it was the sails of a vessel. Mr. Woodfield watched it narrowly as it skimmed lightly over the ocean, and was evidently bearing down upon the rock on which the ruins of Saint Mark's Abbey stood. "It must be the smuggler's vessel," thought Mr. Woodfield, and a hope sprang up in his bosom that he should learn something of Hugh Clifford, and likewise how far his surmises as regarded Angelina were correct. He was soon convinced that was right, for the vessel shot in immediately beneath the rock, and close to the secret entrance to the smugglers' retreat, and eager to have his mind set at rest, he descended the rock, and reached the mouth of the cavern just as some of the smugglers came ashore. He would have been seized upon immediately, and, no doubt, roughly handled, had not Ned Stukely, as Kate had called him upon a former occasion, happened to be there, and soon afterwards Kate of the Ruins made her appearance.

"Where is the villain?—Where is Hugh Clifford?" demanded Mr. Woodfield impatiently, unable to subdue his feelings.

"That am I as much at a loss to imagine as yourself," was the reply of Kate.

"'Tis false!" exclaimed Mr. Woodfield, with much emotion; "you would deceive me; he has acted the part of a villain!"

"How, Mr. Woodfield?" said Kate, sharply; "be not too hasty in forming your conclusions; the name of Hugh Clifford and that of villain should never be associated.''

"Has he not robbed me of my niece?" said Mr. Woodfield, in accents of the most powerful emotion; "if I be wrong, where is he, that he may answer for, and endeavour to exculpate himself?"

"Angelina gone!" ejaculated Kate, in evident surprise; "is it possible?"

"Angelina has disappeared in a most mysterious manner from the house of Mrs. Montmorency, in whose charge I left her," returned Mr. Woodfield, "and, from circumstances that have come to my knowledge, I have but too good reason to suspect that Hugh Clifford is the man who has been guilty of this crime!"

Kate of the Ruins seemed to be much agitated for two or three moments, and appeared to ruminate upon what Mr. Woodfield had said.

"Can it be possible?" she at length said,

" can he have been so rash,—so misguided?—But, no, I will not believe it; there must be some mistake. Mr. Woodfield, I can excuse your expressions under the circumstances that have drawn them forth; but, depend upon it, your suspicions are wrong. True it is that Hugh Clifford by some means or the other, which I am not at present acquainted with, contrived to become acquainted that Angelina was at Scarborough, and, doubtless, urged on by the violence of his love for the maiden, which in one so young and so ardent, it is not easy to subdue; he went thither for the purpose of seeking an interview with her; but as to anything else I am certain he would be incapable of commiting. Had he by persuasion have been able to prevail upon her to become his wife, he, doubtless, would have done so; but if she refused him, I am confident he loves her too fondly, and has too great a friendship and esteem for you, to seek to force her compliance with his wishes. The men who have just now returned, inform me that having put the captain ashore at Scarborough, they waited for him according to his orders; but at the time at which they expected him had long elapsed, and he did not return. In the meantime a storm arose and the vessel was torn away from her anchorage, and they were driven out to sea. The only conclusion I can come to is, that some accident has befallen him, or that he has fallen into the power of the Baron de Morton, and if my suspicions should be verified we have everything to dread. Of this, however, rest assured, that I was not aware of Clifford's designs, or I should have used all my exertions to have persuaded him from such a purpose, and to have frustrated him in any attempts he might make."

Mrs. Woodfield did not make any immediate reply, and he remained buried in deep thought for a short time; but, at last, he said,—

" It is strange; but still I cannot divest my mind of the suspicions that have occurred to it; it is not at all probable, that Clifford would have undertaken a voyage of this description, for the mere purpose of seeking an interview with Angelina. He must have some further design in view. As for the return of his companions, that is a mere subterfuge, invented for the purpose of deceiving me."

" By heaven! I am confident you wrong him!" exclaimed Kate, vehemently, " and that you do me an injustice by surmising that I would attempt to deceive you, is equally certain; indeed, you cannot have the interest and welfare of Angelina more at heart than I have, and—"

" Am I never to understand you, mysterious woman?" interrupted Mr. Woodfield, in a tone of astonishment; " tell me, I desire, who, really, are you, and why should you take such a remarkable interest in the fate of one who, it would appear, is almost a stranger to you?"

" Who am I?" returned Kate, and a melancholy smile overspread her features. " Oh! there may be a time when you will know me; but that time has not yet arrived. It is sufficient that I know you well, and all your former history!"

" Impossible!" exclaimed Mr. Woodfield, gazing more earnestly in the face of Kate. " There is not a person living who really knows me!"

" Methinks you will own yourself mistaken, Sir Eustace Arlingham," replied Kate, with another smile.

Mr. Woodfield started, and turned pale.

" Ah! known!" he cried:—" by Heaven, I am thunderstruck! Again, mysterious woman, I entreat of you to disclose to me who you really are. I have no recollection of your features."

" Indeed," said Kate; " but it is as well that you should not for the present; but I shall, doubtless, reveal myself anon; then will you see how much reason have I to esteem and love Angelina as much as yourself. When you hastily quitted those ancient halls that had long been in possession of your ancestors, you left considerable wealth behind you, which you, no doubt, never expected to receive again?"

" True; but how know you that?"

"No matter ; that I speak the truth, you cannot deny," observed Kate ; "and that I am sincerely your friend, I will presently endeavour to prove to you.   Will you follow me ?"

Mr. Woodfield, in a state of astonishment and impatience, assented, and Kate led the way to the interior of the Abbey : and having proceeded to one of the vaults beneath, in which were deposited the ashes of the dead, she removed the stone from one of the tombs that

FLORENDOS AND ORILLIA DETERMINE UPON DE MORTON'S DEATH.

were ranged around, and Mr. Woodfield (by which name we shall for the present continue to call him) was completely lost in amazement, when he beheld a small iron chest, which had formerly been in his possession ; and Kate having raised the lid, he was still more surprised to perceive that it was full of gold, and on the top of which was placed some private documents, which did not seem to have been disturbed since he had himself deposited them there, which was many years before.

"That wealth, I need not inform you," said Kate, "belongs to you. It was saved from the despoilers by one who was sincerely your friend. Now, do you longer doubt that I know you, Sir Eustace?"

"Wonderful!" he ejaculated; "you bewilder me more and more. In vain I have been endeavouring to recollect you, and yet it strikes me that your features are familiar to me."

"They should be, Eustace," said Kate, in a peculiar tone of voice, "but no matter; for the present it is, perhaps, as well that you do not. The time, however, is not far distant when you will not only know me, but when you will——. However, no more of this just now. We must see what is best to be done to find out the place in which Angelina is confined, and what has become of Hugh Clifford."

"Nay," exclaimed Mr. Woodfield, "we must not part thus; ere I leave you, I must know to whom I am indebted for these acts of kindness, and how you have become acquainted with my name, and all the circumstances connected with me:—my heart yearns strongly towards you, and yet,—ah! you weep—tell me, what means this?"

"It was but a momentary weakness, Sir Eustace," said Kate, dashing away the tears that had gathered involuntarily in her eyes, and recovering her composure in a few seconds; "but it is over now. Oh, Eustace, I cannot marvel that you should feel—but, no, no—not now; but the time is not far distant when all will be unravelled. For the present, leave me; I am in no mood to talk now. I will, rest assured, lose no time in making every inquiry, and seeing after the restoration of that poor girl, who is as dear to me as she can possibly be to you. Farewell for the present, Sir Eustace Arlingham, for by that name I shall in future call you, although no other person shall ever know it from me, until you shall deem it meet;

it is a name that inspires my soul with rapture, and recalls to my memory scenes, many of which are those of happiness, and others, such as I cannot reflect upon without the most poignant anguish. You know where your treasure is deposited, and can use it as you think proper, not a coin of it has been touched by me since it was brought hither. Farewell, Eustace, I go to——"

"Stay, mysterious woman! who have excited such an extraordinary interest in my bosom," exclaimed Mr. Woodfield, or rather Sir Eustace Arlingham, whose feelings were wound up to a pitch of insupportable anxiety and wonder, at the same time he seized her arm with great vehemence of manner, and forcibly detained her; "by Heaven! I will not suffer you to leave me until you have satisfied me upon the points on which you have aroused my curiosity to such an intolerable degree. An instinctive feeling tells me that it is not to any stranger I am indebted for—Ah! what is this?"

Kate of the Ruins, during the time he was speaking, evinced the most powerful emotion, and with convulsive sobs, she struggled hard to release herself from his hold; in doing so, a beautiful diamond bracelet, which encircled her wrist, and which she always contrived to conceal under the folds of her white mantle when she was in his company, became disengaged, and fell to the ground. Sir Eustace picked it hastily up, and as his eyes became fixed upon it, his chest heaved, his countenance became deadly pale, his lips quivered, and in breathless haste he articulated—

"Powers of mercy! what do I behold? This bracelet!—sacred relic of one so dear to me, yet so unfortunate. Woman, for pity sake tell me, how came this into your possession?"

"Leave go thine hold, Eustace, and do not torture me," cried Kate, endeavouring still more violently to release herself from his grasp, and evincing redoubled agony.

"I will be satisfied ere you stir from this

spot," cried Sir Eustace, frantically; "this bracelet—tell me whence you obtained it?"

"It is mine, what would you more?" demanded Kate, her voice almost choked with agony.

"'Tis false!" returned Eustace, hastily, "you would deceive me."

"It was your sister's," said Kate.

"It was—it was—my poor, but guilty Emmeline," returned Eustace, with a burst of agony.

"Oh, Eustace, you wrong her—by Heaven! you do," sobbed forth Kate; "the foul breath of calumny blasted her character, but yet was her soul as spotless as when she first drew the breath of life."

"Ah! how know you that? And who are you, who seem so well acquainted with me and my family? Unfortunate Emmeline! but you are no more, and oh! may the remembrance of your errors sleep with you."

"Sir Eustace Arlingham," observed Kate, in a voice of deep emotion, and struggling hard to subdue her feelings, "your wronged and calumniated sister still lives; Emmeline is not dead."

"Not dead—my sister still living!" cried Sir Eustace, evincing the greatest possible anguish, anxiety, and suspense; "oh, repeat those blessed words again. But you cannot be speaking the truth; you are only tantalizing my feelings, and sporting with a heart already so deeply lacerated;—how should you know? And yet, your looks—your tears;—what feeling is this which comes over me? A mist seems to fall from before mine eyes. My sister living! Oh, if you do, indeed, speak the truth, tell me, where—where shall I find her?"

"And would you receive her with affection? Would you listen patiently to her melancholy recital, which would show you at once how grossly you have been deceived, how much Emmeline has been wronged, and by that man whom you thought your friend?"

"Good God! surely I am labouring under some mysterious delusion—I cannot hear aright," ejaculated Sir Eustace; "would I receive my poor Emmeline with the affection of a brother? Oh, Heaven! thou knowest that I would, and with what transport; even though she be guilty of the vices with which her character has been stigmatised! What a precious boon would she be to my declining years, and—but you rack me, woman; say, where is she? Where shall I find my sister?"

"Eustace! dear, dear Eustace," cried Kate, with a passionate flood of tears, putting back her white hood, and kneeling at the feet of the astonished man; "and has, then, time, care, and the disguise I have assumed, so altered me, that you do not know me? But—but look steadfastly into these features, or if you fail to recognise the likeness of one who was once dear to you, consult the emotions of your own heart, and behold your sister—your long lost sister, Emmeline, kneeling at your feet."

"Emmeline!" cried Sir Eustace, with distended eyes, and his limbs agitated with convulsive emotions, as he fixed his gaze upon the weeping woman kneeling at his feet; "Great Heaven! is it possible? And have we, then, so often met, and yet I not to remember you? But it must be; yes, yes, my heart would not thus instinctively throb for any one but my sister. She is restored to me—Eustace is not left alone in the world—Emmeline—dear, dear Emmeline, sister, and mother of—no, I dare not utter that name; it is coupled with disgrace and shame, and at once dashes away the honied cup I had just raised to my lips, and replaces it with one of poison. No, no, Emmeline, I pardon you, but I dare not—will not recognize you as the mother of my Angelina."

"And if you did, you would be wrong," said Emmeline, (for such, our readers will perceive, that Kate of the Ruins, as we have hitherto called her, was). "Angelina is not my daughter!"

"Not your daughter!" gasped forth Sir Eustace, with increased astonishment; "what strange mystery is this?—Do not seek to deceive me, Emmeline, or you will drive me mad;

if she be not your child, who, then, are her parents?"

"Her father has long been no more," replied Emmeline, solemnly, "he fell by the blade of an assassin. Her mother has also for many years been considered dead, but she lives."

"Keep me not in this torturing state of suspense," said Sir Eustace, unable scarcely to contain himself, "of whom do you speak? For the love of Heaven, tell me."

"Of Matilda, Baroness de Morton," replied Emmeline.

"Merciful Heaven! is it possible?" ejaculated Sir Eustace; "our cousin!"

"The same!"

"And Hugh Clifford?" gasped forth Sir Eustace, with breathless eagerness.

"Is my son;—the child, as you imagined, of shame," answered Emmeline, "but he knows it no'."

"Great God! thy ways are wonderful!" cried Sir Eustace, "but, oh, Emmeline, why was I so deceived?"

"Dear Eustace," said his sister, affectionately, "do not condemn me unheard; at a more fitting opportunity I will explain everything to you; but, for the present, rest assured that all I have done has been under the impression it was for the best."

"But you say Matilda lives?" observed Sir Eustace; "where, where?"

"Beneath this abbey, among the vaults; where she has been secreted for years," answered Emmeline.

"Is it possible?—But oh, my sister, how could she remain so long without claiming and seeking the restoration of her child?" demanded Sir Eustace.

"For particular reasons, that will be afterwards explained," answered Emmeline; "but think not, Eustace, that she has not watched over her—been almost constantly near her, and that she has not been the object of her constant solicitude. Alas! no;—what a life of suffering has been hers and which she was con-

strained to adhere to for awhile, to prevent the sacrifice of the lives of both her, myself, and Angelina."

"And who is the villain who who has occasioned all this?" asked Sir Eustace.

"Who, think you," returned Emmeline, "who think you, but the murderer, the seducer, the wretch, the usurper, who calls himself the Baron de Morton!"

"Ah!—I thought so!" ejaculated Eustace, "the miscreant! But, by Heaven he shall not escape my vengeance. But Emmeline, my sister, restored to me after the lapse of so many years! I can scarcely believe my senses; it seems more like a dream than reality!—Dear, dear Emmeline; one more fond embrace, and——"

"Hold!" exclaimed Emmeline, drawing herself back, as he offered to enfold her in his arms. "Do you believe me guilty of the vices with which I have been charged?"

"You have asserted your innocence, Emmeline," replied Eustace, "solemnly protested it; and can I doubt the solemn asseverations of my sister? Oh, no, Emmeline, I cannot, I dare not. I will not believe you capable of the errors that have been attributed to you, and, by Heaven, on the heads of your base calumniators shall descend the vengeance of your brother."

Once more did Sir Eustace Arlingham, and the sister from whom he had been so long parted, and had never expected to meet again, ardently embrace, and, unable to repress the power of their feelings, they wept upon each other's bosoms.

"But come, my dear brother," said Emmeline, "I will introduce you immediately to our much-injured cousin, and the fond mother of Angelina, whom, my heart tells me, will soon be restored to us, and then I will enter into a full detail of the many painful and singular events that have happened to me since last we met."

Sir Eustace Arlingham offered not a word in reply; in fact, his heart was at present too full to speak, but dashing the tears from his manly brow, he followed Emmeline to the interior of the abbey.

———

CHAPTER XXX.

WE need not attempt to describe the manner in which the Baron De Morton behaved towards Hugh Clifford from the time he got him in his power; suffice it to say, that it was brutal in the extreme; but Clifford received his taunts and persecutions with the most superlative contempt, and mocked at his threats. To know, however, that Angelina was in his power, and that he was prevented from rendering her any assistance, greatly tormented his mind, and he felt truly wretched. As regarded his own fate, he felt quite indifferent; but to know that she to whom his heart was devoted, was left to the tender mercies of the villain De Morton, filled his bosom with the most poignant anguish, and there were moments when his anxiety and fear became insupportable. He was placed in a dungeon under the left wing of the tower, and heavily fettered, and his fare was of the coarsest and most loathsome description. The place, too, was horribly damp, and always buried in impenetrable darkness, and the rats and other vermin used to crawl about in abundance, and over him, as he stretched his limbs upon the heap of straw which formed his pallet. Tedious and painful were the hours that the young man passed in this horrible place, and the baron daily visited him to glut over his anguish, and to exult in the success which crowned his villanous schemes. He threatened him with perpetual imprisonment, and in tones of irony informed him, that he would suffer him to live to know that Angelina was living with him as his mistress. At these times it was with the utmost difficulty that he could restrain his temper, or bear with it with the least degree of patience. In spite, however of the threats of the baron, and the wretch Rufus, Clifford did not give way entirely to despair, and there

were moments when his hopes were so strongly raised that he could not help believing he should not only be able to effect his liberation, but also to rescue Angelina, uninjured, from his power. He had not the least doubt but that the men who had come with him on the expedition, when they found that he did not return, would conclude that something had happened to him; and having made the circumstance known to Kate of the Ruins, some means would be immediately adopted by her to ensure his restoration to liberty, and the liberation of Angelina.

Thus passed away several days, and Clifford suffered no change in his circumstances, nor saw any prospect of being released from his present painful confinement. He suffered considerably from the effects of the wound which had been inflicted on him when he and our heroine were seized by Rufus and his accomplices, more especially as he was supplied with no remedy for it, and the cure of it was left entirely to chance. However, he had naturally an excellent constitution, and, in a short time, it entirely healed, without his feeling any further bad effects from it. As day after day glided on, and still he saw no prospect of being released from his gloomy dungeon, his impatience grew stronger, and at certain times the pain he felt was intolerable; and he raved in the most violent manner against the villany of the baron, who only mocked at and reviled his sufferings. And must he, then, end his days in that awful place, and Angelina so near him and yet be unable to approach her, or to render her any protection against the power of the villain by whom she was persecuted? Alas! it appeared not at all improbable; for what prospect had he to the contrary? Should De Morton discover that it was found out he was confined in the Grey Tower, he would adopt sure means of frustrating every scheme to rescue him from his power; and he was aware that the baron had the means of placing him in the hands of the law, and thus gratify his vengeance, without taking the responsibility upon himself. His mind was dreadfully tortured when he thought upon the sufferings Angelina was, doubtless, enduring from the cruelties of De Morton, who, it was very evident, was a villain that would not stick at anything to accomplish his desires.

One day Rufus missed coming to him, and in the evening he was visited by another man, who brought him his provisions, and it appeared was in future deputed to attend upon him. To the astonishment of Clifford, he discovered in this man, one who had formerly been one of his crew, and the surprise of Winton (which was the name of the man) was no less than that of Clifford. Hope was in a moment restored to the mind of the latter, who could not but think that Winton would not be able long to resist the entreaties of his old captain, but assist him to escape. In this he was not mistaken. Winton promised at the earliest opportunity to aid him in his flight; and the following night he kept his word. The door of his dungeon was opened to him—he was released from his heavy fetters, and himself and Winton (who had determined to fly with him) were soon far away from the Grey Tower.

As he could not learn anything of the men who had come there with him, or the vessel which contained them, Clifford took the advice of his companion, and having procured a boat, proceeded across the water to a fisherman's hut on the opposite shore, the fisherman being a relation of his (Winton's), and where he purposed that they should remain for a day or two, until he could come to some determination or another, what it would be best should be done.

It is unnecessary to state that it was in consequence of the escape of Hugh Clifford that the baron had come to the determination of so abruptly removing Angelina from the tower, and it was now his intention to convey her to France, where, he had not the least doubt, she would be secure from discovery; and he was resolved that he would no longer delay the gratification of his desires, which she resisted so obstinately. Scarcely, however, had they quitted the shore, when a violent storm arose, and the vessel was dashed about like a straw. In vain she struggled with the furious elements—she soon went to pieces, and those who were on board of her, were immersed in the deep, and all expected, of course, a watery grave. The unfortunate ship was wrecked within sight of shore, and before any of the fishermen could render assistance. Our heroine, who had clung to a piece of the wreck, floated, and was at length picked up, but in a state of insensibility, by the very same fisherman at whose hut Hugh Clifford and Winton were staying. What became of De Morton and the other persons, it was not known, and it was, therefore, concluded that they had perished.

The transport, the astonishment, and the delight evinced by our heroine and Hugh Clifford, on being thus miraculously restored to each other, exceeded all bounds, and it was some time ere they could speak or do anything but embrace each other; but when the power of speech was restored to them, they returned their thanks to the Almighty in the most earnest and enthusiastic manner. When they related what had happened to them, and the manner in which the baron had served them, their indignation against that guilty nobleman was greatly increased, and they could not help thinking that the untimely death he had most likely met with, was only the just retribution of offended Heaven.

The next day was the time fixed upon by them both to take their departure, and to make the best of their way to Mr. Woodfield, and in the meanwhile Angelina was accommodated in the cottage of an old woman who lived near to where Hugh Clifford was staying. We will pass over the voyage, and bring the lovers at once to St. Mark's Abbey, where the arrived the day after the scene took place between Sir Eustace Arlingham and Emmeline, his sister, which we have described in the previous chapter. The surprise and delight of Sir Eustace and Emmeline (for they were together in the abbey at the time), baffles all description, but at first Sir Eustace was fearful that his apprehensions as regarded the clandestine marriage of Angelina and Hugh Clifford was too well founded; but when they briefly explained what had happened to them, he, of course, was quite satisfied, and gave free indulgence to his happiness, at the restoration of two beings who were both now, he had discovered, attached to him by the ties of consanguinity.

Angelina could not but notice, with no small degree of astonishment, the unusual affectionate manner in which they were both greeted by Kate, which was the only name they at present knew her by, and she felt confident that something particular had happened, and their hearts forebeded that something of importance was about to take place. The congratulations being over, Sir Eustace showed considerable emotion and tenderness of feeling as he addressed himself to our heroine—

"Angelina," exclaimed he, "you must prepare yourself for a surprise; but it will be a joyful one;—the secret which has been kept so long regarding your birth, I am now about to divulge!"

Angelina turned ghastly pale at these observations, and she looked at him and Emmeline alternately, but without being able to speak, while Clifford was scarcely less agitated than herself.

"Compose yourself, my dear girl," said Emmeline, in accents of the greatest tenderness, "or you will not be able to support the surprising intelligence which is about being imparted to you; and you, Clifford, you will also be no less astonished, and, I doubt not, delighted, for I have also some information for you that——"

"For goodness sake, do not keep us any longer in suspense, my dear friends," said Clifford; "what can be the surprising intelligence to which you allude?"

"Angelina," said Sir Eustace, "in this lady, whom you have hitherto known only as Kate of the Ruins, you behold my sister, the Lady Emmeline Dalton, and in me, Sir Eustace Arlingham!"

Angelina was thunderstruck, and stood gazing upon them for a moment or two in stupified amazement, unable to say a word; but in an instant she found herself clasped close to the bosom of Lady Emmeline, whose tears of ecstasy were shed upon her countenance as she pressed her lips fervently to those of our heroine.

"Good God!" at length gasped forth Angelina, "is it possible that I can hear aright, or do my ears deceive me! I am bewildered, and scarcely know what I am saying. Am I then, indeed, not related to you, sir?"

"Yes, my child," said Sir Eustace, in his usual affectionate manner, "your mother is my first cousin."

"Mother!—mother!" repeated our heroine. "How that name agitates me. Oh, tell me, who was my mother, and why have I been so long separated from her, and left alone to your protection?"

"I have a long explanation to give you, my child," said Sir Eustace, once more embracing her passionately, while Clifford was so astonished at all he heard, that he was unable to utter a syllable, but stood gazing first at one, and then at the other, with an expression that may be imagined; "but not now: suffice it to say, that your mother has been the victim of cruelty and injustice, and that the blood of your murdered father calls aloud for vengeance on his assassin. Matilda, Baroness de Morton, is the name of her who gave you being!"

Had an avalanche at that moment descended on the head of Angelina, she could not have exhibited greater surprise than she did when Sir Eustace gave utterance to these words.

"God of Heaven!" she cried, "can this be true?—Ah! I see it all now!—the terror and behaviour of the baron is sufficiently explained! But, oh! tell me, does my mother still live?"

"She does," answered Lady Emmeline, "and in this very abbey, where she has been so long secluded, and watched that adored child she was afraid to acknowledge. She is even now close at hand, ready to clasp her daughter to her bosom."

"Oh, let me fly to her arms!" exclaimed Angelina, frantically; "do not keep me longer from that blessing I have never yet experienced; My mother!—Oh, what rapture is there in that sacred name! A tide of feelings rush to my heart I have never experienced before! Oh, do not, pray, do not detain me!"

"But a few minutes, my dear girl," returned Sir Eustace; " and pray calm the violence of your emotion, or your feelings will overpower you."

Angelina gasped for breath, but she could not speak, and sinking into a chair, she looked imploringly into the countenances of Sir Eustace and his sister alternately,

"This is wonderful!" observed Clifford. "But what is it that you would impart to me? I am certain that there is something in this that——"

"Clifford!" interrupted Lady Emmeline, with extreme emotion, while tears trembled in her eyes—"Clifford, you ever believed, at least, I so instructed you, that Captain Clifford was your father, and that I was only some distant relation to you; but it is not so. Oh, Clifford, does not your heart tell you that there must be a nearer tie than that one to draw us together?"

"For Heaven's sake be explicit," gasped forth Clifford, as a strange foreboding flashed across his brain.

"Captain Clifford was in no way related to you," answered Lady Emmeline; "but he was a sincere and well-tried friend to me and mine; your father (I know not if he still live) was Lord Edward Dalton, and your mother——"

"Ah! what of her?"

"She stands before you!—My son!—My darling boy!"

Clifford in a moment was locked in the arms of his mother, and surprise, rapture, and a variety of feelings took from him all utterance.

"Good God!" at last he observed, "is it possible that I am pressed to the heart of my mother! Oh! yes, it must be so; an instinctive feeling tells me that it is; none other than a parent could ever have behaved so kind to me. But why did you not reveal yourself to me before? Why has this mystery remained so long without being unravelled?"

"Oh, my son," answered Lady Emmeline again embracing him with fervour, "when you have been made acquainted with my melancholy story, you will not be surprised that I did not discover myself to you before. But you shall know all."

"Wonderful!" said Clifford; "and in Sir Eustace Arlingham, whom I have hitherto known as Mr. Woodfield, I recognise my uncle?"

"True!"

"For pity's sake, do not longer rack my mind," said Angelina, who, while this conversation was going on, had been sitting in a state of agony and suspense, which, after the explanation given by Lady Emmeline, may be very easily conceived; "if you have, indeed, not deceived me, and it is true my mother still lives, oh, take me to her, that I may receive her maternal embrace, and hear, for the first time, a mother's blessing."

She had scarcely given utterance to these words, when the room-door was sudddenly thrown open, and the next moment the form of the Baroness De Morton, and the supposed phantom, stood before her. Angelina fixed one look of intense affection upon her, uttered a faint scream, and the exclamation of "Mother," and rushing frantically towards her, fell insensible at her feet.

————

CHAPTER XXXI.

WE will now proceed to detail the particulars of the "strange eventful history" connected with the principal characters in our narrative, and with which the reader is, no doubt, anxious to be made acquainted.

The noble and Gothic hall of the wealthy family of Arlingham, was situated in a beautiful and romantic spot, near the river D——, and from its casements it commanded a delightful prospect of the full extent of the river, slowly and calmly winding its silvery course through plains and meadows, until it was lost in a distant forest, whose tall trees rose in picturesque and mountainous clusters on the distant horizon.

This spacious and venerable edifice had been in the possession of the Arlingham family

HUGH CLIFFORD A PRISONER IN THE GREY TOWER.

from time immemorial; and many were the noble deeds attributed to its members, and numerous were the records transmitted to posterity of their gallant achievements on the battle-field.

The father of Sir Eustace Arlingham and Lady Emmeline, was one of the most noble and virtuous of men—the favourite of his sovereign, in whose service he had fought with a valour which had excited the wonder and admiration of every one who esteemed and were anxious to maintain the liberties and institutions of their country, and was beloved no less by his dependants at home, for philantrophy was his prevailing passion; and many were the unfortunate beings who had good cause to bless and revere his name.

Lady Arlingham (to whom Sir Edward Arlingham had been united when very young) was every way worthy of such a husband—mild, affable, amiable, and benevolent. He sole delight seemed to be in doing good—in seeking to make her husband happy—in instructing her children, and inciting them to those deeds of virtue that had rendered her and her husband such bright ornaments of society.

Eustace Arlingham was several years the senior of his sister, Emmeline, and early evinced all those noble and excellent qualities which his father possessed. Emmeline, too, answered all the expectations of her fond parents; and as she increased in years, so likewise did her virtues and her beauty.

There was but another being who formed one of this happy family, and that was Matilda, the orphan daughter of Lady Arlingham's sister, whose parents having died when she was very young, she had since been brought up under the protection of her uncle and aunt, with the same care and affection as if she had been their own child. And well did the beauteous Matilda repay their kindness, for her mind being endowed with every virtuous and amiable quality, it was her constant study to please them, and to show how well she had profitted by the brilliant example they had set her. She was only a year younger than Emmeline, and they loved each other with the same passionate fondness as if they had been sisters.

Lady Arlingham died suddenly, when Emmeline was not more than sixteen years of age, and Sir Edward was so deeply affected, that he never recovered, and in the course of a few months followed his wife to the tomb, leaving his son, Eustace, in the possession of his title and estates, and appointing him the guardian of his sister and Matilda, until they became of age.

This task he was prepared to fulfil in the most excellent and praiseworthy manner, for never was brother more fondly attached to a sister, than he was to Emmeline; and on his cousin he bestowed the most unbounded affection.

Two years passed away—years of uninterrupted happiness, unless it was the sorrow occasioned when they recalled to their memory the irreparable loss they had sustained by the demise of the late Sir Edward and Lady Arlingham. At this period, Sir Eustace led to the hymenial altar Amabel, the fair and accomplished daughter of Lord and Lady Hammersford, in his union with whom he anticipated every earthly felicity. But, although Lady Amabel ever behaved with kindness and attention to Sir Eustace, there was not that passionate fondness in her conduct which he had been sanguine enough to expect; and there were times when she would be buried in a profound melancholy, from which he found it impossible to arouse her, and was equally unable to penetrate. This, of course, caused him considerable uneasiness, and he endeavoured all in his power to dissipate it. He redoubled his affectionate attentions, was most studious to anticipate her every wish, and tried every effort his mind could suggest to enliven her, in which task he was ably assisted by his sister and Matilda, who had formed the most fervent attachment to the Lady Amabel, the graces of whose mind shone forth, upon all occasions, most redundantly. She, too, was not unmindful of their love, and frequently repaid them by her earnest assurances of a reciprocal affection.

At length, however, the ennui that had formerly at times afflicted Lady Amabel, entirely disappeared, and she seemed studious to show her husband, by the most fervent affection, the gratitude she felt for the love he had honoured her with, and the manner in which he had sought to make her completely happy.

Emmeline and Matilda were now fast blooming into all the charms of womanhood, and had had many suitors ; but Emmeline had not yet seen one she could love sufficiently to bestow on him her hand. Matilda, however, had captured the heart of Algernon, Baron de Morton, and she was soon compelled to acknowledge that her heart throbbed with a responsive sentiment, for the baron was every way worthy of her, both from his rank, his wealth, his personal and intrinsic recommendations. Sir Eustace offered no opposition to their addresses, and the baron was recognised as her affianced husband.

Upon the terrace, of which we have before spoken, and which commanded so delightful a prospect, it was the custom of Sir Eustace, Lady Amabel, Emmeline, her fair cousin, and her lover, to sit for hours, engaged in charming conversation, and contemplating the boats as they lightly skimmed over the river's surface.

It was a lovely day in June, when the sun was in its meridian, that they were seated on this terrace as usual, and had been for some time amused by watching a race between two small boats, which were occupied by four young gentlemen, when they accidently came in collision with each other, and in a moment they upset, precipitating them all into the water. Some persons on the shore immediately put off to their assistance, and succeeded in saving three of them, but the other met with a watery grave.

The consternation of the friends, particularly the ladies, on beholding this catastrophe, may be easily imagined ; but Sir Eustace immediately summoned two or three of his domestics, and ordered them to hasten to the spot, and desire that the gentlemen should accept of an invitation to the hall, until they had recovered from the effects of their immersion in the water. The gentlemen gladly availed themselves of this offer ; and having changed their apparel from the wardrobe of

Sir Eustace, they were introduced to him, the Baron de Morton, and the ladies. Lady Arlingham no sooner beheld one of them, Sir Vincent Rosenford, than she turned ghastly pale, clung to the back of a chair, and seemed nearly sinking, while Sir Vincent himself exhibited considerable confusion, and went through the ceremony of introduction very awkwardly.

Sir Eustace noticed this circumstance with some surprise ; and Sir Vincent, no doubt observing it, said, in a faltering voice,—

" I pray you excuse this confusion, Sir Eustace ; but I have had the honour of meeting Lady Amabel frequently before at her father's, and the agreeable surprise of again seeing her so unexpectedly——"

" I beg you will make no further apology, sir," said Sir Eustace, in a tone of satisfaction ; " I am happy to think we have been introduced to each other, although I would much rather it had been under more pleasant circumstances. I hope this will be the commencement of an intimacy that will afford pleasure to us all."

Sir Vincent bowed politely, and returned some appropriate answer ; but Lady Amabel evinced very little more composure, and begged to be permitted to retire, attributing her illness to the sudden shock her feelings had sustained through witnessing the fatal accident on the river.

Sir Vincent Rosenford was a fine, handsome young man, and highly accomplished. His address was easy, and his manner prepossessing ; yet, with all, he possessed passions the most licentious and unprincipled. He had, however, the means of concealing his real sentiments in such a manner as to deceive the nicest observer ; and his conversation and general demeanour were so insinuating, that he readily ingratiated himself into the esteem of those who beheld him.

His two companions were Lord Edward Dalton and the Marquis Le Clair, a French nobleman. They had come down to D—— for a short time, in order to enjoy the scenery, when the accident ccc rred which we have just related, attended with such fatal results.

Sir Eustace Arlingham was so well pleased with their new acquaintances, that he warmly invited them to honour him by frequently becoming his guests, and they accepted his invitation with much apparent pleasure, especially Lord Dalton and Sir Vincent. Scarcely a day passed without their visiting Arlingham Hall; and it was soon evident, from the marked attention which Lord Dalton paid to Emmeline, that she had taken possession of his affections; and all doubt upon the subject was very shortly removed, by his confessing his passion to Sir Eustace, and requesting his sanction to his paying his devoirs to his lovely sister.

Sir Eustace, who had formed a very high opinion of the young nobleman, gave him every encouragement, and referred him to the object of his love herself. Lord Dalton obeyed : but his hopes were blighted ; Emmeline informed him, that although she could esteem him as a friend, he could never possess her heart.

Had the beauteous Emmeline spoken sincerely the sentiments of her heart, she must have owned that that heart had been taken possession of by Sir Vincent Rosenford; and though, whenever their eyes met, the glances they bestowed upon each other was a convincing proof that their passion was mutual, they had never spoken of it, nor had they given utterance to a word in the presence of one another, or their friends, which could create the least suspicion of their sentiments.

Sir Eustace was extremely vexed at the peremptory manner in which his sister had rejected the suit of Lord Dalton, for he was greatly prepossessed in his favour, and considered himself in every way worthy of her hand; and in his anxiety to see her happy, he became unjust in seeking to bias her affections, and to make a sacrifice of her hand to a man whom she had candidly acknowledged she could esteem as a friend, but could not love. He desired a private interview with Emmeline; and after informing her that he, as her guardian, had

given his assent to the addresses of Lord Dalton, expressed his surprise that she should so abruptly decline his suit. He then affectionately addressed her, pointed out the merits of his lordship, and the advantages of an alliance being formed between the houses of Dalton and Arlingham, and he trusted that she would maturely consider it, and give her assent to a union upon which, he admitted, he had fixed his mind, being only guided by a wish of seeing her happy.

Emmeline evinced the strongest emotion upon this address. Since the death of Sir Edward, she had been used to look up to Sir Eustace not only as a father, but a brother, and it grieved her sincerely to be the means of acting in any way which might cause him uneasiness; although, at the same time, she could not help thinking that he was asking too much of her to expect her to sacrifice her own wishes entirely to his will. She, however, did not confess her real sentiments, but begged her brother to forbear to urge a proposal to which she was herself averse. She admitted the virtues of Lord Edward, but told her brother that she was too young to think of a change in her situation at present, and that she had no desire to leave him ; but that, if even she should be compelled to that alternative, Lord Edward Dalton was not the man of whom her choice would fall as a partner for life.

"Nay, Emmeline," said Sir Eustace, "this is folly. It is childish. Lord Edward is a noble and amiable youth, and every way worthy of becoming your husband, and I cannot see what reasonable objection you can make to him. You know, my dear girl, I would not advise you wrongfully, or urge anything which I thought would be the means of detracting from your happiness; but this alliance seems to be so desirable, that I must, indeed, request you will think better of it, and urge you not prematurely to reject an offer which, I believe, will be so advantageous, and on which I have fixed my mind."

With these words Sir Eustace quitted the

room; and, with a heart full to bursting, Emmeline hastened to Matilda and Lady Amabel, to whom she imparted what had taken place between her brother and her, and to them acknowledged the love with which Sir Vincent Rosenford had inspired her, but begged that they would not make Sir Eustace acquainted with it, urging them only to endeavour to persuade her brother not to persist in wishing her to unite herself to Lord Dalton, which, although she honoured his virtues, would make her wretched for life.

At the mention of the name of Sir Vincent Rosenford, Lady Arlingham uttered a scream, and turned ghastly pale, trembling violently at the same time.

" Recal your words, Emmeline," cried Lady Amabel, in a voice of the deepest emotion; " for Heaven's sake endeavour to stifle your fatal passion; for——"

" Gracious heaven! Lady Amabel," interrupted Emmeline, she and Matilda gazing upon her ladyship with the greatest astonishment, " what do you mean? why are you thus dreadfully agitated?"

" Oh! do not ask me," gasped forth Lady Arlingham; " do not ask me, unless you would drive me mad; do not give any encouragement to the sentiments with which the too powerful accomplishments and graces of Sir Vincent have excited in your bosom. I cannot say more;—pray leave me to myself for a few minutes;—this intelligence has——. Leave me, my dear girls, I implore ye!"

Completely bewildered and astonished at the singular and mysterious behaviour of Lady Arlingham, Emmeline and Matilda did as she desired.

Weeks passed away, and Lord Dalton was unremitting in his attentions towards Emmeline; and her brother urged her to encourage his vows with even more earnestness and perseverance than ever; and suffice it to say, that, after the lapse of a few months, she reluctantly yielded, and became Lady Dalton, at the same time that the Baron de Morton was

united to her cousin Matilda. Lord Dalton purchased a beautiful estate near Arlingham Hall, so that he might not separate his lovely bride from her brother; and if Emmeline was not supremely happy, the fondness and attention of Lord Edward rendered her at least contented, or so she appeared to be. A few months, however, had only glided away, when the whole of the family were thrown into a complete state of distraction, to find that Lady Emmeline had eloped, and it was ascertained that the companion of her flight was Sir Vincent Rosenford.

It is quite unnecessary for us to attempt to describe the grief, surprise, and disgust, excited in the breasts of Sir Eustace and the friends of Lady Emmeline upon the discovery of her flight; and after they received such indubitable proof that Sir Vincent Rosenford was her companion, it is quite sufficient to state that it was of the most intense description, more especially that of Sir Eustace, who was completely thunderstruck at the circumstance, and (although after being aware of the sentiments of Emmeline as regarded her husband, and the preference she had given to Sir Vincent, it ought not to have been any matter to him) he not only condemned her for her adultery, but was firmly resolved that nothing should ever induce him to acknowledge her for his sister again, unless she could fully, and most unquestionably, establish her innocence of what now appeared to be so apparent. As for the unhappy husband of Lady Emmeline, he was in a complete state of distraction at her unexpected elopement; and, for several weeks after the distressing circumstance, he was in a state of utter phrensy. Every possible search was instituted after the fugitives, but all efforts to discover any clue to the course they had taken were without effect. Lord Dalton's heart was completely broken; he assured Sir Eustace of his forgiveness of his wife's fatal indiscretion, but at the same time declared that nothing should ever make him pardon her guilty seducer, and that if fate ever caused them to meet again, death to both or one of them must ensue before they parted. After this, and having given up all hope of discovering the retreat of his wife and her guilty paramour, his lordship bade a melancholy and affectionate adieu to Sir Eustace Arlingham and the Baron and Baroness de Merton, and then took his departure for the continent, expressing it as his determination never to return to England again.

Ever since the elopement of Lady Emmeline and Sir Vincent, the illness of Lady Arlingham had increased, and there were times when she was completely delirious, and uttered strange and incoherent sentences, which her auditors tried, but in vain, to comprehend. She raved, however, continually of the ill-fated Emmeline and Sir Vincent ; and at the mention of the latter's name, her agitation would become so intense, that it was not expected she could survive one moment from another. The first medical aid that the country could produce, was called in by her distracted and affectionate husband, but after having tried the very utmost of their skill, they gave him not the least hopes of her ultimate recovery, and Sir Eustace, to his sorrow, found that their predictions were just.

At length the fatal moment approached, Lady Amabel had been worse for the last few days, and it was very evident to those who attended her, that her end was at not great distance. For three days she had been delirious, and raved in the most awful manner, accusing herself of crimes at which human nature shudders. Although most of those who attended her felt convinced that most of what she uttered was only the wild ravings of a distemperd brain, they could not help thinking that there was something upon her conscience which she was anxious, yet fearful to divulge, and a few hours before her death verified these conjectures. Sir Eustace had only left her bedside for an hour or two at intervals to gain a short period of rest, when suddenly her reason seemed to be restored to her, and looking upon

him earnestly, she, in a voice perfectly calm, desired him to approach nearer to her. He obeyed her, happy to see such a change, and taking her hand, expressed a hope that she was better.

"Better," she repeated in a melancholy tone "oh, yes, I am indeed much better, better that Heaven has been merciful enough to grant me reason before I quit this world, to confess my errors and to pray to Him for mercy. Eustace, draw nearer."

Sir Eustace, almost choked with emotion, yet striving all in his power to stifle his anguish, advanced closer to the side of her couch, and with eyes brimful of tears, he clasped the hand of his dying wife, and without being able to give utterance to a syllable, awaited with the most poignant agony to hear what she had to impart to him.

"Eustace, dear Eustace, if such I dare call you," said Lady Amabel, looking up into the face of her husband with an expression of the most indiscribable emotion, "dry your tears, and abate your anguish, I am unworthy of either; eh! that I could have repaid your love as it deserved, or that the Almighty had taken my life ere I betrayed the confidence you reposed in me. Eustace, you behold before you a poor penitent, but guilty wretch, unworthy of your pity, deserving only of your abhorrence. Say, were I to confess myself an adultress, were I to say that another has revelled in those enjoyments I swore at the altar none other but you should possess, would you not curse me, would you not hate, despise, loathe me? Yes, I know you must, you will."

"Oh, my love, my adored Amabel," sighed forth the deeply afflicted Sir Eustace, half choked with sobs, "why talk in this manner? What should so deeply agonize you? Why should you give way to such wild, such inexplicable expressions? Nay, nay, my love, your brain is disordered, you know not what you say, you——"

"Eustace," interrupted Lady Arlingham, in tones of the deepest solemnity, "I feel that there are but a few minutes intervening between me and eternity! I am certain that ere long I shall be in the dread presence of my Almighty Judge, and it is my most earnest wish, ere I go before that awful tribunal, to make all the earthly atonement in my power, by confessing to you my guilt. Eustace, I am an adultress! I have been false to those vows I plighted with you at the connubial altar!"

Sir Eustace turned deadly pale; he gazed upon the features of his expiring wife with an expression of the most unutterable horror, and he was unable to give utterance to a single word.

"Yes, I see how it is, I but imagined right," gasped forth Lady Amabel; "but what else could I expect? What else could I hope? What deserve? Nay, my husband, if I dare now venture to call you by that name, think not that I know not what I am uttering. Alas! would that it were untrue; Eustace, Sir Vincent Rosenford———"

Sir Eustace started at the mention of that detested name, his lips quivered, a palsy shook his frame, and it was with difficulty he could support himself; he tried to speak, but his tongue clave to the palate of his mouth, and he with distended eye-lids fixed his gaze upon the pale countenance of his wife, and awaited what she would next say with the most breathless and indescribable anguish.

"Ah! well may you shudder with horror," ejaculated Lady Arlingham, "well may you look at me agast; but now will you hate and curse my memory, when I tell you that Sir Vincent Rosenford, since he has been your accepted guest, has become the seducer of the poor, unhappy, guilty wretch, who now lies before you."

"Horror! horror! great heaven! let me not hear this dreadful acknowledgment, and be convinced of its truth!" exclaimed Sir Eustace.

"But you must hear it, Eustace," said his wife, "yes, your guilty wife cannot quit this world without———"

"My God!" interrupted Sir Eustace Ar-

lingham, "can this dreadful tale really be true; and my stster———"

Lady Arlingham groaned, and covering her face with the bed-clothes remained silent for a few seconds, while her husband, clasping his burning temples, paced the room with hasty and uneven steps, and the deep sobs that ever and anon escaped his heavily surcharged bosom, told too plainly how severely he suffered. At length, however, Lady Amabel once more looked up, and with more composure in her manner than might have been anticipated, she said—

"Sir Eustace, I feel my end rapidly approaching, and that my moments are numbered; let me then employ them in disclosing that, which at the same time will, perhaps, be a source of everlasting unhappiness to you, I cannot quit this world without disclosing. Before you sought my hand, Sir Vincent Rosenford had gained full possession of my heart. When my father bade me look upon you as my future husband, I feared to offer any opposition to his will (which I knew was peremptory) or to inform him of my affections, and throwing myself upon your mercy to withdraw your suit, but from that also I shrank with a feeling of dread which I found it utterly impossible to vanquish, and the fatal time arrived, we were united. Still, Eustace, think not, although another held possession of my warmest regard, that you were despised, that you have never held any place in my affections. Heaven knows that next to my guilty seducer, you have been, and you are dearer to me than any other being in existence; but who can control the strength of the first and ardent attachment? We were married; time passed on, and you saw the manner in which I behaved to you; the way in which I attempted to struggle with and conquer my feelings. Heaven knows that it was my most sincere wish, my hourly prayer, that nothing should ever make me swerve from the duties of a wife, and hard did I strive to forget that individual who was fated to be my greatest curse. You recollect the accident which first introduced Sir Vincent and his friends to you? You remember the deep emotion, the uncommon agitation I evinced upon that occasion, and after what I have mentioned, you cannot, you will not, be surprised at it. Oh, Eustace, how shall I give utterance to the guilty sequel? But it must be told! Sir Vincent, in spite of my situation, renewed his vows, and weak, guilty fool that I was, I yielded to his base wishes—"

"Almighty powers!" gasped forth Sir Eustace staggering and dropping into a seat; "and my sister, Emmeline, too!"

Lady Amabel made a powerful effort to speak, her bosom heaved with convulsive emotion, her countenance turned completely black, and sinking back on her pillow, with a groan, she yielded her spirit into the hands of her Creator.

Let us pass hastily over the painful scene which followed this dreadful disclosure. Suffice it to say that for a few days after the demise of his wife, Sir Eustace Arlingham was quite delirious, and it was feared by his medical attendants that he would never recover the severe shock his feelings had received; but at length his reason was restored to him, but not until the remains of his unfortunate but guilty wife were consigned to the tomb. Upon the head of the villain Sir Vincent Resendford he invoked a dreadful curse, and although he did not make any vow, he felt almost confident that he could never pardon his sister Emmeline, who had not only brought eternal disgrace upon their hitherto unsullied name, but had also broken the heart, or ruined the peace of mind for ever, of a fond and indulgent husband.

Fast did the clouds of misfortune gather over the once happy and proud house of Arlingham. Scarcely six months had fled from the time of the elopement of Lady Emmeline, and the death of his wife, when Sir Eustace, who had two or three most implacable enemies at court, who were jealous of the favour he had by his merits gained in the eyes of his sovereign, was accused of high treason; and so well concerted

was the villanous plot which had been formed against him, that his monarch, who had hitherto placed such implicit confidence in him, was persuaded of his guilt; and he was committed to prison upon the charge, and would, no doubt have been found guilty, but he escaped, and got on board a ship in disguise, with not any property in his possession, and by the assistance of a friend, made his way to Flanders, where, under an assumed name (that by which he was first introduced to our readers), and the exertion of that friend who had never deserted him in all his misfortunes, he set up in business and after remaining there upwards of two years with but indifferent success, during which time he had made every inquiry after his sister and her villanous companion (as he suspected) to no purpose, he resolved, having married his present wife, to return to England, he being so altered in personal appearance and in circumstances. that he thought it would be impossible for any one to recognise him. He did so, and settled in a remote part of the country, where by frugal habits and industry (for he had learnt to forget his rank, and had found even a source of pleasure and amusement in turning his hand to labour), he managed to live comfortably.

In the interim his property had been confiscated, and a price was set upon his head, either dead or alive. Another year elapsed, and Laura was born, when one night soon after they had retired to rest, they were awakened by the cries of a child, and Mr. Woodfield (as he then called himself) having hastily arisen, and slipped on a portion of his clothes, hastened to his cottage door, and was completely thunderstruck to behold, huddled up in one corner of the threshold, a child, apparently little more than two years and a half old, but the beauty of whose countenance surpassed everything he had beheld before. He took her hastily into the cottage, and calling to his wife, they trimmed the fire, which had not yet expired, and proceeded to examine the little stranger. She could only lisp out a few words, and from them they could not gather anything which could throw any light upon the subject, or give them the slightest idea as to who she was. The only words that they could distinctly make out were, that "strange woman, not mamma, had left her; that mamma would so cry if she did not go back," and many other expressions of a similar description, which they were at a perfect loss to understand, although they were strongly of opinion, that the child had been abandoned by its unnatural mother, and Sir

THE DEATH-BED OF LADY AMABEL.

Eustace could not help being particularly struck with the sweetness of its features, which bore a forcible resemblance to a countenance he had often seen before, but could not at the time recal to his memory where.

Having placed the poor little thing, who was handsomely dressed, under the care of his wife, Sir Eustace sallied forth from the cottage, thinking he might see some person who might answer the faint description of the female the child had given, but in this he was totally disappointed, as may be expected, and on his return, he found the child fast asleep on the lap of his wife, and she placed in his hands a scrap of paper which she had pinned in her bosom, and which contained the following lines—

"A much wronged and heavily afflicted woman, who was once acknowledged the sister of Sir Eustace Arlingham, submits to his care and affection her child, trusting that however prejudiced he may be against the unfortunate, but not guilty Emmeline, he will not despise or cast away the little innocent, whom it is no longer in her power to support ! The eyes of her mother will constantly watch over her, until those eyes are closed in death ; and when the clouds that at present obscure her happiness shall have dispersed, that mother with transport will reclaim her offspring, and hopes to be received once more with affection by that brother who now entertains so unjust an opinion of her conduct. In the bosom of the child, whom I wish to be called Angelina, you will find a purse of gold ; I wish you to appropriate a portion of it to the education of the child, and as you comply with these wishes, may the blessings of Heaven descend upon your head.

"EMMELINE."

Astonishment completely tied the tongue of Sir Eustace ; but when he had partly recovered from the emotion into which this unexpected and remarkable circumstance had thrown him, he snatched up the child in his arms, and after gazing rapturously upon its innocent features, he kissed it frantically, and burst into a violent paroxysm of tears. Suddenly, however, as an agonizing thought flashed across his brain, he replaced the little Angelina in the lap of his wife, and turning away with a shudder of horror and disgust, he said—

"But no ! is it not the child of shame ? The offspring of the villain who—Oh, God ! I shall go mad if I think of it !"

Clasping his forehead, he rushed away from her room, and hastening to his chamber, endeavoured to bury all recollection of the circumstance. Dreadful were the sufferings the power of his thoughts inflicted upon him that night, but by the dawn of the morning his thoughts had undergone a complete revolution, and he vowed to protect and love Angelina the same as if she had been his own child.

Sir Eustace had never imparted to his wife the minute details of his melancholy history ; she knew that he had been unfortunate ; she knew that he had had a sister ; but whether she was living or dead she was not acquainted ; she was also aware of the rank he had formerly held in society, and of his just title ; but finding that it ever caused him pain, she never ventured to mention the subject to him. She herself was of a humble family, and Sir Eustace had united himself to her entirely out of love for her numerous excellent qualities, which more than compensated for her want of education and polite attainments.

One particular circumstance we have forgotten to mention, and that is, when Sir Eustace, through the false accusation which had been brought against him, was compelled to fly his country, he became unavoidably estranged from the Baron and Baroness De Morton, who retired to their castle, and not long after he had been over in Flanders, he received intelligence of the sudden and mysterious disappearance of the baron, and to his most indescribable amazement and disgust, a short time only elapsed when he heard that Matilda had actually accepted the hand of her deceased husband's brother, who had been one of his greatest enemies at court, and to whom she had previously ever evinced the utmost repugnance. So thunderstruck was he with this intelligence, that he was some time before he would believe that it was true ; but when he was fully convinced that such was the case, he became so exasperated, that he resolved to endeavour to erase her name from his recollection for ever. The circumstance of the supposed death of the baroness has already been mentioned, and having now fully explained the melancholy events of Sir Eustace Arlingham's life, we must let the Lady Emmeline explain herself in her own words, as they were spoken to her brother on the night when she revealed herself to him.

CHAPTER XXXIII

"Eustace," commenced Lady Emmeline, "I am certain you will pity me, I know you must heartily feel for me, when you hear my painful narrative, for the sufferings to which I have, I can safely say, been most undeservedly subjected, and the unjust aspersions that have been cast upon my character. To you, Eustace, must I also attribute much blame, for so hastily condemning her to whom, I had ever cause to believe, you were so fondly attached, and who never gave you any reason to suspect her capable of acting in any way dishonourable to the name of Arlingham, or to that noble house to which I had allied myself. Oh! my brother, did you but know the nights, the days, the hours of intense, of indescribable anguish which I have for so many years endured, and yet, amidst it all, how constantly my prayers were offered up for you, and that dear girl whom I loved as fondly as if she had been mine own offspring, how sincerely would you reproach yourself for——but, no matter, let me pass this painful subject over as quickly as possible! Heaven knows, you have had your share of affliction, and I ought not to reproach you after the dreadful confession which the unfortunate, the ill-fated Amabel made to you on her death-bed. Ours has been an unfortunate family, Eustace; marked, as it were, by fate to be its sport—buffetted about as its caprice. But I become tedious. Alas! the recollection of the many sorrows I have endured, so bewilder my mind, that I scarcely know what I am talking about.

"I am ready to admit, Eustace, that I was wrong in one thing, and that was in not making you acquainted with the sentiments I had imbibed for Sir Vincent, when you urged the suit of Lord Dalton; but at the same time you should not have enforced me to unite my fate with a man whom I had candidly acknowledged to you I could not love, although I could sincerely esteem him as a friend. Had you not been so peremptory, and had I not been so tenacious of opposing the wishes of a brother, whom I had always revered as a superior being, how many misfortunes, how many cares might I have saved myself. But it is past now, and let me not waste any time in useless regret, but rather come as soon as possible to the conclusion of a narrative, the incidents of which I cannot recal to my memory without the deepest anguish. That I loved Sir Vincent, I have already admitted; but no sooner did I yield my hand to Lord Dalton, than I made up my mind to endeavour to discard him from my thoughts, and I can solemnly avow that, after I became the bride of his lordship, I never harboured a thought that I need since be ashamed of acknowledging. I must confess that I had a hard struggle with my feelings before I could accomplish my wishes: but the uniform affection of my husband, the high regard in which I had always held his virtues, and the duties that I felt were incumbent upon me as a wife, at length triumphed, and I became happy. Alas! it was not to last long; Sir Vincent (whom his friend never suspected for a moment of any guilty design, or the sentiments that really inhabited his mind towards me) was, as you are aware, a frequent, nay, almost a constant visitor at our house; and, although I must do myself the justice to state, I endeavoured as much as possible to avoid his presence, common etiquette would not admit of my always absenting myself, neither could I do so without making my husband acquainted with the secret, which I wished for his own sake and mine too, he might be kept in ignorance of.

"You may imagine what I suffered at those times, Eustace, but it was nothing to what it was my fate afterwards to undergo.

Although I most sedulously avoided all that was in my power being alone with Sir Eustace, he seized every opportunity he possibly could to be so, and to urge his passion. I heard him with feelings of disgust; severely reproached him for the injustice he did my character, and how much he wronged my husband, of whom he pretended to be so sincere a friend ; and when he still persevered in importuning me, and endeavouring to win me to the indulgence of his sensual desires, I threatened to make known his conduct to Lord Dalton ;—he threw off the mask in which he had so long concealed himself, and stood confessed in his true character. He laughed at my threats, mocked what he called my false modesty, and vowed that obdurate as I was, no power on earth should force him to give up the design he had fixed upon, and that in spite of all my opposition and my threats, he would not rest until he had accomplished his wishes, and had me in his power. I paid but little attention to his treats, for I thought them at the time merely to originate in disappointment and offended pride ; but it was not long ere I found out how egregiously mistaken I had been, and then I severely upbraided myself for not having made my husband acquainted with the whole of the circumstances ; but yet it was done from the best of motives ; I was fearful to distract his mind, and render him perpetually unhappy ; while, if he were kept in ignorance of the truth, he would be contented with the love I bestowed upon him, which was really sincere, and not have cause to torment his mind, where there was actually no occasion, by supposing me weak enough to yield to the persuasions of Sir Vincent Rosenford, and doing anything derogatory to the vows I had plighted to him at the altar.

" It was my custom frequently to walk forth in an evening in a neighbouring wood, when my husband was from home, and taking with me a book, I would sit down beneath some cool umbrageous shade, and peruse the contents, in undisturbed enjoyment of its beauties, until darkness set in, when I would return to the castle. It was upon one of those occasions that I was seized by some wretches whom Sir Vincent had employed, and borne away to an estate he had in a remote part of the country. Here I found myself entirely in his power, and was hourly tormented with his importunities. But I will not enter into the particulars of all I suffered from his loathsome addresses ; for loathsome they were to me now ; and I hated him as much as I had before loved him, for the base act of treachery he had been guilty of ; suffice it to say, and I call God solemnly to witness that I speak the truth, I was enabled to resist them, and to defeat him in all his attempts. Before I had been forced away, I had discovered myself to be in a delicate situation, and Sir Vincent, therefore, was forced to relax in his conduct for fear of fatal consequences, and I must do him the justice to say, that in the interval that elapsed prior to my confinement until subsequently, he behaved to me with the utmost kindness and attention, and I had all the advice and assistance my peculiar situation required. In a short time I gave birth to a son, whom it is unnecessary for me to state is that young man, whom you have hitherto known only as Hugh Clifford, but who is the lawful heir of Lord Edward Dalton, my husband. What with the suffering I underwent, in consequence of the manner in which I was situated, and the misery and anxiety I was aware that you and his lordship would be suffering, it was a long while before I was able to leave my bed, and it was then advised by the medical men, that I should have change of air, and the south of France was suggested as the most likely place where I might recruit my strength. In vain on my knees I implored Sir Vincent to restore me to my friends ; he was inexorable, and I was borne on board a ship together with my infant boy. In the night, after our quitting the sight of land, a terrific storm arose, and, in spite of all the efforts of the captain and crew, the ship became unmanageable, and shortly afterwards foundered. Better had it been for me and my offspring, perhaps, had we met with a watery grave at that time, for it would have saved us many, many cares it has since fallen to our lot to undergo. However, we were picked up by a smuggler, of whom a Captain Clifford, as he called himself, was the master; and we were behaved to with a humanity which would have reflected credit on those who take to themselves the sole merit of being christians. Sir Vincent Rosenford was never heard of afterwards, so, doubtless, he perished.

"Captain Clifford had formerly been a naval officer, and had done his country good service, but, like many other brave fellows, had met with the most shameful neglect; and disgusted with the treatment he had received, he quitted the service, and with the residue of a fortune he had been enabled to save from a very unsuccessful course of adventures, he purchased a vessel, and commenced the life of a smuggler, in which he met with the most extraordinary success, and soon accumulated a large sum of money. His principal retreat, or the place where he used to deposit his contraband goods, was in the cavern of the rock underneath the ruins of this abbey, and which I need not describe to you, as you have been in it several times. And the better to keep the place secure, a most awful report of the abbey and the adjoining spot being haunted, was industriously circulated, which the ignorant and the superstitious very readily believed, and sedulously avoiding it, Clifford and his companions were left in undisturbed possession of the ancient fabric.

"Captain Clifford was a married man, and had a family; and although his occupation was what is termed lawless, he was an excellent and humane man, and would have formed a bright example to many who pretended to far more rectitude of conduct. He sincerely pitied my situation, and looked upon my poor infant with the most unbounded compassion.

"'Poor little innocent,' he exclaimed, 'if your father will not receive you, I will replace his loss, and always be to you a protector and a parent!'

"I thought little of these words at that time, but I was not long before I was able to test their sincerity. Mr. Clifford brought me safe to England, and landed me at this spot, from which place, accompanied by one of his confidential men, with a heavy and foreboding heart I set out for Arlingham Hall. I will not attempt to describe my feelings as I proceeded thither—the hopes, the fears, that by turns distracted and perplexed my mind. At length I reached the well-known spot. My God! but to what a dreadful change did I return! The venerable home of my ancestors was in the possession of another; I was informed of your disgrace, Eustace; I was told of the distraction of my husband—his abrupt departure for the Continent, but to what particular part no one knew; and the guilty wretch I was supposed to be, not only by him, but by you, my brother, and almost everybody else. Guilty! yes—a guilty wretch, unworthy of pity or a thought. It is a wonder I did not go mad at that time, or that I did not destroy myself; but my little innocent's smiles withheld my hand, and for his sake I resolved to live.

"Captain Clifford took me to his house, and introduced me to his wife, who received me with the utmost kindness, and did all in her power to soothe me under my heavy afflictions, and at length she did partially succeed. I took up my residence with her, and the utmost attention was paid to me and my child. I had heard of the mysterious death of Lord De Morton, and of the second marriage of Matilda to his brother; I knew that brother to be a very base man, and that Matilda had ever viewed him with a feeling of hatred and dread, therefore was I certain that she had never willingly assented to become his wife. After considerable reflection upon the subject, I determined to seek an interview with her, and chance the reception she might give me. I left my child in the care of Mrs. Clifford, and set out for De Morton Castle; I asked an interview with the baroness; but judge of my astonishment when I was told that she was no more, and had been consigned to the tomb only the day before. It was from the baron himself that I received this information, and unable to suppress a feeling of disgust and horror that came over me in his presence, and extremely shocked at this unexpected intelligence of the death of my cousin, I hurried from the castle. I had only just entered the wood, when I found myself forcibly seized by the villain Rufus and another; and in spite of my screams for help, they forced me back to the castle, and taking me by a secret way, I was conveyed to an apartment, in which I was locked, and remained till the morning without seeing any person. The wretch De Morton then made his appearance, and after entering into a long and hypocritical apology for his conduct, vowed the most undounded passion for me, and offered me every enjoyment if I would yield to his base wishes. You may guess the answer I made him, the maunner in which I upbraided him for his villany; and, in a terrible rage, he left me, vowing that I should be his, and if I did not yield a compliance with his desires, he would use force to compel me. I will pass hastily over all that I endured while a prisoner in De Morton Castle, and the difficulty I had in resisting his nefarious designs; but at length, rumour having reported my being a prisoner there, I was removed secretly one night, and conveyed to the old Grey Tower, but unaccompanied by the baron, who intended to follow me as soon as he had an opportunity. Here I endured all the agony which the peculiarity and horror of my situation were calculated to engender; but the principal cause of my anguish was the idea of my infant, my little Hugh; not but that I felt confident Mrs. Clifford would behave with the greatest kindness towards him, but yet what was the utmost attention without the mother's fostering care?

"Providence, however, interfered in my behalf, and a short time after this I contrived to make my escape, and travelled with the utmost expedition until I reached the house of Captain Clifford; but was distracted when I found it closed, learned that Mrs. Clifford had died suddenly, and that Captain Clifford had gone to sea again, taking the child with him under the care of a nurse.

"You may judge of the state of my mind when I became acquainted with this, and for some time I scarcely knew what I was doing. Fortunately, I had a purse of money, which I had about me when I was seized by the order of the baron; and I therefore resolved to make the best of my way to one of the daughters of Captain Clifford, who was married, and endeavour to learn further particulars from her, or at any rate seek a shelter beneath her roof until Captain Clifford might return, which would be in a short time, no doubt.

"From the same individual who furnished me with the intelligence I have mentioned, I was told of the abrupt departure of the Baron De Morton from the castle to the continent, and thus I considered I had nothing to fear from him. In my way I had to pass this abbey, and just as I did so a violent storm came on, and I was forced to seek a shelter in the ruins. I recollected, too, a circumstance which had quite slipped my recollection in the multifarious and afflicting events which had recently occurred to me, and that was the chest of gold which you, Eustace, had buried in those troublesome times in the grounds of Arlingham Hall, and which, by my instructions and the aid of the smugglers, had been secretly removed to the abbey ruins, and I determined to see if it were safe. To my great satisfaction I found it in the same place where it had been first deposited, and which did not seem to have been touched since. I looked at it, and closed it up again, without touching a coin. No, I was determined to suffer any difficulty rather than take the smallest portion of the coin which belonged to my brother, and who could do me the injustice to suppose me the guilty wretch that I was reported to be, I was turning away from the spot, when I was surprised to behold a light glimmering at the further end of the vault, and almost immediately the shadow of a human form met my gaze, which flitted beneath the arch-way with the greatest precipitation.

" I was, as you may guess, somewhat startled at this circumstance; but I speedily recovered myself, and hastening to that part of the vault whence the form had vanished, I called in a firm voice, and demanded who was there. Instantly a loud scream struck my ears, and then the fall, as if of some heavy substance, upon the pavement. With a courage I never remember to have felt before, and for which I have never been able to account, I rushed immediately forward in the direction which the form I had seen had taken, and almost immediately afterwards I beheld the rays of the lamp which it had carried, and which seemed to be at no great distance from me. I came up to the spot—I beheld a human form—the form of a female clad in white, stretched prostrate and insensible on the pavement. With tremulous haste I raised her in my arms. The rays of the light fell full upon her countenance; and judge of my astonishment when I recognised in her features those of my cousin, our dear Matilda, whom I had been informed was no more. But here, perhaps, it would be better for the baroness to relate her own story."

"Oh! no, dearest Emmeline," ejaculated the still beauteous Lady de Morton, who was seated between Angelina and Sir Eustace, and listening with a melancholy interest to her narrative. "Pray proceed; I should never be able to collect myself sufficiently, at this moment, to do justice to it."

"Well, then, Matilda," resumed Lady Emmeline, "since it is your wish, I will briefly relate the circumstances as I recieved them from your own lips. Our emotions at so unexpectedly meeting, and under such singular circumstances, I shall the liberty of passing over; they can easily be imagined by all present.

"The brother of Matilda's husband, from the very moment he beheld her, had viewed her with an eye of desire, and had doubtless resolved within his own mind to possess her; but she had ever looked upon him with detestation and a feeling approaching to horror. Of the mysterious disappearance of Lord Edward de Morton you have heard, and Matilda's subsequent marriage to his brother. But think not it was by her consent. Oh, no; she was forced to the altar at midnight, and the ceremony was solemnized in secret. A short time afterwards Matilda was delivered of a girl, which they told her had died, and it was taken away from her sight. She became distracted, and accused the baron of murdering it, and also with the murder of her husband—for a dreadful suspicion had always haunted her imagination to that effect, and she had heard De Morton utter certain broken sentences in his sleep, which served to strengthen it. The baron appeared conscience-stricken, and turning very pale, he rushed immediately from the chamber. Matilda saw no more of him, and the nurse who attended her was a woman of the most repulsive character. In spite of all, however, a natural strong constitution enabled her to combat with these heavy trials, and she recovered from her accouchement; but her alarm and grief was increased, when she was informed it was the baron's orders she should be confined to her room.

"Here she was treated with every cruelty and indignity, her only attendants being the old nurse and Rufus—the latter created an indescribable sensation of horror whenever she beheld him.

"She had been confined in this manner about a month, when one night Rufus came to the room, and from the peculiar and awful expression of his countenance, she guessed that he was come upon some dreadful errand as soon as he entered. He brought with him a bottle and a glass, which he laid upon the table, and Matilda, quite overpowered by her terrible apprehensions, directly he came in, fell upon her knees before him, and with clasped hands and in piteous accents, she implored his mercy. The ruffian only answered her with a scornful laugh, and then stood gazing at her emotions for a second or two, as though he exulted in the blood-thirsty deed he was employed to perpetrate.

"'This night settles your business,' said the blood-thirsty miscreant, coolly taking a poniard from his bosom, and then proceeding to pour a dark brown liquor from the bottle into the glass—'the baron has doomed you to death!—You may take your choice, either to swallow the contents of this glass, or die by the poniard—it is a matter of indifference to me!'

"Let me hasten over this revolting scene as quickly as possible; in vain Matilda supplicated; her prayers and her tears were alike unavailing to a wretch who was destitute of all sort of feeling; and seizing the fatal glass, she commended her soul to Heaven, and drank the contents, Rufus standing over with the dagger pointed to her breast, while she drained it to the dregs. Her brain immediately seemed to whirl round; flames appeared to flash before her eyes—a mist gradually gathered before them, and she remembered no more.

"When Matilda recovered her senses, she felt an icy chillness all over her limbs, and a burning sensation in her head. She was involved in complete darkness; but feeling around her, her hand came in contact with damp stone walls, and she then recollected all that had passed, and imagined she was consigned to one of the dismal vaults underneath the castle, being supposed to be dead; but, after drinking the dreadful draught, what astonished and bewildered her more than all was, that she should be still alive; the only conclusion she could come to was, that the wretch, Rufus, had made a mistake, and given her some strong opiate instead of poison. But oh! how awful was her situation, enclosed, as she imagined, in that awful place, where she would be left to perish of hunger. She wrung her hands in despair, and groaned aloud with the agony of her mind. She felt around the walls until her hands met the door, which, to her astonishment, was open; and with the speed of lightning she emerged into the subterranean passage beyond. She then found that she had conjectured right, that she was underneath the castle. So overjoyed was she, that she fell upon her knees, and returned her most heartfelt thanks to Omnipotence, for she knew she could easily regain her liberty, being acquainted with all the secret passages with which this place abounded. She was not mistaken; and in a short time found herself in the open air. For some time she remained in a state of doubt and uncertainty in what manner she should act; but at length she took her course through the wood, without having made up her mind as to what point she should direct her steps. It was but just the dawn of day, and upon the weakened frame of Lady de Morton the fragrant breeze came most refreshing.

"At length she remembered that the cottage of her old nurse was situated on the skirts of the wood, and she resolved to hasten to her, and there seek a shelter for the present, knowing that in her she could confide. She was not long in reaching the cottage, and the old woman was at first very much alarmed—for, thinking that Matilda was dead, she thought it was her spectre she beheld. The poor old woman shuddered with horror when Matilda briefly related to her all that she had undergone; but a surprise, a delightful and unexpected circumstance awaited Matilda, which at first was nearly the means of driving her mad.

"The daughter of old Margaret lived in the adjoining cottage to her, and about a month or two before, her husband—so Margaret informed Lady Matilda—in crossing the wood, heard the cries of an infant, and coming up to the spot, saw a wicker basket lying upon the ground, which, on opening, a female infant, apparently but a few weeks old, met his view. He immediately took the child home to his wife, who had not long recovered from her confinement, and they resolved to adopt it for their own, thinking that its inhuman parents, whoever

they might be, would never acknowledge it should they discover that it still survived; and although they were poor, they could not have the heart to abandon the poor little innocent to the mercy of strangers, or consign it to the same fate from which they had so recently rescued it. When Margaret was relating this, a strange emotion filled the bosom of Matilda, and she trembled so violently that she could scarcely support herself. She asked hastily to see the little foundling—and hastening to the cottage of Margaret's daughter, judge of her feelings, when, the moment she beheld the infant, she knew it was her own child; but if any confirmation of her conjectures was wanting, it was soon obtained; a mark of a peculiar description on the left arm, was an indisputable conviction; the frantic mother hugged her child (you, Angelina) to her bosom."

Lady Emmeline was so overcome by her feelings, as was also was everybody present, that she could not proceed for a few minutes. Lady de Morton's eyes filled with tears as she clasped the sobbing Angelina in her arms, and pressed her with all the ardour of maternal fondness to her heart; and every one present admired the wonderful ways of Providence. At length, Lady Emmeline resumed in the following words:

" Those good and humane people, who had rescued you from death, Angelina, were the parents of Bridget."

" Good God! is it possible !" ejaculated our heroine, with a shudder of horror, as she thought upon the fate of that unfortunate woman, of whom she had not heard anything since the shipwreck.

Lady Emmeline continued—

" I shall not tire your patience with a long detail of what feelings of transport filled the bosom of the fond mother upon this discovery; imagination may picture them, but the tongue cannot describe them. It was agreed that Angelina (which was the name the child afterwards received) should remain with its present affectionate nurse, and Matilda could never sufficiently return her thanks to Heaven for the miraculous way in which it had been restored to her, and for her own wonderful preservation from a dreadful death; but, alas! what was to become of her now she was at liberty?—She had not any money, or means of supporting herself, and from becoming a burthen upon those poor people as well as her child, she revolted. But, alas! she had no other alternative, until such time as she ob-

tained retribution for the wrongs she had sustained from the baron. But, then, her personal security would be at risk. For a long time she racked her brain to no purpose; at length, an idea struck her. The ruins of St. Mark's Abbey had long been deserted, and reported to be haunted, and Matilda, who believed not the ridiculous stories that were circulated concerning it, knew that there were many parts of it that were not only habitable, but in a very good condition, In this venerable abbey, then, did Matilda resolve to take up her future residence, feeling assured that the wild superstition connected with it, would be her best security.—Here, as I have before stated, we met. The resolution of Matilda pleased me, and was exactly in accordance with the state of my mind. I was tired of the world, and was resolved, therefore, to become her companion, and, in future, to exert every nerve to bring about that retribution for our wrongs, and destruction upon our enemies, we both were so anxious to obtain. I had money, and, therefore, we could put such a plan into execution without any inconvenience. In a few days, Captain Clifford returned, stopping at the abbey, and I had then once more the delight of clasping my child to my bosom. Mr. Clifford was astonished and enraged when I related to him the particulars of the wrongs I had endured, and the sufferings of my unfortunate cousin; yet he, at first, was opposed to the singular resolution I had formed, but yielded at last to my arguments, and insisted upon becoming the protector of my boy, whom he put under the care of a nurse, in a place so adjacent, that I could see him every day. Behold me, then, as ' Wild Kate of the Ruins,' which was the character I thought proper to assume, while Matilda acted the part of the spirit which was supposed to haunt this ancient fabric. We were not long, Eustace, in discovering where you resided, but still we determined not to reveal ourselves, until such time as Providence should be pleased in its own infinite wisdom, to bring about our restoration to that rank and reputation in society, of which we have been so unjustly deprived, and likewise to place us in a fair situation of gaining a just retribution upon the heads of our oppressors. The idea of committing Angelina to your care, and endeavouring to make you believe she was my daughter, was mine—for I felt convinced, Eustace, that however you might condemn me, you would not act otherwise than as a parent towards my offspring; and, therefore, Matilda readily yielded her consent to the arrangement, more especially as Ellenor, the mother of Bridget, was attacked with a severe fit of illness, and was, consequently, unable to attend upon it with that care which she had hitherto done. Besides, under your protection, we both considered that Angelina would be more secure; and therefore, without any farther hesitation, we decided upon the plan, which you afterwards know we put into execution. We forgot, however, to remove a small miniature likeness of her mother, and we were fearful that this circumstance would lead you to suspect who she really was."

"Why," interrupted Sir Eustace, "I certainly, at first, did think it rather remarkable; but afterwards I concluded it was one which Matilda had presented to you, and that, when you committed the child to my care, you placed it round her neck for the purpose of recalling to my memory the features of her we both so tenderly loved."

Lady Emmeline concluded her extraordinary recital in the following words:—

"I have a little more to relate, with which you are unacquainted. I so disguised myself, that I thought it was utterly impossible for any one to know me, and it appears I succeeded to a marvel. Years flew on, and Captain Clifford well fulfilled his promise as regarded my son; no parent could behave better to him, and as he grew up, he felt as ardent an affection for him, I believe, as if he had been his son; in fact, he knew himself for no other; as for me, he imagined that I was related to him, but that, owing to some heavy calamity, I chose the wild life and air of mystery I did. He became attached to the life of Captain Clifford, although the latter did not encourage him in it; and when the captain died, he assumed the command, and has ever since been in the situation in which you first knew him. It was I who urged you, Eustace, in the first instance, and continued to do so, to discourage the passion of Hugh and Angelina, and to refuse your assent to their paying their addresses to each other; for I foresaw that if I had not done so, it might have been productive of much misery, and when the real facts of their birth were revealed, have given you cause for reproach. I have now stated all the particulars of this extraordinary narrative."

CONCLUSION.

We will draw a veil over what passed after Lady Emmeline had finished her narrative, or the powerful emotions that were experienced by every one present. It was finally determined that Sir Eustace should hasten immediately to Court, and, seeking an audience of the king, solicit the restitution of those rights of which he had been so unjustly deprived, and afterwards to state the whole particulars of the events that have been related here, and pray for justice on the guilty, if they still survived. Sir Eustace lost no time in putting this plan into execution; and having arrived in London, by the interest of an old and tried friend, whom he found out there, he obtained his wishes, and threw himself at the feet of his monarch. The king, who had many times repented of the harsh treatment Sir Eustace had received, and had cause to suspect the truth of his accusers, received him affably, and promised him that a proper inquiry should be immediately instituted, and every justice rendered him. While this was pending, news reached the court of the death of the Baron de Morton, who had been attacked by robbers while travelling, and so severely wounded that he only survived a few hours. He had been preserved from the shipwreck, but the villain Rufus had perished. Before he died, he had made a confession of all his crimes, in the presence of the gentleman to whose house he had been conveyed, and among others, he accused himself of having been guilty of the treason he had been the means of laying to the charge of Sir Eustace Arlingham. It is unnecessary to add that justice was immediately done to the latter, and before he quitted the court he was fully reinstated in those possessions and that title he had been so unjustly deprived of. But a more joyful surprise than all awaited Sir Eustace; on the last day of his appearance at the palace he encountered Lord Edward Dalton, whom he had supposed to have been dead, or never expected to see again. The meeting may well be imagined; but when Sir Eustace informed him of the sufferings his unfortunate wife had undergone, and the certainty there was of her innocence of the guilt of which she had been suspected, his agitation was so great that it was almost more than he could support. In a few days, Lady Emmeline Dalton was restored to the arms of her husband, from whom she had been so many years separated, and to her former rank in society; while Hugh, for the first time in his life, received the embraces of his father, and heard his blessing invoked upon his head.

No sooner did Orillia hear of the death of the baron, and the confession he had made, than, unable to meet the disgrace which would follow such disclosures, she fled, with the Marquess Florendos for her paramour, and ended her days on the continent, in a career of profligacy, dissipation, and shame. Lady Matilda de Morton was, without any difficulty, recognised, and the wealthy possessions of the family restored to her.

For the purpose of being near Lord and Lady Dalton, and Lady Matilda and Angelina, Sir Eustace purchased an estate near De Morton Castle; and Hugh and Angelina having shortly afterwards plighted their vows at the hymeneal altar, hey all became united

as one family, and their future happiness knew of no interruption.

Not long after these events had taken place, our heroine was transported with pleasure one morning when the faithful Bridget, who had suffered so much for her sake, and whom she had supposed to have met with an untimely death, presented herself before her. She had been preserved in a most miraculous manner; and hastened, as soon as she learnt that Angelina was also saved, and where she could find her, to rejoin one to whom she was so devotedly attached. Angelina was determined that she should never leave her again as long as she lived, and she kept her resolution, Bridget residing in the castle, and being treated as a sister by our heroine, and with the most distinguished esteem by every other person.

Angelina and Hugh were supremely happy in each other's love, and in seeing a family of virtuous and beauteous children around them, never looked back upon the sorrows of the past with any other feelings than those of satisfaction, as they taught them more duly to appreciate the felicity of the present, and the unbounded goodness of Providence.

Laura Arlingham, in the course of a year after these events, was united to a gentleman every way worthy of her, and they passed a long life together in mutual happiness and content.

Lady de Morton caused St. Mark's Abbey to be restored to all its pristine beauty, and it became the favourite residence of her son and daughter.

It may be as well to explain, that the skeleton which Angelina had seen in the chest upon one occasion of her visiting the ruins, had been placed there at the desire of Lady Emmeline, by the smugglers, to alarm any person who might be bold enough to examine the place, and it was removed from one of the vaults underneath the old abbey. Thus, then, do we end

" This round unvarnished tale."